"You Shan't Have Her, Bouchard. I'm the One What Found Her, and She's Mine!"

"Stand aside, Grosbeck," Bouchard ordered.

Another sailor stepped up beside Grosbeck. "Remember you well," he said to Bouchard, "you're our captain by vote of the crew. We made you, and, by God, we can unmake you as easily." The men behind him murmured their assent.

"You sons of bitches," Bouchard shouted in a high-pitched voice, "are you all mad with lust?"

"We ain't in action now," Grosbeck said sullenly. "Have we ever disobeyed you in the face of an enemy?" He turned to the other men.

A chorus of noes answered him.

"Is the señorita mine by right?"

"Aye!" the men shouted.

"After all, we don't mean to kill her. She'll still fetch a goodly ransom when we're through with her."

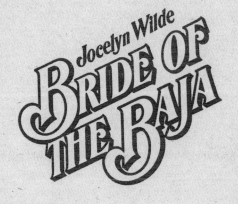

Jocelyn Wilde

BRIDE OF THE BAJA

PUBLISHED BY POCKET BOOKS NEW YORK

A POCKET BOOKS/RICHARD GALLEN *Original* publication

POCKET BOOKS, a Simon & Schuster division of
GULF & WESTERN CORPORATION
1230 Avenue of the Americas, New York, N Y 10020

ISBN: 0-671-83682-X

First Pocket Books printing July, 1980

10 9 8 7 6 5 4 3 2 1

POCKET and colophon are trademarks of Simon & Schuster.

Printed in the U.S.A.

BRIDE OF
THE RAJA

chapter 1

FROM THE DECK of the *Flying Yankee*, Alitha Bradford idly swung her white bonnet of pleated silk by its ties as she watched the rising sun burn through the Valparaiso harbor mist. A dark shape slid from the fog in front of her, a brig taking advantage of the first of the ebb tide to weigh anchor and sail out into the Pacific.

She looked up at the red, white and blue flag fluttering from the halyard at the stern. It was an American ship, the first she had seen since her father had sailed the *Flying Yankee* around Cape Horn three weeks ago. Seeing the flag with its fifteen stars and fifteen stripes in this foreign port thrilled Alitha, and she peered into the mist at the brig as it plowed slowly past the *Yankee*'s bow.

Suddenly she drew back, one hand clutching at her cashmere shawl to draw it together across her breasts. A man stood at the brig's taffrail, hands on hips, staring at her; a tall man with black hair and a short black beard, wearing a visored cap. He was the captain of the brig, she was sure; he looked like a man accustomed to command. His eyes left her to probe the mist ahead of his ship as though, Alitha thought, he could see to the next landfall, see across the Pacific to the Sandwich Islands.

She sighed. Thomas. Thomas Heath awaited her on the Sandwich Islands. If only *she* could see that far, and not only beyond the great expanse of the ocean but into the future as well. If only she could discover the fate predestined for her on those islands thousands of miles to the west. She shook her head, impatient with her fancy. Time will tell, she thought.

Don't be afraid of the day you never saw, she remembered her mother telling her. What made her think of that? She wasn't afraid. Not of Thomas, certainly, for he was a gentle man; nor was she afraid of marriage. She wanted to marry. And have children, of course. That was what all young women of eighteen wanted. Then why did she feel this unease, this uncertainty? Was it because of that night on the banks of the Charles, that night she and Thomas had agreed never to mention? *Was* there something wrong with her?

Alitha's eyes returned to the taffrail of the two-masted brig. The captain had turned toward her again, raising his hand to his cap in a salute. The sound of his voice drifting over the water was so faint she couldn't make out his words.

Should she acknowledge a man she'd never met by waving back? Alitha glanced down at her green-sprigged lawn gown, at the frills of her petticoats below the gown. Hastily she put on her bonnet. Perhaps he hadn't thought her a lady. But this isn't Boston, she told herself; manners are freer here and besides, she would never see him again. Who would know if she waved? Taking a handkerchief from her sleeve, she returned his salute with a flutter of the handkerchief, seeing him smile at her as he raised his hand to his cap once more before he and his ship were shrouded by the fog.

She strained to make out the name on the brig's stern. She saw two words, the first beginning with a *K*. And then the brig was gone. What was its name? And who was her black-haired captain?

"Mr. Jordan Quinn, master of the *Kerry Dancer* out of the city of Portsmouth in the state of Maine."

Alitha whirled to find herself face to face with Amos Malloy. The *Yankee*'s first mate, only inches away, smiled down at her. She tried, with only partial success, to smile back.

"Thank you, Mr. Malloy," she told him. "I couldn't help noticing the brig was from the States. I was only . . ." She stopped; she would not make excuses to Amos Malloy.

"The pleasure was mine in being able to help you." Malloy's bow was as stiff as his words.

Looking up at him, Alitha pulled her shawl yet closer together, resisting an almost overpowering impulse to move away. Why? She had no reason to fear him. Amos had never been other than a gentleman, both before he had asked for her hand two years ago and after she had refused him. He seemed to harbor no grudge against her because of her refusal, was always civil and courteous, even going out of his way to be helpful.

Why, then, was she so wary of him? He was good-looking, clean-shaven with curly black hair and long side whiskers; a well-built, stocky man. Yet with his fair complexion, reddened now by the wind, his eyes, which should have been as blue as her own, were a dark, mottled brown. Small, furtive eyes. Yet there appeared to be nothing else furtive about him. Slow and steady, that was Amos Malloy. And a good seaman.

"One of the best mates who ever sailed with me," her father had told her. "In time he may be the equal of Mr. Jones." Although Ephraim Jones, now dead, had sailed under her father for ten years, he was still "Mister" to Captain Bradford.

Was it Malloy's hands, Alitha wondered. How foolish, to dislike a man because of the size of his hands. He couldn't help it if they were the largest hands she had ever seen, huge work-hardened hands with long, thick fingers, hands large enough to encompass a woman's waist and still have the fingers interlock at the small of her back.

Amos shoved his hands into the pockets of his jacket. She frowned; she must have been staring at them.

"If I might, Miss Alitha," he said, "I'd be pleased to accompany you into the city this forenoon. I've been to Valparaiso before, as you know." He nodded to the white buildings only now beginning to emerge from the morning mist.

"I'm sorry, Mr. Malloy," she told him. "I'm going with my father to visit Mr. Burns, the American consul."

"Of course, I understand perfectly. Perhaps later in the day then?"

"Perhaps, Mr. Malloy."

He bowed, turned on his heel and crossed the deck to the wheel. Alitha looked past the *Yankee*'s bow, trying to catch a last glimpse of the *Kerry Dancer*, frowning with disappointment when all she saw was a gray swirl of fog.

Holding the rail with both hands, she breathed

deeply of the salt air. A gull screeched above the mizzenmast; under her feet she felt the anchored ship's gentle rise and fall. How she loved the sea! How she savored the blue expanse of water on a clear day when white puffs of clouds scudded overhead and the sails billowed in a freshening breeze. How she thrilled to rough weather when the wind sang in the rigging and heavy seas crashed onto the maindeck. The excitement and danger of a storm were best of all, rousing something within her, making her want to brace herself at the bow with the salt spray lashing her face, making her want to cry out her defiance and her joy.

She could understand why her father loved the sea. It had been different for her mother, waiting, always waiting at home. *She* would never marry a sailor and spend the rest of her life waiting.

Aware of being watched, Alitha turned her head slightly, seeing Amos Malloy staring down into the binnacle. He couldn't really believe she would think he was taking a compass reading while they were anchored in this well-charted port. Actually, she knew, he had been watching her. She shivered. This was why she disliked him, she decided, this sensation of having his gaze constantly following her. Only in her cabin with the door closed and latched did she feel safe.

She would not be intimidated! She turned so her back was against the rail and for a moment their eyes met. He lowered his glance, yet she felt him still appraising her, almost as though he could see through the cotton cloth of her high-necked dress, through her petticoats and chemise, almost as though he knew . . .

Reddening, she looked quickly away and thought she saw him smile. As if he had read her mind, suspecting the truth—that she felt not only distaste, not only apprehension, not only the beginnings of fear, but something else besides. Alitha pushed the unwelcome idea away.

No! she told herself. Face the truth. You promised when you left Boston that you'd be true to yourself. And to Thomas as well, of course. Her mother's fault would not become hers—she would not practice self-deception. Alitha frowned as she thought of her mother during her last illness the year before.

"Nehemiah's been a good husband to me," Norah Bradford had said, "all in all. He's been a good provider and a temperate, God-fearing man."

And an adulterer, Alitha thought. *Adulterer.* What a terrible word. A terrible word for a terrible sin.

Alitha remembered her horror when her mother, delirious with the fever that went with her consumption, had told her the truth. The shock had overwhelmed her. Her father, the man she loved, the man she respected above all others, had been unfaithful. Yet her mother had never told him she knew. How could she maintain her silence, blinding herself to what her husband was? A man who broke one of God's commandments placed himself beyond the reach of Christian charity.

At least she'd never have to worry about Thomas in that way. Hadn't he pledged his life to serving God? Hadn't he ventured forth to the Sandwich Islands as a missionary to lead the heathen natives to the Savior? Thomas was, in fact, much too good for her; he was an idealist in all things. If only . . . No, she mustn't doubt. She was unworthy of him. She could only hope to become more like him, a better Christian. Perhaps then she would find a way to forgive her father.

Alitha had vowed never to practice self-deception as her mother had. No matter how painful it might be, she would face the truth. And it *was* painful to admit that she didn't find the attentions of Mr. Malloy completely unwelcome. After all, he was a fine-looking, capable man; any of the girls she'd known in Boston would have accepted his proposal in a minute. I'm glad I waited for Thomas to ask me to marry him, she told herself. I love Thomas more than I could ever love a man like Amos.

Yet when Alitha saw Amos watching her, she admitted she felt more than an instinctive distaste. That was her secret and her shame. She felt more than an innate revulsion. In fact, at times when she lay restlessly in her bunk listening to the rush of the sea only a few inches away on the other side of the oak hull, as she tried to let the cradlelike rocking of the ship lull her to sleep, she had imagined Amos Malloy touching her, imagined the feel of his strong hands circling her waist and drawing her to him.

As Alitha relived her daydream, the memory returned of that soft September night along the Charles where she and Thomas had strolled hand in hand listening to the murmur of the water below them. She remembered the two of them stopping, as though of a single mind. His lips found hers in the chaste kisses she was accustomed to, then, as a kiss lengthened, his lips grew more insistent, more demanding. His hands slid awkwardly up along her sides to her breasts, touching them tentatively and, when she didn't thrust his hands away, cradling them.

She lay on the grass of the riverbank, her hands behind her head, and he lay beside her. His lips met hers again, and she drew in her breath as she felt the length of his body touching hers. Quite unexpectedly an unbidden fire rose in her, a trembling starting in her legs and pulsing up through her, a surging response to his touch, a feeling she had never experienced before, a sensation she had never imagined possible.

"Thomas," she whispered.

"Thomas," she said again, wanting to hear the sound of his name. Her cold hand slipped under his shirt to the warm flesh of his back, and she felt him shiver at her touch. His hands clumsily caressed her breasts, cupping them through her dress and chemise, his fingers circling her breasts as the fire mounted higher and higher in her.

He leaned over her, his lips still locked to hers. Her mouth opened to say his name and she felt his tongue lightly touch her lips and, as quickly, withdraw. She moved back but he kept kissing her, almost angrily she thought, as though to punish her, his mouth nipping her neck and ear until his lips covered hers again. Her arms circled his neck, drawing him to her, her body arching to his, pressing against a hardness that thrilled and frightened her at the same time. She wanted, she wanted—oh, what did she want?

Thomas rolled away, his lips and hands leaving her. He stood up and in the moonlight she saw him standing a short distance away, with his back to her.

"Thomas," she cried without thinking, "don't go, don't leave me now, you can't."

Through a humming blur of passion she heard his quick breathing, saw him walk away to stare out over the river. Slowly she sat up, then rose to her feet, pushing her hair from her eyes. She went to him, her arms going about his waist as her breasts pressed against his back. He disengaged her arms and stepped away. She seemed to hear his words indistinctly, in snatches, words she didn't want to hear yet, afterward, words she couldn't forget.

"Sins of the flesh," he said. "Wait . . . wrong . . . evil . . . don't tempt me, Leeta, don't tempt me . . ."

She ran from him, ran as fast as she could, finally

tripping over a root and sprawling on the ground with her hands clutching at the mounds of grass, her fingers clawing the loose earth, hearing, as from a distance, sobs. Only after several minutes did she realize they were her own.

She sensed someone beside her, felt Thomas's hand on her shoulder. He gently smoothed her hair.

"Tell me the truth," she said, looking over her shoulder at his face dark above her. "Is it wrong to feel as I did? Is there something wrong with me? Is there, Thomas?"

He hadn't replied, not then or later. She had answered the question for him, though, a hundred times and more, in the lonely emptiness of her room, later as she slept on the cot in her mother's sick chamber, later still in her cabin on the *Yankee* during the long voyage around the Horn.

Yes, she told herself, there is something wrong with you. You're weak, Alitha Bradford, your flesh is weak, a prey to temptation. If you don't beware you'll become a handmaiden of the devil.

Yet no matter how many times she told herself this, she never completely believed her own words. There was always a part of her that seemed to stand aside and protest, "No! It's not true!"

"Alitha, are you ready?"

Startled, she swung about to see her father standing at the top of the companionway leading from his cabin. He wore his best shore clothes—his blue trousers, the blue jacket with the gold buttons and gold braid and a black cap set squarely on his head—Nehemiah Bradford could never be accused of being rakish. He had trimmed his beard and shined his boots mirror-black.

Alitha wanted to run to him, throw her arms about him, press her face against his chest. She couldn't. Six feet tall, a head higher than his daughter, Nehemiah seemed to her the reincarnation of a Biblical patriarch.

She could never really talk to him. Their conversational voyages, she fancied, took them on a triangular course from the weather to their journey to her mother. Then back to home port, the weather. Could you talk to a Noah, to a Moses? If only there were someone to hear whatever outrageous thoughts, dreams and desires might sail through her head. And understand. Someone—a man, yes, it had to be a man—who would accept her as she was. Not someone who wanted to change her. Change her for her own good, of course.

"I'm ready, father," she said, going to him and brushing a fleck of lint from his jacket collar. "My father is the handsomest man in the entire Southern Hemisphere," she told him.

Nehemiah stared down at her in surprise. "And you, Alitha," he said awkwardly, "must be by far the most beautiful woman."

As he looked at her, she saw his eyes mist and she knew he must be thinking of her mother, seeing her mother in her. Nehemiah reached out and for a moment Alitha thought he meant to take her in his arms. If he did, she thought, she could almost forgive him. His hand held in midair and, after a pause, he crooked his arm. She pulled on her gloves, laid her hand on his sleeve and they crossed the deck to the ladder and the waiting ship's boat.

As they were being rowed to the wharf, Alitha glanced behind her toward the Pacific. The fog had risen, and in the distance she saw the *Kerry Dancer* under full sail.

"Jordan Quinn," she said half-aloud.

"I beg your pardon," her father said.

"Nothing, father. I'm just daydreaming again."

Jordan Quinn. She repeated the name to herself, liking the sound. I don't know when, Jordan Quinn, she thought, and I don't know where, Jordan Quinn, but one day we'll meet, you and I.

The compass read north by northwest. Captain Quinn nodded with satisfaction.

"Steady as she goes," he ordered the helmsman. Already he could feel the well-remembered surge of the ocean beneath his ship.

"Aye aye, sir," Jack McKinnon said.

"Ah, and wasn't she a beauty, Mr. McKinnon? Have you ever seen her like before?"

"The *Flying Yankee*'s been the pride of the Beachum yards ever since she was launched."

"You know as well as you know port from starboard that I wasn't referring to the ship."

"Might you mean the lass who waved to you from the rail then? The bonny lass with the long golden hair?"

"You know damn well I mean the lass. Did you ever see such a beauty in all your days?"

"A likely looking wench, I'll admit, but not one for me nor for you, either. Myself a happily married man and you about to join our fraternity. In another two months or sooner if this wind holds." He tapped his knuckles on the kingspoke of the wheel.

"A bit of dreaming never harmed a man."

"In another year," McKinnon went on, "if I know the ways of these *señoritas,* your new bride'll have you living ashore, a Californio like the rest of them, complete with a *rancho,* herds of cattle and all."

"You're mistaken, Mr. McKinnon. I'll never leave the sea; not for long, certainly not for any woman. My father always said if they sliced into a Quinn's veins they'd find a generous portion of salt water mixed with the blood. When my time comes, I'd like to go as he did, struck down on the deck of a frigate trading cannon shot with a Limey man-o'-war."

"You may have your wish, Captain. These are troubled times."

Jordan smiled. "All times are troubled, Mr. McKinnon, to the men who have to live through them. It's only later we forget the bad and remember the good."

"Aye, there's truth in what you say. You'll have to write that in your journal."

Jordan tensed, ready to lash back at McKinnon with angry words. Though he knew his journal was no secret, he didn't like having it mentioned. At sea being labeled a literary man was a sign of weakness, even in a captain. Jordan checked himself, though. McKinnon's words had been lightly said; the man meant no harm. Jordan prided himself on running a good ship and knew men were eager to sign aboard the *Kerry Dancer*. He didn't want that to change; he said nothing.

Jordan broke a long silence. "You're right enough about the times," he said. "No sooner is the war with England won than we're on the verge of another with Spain over Florida. Not that the Spaniards don't have enough on their hands with revolutions up and down the length of South America. And in Mexico. The consul in Valparaiso even passed on a report of pirates off Acapulco."

"Pirates? In the Pacific? I thought Lafitte and his crew kept to the Caribbean."

"These buccaneers claim to be patriots fighting for their freedom from Spain. According to Burns, they're led by a renegade Frenchman named Bouchard who's set himself up as an admiral in the navy of the Republic of Buenos Aires, whatever in the name of God that might be."

"Pirates ahead of us and pestilence behind," McKinnon said.

"Pestilence?"

"Last night while I was enjoying a drop of rum, I heard whispers of cholera in the city. The *alcalde* isn't admitting it, of course, but I was told a hundred or more have died since last February."

"I'd rather face pirates than the plague," Jordan said. "Not that we'll have to face either. We keep a spruce ship and I have a feeling we'll have a good wind and calm seas all the way to Santa Barbara."

McKinnon nodded. This time the helmsman didn't tap his knuckles on the wood of the wheel—Captain Quinn's hunches had earned his respect.

Jordan's experienced gaze swept up along the rigging and across the sails as he walked to the rail. Putting his foot on a deck cleat, he looked back at the foaming wake of the *Kerry Dancer*. To the east fishing boats clustered near shore, and in the distance he saw the purple peaks of the Andes. The city of Valparaiso was a receding shimmer of white to the south. He couldn't see the *Yankee*.

"Probably if you got close up," McKinnon said as though he had followed his captain's thoughts, "you'd find your blond lass had the scars of the smallpox."

"Worse, she's undoubtedly a shrew. I could tell by the cut of her that she has a mind of her own. Give me a *señorita* any day."

As he looked across the sun-glittered sea, in his mind's eye Jordan pictured the girl on the *Yankee*. Tall for a woman, slim but generously fashioned—the wind had shown him that, blowing her gown against her body. Hair the color of a new-minted gold piece. And her eyes, he knew, must be as blue as the Caribbean. Suddenly he had a feeling—a premonition, a hunch, call it what you will. He knew, as surely as he had ever known anything in his life, that he would see her again.

And soon.

chapter 2

ABLE SEAMAN PETERS was on his knees swabbing down the deck as the *Flying Yankee,* three days out of Valparaiso, sailed north before a strong southwesterly wind. Sam Peters moved sluggishly, stopping often to rest.

"Get the lead out of your ass, sailor," the bosun shouted.

Sam nodded and doggedly returned to his work. All at once he dropped his brush, staggered to the rail and vomited over the side. He leaned on the rail, retching.

"Peters!" It was the mate. "Haven't got your sea legs yet?"

Sam shook his head. Amos Malloy took the seaman by the shoulders and turned him so he could see his face. Peters looked wretched, shivering and hunched over. The mate frowned.

"How be you?" he asked, not unkindly.

Peters took a gulping breath of air. "My bowels feel like the hand of God's twisting them."

"Best go below," Malloy told him.

Sam turned and began weaving his way toward the forecastle.

"Wait," Malloy ordered. "Not to your bunk—take the one fore of the galley. Best to keep away from the others, whatever it is you have. I'll see you get a good dose of laudanum."

Sam Peters looked fearfully at the mate. "My bowels are loose, too, sir. What do you reckon it might be?"

"You had shore leave in Valparaiso?"

"That I did, sir."

"No doubt something you ate. Don't worry, you'll be good as new by tomorrow's sunrise."

Sam nodded and, one hand clutching his belly, shuffled to the ladder. As soon as he was out of sight, the mate strode aft, hurried down the companionway and knocked on the paneled door at the bottom.

Captain Bradford opened the door and motioned the mate into his cabin.

"It's Seaman Peters, sir," Malloy said. "He's come down with the cholera."

The captain's eyes narrowed. "Are you sure, Mr. Mate?"

Malloy described the symptoms.

"Aye," the captain said heavily. "Nine chances out of ten it's the cholera. I'll see that Alitha gives him laudanum and brandy. After that, he's in God's hands."

"Do you think that's wise, sir?"

"I don't follow your tack, Mr. Malloy." The captain drummed his fingers on the table. "Laudanum and brandy are the best remedies for cholera. Are you questioning my judgment, mister?"

"No, sir. Not at all, sir." Malloy shifted his feet. He couldn't help recalling the ancient law of the sea: The crew reports to the mate, the mate to the captain, and the captain to God. "Not the treatment, sir, I didn't mean that. I was thinking of your sending Miss Alitha to nurse the man. After all, we don't know how cholera is passed along."

"Don't say 'we don't know,' Mr. Malloy. Because *you* may not know the cause of cholera doesn't mean *I* don't. Filth, that's what brings on the disease. Filth, swamplands, miasmas. Dirt. That's where cholera breeds, Mr. Malloy, in filth and dirt."

"Aye aye, sir." Malloy felt the tic start at the corner of his mouth. He tightened his lips to a thin line but he couldn't stop the twitching.

"We'll scrub the ship from stem to stern, Mr. Malloy. We'll hunt down and kill every rat in the hold and we'll kill every other vermin as well. See to it, Mr. Malloy. See to it now."

"Aye aye, sir."

"One other matter, Mr. Malloy."

"Sir?"

"I don't need your assistance in looking after the welfare of my daughter. Understood?"

"Aye aye, sir."

Malloy spun on his heel and climbed the companionway. As soon as he reached the deck, he began shouting his orders. Damn him, he thought. Clenching his fists at his side, he directed his fury at the job at hand. I'll show him. Before I'm through, he vowed, Captain Bradford will be able to eat his dinner off the deck of the *Yankee*'s hold.

In his cabin Captain Bradford stared after his mate. He'd noted the twitch, of course, as he'd noted it before in times of stress. As he had many times, he asked himself whether Malloy was ready for command, whether he would ever be ready. He was a good mate, worked hard and knew the ways of the sea. And yet Captain Bradford, without knowing precisely why, didn't completely trust the man. The captain shrugged. He was probably finding flaws where none existed . . .

Samuel Peters died shortly before noon on the following day. After his body was washed and toweled dry, it was sewn into a length of canvas sail to which lead weights had been attached. Alitha, head bowed, stood beside her father while he read the burial service. The seaman, she knew, was only a half-year older than she was. So young to die. She blinked back tears as, with the captain's final "Amen," the earthly remains of Samuel Peters were lifted on a canvas stretcher to the rail and committed to the waiting sea.

Alitha walked to her cabin knowing that the dead man's belongings would now be brought to the main-mast so the bosun, as was the custom, could auction them off to the rest of the crew. Alitha had opened Peters's sea chest and listed his effects so her father could make a record in the ship's journal: three shirts, two pairs of trousers, boots, a knife, a pocket watch and a Bible. The man who bought the dead man's clothing, she knew, would not wear them until his next voyage—to do otherwise was to tempt fate.

Five more men died in the next three weeks, the disease striking with lightning suddenness and seeming-ly at random. Two healthy men would bunk down across from each other and in the morning one would wake to find the other dead. By the end of the fourth week, half the crew had become ill, and even those who recovered—only one in three did—were too weak to climb the shrouds.

As day followed day with no break in the epidemic, Alitha noticed a change in her father. The captain, always a taciturn man, became even more uncommunicative. He stood for long hours on the poop deck staring at the rise and fall of the empty sea, always looking off the port side toward the islands thousands of miles beyond the horizon, the islands of the South Seas where he had sailed as a young man. On other days Nehemiah Bradford took to his cabin, and Alitha wouldn't see him for twelve hours or more at a time.

Nothing favored the *Flying Yankee* except the weather. The ship sped north, the days blue-bright, the nights lit by a thousand stars. They crossed the equator, sailed along the west coast of Mexico, heading for their next port of call, Yerba Buena in San Francisco Bay. From Yerba Buena they would sail westward to the Sandwich Islands.

Where Thomas Heath waited.

Alitha, with most of her waking hours spent in the forecastle nursing the crewmen, rarely thought of Thomas now. When she did, her memory of him seemed faint, almost dreamlike, as though he belonged to another time, to another Alitha—a younger Alitha who intended to marry a man she scarcely knew.

Strangely, her thoughts turned more and more to the captain of the *Kerry Dancer*, Jordan Quinn. She could no longer recall exactly what he looked like. Was he tall? Did his black hair curl? Had he smiled when he saluted her? She thought his eyes must be blue.

Alitha shook her head. Forget Jordan Quinn, she told herself. As for Thomas, there'd be time enough for Thomas and marriage when this voyage, so well begun and now so ill-fated, was over. She poured brandy into a glass and held it to the lips of the man the crew called English George, the ship's carpenter. English George, in the third day of his torment, weakly shook his head.

"You'll feel better if you drink some," she told him.

When he shook his head again, she put the glass on

the deck beside the bunk and raised her scented handkerchief to her face, trying to breathe as little of the stench of the cabin as she could. When a man moaned from a bunk near the bow, English George opened his eyes and began mumbling to himself. Alitha lowered her head to hear his words.

"I pray the Lord my soul to keep . . ."

She whispered the rest of the child's prayer along with him. "If I should die before I wake, I pray the Lord my soul to take."

English George's mouth twisted into what could have been a smile. His head fell to one side. Alitha took a small magnifying glass from her pocket and held the lens close to his mouth. Nothing. Opening his shirt, she laid her hand on his chest. Again nothing. She drew in her breath; another man gone to meet his Maker. Would the dying never end?

She clenched her right hand into a fist and raised it above her head. "How can you be so cruel?" she demanded. Instantly ashamed, she lowered her hand, closed her eyes and repeated a silent prayer.

When she opened her eyes, she saw Amos Malloy standing just inside the forecastle, his hair matted, a beard blackening his usually clean-shaven face. In the dim light from the spirit lamp, his eyes seemed even smaller than usual.

"I must speak to you, Miss Alitha," he said.

Reluctantly she followed him up onto the deck, where she blinked in the light of the warm April sun rising between streamers of red-hued clouds. The wind disarranged her hair and she had to put her hand to her forehead to keep the loose strands from blowing into her eyes. Spray wet her face as the ship, still under full sail, swept northward.

"It's about your father," Malloy said.

"Is there something the matter with him?" she asked, suddenly alarmed.

"No, no; it's that he's kept to his cabin these last twenty-four hours and more. Some of the crew think he's afraid."

"Afraid? How could they think that? A man who's rounded the Horn ten times?"

"They think he fears the cholera, miss. There's a difference between outlasting a gale at sea and facing cholera."

Not so different, she thought; both are the will of God. She recalled a verse from one of Thomas's favorite poems:

> God moves in a mysterious way,
>   his wonders to perform;
> He plants his footsteps in the sea,
>   and rides upon the storm.

"What do you want from me?" she asked Malloy.

"I want you to talk to your father. See if you can get him to show himself on deck where the crew can see him. As it is, I don't have enough able-bodied men to handle the sails, if worse comes to worst. We don't need grumbling besides."

"Is there foul weather coming?"

"The glass has been falling fast for the last eight hours." Malloy nodded to the clouds building in the east and south. "I don't rightly like the looks of it."

"I'll talk to my father," Alitha told him.

Fearful of Malloy's forebodings, she tapped on the door of her father's cabin. There was no answer. When, after she knocked again, louder this time, there was still no reply, she pushed against the door. It was unlocked. Alitha stepped into the captain's cabin, drawing back momentarily when she found the air so fetid she had to put her handkerchief to her face. The spirit lamp had burned low and at first, seeing his empty berth, she thought her father had left the cabin for the deck above. She gasped as she realized that what she had thought was a pile of discarded clothing on the deck was a man's body. Her father's. She ran to him and knelt at his side.

He's dead, she thought, my father's dead. Then he moaned, turning to her and opening his eyes. She was shocked by his appearance. His graying beard was unkempt and matted with vomit, his pale face shriveled, his eyes sunken and staring. He opened his mouth to speak, but his words strangled on his phlegm.

Looking around the cabin, she saw a whiskey bottle on the deck next to his bunk. She found a mug, poured the liquor and held the drink to her father's lips. He swallowed, gagging and coughing. She wiped his face dry with her handkerchief.

"Norah," he said. "Norah, my love."

How can he call her that, Alitha wondered, after betraying her.

"I'm not Norah," she told him. "It's Alitha."

"Alitha?" He struggled to sit up, his back to the bulkhead. "I'll take her to look for mayflowers," he said.

What was he talking about? Then Alitha remembered. She must have been five or six when her father, home on one of his infrequent visits, had walked hand in hand with her to Shelby's Pond and through the small wood beyond, up the sun-swept slope of a field with a long lightning-blasted pine, across a cow path and into another wood. Following a dirt road, they had crossed a wandering creek on a succession of stone bridges. On the far side of one of the bridges, where the creek curved to hug the side of a wooded hill, they climbed a knoll. When they reached the top, her father had pointed ahead into a shaded glen. Alitha ran to kneel on the soft moss, her fingertips touching the flowers, the blood-red flowers shaped like hearts. A short way on she could see the delicate pink blooms of mayflowers.

"I remember, father," she told him. "I remember. Years later I tried to find that spot and I never could."

He took her arm, his fingers surprisingly strong. "Norah," he said, "help me dress."

"No, you should be in your bunk, resting. You're sick, father; let me help you get well."

"I'm dying, Norah, I know that." His voice rose and sharpened into a command. "Help me dress."

Alitha found a basin of water and used a cloth to bathe his face before she helped him off with his soiled shirt and trousers; he was already in his stocking feet. Her father sat on the edge of his bunk watching as she opened his wardrobe.

"The blues," he said, his voice now low and indistinct, infinitely tired.

He wanted his best clothes. She nodded and took down the blue trousers and the blue jacket with the gold buttons and the braid, then helped him put them on. She sat on the deck beside him and pulled on his boots.

"Give me a hand up," he said. She grasped his arm and guided him to his feet. Leaning against her, he staggered to a mirror nailed to the bulkhead. "My hat," he said as he smoothed his hair with his hand. She found the visored cap in the wardrobe and set it squarely on his head.

As he started for the companionway, the ship rolled and he fell, striking his shoulder on the bulkhead.

Alitha steadied him and put his arm around her shoulders.

"Take me to the wheel," he told her.

"No, there's no need for you to go on deck. Mr. Malloy can handle the *Yankee*. Stay here while I get you laudanum."

He ignored her, making for the companionway. She sighed, realizing he wanted to command his ship for the last time, see the billow of the sails over his head, hear the creak of the masts, feel the rise and fall of the deck under his feet. How could she blame him? He will not die, she vowed. He'll live; I'll make him live.

"Don't believe them, Norah," her father said in a hoarse voice as, together, step by tortuous step, they climbed the companionway. "Don't believe the preachers. They lie. They say there is a God and there is none. Enjoy life while you can, Norah. Don't listen to them; pay no heed to the preachers."

Alitha had never heard her father talk this way before. He's delirious, she told herself, he doesn't know what he's saying.

They reached the deck, where the wind and spray stung her face. As they made their way slowly to the wheel, she saw, from the corner of her eyes, Mr. Malloy approach, look into her father's face, then motion the helmsman from his place at the wheel. She had the impression of several crewmen staring up at them from the quarterdeck, heard Malloy shout at them to get on about their business.

Her father gripped the wheel with one hand while Malloy steadied it from the far side. The ship crested a wave and shuddered, and for a moment Alitha thought her father was about to fall. Instead he seemed to call on an inner strength, pulling himself erect and looking up into the rigging.

"Furl the sails, Mr. Jones," he called out. Ephraim Jones, she knew, had been dead more than seven years.

"Aye aye, sir," Malloy answered.

The captain's gaze went to the port side, where whitecaps flecked the sea. With his right hand on the wheel, he raised his left, pointing ahead. "Land," he shouted. "Land ho!"

He glanced down at Alitha. "That's where we saw their fires burning in the night," he said softly. "Look, isn't she a beauty? Did you ever see such a wonder of an island? The mountain shaped like a woman's breast, rising into the clouds, the waterfall cascading from her flank, the palms, the white sands. Can you see it yet, Norah?"

"No, I can't, father," she said.

"You will, once we're closer in to shore. My eyes are sharper than most. Wait till we're anchored in the bay. Look you there." He raised his arm again. "The natives, they're rowing to meet us in their outriggers, bringing coconuts and bananas to barter. And they're bringing women. See the bare-breasted women, brown Venuses they are. And there . . ." He leaned forward. "And there . . ."

He looked back at Alitha as though confused. "Norah?" he asked.

"I'm Alitha," she said.

"Alitha? Of course, Alitha, how quietly she sleeps. She's the most beautiful child in all of New England."

Nehemiah Bradford looked seaward again. Releasing the wheel, he took a step toward the rail as Alitha hurried forward to support him. He took another step and another, at last clutching the rail with both hands and staring across the water to the west.

"She's there in that outrigger," he said. "Do you see her?" He half-turned to Alitha and, because of the spray wetting his face, it was a moment before she realized he was crying. He grasped her upper arm, hurting her. Though she flinched she refused to cry out.

"Do you see her?" her father demanded.

"I see her," she told him, not understanding what he meant.

The captain stumbled along the rail as though to get closer to the outrigger only he could see.

"Just as she was when first we met," he said. "Her hair so golden, her skin so fair, a broad-brimmed hat on her head tied beneath her chin with a red ribbon. So lovely. So lovely. I knew she'd come. Look, she's smiling up at me; she's holding her arms out for me."

Her father straightened to his full height, smoothing his jacket with one hand, his other hand going to his cap. He lifted the cap from his head and swept it across his chest, bending forward as though in a bow. He groaned, lurched back from the rail and fell to the deck. Alitha threw herself beside him, turning him from his side onto his back and burying her face in his chest, sobbing.

"Norah," he whispered. His hand found his daughter's hand and he interlaced his fingers with hers. "Norah," he said. "Do you forgive me?"

He was dying, she could no longer deny it. He would never sail the seas again with a fresh wind at his back and a good ship under his feet. She would never see him smile again, never hear his voice, never feel the comfort of his nearness.

"I forgive you," she told him, speaking for her mother.

"I forgive you," she repeated, speaking this time for herself.

"Then I'm . . ." he began. He gagged, mumbled

words she could not hear. ". . . peace," he said clearly and then lay still.

How long she clung to him Alitha never knew. Her numbness was not broken until the mate lifted her away. Her hand was still laced with her father's, and Malloy had to loosen the fingers one by one. The mate knelt beside the captain.

"He's dead," he told her.

"Yes," was all she could say.

"Go below now, Alitha."

She drew in her breath, quelling her sobs. "Who are you to tell me what to do?" she demanded.

"I'm the master now," he said.

She stood straight and looked him in the eye. "You're mistaken, Mr. Malloy. You are not the master of the *Flying Yankee*."

"If I'm not master, who is?"

"I am, Mr. Malloy."

chapter 3

Amos Malloy stared at Alitha, not knowing what to say. He felt the tic begin at the corner of his mouth.

"The *Flying Yankee* belonged to father," Alitha said. "Now that he's . . ." Her voice broke but she went on. "Now that he's dead, the ship is mine."

"What do you know of sailing a square-rigger? Even if the crew was fit you'd likely run us aground on one of those God-forsaken isles off the California coast."

"Perhaps I'm not making myself clear, Mr. Malloy. You're quite correct. What do I know of navigation other than the little my father taught me on the voyage around the Horn? I'm not intending to pilot the *Yankee*. I just don't want you to have any question as to who her master is."

"And who *shall* captain the ship?"

"Why you, Mr. Malloy, of course." She sounded surprised by his question. "You will, won't you?"

He smiled at the doubt he heard in her voice. Damn her, he thought. Damn women, damn them one and

28

all. A female master! Women had no place on board a ship; he'd said it before and he'd say it again. They brought nothing but trouble in their wake. Once a woman was aboard, bad luck followed. They were Jonahs. From the moment Nehemiah Bradford had escorted his daughter up the gangplank in Boston, the *Yankee* was a cursed ship.

"You will captain the *Yankee*, won't you?" Alitha asked again when Malloy remained silent.

"And why should I?" he said at last. "This ship is hoodooed, half the crew's dead or dying. Who'll be next? Me? You? There's naught to be gained from captaining a ghost ship."

"The cholera is the will of God, not a curse," she said. Alitha reached out to put her hand on his arm, stopped, then touched him briefly on the sleeve before drawing her hand quickly away. "You've been my father's first mate all these years," she said. "He trusted you, he taught you all he knew; now you're the man who must captain the *Yankee*. You're the only man who *can* captain her. The entire crew's depending on you, Mr. Malloy. And I'm depending on you."

"I'll bring the *Yankee* into Yerbe Buena," he said stiffly, trying to hide the glow her words made him feel. "I only wanted it clear that I'm captain of this ship and my orders are to be obeyed. By the crew and by you. Is that understood, Alitha?"

She frowned at his familiar use of her name. "Perfectly, Mr. Malloy," she said.

The ice in her voice made his anger flare. He gripped her chin between his thumb and forefinger and looked down into her face. She started to twist away, then appeared to decide to suffer his touch. When he saw the dark shadows under her eyes, Malloy's anger softened.

"You should rest," he told her, dropping his hand to his side. "You've been up most of the night with the men."

She nodded, pulling out her handkerchief, then glanced across the deck to her father's body.

"I'll see the captain's buried as soon as possible," Malloy said, following her gaze.

Seeing the tears start in her eyes, he felt a rush of sympathy. She had suffered a great tragedy, losing her mother and father in the span of a year, and now she was alone, with no one to turn to. He wanted to help her, take care of her, tell her he understood her sorrow. He, Amos Malloy, would protect her. When he started to put his arm about her comfortingly, Alitha glanced up sharply and stepped away with a glint of fear in her eyes.

"I—" Malloy began, wanting to soothe her fears, to show his sympathy. Why didn't he know what to say? Why wouldn't the right words come? He stepped toward her.

"I'm sure you have a great deal to do," she said. Before he could answer, she turned from him, walking to the companionway and going below.

Damn her to hell, he thought. She thinks she's too good for me because I never had book learning, because I had to fight my way up from the gutter. Old Nehemiah Bradford spoiled her and now she thinks she's better than the rest of us mortals. She needs to be humbled, that one.

The ship rolled drunkenly in the trough of a wave, forcing Malloy to steady the wheel. Signaling the helmsman to return to his post, he strode to the rail above the quarterdeck.

"Bosun," he called, seeing Jonathan Linton making for the galley. He had to hail the man a second time before Linton heard him above the pounding of the sea and came aft.

"The captain's dead of the cholera," Malloy told him, nodding to the body huddled on the deck.

"May God rest his soul," the bosun said. "And may God have mercy on us all."

"See he's made ready for a Christian burial. English George as well."

"Aye . . ." Linton hesitated for an instant before he added, "Captain."

Captain! After all these years, after all his back-breaking toil for a pittance of a wage, the taking of orders, the constant "Aye aye, sir," the groveling before men who knew less of the sea than he, at last he had a ship of his own. A plague ship.

"I've studied the charts," Malloy told the bosun. "Our latitude's 33 degrees 45 minutes north, so we're north of San Diego in Alta California. As for our longitude . . ." He paused for a fraction of a second, then wondered if Linton had noticed. Malloy had never been good with figures; angles and interpolations confused him. He was both slow and impatient yet wise enough to recognize this as a dangerous combination of traits.

"By my dead reckoning," he went on hastily, "I judge we're some four hundred miles off the coast."

Linton's eyebrows went up ever so slightly. "I'd 'spect we'd be closer than that," he said, his fingers massaging his grizzled chin. "There's been gulls following us for the last day or so, and this morning I saw a cloud to starboard. A cloud that didn't move with the wind, like fog sitting offshore."

Malloy nodded. He respected Linton's judgment, knowing the bosun had been to sea for more years than he, Malloy, had lived. Linton was probably one of those seamen who, when they reached the age of, say, fifty-four, accidentally signed on their next ship as forty-five and started anew from there.

"Keep a lookout at the fore topmast," Malloy ordered, "as long as the weather allows."

"Anything else, sir?"

"No, bosun. See to the burials. See to them now."

After he spoke Malloy realized that he had imitated Captain Bradford's way of giving commands and, catching the amused curl of the bosun's mouth, knew he'd been caught out. As Linton went forward to organize a burial crew, Malloy silently cursed himself.

Within an hour the two bodies had been committed to the deep and, as though appeased by this human sacrifice, the storm held off. The seas ran high, yet the wind, though still strong, diminished, and the clouds to the south held their distance as the *Yankee* fled north.

Only after the sun had set behind sullen clouds did Malloy finally go below. He was tired, satisfied with his first day as captain, yet still uneasy. The bosun's warning of the possible nearness of land had nagged him into going to the chart room and laboriously recalculating the ship's position. When he had finished, he nodded to himself. They were a good three hundred miles from shore, approaching the coast at an angle that would keep them out of sight of land for at least two more days. Pushing down the last of his doubts, Malloy sat heavily on the edge of his bunk and looked around his small cabin.

Damn! He was captain; he didn't have to stay in this hovel. He strode along the passageway and pushed open the paneled door to the captain's cabin. Once inside he paused, half-expecting Captain Bradford to appear and order him out. Then he sat in front of the

desk clamped to the bulkhead, putting his feet on
Captain Bradford's sea chest and nodding in satisfaction. This was more like it! This was a cabin befitting a
man responsible for a three-master.

Spying a whiskey bottle on its side in the bunk, he
pulled out the cork and poured himself a full measure.
The whiskey burned his throat; in a few minutes his
spirits lifted. He'd worked hard, he told himself; he
deserved a drop of good cheer. He refilled the glass,
sipping the liquor this time. Closing his eyes, he smiled.
Wait until he sailed into San Francisco Bay to exchange
the *Yankee*'s woolen goods, linen, lead shot, tools and
guns for a cargo of fur and hides. Wait till he returned
to Boston with a ship of his own and a generous profit
from the voyage besides.

Opening his eyes, he watched the light from the lamp
glinting on the empty glass. One more measure to
hurry sleep wouldn't be amiss, he decided.

He'd have to hold off the Boston women with both
hands. And Alitha. That bitch'd be singing a different
tune by then. Why, she acted as if she was afraid he'd
touch her. He looked down at his hands. They were a
man's hands. He splayed his fingers in front of him. A
sailor's hands. Suddenly he folded his arms across his
chest, his hands hidden beneath his biceps.

Alitha. By God, she was a beauty. A beautiful bitch
who thought she was too good for him.

He remembered the night she had turned down his
proposal of marriage, how he'd smiled and nodded,
shaking hands ever so politely with her father as he bid
the captain goodnight. Remembered how he'd stormed
into town thinking to lose himself in drink. After a few
rounds he'd spent his last dollar for an hour with one of
the girls in the house on Dock Hill Road. One of the
girls? Malloy snorted. Like hell she was a girl! That one

hadn't been a girl for a good twenty years or more. He'd had to take the leavings, a man-worn harridan with orange-red hair and sagging tits. He grimaced with distaste.

How different it would be with Alitha. He took a swallow of the whiskey, thinking of Alitha's soft hair cascading over her shoulders, her blue eyes that made him catch his breath whenever she looked at him, the whiteness of her skin above the scooped neckline of her dress, her breasts high, full and firm and her body slim as a girl's yet as rounded as any woman's.

He had often imagined her taking his hand, the fingers of her other hand going to her lips to silence his questions as she led him into her cabin on the *Yankee* and bolted the door behind them. She turned to him, tall and proud, unbuttoning her dress and stepping out of it, pulling her undergarments over her head and hastily slipping into the bunk and clutching the covers to her neck, leaving only her slim white arms exposed. She reached for him, whispering, "Come to me, Amos. Hurry."

Thinking of her white and naked body, Malloy felt his maleness grow. He slammed his fist on the desk in front of him. It would never happen. She hated the sight of him, shunned his touch. Once he had her abed, though, that would change, he told himself. She was a virgin, he was sure, but once she had a man she'd be a hellcat—she wasn't one of these prissy once-every-two-weeks women like some of his friends had married; he could tell by the way she looked at him sometimes, as though she too had secretly imagined their bodies intertwined.

He was tired of whores. He didn't want another man's leavings, he wanted a woman who would be his and his alone. Where were the girls he'd known ashore? Married, the lot of them, most at fifteen or sixteen and none too soon at that, their bellies already swelling beneath their wedding gowns. He didn't want that either, not a life sentence as punishment for a few minutes' roll in the hay.

Malloy sipped his drink. What a fool you are, Amos Malloy! he told himself. Calling this your ship. Dreaming of returning in triumph to Boston with Alitha at your side. He looked down at his hands. You'll be naught but a horny-handed seaman for the rest of your life, Amos Malloy. A short life at that, he feared, one fated to end in a watery grave. It wasn't right; it wasn't fair.

And then slowly, one thought laboriously added to another, as a ship's carpenter might fashion a sea chest, he began to construct a plan in his mind. He crafted it with care, and when he had finished, he inspected it from every side. He could find no flaws. Malloy smiled. Soon the *Yankee* would be his, Alitha would be his. He stood up, ready; there was no reason to delay. Picking up the bottle, he emptied the last of the whiskey and raised his glass in a toast.

"To Captain Amos Malloy!" he said aloud.

After her father's burial service Alitha returned to the forecastle, where she meted out swallows of the ship's precious water to the sick crewmen. She cleaned and bathed them, trying to soothe them in their misery. When she saw there was no more she could do, she hurried aft, warily keeping out of Malloy's sight. She went to her father's cabin and closed the door behind her.

Such a small cabin, she thought, though it was the largest on board. The ship seemed so small, so cramped. After they left Boston, while they sailed south into the Southern Hemisphere's summer, the ship had seemed spacious, with each day offering her new vistas of sea and sky as they left the bitter New England winter behind. Now, with seas running high and a storm bearing down on them, and with her father dead, she felt trapped aboard the *Yankee*, a prisoner on her own ship.

Dropping to her knees in front of her father's sea chest, she took his keys from her pocket and tried them one by one in the lock. After the lid sprang open she laid her father's folded clothing to one side until she found, at the bottom, a Bible and an intricately crafted rosewood case. She opened the Bible, a small black volume with pages edged in gold, and, as she often did when she needed guidance, read aloud the first verse she saw:

And he shewed me Joshua the high priest standing
before the angel of the Lord, and Satan standing
at his right hand to resist him.

Alitha shook her head. What did the verse mean? How did Ezekiel's words apply to her? Closing the Bible and returning it to the sea chest, she removed the rosewood case.

Taking the case in both hands, she turned and placed it carefully on her father's desk. She raised the lid. Inside, lying on the purple velvet lining, was a pistol with a silver barrel and a carved wooden handle. She tested the weight of the gun in her hand, finding it heavier than she had remembered.

She frowned. Could she load the weapon? Her father had taught her how long ago, even letting her practice firing the pistol. She remembered closing her eyes when she pulled the trigger and missing the tree-stump target by several feet.

Now she removed a cartridge and ball from a packet in the rosewood case, tore off the paper end and poured a small amount of the powder into the pistol's hollow pan and the rest down the barrel. She dropped the ball and the paper wrapper into the barrel and rammed them down with a rod. After relocking the sea chest, she picked up the pistol gingerly by the handle and carried it to her cabin.

Once she had slid home the bolt on her cabin door, Alitha laid the pistol on her bunk. She removed her shoes, unbuttoned and stepped out of her dress and petticoats, then pulled her chemise over her head. She held a sheer white batiste nightgown in front of her, admiring for a moment the delicate blue of the ribbons threaded through the bodice, then put her arms in the sleeves and shrugged the gown down over her body.

The pistol. Where could she hide the pistol? She was afraid of leaving the gun on the desk or deck, fearful that a sudden lurch of the ship would send the gun slamming against a bulkhead, firing it. Finally she raised the goose-down mattress from her bunk and put the gun between the mattress and the canvas underneath.

Satisfied, she turned the spirit lamp low, lay on her bunk and pulled the blanket over herself, telling herself she would surely fall asleep at once, she was so tired, so exhausted. But she did not. Thoughts of her father, her mother, Thomas and Amos Malloy whirled through her mind, even thoughts of Jordan Quinn and the *Kerry Dancer*.

She forced herself to picture the Sandwich Islands as she imagined them to be, with the *Yankee* sailing into a sheltered cove where palm trees arched over white sand beaches. Her imaginings mingled with reality as the ship rose and fell to the rhythm of the sea and she heard the creaking of the *Yankee*'s timbers as the ship bore her on toward her destiny.

She was swimming in warm, milk-white water. Turning onto her back, she floated, feeling the sun on her face. When she looked down she drew in her breath at the sight of her uncovered breasts breaking the surface of the water. She ran her hands down along her sides. She was naked.

Rolling over in the water again, she swam toward shore, feeling freer than she had ever felt before. When her hand touched bottom she stood up, wading to the beach. She turned, standing at the waterline with her hands on her hips as she looked at the breaking surf. Her nakedness did not shame her; rather, she felt a pride in her body.

She sensed someone behind her.

"You are a thing of Satan, a creature of the devil." It was Thomas's voice. "Cover your lustful body, woman."

Her hands went to her breasts and she began to run, her hair jouncing damply on her shoulders, her toes digging into the wet sand. When she could run no more, she climbed the slope of the beach and threw herself on the sun-baked sand, feeling the granules hot against her breasts and thighs.

A man's hand closed on the nape of her neck, his fingers moving down to the small of her back. A rough hand. Alitha looked over her shoulder and . . .

. . . woke up. The cabin was totally dark; the spirit lamp was out. The ship was pitching more violently than before, rising high to meet each wave and crashing down into its trough. Had she heard a sound in the cabin? Had something or someone touched her? Wakened her? She held her breath, listening. Yes, there was someone here, close by. She hunched herself up in the bunk, holding a blanket in front of her.

A hand grasped the blanket and tore it from her. She screamed although she realized no one could hear her above the wail of the storm. She felt a hand on her shoulder; the hand felt its way to the neck of her gown and yanked downward. The ribbons pulled loose and the gown opened to the waist, exposing her breasts. She clutched at the cloth.

The gun. She had hidden the gun beneath the mattress. Shifting her body to the far side of the bunk, she whispered, "Who are you?"

"Why, 'tis Amos Malloy," a voice answered, "your husband-to-be."

"You've lost your senses." Her hand slid down between the bulkhead and the mattress, her fingers searching for the gun.

"You'll never say no to me again," Malloy told her. "Once I've had you, you'll have no choice but to marry me. You'll be begging to marry me."

Her fingers closed on the gun's barrel and she pulled the weapon from beneath the mattress. Shifting her grip to the handle, she pointed the pistol where she had last heard Malloy's voice. "I have a loaded pistol in my hand," she said. "If you touch me, I'll kill you."

He laughed in disbelief. When she felt his huge hand close on her knee, her finger tightened on the trigger and she heard a snap. The gun had misfired. She pulled the trigger again. Still the gun failed to fire. What had she done wrong when she loaded it? She took the weapon by the barrel and swung it at Malloy, the butt grazing his head. He cursed her and his hand found her wrist, twisting her arm until she cried out in pain. He seized the pistol and tossed it behind him to the deck.

"You bitch, you did have a gun," he said.

He gripped her ankle and pulled her down so she lay full-length on the bunk. His hands went up her body beneath her gown, closing on her hips and pulling her to him. When his chest brushed against her breasts, she knew he was naked. She screamed, fighting him, clawing at him. He laughed and grabbed the open front of her nightgown so that the thin cotton tore. A moment later her entire body was bared to his hands. Those terrible huge hands.

"I've waited a long time for this," he said.

chapter 4

ALITHA STOPPED STRUGGLING. I must think, she told herself desperately. I can't outfight Malloy; my only hope is to outwit him.

His fingers slid roughly up her leg to her inner thigh and, though she felt her flesh shiver in revulsion, she forced herself to lie still. He pushed her thighs apart with his hands and knelt on the bunk between her legs, his hands going to her breasts.

Her breath came rapidly, not with desire but with fear. Every touch of Malloy's enormous hands made her cringe. How could I have imagined wanting this man to hold me in his arms, she wondered. She wanted to hurt him; yes, to kill him if she could. Still she made no move to defend herself. Though her tense body quivered, she lay before him as though defeated and helpless.

Malloy's hands left her breasts and she felt the mattress shift under his weight as he leaned toward her. His lips touched her breast. When his tongue circled her nipple, she gagged. Swallowing, she raised her hands and put them on his shoulders, her fingers kneading his flesh in the briefest of caresses—she couldn't force herself to do any more to make him lower his guard. She heard Malloy draw in his breath.

With all the strength she had left, she shoved against his shoulders with both of her hands, at the same time hurling herself away so she fell backward from the bunk, her shoulder slamming heavily on the deck. Malloy grunted in surprise and she heard him scrambling to his feet. She rolled sideways until her leg struck the sea chest, and then she was on her feet plunging toward the cabin door.

Malloy was there ahead of her. Catching her by the arm, he held her as she struggled, then forced her back step by step, his strength overpowering her. She felt the edge of the bunk pressing against the backs of her legs.

A pounding came from the passageway outside the cabin. Malloy hesitated and, with both of them frozen in surprise, they listened. A voice called out.

"Captain. Captain Malloy." Linton? Yes, surely it was the bosun.

Malloy's hand closed over Alitha's mouth. She heard more pounding, as though Linton had gone from Malloy's cabin to her father's.

"Captain, Captain Malloy," Linton called again. "Surf to starboard, Captain."

Malloy cursed, shoving Alitha from him so she fell back across her bunk. She lay exhausted, feeling pain stab her shoulder while she listened to Malloy searching in the dark for his clothes. Only after several minutes did she hear the cabin door bang open and then closed.

"I'm coming," Malloy shouted to Linton from the passageway.

Surf! The storm was sweeping the *Yankee* toward the

California coast. Alitha had been so numbed that at first the meaning of the bosun's words had almost escaped her. Above the sound of the wind and waves, she thought she heard a distant rumble like the roll of thunder in the mountains.

She pushed herself from the bunk, hurriedly slipping a chemise over her head. Taking the first dress her searching fingers found, she put it on, then slid her feet into slippers and ran from the cabin. She climbed the companionway, having to stop and cling to the railing as the *Yankee* listed precipitously to port. The ship shuddered, righted herself, and Alitha climbed the rest of the way to the deck.

The wind struck her a savage blow from behind and she went to her knees to keep from falling across the wet deck. The night was so dark she saw only the faint outline of the ship; the huge waves rose and fell blackly against the dark gray of the sky. When she stood up, a rain-soaked cloth slapped her face. Reaching over her head, she felt the cloth and recognized it as a torn section of sail. Without enough crewmen to work aloft, the *Yankee*'s sails had been shredded by the wind.

A wave roared across the deck as though trying to sweep her into the sea, but she had found a rope along the starboard side and kept her feet. Though she peered to both port and starboard, she couldn't see the telltale white of the surf nor could she hear its boom above the howling of the storm and the shrieks and groans of the ship around her.

A brilliant flash illuminated the deck. Lightning! The flash, gone in an instant, was followed by a crack of thunder that seemed to rend the sky. In that moment of intense light, Alitha had stared in horror at the shambles of the once-proud *Yankee*—the mizzenmast was gone, carried away; rigging and sails hung over the port side in a jumble of ropes and spars. Forward, near the forecastle, she had seen men in black oilskins and sea boots straining to free the ship's boat from beneath a tangle of debris. Were they abandoning ship?

She waited until another wave crashed across the main deck. Then, holding the rail with both hands, she inched her way forward, slipping and sliding on the wet, pitching deck. Her hair was soaked and her dress clung to her legs, the cold of the water sending chills coursing through her body.

Lightning flickered in the distance. Seeing a man looming ahead of her, Alitha took him by the arm. He turned to her with an oath.

"It's Alitha Bradford," she shouted.

When he recognized her, he leaned toward her and bellowed in her ear.

"Get thee to the starboard side. We'll soon have the boat ready for launching."

So they did mean to launch the boat—they were abandoning the *Yankee*. Alitha couldn't imagine her father giving up this ship, his ship, without more of a fight. Could they have been swept closer to the shore than she realized? Had they fought the sea and the storm and lost?

She tensed, waiting for her chance to let go of the rail so she could cross the deck to the starboard side. The ship pitched and tossed, the sea rougher than she had ever known it. Now? No, the *Yankee*'s bow rose high on the next wave, and she had to wrap her arms around the rail. If only we had a full crew, she thought, even now we could outrun this storm and save the ship. If only the cholera hadn't . . .

She gasped. She had forgotten the men in the forecastle. They probably lay huddled helplessly in their bunks, deathly ill yet confident the ship would ride out this storm as she had so many others. After all, the *Flying Yankee* had faced the worst of the Cape Horn gales and survived.

When the ship steadied, Alitha clambered up the sloping deck, pushed open the door and climbed down the ladder into the terrible stench of the forecastle. A lamp, swinging with every rise and dip of the *Yankee,* burned dimly overhead. All around her men lay groaning in their bunks; the deck was aslop with sea water and vomit.

"You have to get out," she cried, steadying herself in the doorway. "They're abandoning the ship."

None of the men seemed to hear. Lost in their misery, they lay curled on their bunks, some dead, others unconscious, the rest heedless of all but the extremes of their agony. Alitha sloshed across the forecastle deck to Jenkins's bunk—he had been more alert than the others that afternoon when, together, they had prayed for his recovery. She looked down into his unseeing eyes. Jenkins was dead.

She returned to the ladder, recalling a phrase from Shakespeare. The men were "past hope, past cure, past help." After one last despairing look around the forecastle that burned the scene into her memory forever, she climbed to the main deck. The ship still raced forward, but the wind had lessened and the *Yankee*'s pitching had abated. They'll launch the ship's boat now, she told herself. When lightning flickered again, she looked to where the boat should be.

The deck was empty; the boat and the men were gone; only the litter of sails and rigging remained. She looked ahead—during the lightning's flash she thought she had seen something from the corner of her eye— and saw a line of white to starboard only a cable length from the ship—the white line of surf.

A grinding crash shook the ship. The deck tilted and she heard a pistollike crack from above and a thudding from behind. A yardarm must have splintered, she told herself, and come hurtling to the deck. The ship no longer plunged ahead. She had grounded on rocks and, listing at least thirty degrees to port, offered no resistance to the waves thundering over her stern. For the first time Alitha felt gusts of rain pelting against her face.

She froze. She should stay with the ship, she told herself, until the storm abated and she could reach shore. Surely the crew had abandoned the *Yankee* too soon. No, she argued with herself, the waves would surely break the ship apart on the rocks. She should lower herself from the side into the sea and try to swim to shore even though she was a weak swimmer. Undecided, she felt a quiver of fear for the first time since she had fled from her cabin.

Fighting down her fear and hopelessness, she pulled herself along the rail, making her way aft. She would go to her father's cabin. Only there would she be safe.

A roar filled her ears as the ship shuddered. Water cascaded over her and she grasped for a rope, found none and was swept forward and over the port side into the sea. Fighting her way to the surface, she gasped for air. When she tried to swim, her dress tangled around her legs, so she held her breath and went under as she frantically unbuttoned the front of the dress and shrugged her arms out of the sleeves. After long moments she felt her legs kick their way free, and she surfaced once again.

She couldn't swim in the strong current. Time after time she struggled to the surface and gulped air into her lungs, only to be pushed under again as she was borne forward by the sea. An object struck her arm and her fingers closed on a board as she dimly realized it must be planking from the ship or a piece of crating wrested loose from the hold by the waves. Wrapping her arms around the board, she shut her eyes, concentrating all her energy on holding fast as she let the current sweep her on.

When Alitha opened her eyes, she found herself on a rocky shelf of land with her feet entangled in strands of a brown tubular growth. Water flowed up along her legs, fell away, then rose again. Rain beat down on her back, and the wind moaned mournfully overhead. She had no strength left, her shoulder ached and every muscle in her body seemed sore. She kicked her feet free of the kelp and crawled a few yards higher on the beach, cradled her head in her arms and slept.

When she wakened, the rain had stopped. A strong wind off the Pacific sent dark clouds scudding overhead and drove menacing waves onto the rocks below. The *Flying Yankee* was nowhere to be seen; the only evidence that the ship had ever existed was the timber scattered on the shingled beach.

Alitha pushed herself to her feet, her body aching, her legs and arms blackened by bruises. The torn white chemise, which came only to her thighs, clung wetly to her body and she shivered in the cold wind. Climbing in her bare feet to the top of a rise behind the beach, she looked around and saw that she stood on a point of land thrusting into the sea. A few hundred feet inland the ground rose to twin hills. There were no trees, only the barren, black rocks along the shore and the fields of April-green grass on the hillsides.

She walked along the water's edge—the clouds hid the sun so that she had no idea of the direction she was taking—and found nothing except more timbers and shattered crates washed up on the shore. Overhead, gulls screamed at her, the birds hovering almost motionlessly above her as they fought against the force of the wind. When she had walked about a mile, she stopped and began retracing her steps, passing the place where she had come ashore during the night.

At first she thought the black mass ahead of her on the beach was just another rock. When she realized it was a man with one arm outstretched, the other curled under him, she ran toward him. One of the crewmen, she thought, thrown onto the rocks as she had been. When she drew near, she saw the fingers of the man's huge hand spread out on the black of the rock and knew it was Malloy.

She put her hand on his chest and felt the slow rise and fall of his breathing. He was alive! She stood up and looked both ways along the beach, glanced inland and then out to sea as though seeking help while knowing she would find none. When she looked down at Malloy once more, she remembered his hands on her body and the taste of bile rose in her throat.

A few feet away she found a large boulder. Lifting it, using all her remaining strength, she returned to stand next to Malloy, holding the rock above his head. She would dash it down on him, kill him. She raised the boulder to her chest, then higher, to her chin. Now! she told herself.

She swung around, staggering away and letting the rock fall from her hands. No, she couldn't kill him. The day before, in the cabin, she could have shot him and felt little remorse. Here, with Malloy helpless at her feet, she found it impossible. She lowered her face into her hands.

"You meant to kill me."

She looked down to see Malloy's brown eyes flick away from her face. He raised himself on one arm, then sat with his arms around his knees, staring at the ground between his legs.

"Why didn't you kill me when you had the chance?" he asked. "You had cause enough."

"I don't know," she told him. "I couldn't."

He looked to sea. "They managed to get the boat away," he said slowly. "I stayed with the *Yankee* until she broke up on the rocks."

"Do you know where we are?" she asked.

"No. On the California coast, surely, but just where I can't say. Not within a hundred leagues. I thought the ship was far from shore. I was wrong."

She had never seen Malloy so humble. The loss of the ship, his ship, must have come close to destroying all his faith in himself.

"We have to join forces," she told him. "We can't afford to be enemies, not here. We'll do much better with two pairs of eyes to look for ships, with two of us instead of one to search for food and water."

"Have no fear, I'll not harm you."

For the first time he looked at her, and she followed his glance down to her bare arms and legs, to the damp chemise outlining her breasts and hips under its thin cloth. Instinctively she folded her arms over her breasts as she saw the sudden glint in his eyes. When he pushed himself to his feet, she drew back.

"I'll not harm you," he said again.

He walked from her and stood at the top of the beach looking about him.

"Can you recognize any of this from the charts?" she asked.

"No, none of it. I'd best climb one of those hills and have a look."

"I'll come with you."

"There's no need."

"I want to. You lead and I'll follow."

He shrugged and made off with his rolling sailor's gait across the rocks toward the grassy hills, with Alitha a few steps behind. She felt the wind change; a warm sun came out from behind the clouds. After a time, without looking back at her, he said, "Why do you hate me, Miss Alitha?"

"I don't hate you. I don't hate anyone. It's not Christian to hate."

They walked on in silence. Did she hate him? Was he right? Yes, he was; admit it, she told herself. "You—you tried to force me," she said.

"I mean even before. All during the voyage from Boston. Is it my hands?"

"Of course not," she said quickly. "How can I explain? There are some men, when I first meet them I know I don't want them to touch me, ever. I can't explain why. Perhaps they remind me of someone who hurt me when I was a child. I can't give you reasons, Mr. Malloy. It has nothing to do with the man, how good a man he might be or what he does to earn his livelihood."

"You think you're too good for me." He sounded sulky, like a small boy.

"No, I don't. When I marry, it might be to a laborer or a sea captain or a farmer or a merchant. How well-to-do he is will have no bearing."

"I thought your intended was a missionary."

She stopped in confusion, realizing she had forgotten about Thomas. Of course she meant to marry Thomas. After all, she was betrothed to him.

"I was speaking in a general way," she said. "Not about myself."

She looked to see if Malloy had noticed her white lie.

Seemingly not, for he was walking quickly ahead toward the sheltered side of a rise of ground.

"Look you." He pointed near his feet. When she stood beside him, she saw the wet, charred remains of a fire. "We're not the only ones here," he said.

"Another shipwrecked sailor?"

He poked at the dead fire with his toe. "I don't rightly know; he's left no other signs. They do say there are savage Indians in these parts."

They resumed their climb, going more slowly now, stopping often to glance around them. When Malloy reached the top of the first of the twin hills, he looked about him and then turned to face her as she came up the last slope.

"I feared as much," he said, swinging his arm in a circle.

Shielding her eyes from the sun, she gazed down and saw the sea crashing against the rocks to her right, saw a small sheltered bay ahead of them, the open sea to her left and behind her. They were on an island. This wasn't the coast of California at all but an island. Though she peered across the sea, vainly searching for the mainland, low clouds prevented her from seeing more than a few miles.

"There's isles all up and down the coast in these latitudes," Malloy said. "The Santa Barbaras, they're called." His shoulders seemed to slump.

"We'll find a way to the mainland. We'll hail a passing ship or build a boat of our own. There must be a way."

"No ships approach these shores. Unless they have a fool for a captain," he added bitterly. "And from the looks of it there's nary a tree on the island, nor food."

"We have the timbers from the *Yankee*. And there

must be fish in the sea we could catch. And I saw pools of water left by the storm."

"I should be the one encouraging you," he said. He sighed. "We'd best find out what we're faced with."

They spent the rest of the day exploring. The island, she judged, was some seven miles long and three across, with the one bay protected by a reef. As Malloy had said, there were no trees, none at all; only the grass and a few shrubs growing in gullies. They found sand dunes on the lee side; the rest of the shoreline was black rock inhabited by thousands of birds. Other than the remains of the fire, they saw no other signs of human life.

As the day darkened, Alitha came upon a sheltered cranny near the dunes and dropped to the sand, exhausted. She was hungry, her head ached and she was beginning to shiver from the cold. Her throat hurt when she swallowed and her bruised muscles throbbed. She watched Malloy warily. During the day she had seen him staring at her, seemingly fascinated by the way her nipples pressed against her chemise and, when she walked ahead of him, by the curve of her buttocks.

Now he came and stood over her. "I mean to have you," he said.

Alarmed, she looked up. "You agreed," she protested.

"All day you've flaunted yourself at me. It's more than a man can stand."

"Amos," she said placatingly as she got to her feet. He watched her, waiting.

She turned and ran. When she left the sand, she heard his boots pounding after her across the shingle. Pain sliced into the soles of her feet and she winced. He would be upon her in a moment; already she could imagine him grasping her by the shoulder, spinning her about and throwing her to the ground.

Malloy grunted and she heard him fall. Slowing, she looked behind her. Malloy lay sprawled on the black rock with the shaft of an arrow protruding from his back.

chapter 5

JORDAN QUINN RODE the bay gelding slowly up the dirt road from the beach with Señor Huerta, the Mendoza rancho overseer, riding beside him while behind them Jack McKinnon sat next to an Indian driver on the raised seat of a mule cart. Jordan envied his first mate, able to ride in comfort while he had to make the four-mile journey on horseback. Damn, he was sore already.

In the distance he saw Indian workmen carrying mortar up long ramps to one of the unfinished towers of the Santa Barbara Mission. In front of the church water spouted from the stone mouth of a statue of a bear, flowing into a basin where Indian women bent over their washing.

"Don Esteban," Huerta said, speaking in Spanish because he knew Jordan was fluent in the language, "asked me to extend a thousand pardons for his unfortunate delay. He hoped you would accept my own humble presence as a small sign of his regard for the esteemed American captain who has come from far across the oceans to marry his sister."

This was at least the fourth time Huerta had proferred Esteban's regrets for being absent when the *Kerry Dancer* anchored in the Santa Barbara channel. Jordan controlled his impatience.

"I appreciate Don Esteban's concern," he said, "and I know that only the most urgent business would have kept him from greeting me himself. I will not neglect to inform him that you, Señor Huerta, represented him with all the courtesy and hospitality for which the Mendoza family is so rightly renowned throughout Alta California."

In fact, Jordan thought, he'd just as soon not have to see Esteban Mendoza at all. He'd never liked the man even before he'd learned that Esteban opposed his sister's marriage to a foreigner. Jordan was here for one purpose and one only—to marry Margarita Mendoza as quickly as possible and take her with him aboard the *Kerry Dancer* to Monterey.

Señor Huerta smiled. "You are too kind," he said, "to a humble emissary."

Ahead of them two California oaks flanked the roadway at the entrance to the Mendoza *rancho*. Jordan, who had been a guest of the Mendozas the year before, knew that their lands extended from the *rancho* for many miles west along the coast.

"So must the gates of Paradise seem," Jordan said as they rode under the oaks with the scent of orange blossoms in the air all around them. He could match false sentiment with false sentiment any day, he told himself.

"The orange groves are white with blooms," Huerta told him. "This year will be a good one for all of us. The cattle are branded, the sun following the rains will

speed the crops, the orchards are in leaf and—a crown
upon our crown of happiness—Señorita Margarita will
soon wed the man of her choice, the gallant Capitan
Jordan Quinn of the stout ship *Kerry Dancer*."

Jordan sketched a bow, reluctant to do even that for
fear of losing his balance in the saddle. He made no
reply, realizing when he was clearly overmatched in the
contest of exchanging empty compliments.

They rounded a turn in the road and saw the
two-story Mendoza *casa* set against the green back-
ground of the Santa Inez Mountains. A horseman, his
black steed at a walk, the silver ornaments of his jacket
glistening in the sun, came around one of the ranch
buildings onto the road in front of the house.

"*Bueno*," Huerta said. "Good, Don Esteban has
returned."

As Esteban approached, Huerta raised his hand to
his wide-brimmed hat while Jordan clumsily shifted the
reins to his left hand. He'd be damned if he'd salute the
man. Should he offer to shake hands? On horseback
he'd be risking life and limb if he did.

Esteban reined in beside Jordan, leaned from his
horse and clasped the sea captain to him, then guided
his black stallion a few paces to one side, rider and
horse moving as one. The man can certainly sit a horse,
Jordan thought with reluctant admiration. He'd like to
see him, though, on the deck of the *Dancer* for a few
days; he'd be sick as a dog. Jordan smiled at the
thought.

Esteban smiled back, his white teeth flashing. He's a
handsome devil, Jordan admitted to himself.

"I welcome you as brother greets brother," Esteban
said, "not with great ceremony but with pleasure and in
the spirit of comradeship. My people are your people.
My home is your home."

"Don Esteban, whatever pleasure you have in welcoming me only equals half the joy I feel in being at last at the home of my betrothed and her gracious family."

"Well said; already you speak like a Californio. In truth, soon you will become one."

"Never; I'm a sailor. I've been a sailor all my life and I intend to remain one."

"As for myself," Esteban said, "I love the sea. I have sailed to Spain, to Acapulco, San Diego and Yerba Buena many times. Never have I suffered from the *mal de mer*. Forgive me, I did not intend to appear boastful; I only wished to state a fact."

"*De nada*. It is nothing."

How I'd like to take you down a peg or two, Don Esteban Mendoza, Jordan thought. Why did Margarita's older brother always have this effect on him? Each time he met Esteban, Jordan's intentions were of the best. I'll make a friend of the man, he'd assure himself, and each time, after a few minutes, he found himself gritting his teeth.

Could he be envious of Esteban, Jordan wondered. Though he was not as tall as Jordan, the Spaniard who, at thirty, was Jordan's age, was muscular and lithe and sat his horse as though the animal were an extension of himself. The man had charm, too, Jordan admitted, or at least women seemed to think so. Perhaps he was put off by Esteban's small black mustache. Jordan distrusted men with mustaches even though he himself wore a beard. There was something almost effeminate about a mustache, he thought.

"Señor Huerta will escort Señor McKinnon to his room," Esteban said as they dismounted in the courtyard in the center of the Mendoza *casa*.

"I'm anxious to see Margarita," Jordan told him,

glancing up at the gallery in the vain hope of catching a glimpse of her. "It's been almost two years."

"A lengthy absence kindles the flames of love. Be patient; she will come to us soon. I can attest that her impatience is the equal of your own."

The *casa* appeared little changed, Jordan thought, with the living quarters for the Indian house servants, the bathing rooms and the offices on the lower floor. The two men climbed the stairs to the gallery, which ran completely around the inside of the house and overlooked the courtyard in the center. Esteban pulled aside a beaded curtain and they entered the *sala*, a dark, cool apartment furnished with tables, two chaise longues and armchairs made of cane. Candles flamed in brass and iron sconces on the walls.

Esteban went to a side table and returned with a bottle of white wine and two glasses. He handed a glass to Jordan and poured the wine.

"To the marriage of Jordan Quinn and Margarita Mendoza," he said, raising the glass. "May their union be blessed with every happiness known to God and man."

They sipped the wine in silence.

"I deeply regret that I was unable to meet your ship," Esteban said after a time.

"Your emissary, Señor Huerta, was most profuse in expressing your apologies."

"Three days ago I and others were summoned to the *rancho* of Don José Ortega at Refugio Bay. He had received a report that Monsieur Bouchard and his men were about to mount an attack. Fortunately the report proved false."

"The pirate Bouchard? Then there actually are pirates in these waters."

"Of a certainty. A sea captain arriving from the

Sandwich Islands told of seeing Bouchard's ships anchored there and hearing that they planned to sail east to raid the coast of the Californias. These pirates are men of evil who care nothing for life or property. And, as you know, there are few of us here in California to defend our lands. A few missions, each with one or two *padres,* a scattering of *ranchos* along the coast and *presidios* manned by soldiers who haven't been paid more than a few times since the troubles began in Mexico. We're kept busy controlling the thousands of wild Indians who rob and steal from us at every opportunity. And, though the mission Indians are not wild, who knows if they would fight with us against Bouchard?" Esteban shrugged. "What is one to do?"

"You could join forces with the Americans."

"I must smile. The Americans are two thousand miles away beyond the great mountain ranges. It takes six months and more for one of your ships to sail around the Horn. No, we'll never link our destiny with the Americans. Nor with the Russians at Fort Ross in the north. Our salvation lies with the mother country, with Spain. Or if Spain is too weak to hold Mexico and the Californias, we must make our own destiny."

"Spain is of the past. She loses her colonies one by one. And, as you say, the Spanish in California are too few. The future belongs to America, to the United States."

"Not in our lifetime, Capitán. Ah, I almost forgot. When I was the guest of the Ortegas, I heard ill tidings of one of your Yankee ships. She had the misfortune to run aground in last week's great storm."

"The *Kerry Dancer* had to wait out the same storm in the bay on Catalina Island," Jordan said. "What was the name of this American ship?"

"The *Flying Yankee.*"

"Were there survivors?" Jordan belatedly realized he'd spoken in English, but Esteban answered smoothly.

"Seven men brought the ship's long boat ashore fifty leagues up the coast. They spoke of cholera aboard the ship, the captain dying, and of breaking up on a rocky shore. Only then, or so they said, did they abandon their ship. They had no notion where their ship went aground."

"Seven men." Jordan walked to the far end of the *sala* where three large windows came down to the floor, their green shutters closed against the sun.

"No women?" he asked.

In the reflection in the window glass, Jordan saw Esteban shake his head. "They spoke of none," the Californio said. "Do you know this ship, this *Yankee?*"

"I saw her in the harbor at Valparaiso more than two months ago as we were putting to sea. There was a young woman on deck, the captain's daughter or wife, I suppose. I saw her for no longer than five minutes."

"Many years ago," Esteban said, "in Mexico City, I watched a Spanish *señorita* dance *la zorrita*. I never spoke to her and I never saw her again. I've never forgotten her. I don't think I ever will."

The bead curtains parted and Margarita came into the *sala*. As she paused inside the entrance, Jordan caught his breath as he always did when he first saw her. She was so lovely, with her jet black hair falling in curls to her shoulders, her deep brown eyes, her small hands, her tiny feet just visible beneath her flowered silk gown. So lovely and so vulnerable.

She ran to Jordan, and he circled her waist with his hands, lifting her high into the air. She couldn't weigh more than a hundred pounds, Jordan thought as he let her slide down into his arms. When he embraced her, she offered her cheek for him to kiss. Though Esteban had turned away to pour more wine, Margarita's aunt, Doña Maria Mendoza, had entered the room and was standing behind her.

"I've counted the days," Margarita said, smiling up at Jordan. "As each passing day brought you closer to me, I marked my calendar with an enormous *X*."

"I came as quickly as the wind and the sea would let me." Jordan felt uncomfortable talking to her with her brother and aunt in the room, even though he knew it was the custom.

Margarita took his hands in hers and danced around him, making him turn in a full circle. He grinned down at her; she was so alive, her eyes shining as she smiled gaily at him. He wanted to gather her into his arms where he could hold and protect her forever.

Esteban handed them each a glass and, the mood broken, they stood awkwardly sipping the white wine. With the first excitement of their meeting past, there seemed to be nothing to say. Esteban finally broke the silence.

"The wedding will be held in five days' time," he told Jordan. "We had to delay making our plans until we learned of your arrival."

"Guests are coming from all of California," Margarita said. "Don Francisco Ortega, Don Pablo Grijalva, Don Mario Vallejo and so many others. All with their wives, of course."

"As usual," Esteban said, "my sister is more enthusiastic than accurate." Jordan, seeing Esteban smile fondly at Margarita, felt a grudging warmth for his future brother-in-law. "They are journeying from as far away as Santa Ana," Esteban went on, "the pueblo of Los Angeles, San Luis Obispo and, perhaps, from the capital at Monterey as well."

"And after the ceremony," Margarita told Jordan breathlessly, "there will be a magnificent *fandango* here at the *casa*, with dancing and feasting for many days and a fight between a wild bear and a brave bull and the *vaqueros* will race their horses and draw the cock."

Jordan nodded. He had seen them draw the cock on his last visit, the *vaqueros* burying a live rooster in the ground and, one at a time, riding by as fast as they could, hanging one-handed from their horses to grasp the cock's neck and try to pull him from the ground.

"Padre Luis has given us permission to use the mission church for the ceremony," Esteban said, "even though the work on the tower isn't finished. This time they intend to build a church that will withstand the most violent of earthquakes."

"I expected to find the church finished," Jordan said. All of the day's irritations rose to his mind; his impatience with the elaborate Spanish courtesies, having to wait another five days before he and Margarita could marry, the antagonism he suspected Esteban felt toward him. "Surely they have enough Indian slaves for the work," he said.

There was complete silence.

"Slaves?" Esteban asked quietly. "The Indians are not slaves. You are, perhaps, confusing California with one of your Southern states. This is not Georgia, not Virginia. The Indians are neophytes, as you know, who are being taught Christianity by the *padres*. They were savages when we Spanish came to California, living in the wilds, eating acorns and grass . . ."

". . . and wearing no clothing at all," Margarita

broke in. Her brother glared at her and she quickly covered her mouth with her hand. When Esteban looked away, she winked at Jordan.

"They were pagans who worshipped the sun, the moon, the earth and the mountains. They had no sense of sin, they did not know the difference between right and wrong. The *padres* are instructing them in the meaning of sin."

"By flogging them? Or did they get the stripes on their backs in some other way?"

"They are like children. As a child must be punished by his parents when he disobeys, so must the Indians be punished. The *padres* love them as though they were the sons and daughters they themselves can never have. They feed and clothe and house them."

"And pay them nothing for their work."

"If the Indians were given money, they would buy *aguardiente* and drink and quarrel for days."

"And be unable to carry mortar or work in the mission fields or tend the mission cattle," Jordan put in.

"The Indians are happy living at the mission," Esteban said.

"Is that why they come there only in the winter, sheltering from the rain and cold, and then in the spring steal whatever horses and cattle they can find and try to escape to their homes in the mountains?"

"As I say, they are children. They think as children think and act as children act. Like a child, an Indian sees no farther than a day or two into the future. In many ways, however," Esteban said, "I agree with you, Señor Quinn. The days of the missions are nearing an end. The priests are too little concerned with Christianity; they have become too accustomed to their lands and their wealth. But remember, we are a few hundred white men living on the edge of a wilderness inhabited by thousands of savages. At times we must be cruel to survive. Otherwise we'd all be murdered in our sleep."

Esteban put his glass on the table. "But let us speak of happier events—your marriage, your new life in California. Do you still intend to make your home in Monterey?"

"I do. Margarita will live with the American consul while our house is being built."

"I was surprised you chose Monterey for your home," Esteban said. "Governor Sola, as you know, has long been one of Margarita's many admirers."

Jordan smiled despite the pang of jealousy he felt. Esteban Mendoza, he decided, could give as good as he got.

"Governor Sola," Margarita said, "is a pig."

"Admittedly he weighs two hundred and fifty pounds or more," Esteban said, "and is only slightly taller than you, Margarita. It's true he does eat five enormous meals of meat a day, or did when last he visited here, and his table manners have been described by some as uncouth, but he is not a pig. Pedro Sola is our governor, sent to us from Mexico City by the Spanish viceroy himself, and a man of great wealth."

"He is a pig." Margarita faced her brother, her eyes flashing. "If a man like that, a man I didn't love, were ever to put his hands on me in lust, I would, I would—"

"Kill him?" Esteban asked.

"No, I would kill myself rather than endure the shame." Suddenly she ran to Jordan and buried her face against his chest. "Take me with you," she whispered as he stroked her hair. "Take me with you now."

He was tempted. They could, after all, be married in Monterey. He turned the idea over in his mind, weighing the pros and cons. No, he finally decided, he couldn't afford to make enemies of the Mendozas.

"We should be married here," he told her. "The great feast is planned and the guests are already on their way."

She looked up at him, smiling though her eyes glittered with tears. "I shall count the days."

The night before the wedding Jordan walked to a high hill overlooking the sea. He stood for a long time leaning against the trunk of an oak with the sweet scent of orange blossoms in the air all around him. Overhead, a half-moon shone in a cloudless sky, silvering the mountains, the ranch buildings, the fields and the orchards.

To his left he saw the gray adobe walls of the mission; below him the *Kerry Dancer*'s masts were outlined in black against the sea. The sound of singing drifted to him from the direction of the mission.

I'm in Spanish California, he told himself, listening to mission Indians singing a French hymn in Latin. He thought of the next day, the wedding and Margarita. She was so young, so trusting. I hope to God I know what I'm about, he said to himself as he turned and walked slowly back to the *rancho*.

In the morning he and Margarita rode side by side to the church, on horses covered with silks decorated with pieces of silver, iron and copper, the tinkling of the metal sounding like a hundred small echoes of the tolling mission bells. Margarita's head was crowned with a white mantilla and cascades of lace fell down to cover the rich darkness of her hair.

Was this magnificently gowned woman the mischie-

vous girl he'd courted, Jordan wondered. He saw
gleams of lustrous white satin through the overdress of
fine lace that flowed in tiers from her waist to cover her
feet. "Convent lace from Spain," Margarita had said of
a shawl she'd once worn. Jordan had a sudden vision of
black-garbed nuns bent over flying shuttles, laboring to
produce the lace for this wedding gown. Lace for a
woman who was to taste what they had forsworn.

He tried to catch Margarita's eye, to smile at her, but
she stared straight ahead, unnaturally solemn. Her
breasts rose and fell with her quickened breathing, the
white skin that showed above the gown's pearl-
encrusted bodice fairer than all the costly garments she
wore.

They dismounted at the foot of the steps in front of
the church, where Esteban waited with Jack McKinnon. Margarita took Esteban's arm, and as they
climbed the steps to the open door, the murmur of
voices from inside the church was suddenly hushed.

When he reached the top of the steps, Jordan turned
and looked behind him. He saw a horseman riding
toward the mission from the west. Beyond the road he
caught a glimpse of the *Kerry Dancer* through the
morning mist. As he and Jack McKinnon followed
Esteban and Margarita into the church, Jordan felt a
fleeting pang of sadness, remembering another foggy
morning months before when, in the harbor of Valparaiso, a golden-haired girl had waved to him from the
deck of the *Flying Yankee*.

chapter 6

As Jordan and Margarita knelt at the altar rail while Padre Luis Martinez intoned the words that would make them man and wife, loud voices came from the rear of the church. Frowning, the priest looked up, then went on with the ceremony. Jordan heard approaching footsteps and a swelling murmur of surprise from the wedding guests.

Padre Luis stopped in mid-sentence. Jordan swung around and saw a tall, mustachioed man dressed in black with silver trim, his hat in his hand and a leather pouch slung across one shoulder, come striding down the aisle. The Californios watched, whispering and shaking their heads. Jordan rose to his feet.

"What is the meaning of this interruption of a holy sacrament?" Padre Luis demanded.

The man genuflected before the altar, then stood to face the priest. "A thousand pardons, *padre*," he said. Beads of sweat covered the man's forehead and his clothes were creased and soiled. "There was no other way. I have ridden all night."

"Explain yourself."

"I come from his excellency, Don Pedro Sola, the governor of Alta California, with a message of great importance."

He opened his pouch and handed the *padre* a folded paper sealed with red and green wax. Jordan watched Padre Luis tear open the seals and read the letter. The priest's face gave no clue to its contents.

"His excellency, the governor," the *padre* said at last, pitching his voice so all could hear, "has ordered that the marriage uniting Margarita Mendoza and Señor Jordan Quinn not take place because Señor Quinn has violated the laws of New Spain."

Ignoring the babble of questioning voices, the priest turned and looked up at the statue of the Virgin Mary in the niche at the side of the church. "Under the circumstances," he said, "I cannot go on with the ceremony."

"What right has the governor to interfere?" Jordan demanded. "What law have I broken?"

"Wait." Esteban was at his side. "Permit me to speak to Padre Luis."

"Don Esteban," the priest said placatingly, his voice pitched so only the group at the altar could hear. "What can I say? I am as appalled as you must be. I would have done anything to prevent you from suffering this embarrassment in the presence of your family and guests."

"Does our esteemed governor have the right to order the marriage stopped?"

"Under the circumstances, yes, he does. Señor Quinn is, after all, a foreigner, and if he has violated the law . . ."

"What law has he broken?"

"The governor states that he is accused of using his ship to smuggle goods to California."

"Padre Luis, as you are aware, all American sea captains who trade with California must of necessity be smugglers in the strict interpretation of the law. This is no crime. Why, I have even heard that members of the clergy have been known to visit their ships and bargain for goods from the United States."

The priest shrugged and raised his hands, palms up. "Because a thing is done by the clergy or by yourself or by others does not make it legal."

"*Padre,* the happiness of my sister means more to me than anything else in the world. This is the man she has chosen. A foreigner, yes. A criminal? Who are we to say? You and I know there are ways to accomplish what is in the best interests of both of us. We need one another, you and I. Your mission and the Mendoza *rancho* are only a few leagues apart, while Governor Sola and Monterey are many leagues to the north. Help me, *padre.* Tell me what I can do."

"There is much truth in what you say, Don Esteban. However, I must first write to Prefect García Diego of the Santa Clara Mission for instructions. I will do so at once. I can do no more now."

"We must be patient," Esteban said to Jordan. "Padre Luis will do all he can."

"How long must we wait?"

"*Quién sabe?* Who knows? Perhaps it will take two weeks, perhaps two months. You must realize that the workings of the church and the government are slow and ponderous. The prefect may have to seek advice from Mexico City."

Margarita took her brother's arm. "I've waited a year, Esteban," she told him. "I can wait no longer.

Besides, do you want your sister to be forced to hide her face in shame for the rest of her life?"

"You will not be disgraced," Esteban said. "On the contrary, you will be honored, you will be a woman of reknown. You may even become a legend."

"I don't want to be a legend, I want to be a wife. The wife of Jordan Quinn."

"And you shall. Be patient." Esteban looked about the church and found his overseer sitting in the last row of benches. "Señor Huerta," he said in a voice loud enough for all to hear, "there has been an unfortunate, although temporary, delay. How long we must wait, no one yet knows. In the meantime, I wish the *fandango* to begin."

Jordan heard the whine of a mosquito. Damn, he thought. He snuffed his bedroom candles. Damn the mosquitoes, damn the governor, damn Padre Luis, damn Esteban.

He walked onto his balcony, abandoning his journal for the time being. The night was dark, with the moon hidden by high clouds; from a distance he heard guitars and the sounds of singing and laughing. Jordan smiled grimly. A wedding feast without a wedding. A *fandango* without the bride and groom. When Don Esteban had asked them to come, Jordan had cursed and Margarita had fled to her room in tears.

Looking down from the balcony, Jordan saw, in the faint glow from the lanterns, two men walking unsteadily toward the house. Linking their arms, they began to sing a sad, rambling ballad about *la paloma,* the dove. Suddenly one of the men stopped and stretched full-length on the ground. Failing to rouse him from his drunken stupor, his companion went on into the house, his voice raised again in song.

This is the time to act, Jordan told himself. He crossed his room and walked along the gallery. When he came to McKinnon's room, he knocked, slipped inside and whispered a few words to the mate. McKinnon nodded, walked quickly to the stairs and disappeared into the darkness.

Jordan returned to his room. Pushing the bed curtains to one side, he lay down, intending to rest for a few minutes. Instead, he fell asleep almost at once.

Gunshots awakened him. He sat up, not sure where he was until, through the white netting, he saw the glimmering lights from the *fandango*. He swung from the bed and hurried to the gallery and down the steps.

Men ran past him in the dark; women clustered in small groups. He heard shouts and the clatter of hoofbeats. Another volley of gunshots came from beyond the corral. He smiled to himself. So far, so good.

Jordan found Esteban standing beneath a lantern, giving instructions to men who listened, nodded and then hurried off into the night.

"What happened?" Jordan asked.

Esteban glanced at him impatiently. "Indians. They've stolen our best horses and made off into the mountains. We're preparing to ride after them."

"Can I help?"

"You?" As soon as he spoke, Esteban appeared to realize the scorn in his voice. "If some of them had taken to the sea in one of their canoes," he said in a softer voice, "you could pursue them in the *Kerry Dancer*. In the mountains, no, you would be of no help; we must ride far and fast. We may be gone for many days. I take only the best horsemen and those most skilled with their guns."

Jordan nodded.

"A thousand thanks for your offer," Esteban said.

Without answering, Jordan walked to the courtyard and up the stairs to his room. He waited until he heard the sound of hoofbeats recede in the distance before he sat on his bed and pulled off his shoes and stockings. Going to the balcony, he climbed onto the rail and grasped the tile eaves over his head, pulling himself up onto the roof where, in his bare feet, he climbed across the tiles until he saw the dark dome of the pepper tree beside the house.

Lowering himself from the roof to the balcony nearest the tree, Jordan tapped on the half-open window. He heard a gasp and saw a shimmer of white come toward him.

"Jordan!"

He gently covered Margarita's mouth with the palm of his hand, knowing her aunt slept in the apartment between Margarita's room and the gallery.

"What's happening?" she whispered.

"Indians raided the horses and Esteban's organized a pursuit. This is our chance to escape."

"Do you intend to carry me off on the *Kerry Dancer?*"

"Yes. McKinnon's readying the ship now. We can be miles to sea by the time we're missed. I've had my fill of your Governor Sola." He began to marshal his arguments in his mind, wondering if he could convince her to leave her home and family.

"Hold me," she told him.

He enfolded her in his arms, kissing her hungrily as she clung to him. "My heart, my love," she said.

"Will you come with me?"

"I've already taken what I'll need from my trousseau and packed it in a small chest. All I have to do is put on my gown. I knew you would come for me."

"You're a wonder." He remembered he hadn't thought of her luggage; all he'd need was already aboard ship. "I'll find a rope to lower the chest from the balcony."

"There's no need; I have one hidden beneath my bed." She ran into the room and returned with the rope. "Now turn your back, Jordan. I'll be ready before you know it."

Jordan waited on the balcony with his arms folded across his chest. When he heard the whisper of clothing behind him, he glanced over his shoulder and saw, in the soft light of a candle on the dressing table, Margarita standing in front of a pier glass, naked, her back to him, her body all golden curves and inviting shadows. Jordan stepped into the room, intending to put his arms around her with his hands covering her breasts and his lips burying themselves in her soft, flowing hair.

Margarita put her head and arms into a silky chemise and let it fall down over her body. Clenching his hands at his sides, Jordan turned away. Later, he told himself, there'll be time enough later.

He returned to the balcony and in a few minutes heard her blow out the candle. His gaze searched the darkness of the room without finding her. All at once he felt her arms go around him. Picking her up with his hands on her waist, he held her in front of him, then gathered her body close to his. When she tried to kiss him, he teased her, his lips and tongue touching first her cheeks, then her eyes and the tip of her nose.

Standing on tiptoe, she clasped her hands at the back of his head, holding him while her lips captured his. As the kiss lengthened, his hands slid down her back and over her rounded buttocks, pressing her to him until he felt her breasts against his chest and her leg trapped between his.

They heard a tapping.

Margarita drew back and they both held their breath, listening.

"Margarita, are you all right?" The woman's voice came from across the room.

"Yes, Aunt Maria."

"Sleep well, my child."

"And you."

When she heard the door close, Margarita put her mouth to Jordan's ear. "We must hurry," she told him.

He nodded and lifted her to the balcony railing. Taking her hands in his, he lowered her, leaning over as far as he could without falling.

"Now," she whispered.

Jordan let go. He heard a soft thud and then the rustle of skirts below him.

"I'm all right," she said.

He used the rope to lower her chest, then hung by his hands and dropped to the ground beside her. After manhandling the chest up on one shoulder, he followed her along the side of the house. The heavy scent of orange blossoms sweetened the night. Lantern light shone from behind them and, as Margarita led him to the trees on the far side of the road, he heard a woman laugh.

"The wagon should be waiting near the oaks," he told her.

Margarita took his hand and they followed a path through the grove of trees. All at once she stopped.

"I saw a light," she told him.

He peered into the dark night. He saw nothing, so he waited, interminably, he thought, before a light gleamed for a moment a hundred feet in front of them. The light was gone as quickly as it came.

"It is good," he told her.

Now Jordan led the way, with Margarita's hand small and warm in his. When he neared the place where he had seen the light, he stopped.

"*Erin go bragh,*" he said in a low voice.

"Faith and begorra," Jack McKinnon said, burlesqueing an Irish brogue, "if it isn't the captain of the *Kerry Dancer* and his lady."

"You have the wagon?"

McKinnon unshielded his lantern long enough for Jordan to see the mule cart concealed in the trees near the road. After Jordan heaved the chest into the back of the cart, he leaned against one of the large wheels, catching his breath and massaging his aching shoulder.

"What in the name of heaven do you have in that chest?" he asked Margarita when he was seated beside her in the cart.

"A few dresses," she said. "And a few clothes. Shoes, slippers, hats, gloves. And my wedding gown. I want to be a proper bride for you, Capitán Quinn."

McKinnon switched the mules with a quirt and the cart rumbled slowly down the road in the direction of the beach. No one was abroad in the night; they reached the ship's boat beached on the sand without being challenged. As soon as they were on board, the sailors from the *Kerry Dancer* shoved the boat into the surf and rowed, their oars muffled with canvas, to the ship.

After helping Margarita over the side, Jordan stood on the deck looking around him. "Have all hands been called?" he asked the mate.

"They have, sir."

"See that the *señorita*'s chest is stowed in my cabin, if you please."

"Aye aye, sir."

Margarita touched his arm.

"You may either go to our cabin or else stay on deck," Jordan told her before she had a chance to speak. "Out of the way," he added.

She walked to the rail, watching the crewmen climb the ratlines into the rigging. One man slipped, caught himself before he fell and cursed loudly.

"Silence," Jordan ordered. "I don't want the dons to hear us, Mr. McKinnon." The order was passed from man to man.

"Ready to set sail, sir," McKinnon told him.

"Hands to the windlass, Mr. McKinnon." Jordan turned to the helmsman. "Set a course south by southeast to pass through the channel," he told him.

The windlass clanked as the *Kerry Dancer* weighed anchor. Jordan slipped the ship's spyglass from its case and scanned the shoreline, seeing an occasional light but nothing more. He nodded, so far he and Margarita had not been missed.

He watched the sails unfurl and felt the *Kerry Dancer* gather way before a fair wind that would see her out of the Santa Barbara channel. Already the memory of his time spent ashore had faded; the annoyances, the pettiness, the greed, the tedium of life on land now seemed unimportant. He wondered, for perhaps the thousandth time, how a man could stand to be landbound all his days when he could be free on the deck of a good ship with all the world awaiting him beyond the horizon.

Suddenly remembering Margarita, he looked around and saw her at the rail, looking out over the sea. Motioning McKinnon to his side, he said softly, "I never want her to know we had a part in that Indian raid on the *rancho*'s horses. Do you understand?" McKinnon nodded.

Jordan crossed the deck, coming up behind Margarita and caressing the nape of her neck with his fingers. She leaned back against him.

"Do you love the sea?" she asked.

"Of course; it's my life. I've been coming down to the sea since I was a boy."

"The sea must be like a mistress to a man, like a lover."

"A lover? No, Margarita, there's only one woman in my life. You."

A shout came from the lookout high on the foremast. "A light. A light off the starboard bow."

Jordan released Margarita, retrieved the spyglass and peered across the dark sea, but the light was still below the horizon. In ten minutes' time he saw it, a faint glimmer some four leagues to the west. Jordan turned to McKinnon.

"That light's most likely on one of the Channel Islands," he said. "What do you make of it?"

"A bonfire of some sort. The Indians, I suspect, signaling to one another."

Already the light was fading, and in another few minutes they couldn't make it out at all.

"I expect you're right." Jordan shook his head. The unexplained light troubled him.

"Where are we bound?" Margarita asked after McKinnon left them to go forward.

"To our cabin," he said, deliberately misunderstanding her.

"No, this ship. Where is she bound?"

"To San Diego. We'll be married at the mission before they have a chance to hear of the governor's objections." He guided her to the companionway and down to the captain's cabin, shutting the door behind them.

"This is for the two of us?" Margarita asked, staring around her. "This tiny cramped room?"

"There're no spare cabins on the ship."

She nodded to the single berth. "It's a sin for us to lie together before we marry," she told him.

"I'll do whatever you want, Margarita. Do you want to wait?"

She didn't answer. Instead she reached up and unbuttoned her dress and let it fall to the deck; unfastened her petticoats and stepped out of them; lifted the chemise over her head and threw it to one side. She stood naked before him.

The ship pitched gently and she let herself fall into his arms. With one hand around her bare waist, Jordan began to fumble with the buttons on his shirt with the other.

"Let me," she said.

While she undressed him, she said, "I must learn to speak better English."

"Why?" Her words surprised him; she was continually surprising him. Would she always, for the rest of their life together?

"So I may learn more ways to tell you how much I love you. I do love you, Jordan, with all my heart and soul."

He kissed her, wondering if she noticed he hadn't told her he loved her, wondering why he hadn't, for he knew he did. Why were the words so hard to say?

When he was naked, she lay on the bunk and opened her arms to him. He let her enfold him, trying to enter her gently, yet still she gasped with pain so he waited, moving slowly above her, their lovemaking matching the rhythm of the sea. He felt her cling to him, arch to him as she kissed him, and he sensed that her pain had lessened, replaced by a pounding surge of pleasure until she trembled in his arms. When at last they slept, she lay with her arms and legs wrapped tightly about him.

chapter 7

CAPTAIN JORDAN QUINN paced the lee side of the *Kerry Dancer*'s quarterdeck. The weather had been fair since leaving Santa Barbara two days before, the sky and the ocean were a deep blue and the sea ran in long, unbroken swells beneath the ship. Though Jordan's eyes moved automatically from the rigging to the wake, his thoughts were below decks.

"Margarita."

He said her name aloud while at the same time damning himself for being a romantic fool. He had never imagined a woman could enthrall him as Margarita had—he wanted to be with her now although it was only early afternoon, wanted to feel her arms around him and her smooth skin on his. He wanted to lose himself in her. Now and forever.

"Sail ho!"

Jordan shook himself from his reverie. Seeing the lookout on the foremast point off the starboard bow, he raised his spyglass and detected the barest glint of white to the southeast. Jack McKinnon came to stand beside him.

"Mr. McKinnon," Jordan said, "go aloft and have a look, if you please."

McKinnon climbed the shrouds to the fore topgallant yard, where he stood holding the rigging with one hand as he scanned the sea through the spyglass.

"Appears adrift," he shouted to the deck.

Jordan's first thought was of the *Flying Yankee*. Could her crew have taken to the boats only to have the *Yankee* survive the storm? It wouldn't be the first time a seaworthy ship had been abandoned by a crew. And in this case their captain was already dead. Their tale of being driven onto rocks might be more fancy than fact.

Jordan raised his speaking trumpet. "What manner of ship?" he asked McKinnon.

"Three-masted square-rigger, sir."

The *Flying Yankee* was a three-master square-rigger.

McKinnon climbed down and swung onto the deck next to Jordan. "As far as I could tell, sir, her sails are shredded and she's lost part of her foremast."

"Could you see her colors?"

"No, sir. And there's no sign of life aboard, though it's hard to be sure at this distance. I'd judge her to be four leagues from us."

"We'll tack toward her and have a look," Jordan said, estimating that at the *Kerry Dancer*'s speed of five to six knots, it would take them more than two hours to reach the other ship. When McKinnon remained silent, Jordan glanced at him. "You have doubts, Mr. McKinnon?"

"No, sir, we're duty-bound to take a closer look. There may be crewmen on board who're still alive and 'twould be criminal to leave them at the mercy of the sea. And if she has been abandoned, we can put a crew aboard and sail her to port for the salvage money. That would mean an unexpected bonus for all hands."

McKinnon hesitated. "There was one thought did cross my mind," he said. ·

"Out with it, Mr. McKinnon."

"It was those pirates," he said.

"Bouchard? The much talked about pirate who's never seen? I take it you fear a ruse."

"No, sir, likely the ship's just what she seems, a derelict abandoned in last fortnight's storm. The thought comes to me, though, that was I a buccaneer and feared the *Kerry Dancer* could outrun me—and we can outrun most any ship in these waters—I'd try to lure her as close as I could."

McKinnon wants it both ways, Jordan thought. The mate agreed that they had a duty to investigate the derelict at the same time that he cast doubt on that very course of action. A captain, without the luxury of second thoughts, had to act with alacrity and decision.

As they slowly closed on the drifting ship, Jordan went aloft but could discover no sign of life on the other vessel. Her sails hung in tatters, and the ship rolled as though rudderless. He did make out a flag at the peak, as shredded as the sails, the colors an unmistakable red, white and blue. She could be the *Yankee*. And yet . . .

Jordan tried to recall the lines of the *Yankee;* he had seen her only once in the fog, and, he admitted, at the time he'd looked far more closely at the golden-haired girl than at the ship. He shook his head, not being able to say for certain whether this was the *Yankee* or not.

"Call all hands, Mr. McKinnon," Jordan ordered when he returned to the quarterdeck.

They reduced sail, and soon the *Kerry Dancer* was lying to a half-league from the drifting three-master.

"Get the long boat ready for launching," Jordan told the mate. "We've three hours of daylight left."

The sea rolled under them in unbroken swells as it had all day. The *Kerry Dancer,* no longer underway, bobbed up and down, forcing Jordan to steady his spyglass with his hand as he inspected the hull and then the decks of the other ship. No, it wasn't the *Yankee,* he decided, this ship was broader in the beam. He raised the glass to the forward rigging, suddenly frowning as a premonition of impending disaster swept over him.

"Belay that order, Mr. McKinnon," he called.

"Aye aye, sir."

"Prepare to make sail." Men scrambled up into the *Dancer*'s rigging.

"What do you see, sir?" McKinnon asked.

Jordan handed the glass to the mate. "I don't like the looks of it," he said. "I don't like the looks of it at all. There appear to be snug-furled sails beneath the tattered ones. Her foremast's shattered right enough but a new mast's been jury-rigged behind it. That ship's no more a derelict than the *Dancer* is."

"My God, look." McKinnon pointed.

Men swarmed onto the deck and into the rigging of the other ship. Wooden covers masking gun ports were lifted away, and ten twelve-pounders rolled out into firing position. The Stars and Stripes were lowered and another banner raised.

"The new flag's green and gold," McKinnon reported, "with a star inside a crescent moon. I never laid eyes on her likes before."

A puff of smoke rose from the other ship's forward cannon and a ball shrieked across the *Dancer*'s bow. Jordan saw a man station himself amidships with a speaking trumpet raised to his mouth, while above him sails blossomed and the three-master began to tack toward the *Dancer.*

Jordan heard a faint though clear voice. "Surrender or we'll blow you out of the water."

"They could do it, sir," McKinnon said.

Jordan nodded. The *Kerry Dancer,* relying on her speed, carried only one small cannon and barely enough handguns to arm half the crew. Judging from the horde of men on the deck of the other ship, the *Dancer* was outnumbered five to one and completely outgunned. Putting up a fight would only lead to disaster. Jordan clenched his fists in futile desperation. They were trapped. He had led his ship and crew into the hands of the pirates.

Another puff of smoke came from the other ship. The cannonball whistled overhead, closer this time, and Jordan saw it splash into the ocean a cable's length beyond his bow.

"Order the men down," he told McKinnon. "We'll offer no resistance. It's too late to outrun them and we can't outfight them. See that the *señorita* is well hidden in the hold." As an afterthought he said, "Bring my pistol from the cabin."

The other ship, her captain seeing that the *Kerry Dancer* intended to remain lying to, approached to within three cable lengths and launched a longboat.

Twenty men clambered from the boat over the *Dancer*'s side and ranged themselves on the quarter-deck behind a short, red-faced man who stood facing Jordan with his hands on his hips. The boarding party was well armed, Jordan saw, with pistols, knives thrust in belts and sheathed swords. Four of the boarders were naked except for loincloths, and Jordan guessed they were Kanakas from the Sandwich Islands.

"Allow me to introduce myself," the leader said in

English to Jordan. "I'm Thomas Burns, quartermaster of the frigate *Argentina*."

"How dare you fire on us in time of peace?" Jordan demanded.

"We're not at peace, we're at war. We represent the Republic of Buenos Aires, fighting for our freedom from the Spanish overlords."

"Ours isn't a Spanish ship, as you can clearly see. We're American registered, out of Portsmouth. I'm Captain Quinn of the *Kerry Dancer*."

"Any ship trading with Californios is an enemy of freedom; you should realize that, Captain. Our Admiral Bouchard means to drive the dons back to Spain where they belong. Failing that, he means to destroy them one and all. California must be a free country, not a vassal."

When Jordan started to protest, Burns turned his back on him and motioned three men to the hatch leading below decks. The men disappeared from view.

"If any of your crew is foolhardy enough to fight," Burns told Jordan, "they'll be killed forthwith."

"There will be no resistance," Jordan said curtly.

Burns nodded and walked away, pausing to examine the halyards, the masts and the wheel. He climbed the foremast to the yardarm, looking at the newly tarred shrouds and running his fingers over the furled sails. By the time he returned to the deck, one of his men had come up from below.

"She carries a full cargo of woolens, yard goods and tools," he reported. "And a consignment of bourbon. No gold or specie that I could find."

Burns grunted and turned to Jordan. "You captain a taut ship," he told him.

A second rebel sailor, a redheaded giant of a man with a harelip, appeared at the hatch. "I found me a prize," he announced, his words blurred by his affliction. Climbing down out of sight, he reappeared with Margarita slung over his back. Although she flailed at him with her fists, he carried her easily across the deck, shrugging her from his shoulder in front of Burns. She staggered backward and fell to the deck.

"Jordan!" she cried.

Jordan sprang forward. One of the *Argentina*'s men waved him back with his pistol while Burns reached out and pulled the gun from Jordan's belt and tossed it to a man behind him.

"We'll take the captain and the mate to the *Argentina*," he said.

"And the *señorita*," the red-haired man added.

"And the *señorita*. Lock the rest of their men below."

Leaving a skeleton crew aboard the *Kerry Dancer*, the boarding party rowed its three prisoners to the rebel ship. When Jordan climbed onto the main deck, he found the ship aswarm with a ragtag assortment of men who crowded around staring at their captives.

Jordan held Margarita close. "You'll be all right," he assured her. "I won't let anything happen to you." He wished he were as confident as he sounded.

"These men terrify me." He felt her body shiver against his. "They're like vultures circling wounded animals."

"Make way for the admiral," a voice called out. The men shuffled aside to form a corridor. The companionway door opened and a man came onto the deck.

"Bouchard," someone said and the name was repeated, "Bouchard, Bouchard."

As Hippolyte de Bouchard strutted toward him, Jordan raised his eyebrows. The rebel admiral wasn't at all what he'd expected. Bouchard was a short, dandified man with curling mustaches. He wore a rich crimson damask waistcoat and breeches with a red sash around his waist holding his pistols and dirk. He sported a gold feather in his tricorn hat and, around his neck, wore a diamond cross hanging from a gold chain. His crew, Jordan thought, eyed him with a strange mixture of respect and disdain.

Bouchard stopped in front of each of his prisoners and looked them up and down as though he were a naval officer inspecting recruits.

"Did you appreciate our ruse?" he asked Jordan.

Jordan didn't answer.

"More experienced captains than yourself have been taken in," Bouchard said.

Still Jordan said nothing.

"Would you care to join me in my cabin for a cup of tea?" Bouchard asked, including McKinnon and Margarita in the invitation by a sweep of his hand.

Jordan stared at him, dumbfounded by the question. Finally he nodded.

Bouchard turned to lead them below, only to find his way blocked by the burly redhead who had discovered Margarita hiding in the *Dancer*'s hold.

"You shan't have her, Bouchard." A cleft palate combined with the harelip to twist the crewman's words. "I'm the one what found her and she's mine."

"Stand aside, Grosbeck," Bouchard ordered.

Another sailor stepped up beside Grosbeck. "Remember you well," he said to Bouchard, "you're our captain by vote of the crew. We made you and, by God, we can unmake you as easily." The men behind him murmured their assent.

"You sons of bitches," Bouchard shouted in a

high-pitched voice, "are you so besotted with drink you can't think straight? Have you no sense at all not to know when you're well off? Are you all mad with lust?"

"We ain't in action now," Grosbeck said sullenly. "Have we ever disobeyed you in the face of an enemy?" He turned to the other men. "Have we?" he asked them.

A chorus of nos answered him.

"Is the *señorita* mine by right?"

"Aye," the men shouted.

Margarita shrank back against Jordan, and he tightened his grip around her shoulders.

"Hear me out, you men," Bouchard said. He removed a pistol from his belt and fired it over his head. The crew retreated a few paces, and Jordan thought he saw the glint of drawn weapons in the crowd.

"Hear me." Bouchard's tone had become conciliatory. He lowered his gun and returned it to his waistband. "I propose we take this captured ship, this *Kerry Dancer,* as a legitimate prize of war. Her cargo will bring us a good price in the Sandwich Islands, the money to be divided among you all as we've agreed. We'll leave her crew ashore, where they'll have a long week's trek to the nearest *pueblo.* These three"— he gestured behind him—"are as much a prize as their ship. They'll bring us all a bountiful ransom from the dons. The *señorita,* as you can surely see, is a lady who'll be worth her weight in silver."

"You use fine words, Bouchard," the man who had first supported Grosbeck said, "and I'll admit that much of what you say makes sense. We need a faster and sturdier ship and we need the cargo. But the *señorita*'s ours by right, not yours. After all, we don't mean to kill her. She'll still fetch a goodly ransom when we're through with her." Again there was a murmur of agreement from the men.

Bouchard raised his eyes heavenward as though asking how any man could be so misunderstood. Shrugging, he motioned to two men who came up behind Jordan and pinioned his arms to his sides. Going to Margarita, Bouchard put his finger beneath her chin, tilting her head. He sighed, then took her by the arm and pushed her toward the men. She sprawled on the deck.

"Jordan," she sobbed. "Help me!"

Jordan lunged at Bouchard but the two men pulled him back, twisting his arms behind him.

"Stop!" It was McKinnon. Jordan saw that the mate held a cocked pistol, the muzzle six inches from Bouchard's ear. "If you touch her," McKinnon said, "your captain's a dead man."

The crewmen hesitated, looking from Margarita huddling on the deck to McKinnon with his pistol. Out of the corner of his eye Jordan saw a flash of silver as a sword sliced through the air, slashing into McKinnon's wrist. The *Dancer*'s mate screamed as his fingers opened and the pistol dropped to the deck. McKinnon stared at his severed hand hanging from his wrist by a length of flesh. Blood surged from the wound and spattered onto his trousers and the deck.

Bouchard pulled his dirk from its sheath, stepped next to McKinnon and drove the blade into the mate's side. McKinnon grunted, lurched toward the rail and collapsed into the scuppers. When Jordan heaved forward trying to free himself, Bouchard raised the bloodied dirk to Jordan's throat.

"Are you ready to die, Captain?" His high-pitched laugh was almost a giggle.

Jordan closed his eyes as Bouchard's blade traced a stinging line across his neck; Margarita screamed. Then the blade was gone. Jordan opened his eyes and saw Bouchard shoving the weapon back into his belt.

"Take the good captain below and put him in chains," Bouchard ordered.

Jordan was shoved to the forecastle hatch and manhandled down a ladder into the depths of the ship. As he was thrust to his knees on the deck and manacles were locked on his wrists, he smelled the dank odor of bilge water and heard the scuttling of rats. A door closed and he was alone.

McKinnon had sacrificed his life, he thought. Now McKinnon was dead and Margarita was . . . He couldn't bear to think of the fate awaiting her. He, Jordan Quinn, captain of the *Kerry Dancer,* had failed his ship, his crew, and his bride-to-be. He was a coward.

Jordan shook his head. What could he have done? McKinnon. He whispered the name as though answering himself. McKinnon had given his life while he, Jordan Quinn, had done nothing.

He closed his eyes and felt the sting of tears. He hadn't cried since, when he was a boy, he'd been whipped by his father, but he cried now, for himself, for McKinnon and for Margarita. He vowed that he would redeem himself. He would avenge McKinnon, he would avenge Margarita. And, if he must, he would die doing so.

Grosbeck carried Margarita below over his shoulder as he had carried her from the hold of the *Kerry Dancer.* He laid her in his hammock, but she tumbled herself from the far side and ran. The other men laughed, grasping her, their hands exploring her breasts and buttocks as they pushed her from one crewman to the next.

Grosbeck put one arm around her waist from behind and again lifted her into the hammock, getting on top of her before she could flee. She raked his face with her nails, and the watching crewmen laughed. He slapped her once, twice, three times, his hand striking her face with the monotony of a pendulum. He stopped only when she at last lay still.

He yanked her skirts and petticoats up around her waist. He loosened his own clothing, but when he had bared himself she struck his sex with her fist and he grunted, doubling over in pain. Again the men laughed.

Grosbeck found a roll of twine and bound Margarita's hands beneath the hammock. She screamed, kicking at him as he climbed into the hammock, but to no avail.

Seven other men ravished her after Grosbeck was done with her. At last Grosbeck carried her, bleeding and unconscious, to the captain's cabin. He knocked, and when Bouchard opened the door, Grosbeck held Margarita toward him.

"You wanted her," he said. "Now take her."

Bouchard took Margarita in his arms and carried her across his cabin, laying her gently on his berth. He shook his head sadly as he removed her soiled clothes. Bringing a basin of water, he placed it on the deck beside the berth and used a cloth to bathe the blood and filth from her naked body.

When he had finished, Bouchard dimmed the lamp until the cabin was in almost total darkness. After removing his clothes he folded them carefully over the back of a chair, went to the berth and stood looking down at Margarita. He spread her legs, took her limp body in his arms and entered her.

When she recovered consciousness her body ached and her head throbbed, and when she tried to raise her head, she gagged. Bouchard lay asleep beside her. She crawled from the berth, pulling herself to her feet and leaning against the table. Her hands examined the clothing on the chair but found nothing of hers. Hanging from a peg on the bulkhead, though, she found a pistol and the dirk. After she pulled the dirk from its sheath, she ran her finger along the blade, the dried blood flaking off under her touch.

Margarita turned, holding the dirk in her hand, and looked down at the sleeping figure of Bouchard. She shook her head, then knelt beside the berth, holding the dirk in both hands as though it was an offering. She tried to say the rosary but the familiar words of the prayers eluded her.

"Hail Mary," she whispered. "Oh, Mother Mary, forgive me for what I'm about to do."

She bowed her head and put the point of the blade against her bare flesh beneath her left breast, under her lowermost rib, then plunged the dirk upward into her body to its hilt.

chapter 8

ALITHA STARED AT the spear protruding from Malloy's back. She looked past his fallen body and saw an Indian, naked, brown-skinned, black-haired, running toward her. She edged away, fearfully crossing her hands over her breasts.

The Indian stopped and held out both hands with his open palms upward. The little finger of his left hand, she noticed, was missing. He had a net bag slung over one shoulder and a piece of wood thrust in his thick hair. When she suddenly realized he wasn't a man at all but a boy, she stepped forward, raising her own hands as he had. The boy, who must have been no more than ten or eleven, she decided, stared at her, then lowered his hands and looked down at Malloy.

Putting his foot on Malloy's back, the Indian grasped the end of the spear and levered it from side to side. Alitha closed her eyes. When she heard a wild cry, she opened her eyes to see the Indian standing with the blood-tipped spear held high above his head. Raising his face to the darkening sky, he began a slow, rhythmic chant.

She watched him in wonderment and fear. The chant over, he lowered his spear and stared at her. Alitha drew back. The boy took the spear, pantomimed breaking it over his knee, and threw the weapon onto the rocks at his feet.

He approached and walked around her, looking up at her—he was several inches shorter—seemingly fascinated by her blond hair. Putting his right hand on his chest, he said, "Chia." When she stared at him he again said, "Chia."

Of course, she thought. She put her own hand to her chest and said, "Alitha." He tried to repeat the name. "Leeta," he said. She felt a fleeting pang, for Leeta was the name Thomas always called her by.

"Chia," she said, pointing at him, and he nodded. All this time his face had shown no expression; he seemed incapable, she thought, of either frowning or smiling. But his dark eyes gleamed.

Chia pointed down at Malloy's body and made pawing motions with his hands. He wanted to bury Malloy. Alitha knelt at the mate's side, seeing a dark circle staining the back of his shirt; there was no question but that the mate was dead. She thought of taking the shirt to wear. No, she couldn't, she'd rather wear nothing at all. Alitha looked up at Chia and nodded. When he stared at her, not seeming to understand, she repeated his digging motions.

He trotted a few feet away, stopping near the spot where Alitha had intended to spend the night and, dropping to his knees, began to scoop the sand to one side. She joined him, and when, a few minutes later, they reached wet, close-packed sand, Chia took the piece of wood from his hair and she saw that it was a knife with a tongue-shaped blade made not of metal but of some gray, stonelike substance. The short handle was decorated with mother-of-pearl. By the time the grave was four feet deep, the night was darkening around them. Chia stopped digging.

She followed him back to the mate's body, barely able to see him in the darkness. Chia picked up one of Malloy's legs and, fighting back her repugnance, Alitha took the other leg and together they dragged him to the grave, where Chia rolled him into the burial hole. As Alitha was about to scoop sand over the body, Chia touched her arm. She stopped and watched him.

Chia walked to the water's edge and, seeing him outlined against the sea and sky, she realized the night had become lighter. Looking over the calm sea, she saw a glowing aureole on the horizon. Chia began to chant, not the harsh cries of triumph he had uttered after he had killed Malloy, but an almost lyrical song of thanksgiving.

She gasped, for as the boy raised his arms above his head, facing east, the rim of the three-quarter moon rose slowly out of the sea. She could almost believe that the moon had risen not because of the turning of the earth but because Chia had, in some mysterious way, called it forth.

As soon as the moon's circle was completely above the ocean, Chia lowered his arms and trotted up the beach. Together they covered the body of the mate and, after they were finished, Alitha knelt beside the grave and prayed aloud as she had heard her father do over the bodies of fallen shipmates.

When she stood up, Chia walked away without looking at her, without making a sign to her. He must expect her to follow, she decided, so she ran after him until she was a few paces behind. He retrieved his spear, then climbed a hillock and then another, stopping finally in a grassy hollow protected from the wind by a rise of ground shaped like a breaking wave.

Chia lay in an indentation in the ground, and she knew he meant to sleep. Probably he had spent many nights here. For the first time she wondered what had brought him to this island. He certainly didn't live here. Had he been swept ashore by the storm as she had been?

Alitha found a hollow in the sand and lay down, clasping her knees to her body for warmth, listening to the pounding of the surf. She was no longer afraid of Chia, she decided; she trusted him. He meant to protect her; he must have killed Malloy to protect her. As she drifted toward sleep, she realized that, after her shock when she had first seen him, she had not noticed his nakedness at all.

She woke up shaking from the cold. Though the sun had not risen, the sky was light and a brisk wind drove clouds over the island from the south. She got up, stretched, felt her hair being tousled by the wind. With a start, she saw that Chia was gone.

All at once she smelled . . . What? Something being cooked, she was sure. She realized she was ravenously hungry.

She followed the odor to where Chia sat on his haunches in front of a small, circular pit. He looked at Alitha when she sat beside him and, after a moment, reached out and hesitantly touched a strand of her hair, rolling it between his fingers. She smiled at him and for the first time he smiled back.

Chia turned away and removed the dirt from the top of the pit, exposing a layer of matted grass. When he lifted the grass out of the pit, she saw four fish lying on hot rocks. Picking up one of the fish, Chia held it by the tail and began eating the head. Though Alitha grimaced with distaste, she used her fingers to split open one of the other fish and brought a chunk to her mouth. The taste, though salty, was surprisingly good.

After they had finished eating, Chia motioned her to follow him. He led her to a cluster of small holes, each lined with leaves, each partly filled with water. From the storm, she supposed. She watched Chia scoop water to his mouth and drink. Again she followed his example, but when she put her hands into the water for a second drink, he raised one hand waist high to make a horizontal, chopping motion. Unmistakably he meant no. Water must be in short supply on the island.

Chia leaped to his feet and set off toward the beach. Following him, she was surprised when he turned in the direction of Malloy's grave, stopping next to the mound and pointing to an oblong piece of metal thrust into the sand. He had placed a marker on the grave! He must have learned the ways of the white men from seeing a Spanish burial ground at a mission.

She ran her fingers over the plaque, feeling indentations in the metal. Examining the plaque more closely, she saw that words had been etched into the surface, words so worn by time she could not make them out.

She tried tracing the letters with the tips of her fingers. When she was done, she said the one word she could decipher.

"Cabrillo."

She had heard the name but couldn't remember where. A Spanish name, certainly, perhaps an early *padre* or explorer who had been buried on this desolate island a hundred or more years before. Chia had found his grave and brought the marker here to please her.

"Thank you," she said, nodding to him.

He stood and walked quickly away, and again she

had to leap to her feet to follow him. She wondered if Chia was actually bashful and hid his unease in these sudden bursts of activity.

They followed the beach until Alitha recognized the rocky coastline where she had been swept ashore. Chia led her to a small cover where timbers had been piled on the rocks well above the tide line. Ship timbers and planking, probably from the *Yankee*. Some had been lashed together to form the beginning of a raft, the rope, she supposed, having also been washed ashore from the ship. Chia pointed to the raft and then north across the sea.

He meant to sail to the mainland. She nodded and began dragging timbers from the pile to the raft. Chia stopped her. After pointing to her, he walked along the beach gathering driftwood until his arms were full. He carried the wood back to the cove and laid it on the rocks.

"I understand," Alitha told him. "The man builds the raft while the woman gathers the firewood."

She set out along the beach, returning time after time with armfuls of driftwood. She soon stopped piling the wood at the place Chia had shown her and began carrying her armloads farther inland to the top of a small hill.

Chia could have his wood for cooking, she told herself, but she was going to make a bonfire, one that could be seen for miles. It would be far easier to be rescued by a passing ship than to brave the currents of the ten-mile stretch of open sea between the island and the mainland.

As she gathered the wood, she found herself walking farther and farther from the cove where Chia labored on the raft. Rounding a spit of land, she came to a sandy stretch of beach where she sat to rest with the water lapping over her bare feet.

Her hands and arms were dirty from the wood, and though the sun was behind clouds, she was hot from the unaccustomed work. After first looking cautiously around, she pulled the chemise over her head and knelt at the ocean's edge to rinse it. She was about to struggle into the wet, torn garment when she changed her mind and spread the chemise on a rock to dry.

She ran into the ocean until the water came to her waist, then walked as far out as she could, shivering until she grew accustomed to the cold. As she plunged into a breaking wave, she felt the exhilarating sweep of the salt water over her naked body. She dove into oncoming waves, letting them carry her shoreward until she was exhausted.

Wading to the beach, she found a large, flat rock and lay on her back to let the warm air dry her. Looking down at her body, she brought her hands up over her legs and hips and along her sides to her breasts. She had never been so conscious of her body before. If she had thought of it at all, she had considered her body as something necessary yet vaguely shameful.

A sea gull shrieked overhead as it wheeled above the beach. The sun came from behind clouds, forcing Alitha to shade her eyes with her hand. She stood up, raising her arms skyward as she stretched, feeling the sun's warmth bathe her as she recalled Chia's similar gesture of homage to the moon.

We make such a secret of our bodies, Alitha thought, hiding them beneath layers of cloth. I doubt if many women even let their husbands see them unclothed. Chia doesn't seem to think of himself as naked—is the rest of his tribe the same? If the Indians feel no need to

conceal their bodies from one another, are they also
more open in other ways?

She looked down at the swell of her breasts where
the skin was turning an unfamiliar brown. I'm only
beginning to know my own body, she decided, and I'll
make a vow this minute to never be ashamed of it.

The shadow of a cloud raced toward her along the
beach. Shivering in the cold breeze, she ran to retrieve
her chemise and slip it over her head. All at once she
thought of Thomas. What would he think of her lying
naked in the sun? He'd disapprove, she was sure. Her
memory of him had faded; he seemed far, far away,
and as she tried to picture him in her mind, images of
her father kept getting confused with him.

When she returned to Chia, he was standing on the
rocky shore with his spear in his hand. He removed an
object—a reddish stone, she thought—from the net bag
he wore over his shoulder and rubbed it along the blade
of the spear. The stone, no longer than Chia's palm,
was carved in the shape of a fish and had a cord strung
through a hole in one end.

Returning the stone to his carrying bag, Chia walked
along the water's edge to a boulder above an inlet
sheltered from the waves by a reef. Spear poised, he
waited. Minutes passed. Suddenly he thrust the spear
into the water, and when he raised it over his head, she
saw a fish impaled on the point. He climbed back to
where she stood, removed the fish from the spear and
laid it at her feet.

Men catch the fish, she thought, and women cook
them. There was no reason she couldn't catch them,
too; it appeared easy enough.

She pointed to the spear, reaching out her hand for
it. Chia stared at her, hesitated, then offered her his
weapon. Balancing the shaft of the spear in her hand,

she went to the boulder where Chia had stood. She heard him behind her, turned, and saw him offering her his stone charm. She shook her head, remembered he might not understand, and made a negative motion with her hand. After staring at her impassively, Chia returned to the beach, putting the talisman back into his bag.

Alitha stood on the rock gazing into the deep water. A silvery fish glided into the pool, a fish over two feet long, much larger than the one Chia had landed. She raised the spear, waiting, and when the fish was directly beneath her, she drove the blade into the water.

The fish darted away, and when the spear embedded itself deep in the sand, Alitha was thrown forward. Releasing the shaft, she tried to keep her balance, failed and fell face first into the water. She surfaced, spluttering, and climbed out onto a rock, pushing her streaming hair from her face.

Hearing a sound from the beach, she looked that way and saw Chia bent over with his hands on his knees. He was laughing, laughing at her. Embarrassed, she smiled uncertainly and in a few minutes was laughing as hard as he was.

She pulled the spear from the sand, carried it to Chia and placed it at his feet. For the time being, at least, she decided, Chia would fish and she would cook.

For the next three days Chia worked on the raft while Alitha gathered wood for the fires she used to cook fish twice a day, at the same time adding constantly to the pile of driftwood on the top of the hill. On the evening of the third day, she helped Chia half-carry, half-shove the raft across the rocks to the water. With his charm stone in his hand, Chia walked around the raft, touching each of the four sides with the head of the stone fish.

When he finished, he pushed the raft over the breakers, threw two hand-hewn double-bladed paddles aboard and rowed along the shore. When he returned to the beach he nodded, evidently satisfied with the seaworthiness of the raft.

Using sticks, Chia marked the high-tide line in the sand and waded into the ocean where he indicated where low tide would be. Standing at the low-tide line, he pointed to the raft and, with his hands, showed the incoming flood tide sweeping in the direction of the mainland. Going up on the beach, he drew the rising sun and a curved arrow to represent the arc of the sun from morning to night, again indicating the start of a flood tide and then pointing to the sun at its zenith.

She stared at him for a moment as she thought through what he was trying to tell her. Of course. He meant to sail with the flood tide, and that tide would come the next day at noon. Chia, she thought, may be a savage, but he was a seaman as well.

Alitha nodded, then walked past him, motioning him to follow. He walked after her, keeping a few paces behind until he saw she was heading for the pile of wood on the hilltop. He quickly walked past her and led the way up the hill. Though the sun was down by the time they reached the top, she waited, sitting on the grass with Chia crouched on his haunches a short distance away. Neither spoke.

Finally, after more than an hour had passed, she motioned him to light the fire. He twirled his fire stick in the hollow of a board and in a few minutes sparks showered onto the pile of dry slivers. The wood smoked, Alitha saw a spurt of fire and a moment later flames were crackling up the sides of the pile of driftwood, climbing higher and higher until she and Chia were forced back by the heat.

When she saw Chia watching her expectantly, she frowned, not understanding what he wanted. He looked from her to the flames, his naked body a golden bronze in the firelight. Slowly he raised his arms to the blaze and as slowly lowered them again. Of course, he must be expecting her to perform some rite, make some obeisance to the fire.

The sun, the moon, the sea, the earth, fire—these must be the gods around which his life revolved. If she were in his place, wouldn't she worship them just as he did? He must think this fire was her ceremony to speed their escape from the island.

She knelt, praying the signal fire would be seen, praying for their safe passage to the mainland. When she stood up, Chia nodded, seemingly satisfied.

Already the flames were dying, the darkness crowding around them to reclaim the small portion of the island from which it had been banished by the fire. Had anyone seen the blaze? During her days on the island, she had sighted no ships nor had she seen any signs of human life. Only the morning would tell if rescue was on the way.

When she woke shortly before dawn, the sea on their side of the island was calm but empty. She cooked their morning meal—how she was beginning to hate the smell of fish—and they drank from their fast-dwindling supply of water. Leaving Chia to greet the dawn, Alitha climbed the highest of the hills, the same one she and Malloy had climbed when they first came to the island days before.

The shipwreck seemed long ago. Now she was tanned almost as brown as Chia. At night she fell into a sound sleep as soon as she lay down, and she woke refreshed. She felt better than she could ever remember feeling before.

She stood on the top of the hill looking around her, saw another island to the east, even smaller and more barren than theirs, saw puffy clouds drifting overhead and the dark line of the mainland to the north. Offshore a pelican dove into the sea and emerged with a fish held crosswise in his beak. But there were no ships, no beacon fires on the far shore, no sign that her fire had been seen. They would have to rely on the raft. With a sigh she turned and walked back down the hill.

When the tide changed, they pushed the raft into the surf, waiting until they were beyond the breakers before scrambling aboard. Alitha took one paddle, Chia the other, and they sat on opposite sides of the raft rowing toward the mainland.

Soon Alitha's arms and shoulders ached and she had to sit back with the paddle resting on the timbers in front of her. Looking over her shoulder, she saw that the beach, the grassy slopes and the twin hills of the island were already beginning to look insignificant in the immensity of the surrounding sea. With a start of surprise she realized that she regretted leaving the island, although she knew she had no choice.

Taking a deep breath, she resumed rowing. The sea was calm, rising and falling in gentle swells, but even so water splashed over the sides of the raft, soaking them both. Each time she looked ahead, the land seemed no closer than before, so she bent to her task, her eyes on the furrow made by her paddle in the water.

Finally, exhausted, she laid the paddle at her side and lowered her face into her hands. She didn't look at Chia, but she heard the steady beat of his strokes. She heard the thump of waves on a shore, opened her eyes and saw the mainland a few hundred feet ahead.

She began rowing again, and for a time they were swept parallel to the shore by the current. Seeing a beach, Chia pointed, and they rowed toward it as the current tried to sweep them past. Paddling with all the strength she had left, her arms heavy with fatigue, for a moment Alitha thought they had won the battle and would reach the sand.

She plunged the paddle into the sea with renewed fervor. They were safe—they had challenged the Pacific and won. She smiled across at Chia just as the raft rose on a cresting wave and was borne higher and higher, with the beach to their left and menacing black rocks to their right.

The wave broke in a shower of spray, sending the raft crashing forward onto the rocks and hurling Alitha into the water. As she tried to swim, she heard Chia's grunt of pain above the boom of the surf. Her hand touched a sandy bottom and she waded shoreward, finally pulling herself onto a rock shelf above the churning water.

Looking around, she saw Chia lying on the rocks near her. She stood up and climbed over the rocks toward him, expecting him to get up at any moment to brusquely lead the way ashore. He didn't get up. When she reached him she saw that one of his legs was twisted under his body.

As she tried to turn him over, he raised his head and she saw that his face was drawn with pain. He gestured weakly with his hand in the negative sign she'd learned. No, don't move him. Alitha stared down at the twisted right leg and saw that the foot was turned in at an impossible angle. She knew then that his leg was broken.

chapter 9

ALITHA BOWED HER head in despair as she crouched over Chia. She was wet, she was exhausted; now, without him, she was helpless on this alien shore. He moved, attempting to hunch himself to a sitting position. She looked at him and waved her hand in the negative gesture he'd so often used to her.

Chia's helpless but I'm not, she admonished herself. It's up to me now. She forced herself to touch his twisted leg. Though he made no outcry, she heard him catch his breath. What could she do for a broken bone?

When the seaman on the *Yankee* had fallen from the rigging off the Falkland Islands, her father had used canvas and wood to splint and straighten the man's broken leg, and in time the man had walked again. With a limp, to be sure, but he'd walked. Alitha looked about her. What could she use to splint Chia's leg?

The broken paddle caught her eye. Leaning over Chia, she unfastened the knife from his hair; while he watched with pain-dimmed eyes, she waded into the water and retrieved the paddle. The sharpness of the flint knife surprised her as she trimmed off the splintered ends of the paddle after breaking the wood in two over her knee. But how was she to hold the pieces of wood in place on Chia's leg?

She looked at her ragged chemise. If she took any cloth from it, she doubted if the chemise would hold together enough to cover her. Chia, of course, was naked except for the net bag now wound about his waist. Could she use that? The net was fashioned of some kind of plant fiber; if she could unravel them . . .

Alitha knelt beside Chia, placing the two pieces of wood on either side of his right leg. She slipped strands of the rough twine under his leg and the wood and tied the upper ends. She took a deep breath and grasped his foot, which turned inward, and twisted so that the toes pointed up.

Chia grunted. Holding the foot in place between her knees, Alitha quickly lashed the wood to the leg with the remaining twine. Chia hadn't made another sound after the first moan, but she saw blood trickling down his chin and realized that he'd bitten his lip to keep from crying out.

Tears came to her eyes, but she brushed them away impatiently. He was the bravest boy she'd ever seen, but now she must be equally brave or he was doomed. He needed food and water, he needed shelter. The first thing she had to do was move him away from the beach.

Half-carrying, half-dragging him, she managed to get Chia over a slight rise to where a group of boulders formed a windbreak and also offered shade. Leaving him there, she hurried to cut foliage from nearby bushes, brought the branches back, then collected driftwood. Now he had fuel for a fire and could use the branches for a blanket.

It took her a long time to find and kill a number of the small, scuttling sand crabs, and she was disappointed to uncover only a few clams to bring to him. More of a worry was the fact that she'd found no fresh water. She fussed over him until Chia made the negative chopping motion with his hand.

"*Ranchería,*" he said, pointing west along the beach. His finger then touched her gently. "Leeta," he said. Immediately he pointed west again.

Rancherías. She'd heard her father use that word for the Indian settlements on the Mexican coast. Did Chia want her to leave him and seek help from his tribe?

She pointed to herself, then west along the shore. "*Ranchería?*" she asked.

Chia smiled in agreement. He broke a twig from one of the branches and drew two circles in the dirt, gestured at the sky, then west again.

Two. Two suns? Moons? A two-day journey, is that what he meant? She thought it probable.

Alitha knew she'd have to make the journey, for Chia needed more help than she could give him—she doubted whether she could keep even one of them fed. Now was the time to begin walking west; now, while she had the strength. She leaned over and kissed Chia on the forehead, stood up and started off without a backward look.

The soles of her feet had grown considerably tougher from the days on the island, but by nightfall both feet throbbed with pain. She had walked along the beach as much as possible because of fear of losing her way, but now she turned her back on the ocean, searching until she found a crevice among the boulders where she could huddle until morning. She had no way to make a fire, and she'd returned the knife to Chia.

Though she fell into an exhausted sleep almost immediately, she woke with a gibbous moon still overhead. She was chilled through. Alitha rose, wincing when her feet took her weight. If I have to keep moving to stay warm, she decided, I may as well walk toward the *ranchería*.

The moon made a shining path on the water, a path leading to the west. To the islands and Thomas. What would he think if he could see her now, barefoot, nearly naked and almost as brown as a savage Indian? Would she ever see Thomas again?

Alitha blinked back tears. No, she couldn't afford to waste her energy crying for what was beyond her reach. Just as she couldn't allow herself to grieve for her father. Not now.

An animal howled somewhere in the hills to the north. Another answered, then another. Wolves? Were there wolves in California? She didn't know. The wailing rose eerily until she felt the sound came from all around her. Alitha broke into a run, stumbled on a rock and fell headlong. Curling herself into a protective ball to ward off whatever terror stalked her, she huddled against a bleached log. The howling rose and fell, diminished and died away altogether. Relaxing, Alitha slipped once again into the welcoming oblivion of sleep.

The sun, warm on her bare arms and legs, woke her. Yards away, waves lapped on the sand. She raised her head and two stilt-legged shore birds skittered away from her. She sat up and was immediately conscious of a desperate desire for water. Her tongue felt dry and thick, too big for her mouth. Getting to her feet, she stared westward along the sand. She could see no streams making their way into the sea. She hesitated, then headed away from the ocean toward a stand of pines on a hillside. She needed fresh water to survive. She could easily find the ocean again.

Alitha stumbled among the pines for hours before she finally came upon a stream. She dropped to her knees and plunged her face into the cool water, swallowing it in such frantic mouthfuls that she choked and gasped.

When she'd satisfied her thirst, she sat back and looked around her. Trees crowded in on all sides— there was no sign of the ocean. But all she had to do was follow this stream and it would lead her to the sea.

Alitha walked along the stream bank until she came to a rocky hillside. To her distress, the water ran between boulders and disappeared into a crevice. She detoured around the hill but the stream didn't reappear on the other side. She returned and clambered up the rocks, searching to no avail.

Alitha climbed to the top of the hill, hoping to be high enough to see the ocean, but there were higher hills all around her. She looked up at the sun, trying to decide which way was south, the way back to the ocean. The sun, high in the sky, gave her no idea of direction.

I'm lost, she thought. A bird squawked at her, making her jump. She looked up and saw a flash of blue as it flitted to another perch. Her spirits rose. It was a bluejay; she recognized the color and the call. At last something was familiar in this strange land. The jay was a good omen. Why not go in the direction the stream had been headed before it went underground? Surely that would lead her to the ocean.

She walked and walked, her feet bruised and bleeding from stones and debris on the forest floor. As the sun dropped lower, she saw to her dismay that she wasn't headed south. She changed direction, tears running down her cheeks as she limped along. When she finally recognized the scent of burning wood, she realized she'd been smelling the smoke for some time. Anxiously she scanned the sky above the trees. There! A drifting plume of gray-brown. She broke into a clumsy run.

Alitha splashed through the water of a small stream, wondering vaguely if this was the one she'd found earlier, and was brought up short on the far bank when she caught sight of a large domed dwelling. At the same time she heard a woman call sharply in a language she didn't understand. She turned and saw an Indian squaw staring at her. Behind the woman, smaller domed lodges were scattered in a clearing.

The Indian woman had long black hair cut in bangs across her forehead and wore a band of seashells around her hair. She was bare to the waist, but a two-piece skirt covered her in front and in back, ending at her knees. The skirt looked like deerskin and was fringed at the bottom and decorated with small colored stones and shells. She spoke to Alitha again, unintelligible words, and Alitha shook her head.

"*Señorita?*" the Indian asked.

Alitha knew the meaning of this but she didn't want the woman to misunderstand and think she was Spanish so she shrugged, holding out her hands, palms up.

The squaw turned her head to call to others who were, Alitha now saw, near the domed lodges. Four women hurried toward her. Joining the first squaw, they surrounded Alitha, reaching with curious fingers to touch her hair and the material of her bedraggled chemise.

Alitha tried to control her alarm. She patted her

stomach and pointed to her mouth. Chia had been quick to understand gestures; maybe the women would be, too.

One of the women took her hand to lead her toward the lodges. When she saw Alitha following her willingly, she dropped her hand and went ahead. The three others acted as escorts.

Am I to be a captive, Alitha wondered, glancing at them and recalling all the tales she had heard or read of white women captured by savages. She was almost past caring, if only they would feed her and let her rest.

No! She mustn't forget that Chia was waiting for her to send help. Surely this was the village, the *ranchería*, he came from.

"Chia," she said. "Chia."

One of the women smiled and hurried away as though she had understood. Was she going to get Chia's mother? His father? Alitha looked about. She stood among the large lodges—she counted ten of them—all made of some kind of vegetation, each with two doors. More women came to stare at her but nowhere did she see a man, although small naked boys mingled with equally naked girls. When everybody seemed to want to touch her hair, she finally realized a blond woman must be unknown to these Indians.

Still, they spoke a little Spanish, so there must be some form of civilization nearby. A mission?

One of the women handed her a chunk of cooked food she couldn't identify. It made no difference to her, hungry as she was, and she wolfed it down. A vegetable of some kind, she decided, sweetish, with a flavor rather like wine.

The women smiled and nodded at her appetite. Another brought out a shell filled with a kind of flour paste. Shamelessly Alitha lowered her head and licked the shell clean. One of the women giggled. She was handed what was unmistakably a dried fish, and she ate that, too.

At last, her hunger satisfied, she shook her head at more offerings. "Chia," she said once more.

The woman who had apparently understood the word the first time handed her a small, beautifully woven basket. She removed the lid and the pungent smell of sage entered her nostrils.

"Chia," the woman said, smiling.

Alitha stared from the basket in her hand to the woman. Had she misunderstood?

"Chia," Alitha said and the woman nodded happily.

Alitha had never considered that Chia's name might mean something in another language. How was she to get these women to understand? She reached out and caught the arm of a small boy hiding behind one of the women. Pointing to the boy with her free hand, she repeated, "Chia." She raised her hand a foot above the boy's head, hoping they'd understand she meant a larger child. "Chia," she said again. The boy began to squirm in her grasp and she let him go.

Looking about the circle of staring faces, Alitha knew they didn't have any idea what she meant. She picked up the discarded shell she'd licked clean and drew a jagged circle in the dirt. The island. She drew shallow wavy lines, then a definite deep line to show the coast. Taking two twigs from the ground, she moved them from the island to the coast, then broke one of the twigs and moved the other until it touched her breast.

The women murmured among themselves, frowning.

"Oh, please," Alitha cried. "You must understand me. Chia is hurt; he needs help."

But no matter what she did, they didn't know what

she wanted. At last, exhausted, she allowed a woman to lead her to one of the round lodges. Inside, the woman shyly proferred a hide skirt, the two pieces strung on a fiber band. Gratefully, Alitha put it over her chemise, tying the band firmly about her waist.

"Tapextle," the woman said, pushing aside hanging reed curtains to urge Alitha toward a raised platform. Reed mats lay on the platform, and she saw that it served as a bedstead with the reed curtains shielding it from the rest of the lodge. She climbed onto the mats, stretched out and was almost instantly asleep.

Alitha woke to daylight and the sound of a man's heavy, rumbling voice. She opened her eyes and lay for a moment orienting herself. She was in a *ranchería*. The man's voice rose and fell, speaking words she didn't understand. She sat up, brushed back her hair as well as she could with her hands and slid to the floor. She stood a moment to arrange the sections of the two-piece skirt so she was decently covered and then parted the curtains and stepped through.

In what she thought of as the front doorway, a naked Indian man squatted on his heels. Alitha gathered her courage and stepped forward, all too aware of her bare legs and feet and the fragments of material barely covering her breasts.

The man looked up at her.

"Chia," she said.

She pointed to her left leg, then picked up a small stick from the ground and broke it in two, pointing to her leg again, then to the man.

"Chia," she repeated.

He stared at her, and she could tell that Chia must belong to this man's tribe—the man's dark eyes were set into his face in the same manner, his black hair was arranged so his knife was held fast, he had the same rather heavy features. What could she do to make him understand? Already Chia had been almost two days without water.

Crouching down, she used the broken stick to draw still another diagram. This time she started with a boat sketched atop wavy lines. *"Tomolo,"* she told the Indian, remembering that Chia had used that word for his boat. She drew another boat, broken in pieces, and showed a stick figure on the irregular circle she'd used for the island. Pointing to the stick figure, she again said his name, "Chia."

Suddenly conscious of a noise behind her, she looked up and saw that she was completely surrounded by naked men. Hastily she returned her attention to her drawing, sketching in a larger boat, a ship with sails, on the opposite side of the island. Step by step she tried to show them what had happened—the shipwreck, the raft Chia had made, arriving on the mainland, Chia's broken leg, her journey here. When she was done, she pointed southward at herself, and at them.

"Chia," she said, pointing south again.

One of the men, the only one wearing a garment of skin folded about his hips, said something, and all the men turned away from her. The man squatting beside her got up to join them.

"Wait," she cried. "No, you must understand!" She rose to hurry after them, but the last man turned and made the negative gesture she'd learned from Chia. She stopped.

Someone touched her arm, and she whirled to face the woman who'd befriended her yesterday. The squaw smiled broadly and made signs of eating. When Alitha persisted in looking after the men, the Indian woman tugged at her arm, pulling her toward the house. A horse whinnied; another echoed the sound. Alitha stared all around but couldn't see the horses. She certainly hadn't been aware of horses yesterday.

Alitha followed the squaw, crouching down near the lodge to eat more dried fish. I've got to take one of the horses, she told herself. With a horse I can get back to Chia, and then he'll have a way to return to the right *ranchería*—this can't be his village or someone would have recognized his name.

When they'd finished eating, the woman pointed to the interior of the lodge. Alitha made the negative motion of the Indians but the woman caught her hand and she went with her without struggling. Another smile flashed across the brown face, a finger pointed to the bedstead and the squaw rotated her hips several times, formed the fingers of one hand into a circle and thrust the forefinger of her other hand through it. Alitha didn't understand, but still the sign seemed menacingly familiar.

Alitha swallowed. She chopped her hand negatively but the woman only smiled and tried to push her through the reed curtain toward the nearest bedstead. There were three other similar curtains in the house, Alitha saw. She heard a man call out nearby and her eyes widened in fright. No! She wouldn't get onto the bed.

The squaw said something, and another woman appeared. Together they forced Alitha up onto the reed mats of the *tapextle*, then hurried away. Alitha immediately started to slide down again but a man spoke nearby. She heard another answer, and she realized the men were in the lodge. She drew back her legs and huddled on the mats.

She heard laughter, grunts and throaty cries, but no one came near her. At last she jumped down from the bedstead and peered out between the mat curtains.

Sounds came from the curtained *tapextles*, and near the front door of the lodge she saw a moving mound which, as she stared, she understood was a man and woman who were—they were . . .

Alitha put her hand to her mouth, then turned away. She couldn't bring herself to go near the couple on the ground, so she hurried past the hanging reeds curtaining the bedsteads.

Once she was out of the lodge, she skirted around the other domes, trying to find the horses. Some of the children saw her and stared after her, but there was no adults visible. At last she heard a horse nicker, and she followed the sound to a crude corral where five horses skitted sideways as she approached.

As she looked at the horses, her heart sank. There were no saddles. She'd never ridden any way but sidesaddle, and while she might have managed to ride astride a man's saddle, she didn't see how she could stay on the bare back of a horse. Still, what choice did she have? The chestnut near her did have a rope bridle. If she could manage to stay on his back, at least there'd be a way to guide him.

The Indian children who'd followed her watched as she let down the poles penning the horses among the rocks. One of the bigger boys called to her. Ignoring him, Alitha climbed to the top of a rock and held out her hand coaxingly to the horse. The chestnut flung his head up and down, eyeing her warily until his curiosity became too great for him to resist. When he came near enough, she grasped the guide rope looped under the bridle and pulled him toward her. She threw herself from the rock onto his back.

Leaning forward and hanging onto the horse's mane, she dug her heels into his sides to urge him forward. As he burst from the corral, she saw the boy running back toward the lodges and heard him raising an alarm. The other horses followed the chestnut from the corral. She hoped they'd scatter before the men realized what she'd done.

As they left the clearing, the chestnut slowed and began to pick his way among the trees. Alitha was torn between her desire to hurry and her fear that if the horse went too fast, she'd slip off. She looked over her shoulder for signs of pursuit but saw no one. Nor did she see any of the other horses. She tried to guide the chestnut south but he fought her, choosing his own route. She was seated too precariously to struggle with him so was forced to give him his head. Wherever they were going, it was away from the *ranchería*.

A man shouted from behind her. Looking back, she saw a mounted Indian in pursuit, with several others following him. She kicked the chestnut's sides, and the horse changed gait so suddenly that she almost slid off. Grasping desperately to his mane and clenching her knees to his sides, she hung on, wondering how long it would be before she fell.

The chestnut skidded down an embankment with the Indians crashing through the brush in pursuit. Alitha heard the rhythmic roar of the surf, topped a rise and saw the blue of the Pacific ahead of her. She cried out in relief. The chestnut pounded onto the sand and she managed to turn him away from the surf to the east, urging him on.

There! Wasn't that the jumble of rocks she'd memorized, the rocks that marked where she'd left Chia? She'd been closer to him than she'd thought possible; she must have wandered in circles the day before.

How was she to stop the racing horse? When her repeated cries of "Whoa!" had no effect, she reached out to grab the bridle, slipped sideways and fell onto the sand, rolling over twice. The horse galloped on, oblivious.

When she had her breath back, Alitha rose to her feet and limped toward the rocks, reaching them just as the pursuing Indians came up behind her. She stumbled around to the lee side and saw a motionless figure.

"Chia!" she cried. "Chia, are you all right?" She dropped to her knees beside him as the first of the Indian men jumped from his horse.

Chia's dark eyes seemed sunken in his face, but he pulled himself up to a sitting position and tried to smile. "Leeta," he said. His eyes went past her to the men. He said one word to them, repeating it over and over.

One of the Indians came forward, lifting a hide pouch from his carrying net to hand to Chia. After drinking the water from the pouch, the boy returned it. He began to talk. Once or twice Alitha caught a word she knew—*tomolo,* boat. The men watched him intently, occasionally nodding.

Alitha looked from the men to Chia. He was safe; they'd look after him. They might not be of his clan but they spoke the same language and must be part of the same tribe. But what about her? Chia might be grateful to her, but these men certainly had no reason to be. She'd stolen one of their horses and lost him, besides.

Chia suddenly reached out and put something in her hand, saying her name to the men with other words she didn't understand. The Indians looked at one another, muttering. She looked at what he'd given her and saw that it was his reddish charm stone. She smiled at Chia, knowing he'd given her his most prized possession. Quickly she hung the cord about her neck so the stone fish nestled between her breasts.

At last the men stopped arguing, and the one who'd given Chia the water nodded. Chia nodded back. They all looked at her and she knew she'd been accepted, at least temporarily. Did savages have a sense of obligation, then? Perhaps, now, she could make them understand that she wanted to be taken to the nearest mission.

The man who'd nodded touched her arm, pointing to the boy. "Chia," he said. He looked back at the others and they all laughed. Friendly laughter.

Then the man raised his head and said one curt word. The others instantly fell silent and all seemed to listen. With a quick movement, the first man swept Alitha up onto his horse and leaped on in front of her. One of the others picked up Chia and did the same. Mounted once again, they turned their four horses toward the hills.

Alitha clung to the Indian's waist, at the same time trying to look behind her to see what had alarmed them. She caught a quick glimpse of mounted men and heard the unmistakable crack of gunfire. The man she rode with grunted, flung his hands up and pitched off the horse, carrying Alitha with him. The last thing she was aware of was her own scream. Then she hit the ground and the world was snuffed out.

chapter 10

HORSES GALLOPING. THE crackle of flames. A volley of gunfire. Shouts in Spanish. The odor of dust and horses and burning wood. The creak of saddles, the jangle of spurs. A scream of pain. A cry of triumph.

Another horse, approaching at a walk.

Alitha opened her eyes. Through a haze of dizziness she saw a black-garbed rider come toward her. Her vision gradually cleared as she watched him. When he was a few feet away, he swung effortlessly to the ground, swept off his broad-brimmed hat and knelt at her side. She had an impression of silver and black— silver buttons on a black jacket, silver ornaments, black breeches, black boots with silver spurs.

His eyes met and held hers. Brown eyes. He had black hair and a small black mustache. He was by far the handsomest man she had ever seen.

He spoke to her in unfamiliar words, and she stared at him blankly.

"Give praise to God," he then said in accented English, "for your safekeeping."

Alitha managed a yes, her voice barely a whisper.

"You are fortunate those savages didn't harm you," the man went on. He glanced down, appearing to examine the white trim on his hat. "They did not, did they?"

"No," she said, sitting up. With the tips of her fingers she touched a swelling on the side of her head. She felt bruised and sore but her vertigo was gone and no bones seemed to be broken.

"I will light a hundred candles to Saint Christopher to offer my thanks for your deliverance." He stood up and bowed. "Allow me, *señorita*," he said. "I am Don Esteban Mendoza of the Rancho Mendoza of the *pueblo* of Santa Barbara. A humble servant of Ferdinand VII, Catholic King of Spain and ruler of all her colonies beyond the seas."

Despite her pain Alitha smiled at his grandiloquence. "Miss Alitha Bradford," she told him, "late of Boston, Massachusetts, a free citizen of the United States of America." It crossed her mind fleetingly that she might be expected to add, James Monroe, President.

"I never expected to find a beautiful woman lost in the wilds of Alta California. A delicate and exotic flower blooming amidst our rough native reeds."

Delicate? She glanced down at her torn chemise and her hide skirt. How terrible she must look! She crossed her hands over her breasts, looking away from Esteban in embarrassment. His hands touched her and she jumped; his fingers had seemed like an electric spark on her bare arm. Glancing up, she saw that he was draping his jacket over her shoulders. She slipped her arms into the sleeves and drew the jacket close around her.

"You were most fortunate that we arrived when we

did. Esteban told her. "These wild Indians are unpredictable. They appear quiet and peace-loving until they lull you into complacency, and then they steal and pillage."

The Indians, the *ranchería,* Chia. Alitha's hand slipped inside the jacket and touched the stone charm that hung between her breasts. How could she have forgotten Chia even for a moment?

"Chia," she said, "where's Chia?"

"Chia?"

"An Indian boy with a broken leg. He built the raft we sailed from the island to the mainland. When we came ashore, he broke his leg."

"A raft. Of course, how stupid I must seem. The shipwreck from which seven men were saved. You are the *señorita* from the ship they call the *Flying Yankee,* the ship that was wrecked in the great storm. Is that not true?"

"Yes, our ship broke up on the rocks in a storm. Seven men were saved? I'm so thankful, I was afraid I was the only survivor." She decided not to mention Malloy. That would only lead to more questions she might not want to answer. "But Chia. Where is he?"

Esteban shrugged. "An Indian boy? I am sorry, I did not see him. I expect the other savages have taken him with them into the mountains."

"Why into the mountains? Their *ranchería* is here, only a mile or two away." She remembered hearing, as in a dream, the horses, the gunfire, the shouts.

"Indians must be punished when they steal," Esteban said. "As I told Capitán Quinn only a few days ago, they must be treated as you would treat a child. Do you know him, perhaps, this Capitán Quinn? He is an *Americano.*"

"Quinn? Jordan Quinn? I've heard the name, but no,

I don't know him." Alitha frowned. "The shooting I heard was from the Indian village, wasn't it? You raided the village. You must take me there, Don Esteban." Alitha stood up, steadying herself against the pine she'd been lying beneath. She found herself looking out over the ocean from a rise.

Don Esteban reached out a hand but drew it back before he touched her. "You are hurt," he said. "I will take you to *mi casa*. You are not fit to ride to the *ranchería*. I have told you that you will not find this boy there. The Indians stole horses from our *rancho*, we pursued and overtook them, there was a skirmish and the Indians fled into the hills. We were fortunate to recover some of our horses." He shrugged. "In California it happens time after time."

"If you won't take me to the *ranchería*, I'll find my own way." Alitha started to walk in the direction of the ocean, ignoring the aching throb in her head. She had reached the beach before she heard Esteban's horse behind her. Once he overtook her, he followed a few paces behind.

"I have heard stories of American women," he said, "without ever believing them. Now I find what I heard is true—that they are strong in the head."

"Headstrong is the word," Alitha muttered to herself as she trudged along the sand. She could think of a word to fit him, too: arrogant. She heard hoofbeats and looked up to see another Spanish *vaquero* approaching.

"I capitulate," Esteban said. "Allow me to ride you to the *ranchería*, since you insist on going there."

"I'd rather walk."

"I will suffer great shame if I allow a *señorita* to walk while I ride. Please."

She stopped, and Esteban swung to the ground

beside her. He put both hands on her waist to lift her to
the saddle, then paused.

"Your eyes," he said. "I have never before seen eyes
so blue. They are the color of the sea on a bright day in
June."

She felt herself reddening as he lifted her into the
saddle and mounted behind her

The other horseman reined in and, after sweeping off
his sombrero and bowing to Alitha, spoke in Spanish to
Esteban. Esteban nodded, and they rode on.

"Don Manuel informs me we have regained five of
our horses from the Indians," Esteban told her.

She said nothing, afraid to reveal her turmoil of
feelings. Concerned about Chia, fearful as to what
might have happened to him, she was at the same time
acutely aware of Don Esteban riding behind her, of his
arm holding her in place on the saddle so that she was
pressed against his chest.

As they left the beach and rode along a trail into the
hills the smell of burning wood grew stronger and she
saw smoke curling over the trees ahead of them. They
splashed across the stream and entered the clearing.

Alitha gasped in horror. The domed lodges were
gone, reduced to smoldering piles of charred rubble. A
solitary spear was thrust into the ground beside a horse
lying dead near the ashes of a campfire. Beyond the last
of the burned lodges Alitha saw a naked brown body.
Chia'

She slid from Esteban's horse and ran through the
smoke and debris to kneel beside him. Not Chia,
though she thought she recognized the dead man as the
Indian who had given Chia water from his pouch. She
couldn't be sure because there was a black-rimmed
bloody hole where his right eye should have been.

Esteban dismounted and walked to stand next to her.

Behind him, other *vaqueros* rode into the clearing, leading a group of riderless horses.

"You did this?" Alitha nodded at the dead Indians, then glanced around at what had been the Indian village.

"The Indians only respect men who aren't afraid to fight for what is theirs. When you've lived in California for a time, you'll understand."

"I'll never understand. You say the Indians are children. Is this how you treat children, then? Do you kill them when they misbehave? You with your guns against Indians armed with spears—is that fighting? It's not, it's killing in cold blood. Are you proud of what you've done?"

"I warned you not to come here to the *ranchería*," Esteban said quietly. "You're a woman, Señorita Bradford. Warfare is not a concern of women."

"Warfare? This is more like murder."

She saw Esteban's hands clench. He slapped his quirt against his breeches, started to reply, then turned from her without saying a word.

"You're a coward, Don Esteban Mendoza," she told him, her voice low and intense. "A coward!"

He spun around, gathered the front of her jacket in his hand and yanked her to him. Alitha gasped. She could feel his breath on her face, his body against hers.

"If you were a man and said that to me," he told her, "I'd kill you."

He shook her, making her head jerk back and forth. Suddenly he drew in his breath and thrust her from him, and she stumbled away. Her foot struck the dead Indian and she toppled over him to the ground. Esteban stared down at her for a moment, his brown eyes flashing, then turned on his heel and crossed the clearing to join the other men.

Near tears, Alitha pushed herself from the ground and brushed the dirt from her hide skirts. She walked after Esteban, conscious of the curious glances of the men. She grasped a rope on one of the riderless horses, a bay, and used it to help pull herself onto the horse's back The *vaquero* who still held the end of the rope raised his eyebrows in surprise, then shrugged and tossed the rope to her.

She kicked her heels into the bay's flanks, and he plunged forward, almost throwing her to the ground. As she clung to his mane, the horse dashed across the clearing, leaped a ditch and thudded along the trail toward the beach.

She heard a horse behind her, the hoofbeats coming closer and closer. Holding tight to the bay's mane, afraid to raise her head, she felt someone grab the rope tied to the bridle. The bay tried to yank its head free, then slowed, finally stopping. Alitha looked up at the other rider, not surprised to find that it was Don Esteban.

"Where in the name of God are you going?" he demanded.

"To the mountains," she said without stopping to think. She glanced at the quirt in Esteban's hand, thinking that if she had a riding whip, she would lash out at him with it. "To find Chia," she added.

"You are a fool."

She lowered her head, biting her lips to keep from crying. She ached all over and she was so tired, so very tired. "I suppose you want the horse," she said, dimly aware that she hoped he would deny that was his reason for riding after her.

"No, *señorita,* the horse is yours. I came after you to ask for the return of my jacket. It was made for me by my sister, Margarita."

She pulled off the jacket, rolled it into a ball and threw it at him. "Take your damn jacket," she said.

Esteban caught the jacket deftly, shook out the wrinkles and put it on.

"Muchas gracias, señorita," he said. He gestured in the direction of the horsemen waiting in the clearing. "We return to the *rancho* at once. You are welcome to ride with us if that is your wish." He touched the brim of his hat, wheeled his horse and rode back along the trail.

Alitha sat glaring after him, sighed and then turned her horse to follow his. She really had no choice but to ride with him, she told herself. She hated him, wished the ground would quake and open up, as she had heard it often did in California, and swallow Don Esteban. But she had to follow him; she had nowhere else to go.

When she reentered the clearing, a *vaquero* was riding from the woods with an Indian over his saddle.

"Chia!"

Alitha slid to the ground and ran to him. It *was* Chia. When she took his head in her hands, he opened his eyes and said her name. She hugged him.

Esteban rode by, glanced at the Indian boy and gave an order to the *vaquero*.

"We will take the boy with us to the mission," he told Alitha, spurring his horse and riding off before she could answer. As she remounted the bay, a *vaquero* reined in beside her and handed her a brown *serape*, and she put it on.

Alitha rode in the middle of the column of horsemen just behind Chia, who, despite his broken leg, sat stolidly astride a horse. As they followed a rough trail winding among the low hills a short distance from the shore, she caught glimpses of Esteban riding far ahead.

He was an excellent horseman, she admitted to herself, for whatever that was worth. And handsome, if you like dark Latin men. Beauty, she reminded herself, was only skin deep. Don Esteban was cruel, a boor and insincere—his flowery compliments meant nothing. Undoubtedly he repeated them to every woman he met. What had he called her? Beautiful, a delicate flower blooming in the California wilderness. How absurd!

At dusk they made camp for the night beside a stream. Alitha was so exhausted that she hardly appreciated the luxury of a blanket. She slept soundly until daybreak, when they remounted to ride on toward Santa Barbara. It was mid-morning when she saw Don Esteban, astride his stallion, waiting beside the trail. When she rode by without acknowledging him, he spurred his horse forward and rode beside her.

"At the crest of the next hill," he said, "we shall be able to see the ocean and the *Kerry Dancer* at anchor. That is the ship of Capitán Quinn." Esteban spoke pleasantly, seeming to have decided to ignore their encounter of the day before.

Why should she be the churlish one, Alitha asked herself. Probably Esteban thought her ungrateful after he had, in his view, saved her life by rescuing her from the Indians.

"Why is this Captain Quinn here?" she asked.

"He intends to marry my sister, Margarita. They have been betrothed for almost two years."

"Ahhh." Alitha let her breath out in a sigh, feeling an unexpected disappointment. So Jordan Quinn was to marry soon. Why was she so surprised? He might have been already married for all she knew. And besides, she herself would marry soon.

"If the governor's objections can be overcome," Esteban said, describing the interrupted wedding ceremony.

She glanced at him, for his tone when he talked of the marriage had hinted at his disapproval. "They'll live here in California?" she asked.

"At first they will make their home in Monterey, but this Capitán Quinn is a restless man. I doubt if he will ever settle anywhere for long. My sister, on the other hand, desires a home with many children."

"You make them sound ill-matched."

"A man, when he marries, should choose someone of his own kind."

"Not necessarily," she said. "I believe that . . ."

"Come," he said, interrupting her, "follow me and you shall see his ship." She glared at him, but he had already turned away and left the trail. Fuming, she followed him, climbing to a rock shelf overlooking the harbor and the village of Santa Barbara. Alitha's annoyance slipped away as she gazed out at the beautiful blue expanse of ocean stretching away before them. There was no ship in sight.

Esteban slapped his quirt against his leg and swung his horse about. "Come," he said over his shoulder to Alitha.

"What happened?" she asked. "Where's the *Kerry Dancer* and where's Captain Quinn?"

"A sudden storm might have forced them to put to sea, but there was no storm. I fear the worst. I fear he has defied the laws of God and man."

When they rejoined the *vaqueros*, Esteban left her to gallop ahead. Twenty minutes later, when Alitha and the other horsemen came down from the hills, she saw Esteban and another man riding toward them.

"They have fled," he told her. "My overseer, Señor Huerta, informed me that this Quinn spirited Margarita away the same night the Indians raided our horses. God knows where he might have taken her."

"They've eloped," she said, smiling wistfully.

Esteban stared out over the empty sea. "If he brings her to harm," he said, "I will kill him."

Looking at his grim face and hearing the intensity in his voice, Alitha shivered. She would never want to be the enemy of this man, she thought.

As they left the hills to ride through green fields, she saw a two-story adobe ranch ahead of them. Dogs ran out to bark at the horse's hooves, women waved a greeting from a balcony and one of the *vaqueros* began to sing a spirited Spanish song. In a few minutes the others had joined in the chorus, and they entered the courtyard singing.

As they dismounted, a boy, shouting excitedly, ran up to Esteban. The men gathered around and, although Alitha couldn't make out the sense of what was being said, she heard the word *oso* repeated several times.

Esteban nodded and the boy ran from the courtyard. The men remounted their horses and followed him toward the rear of the buildings. Alitha, unnoticed, hurried after them on foot past a corral to the base of a rocky, wooded hill. When she caught up to the *vaqueros*, their horses were snorting and skittishly milling about near a brush-choked gully. Seeing Alitha, Esteban rode to her and dismounted.

"The bear we captured to fight the bull has escaped and taken refuge in the *arroyo*," he said. "He's dangerous; he was wounded by a shot from one of the stable boys. We must kill him."

She nodded and watched Esteban start up the gully

toward the brush. When two *vaqueros* followed, he stopped them with a wave of his hand, said a few words to them, then walked on alone.

As he reached the brush, Esteban pulled a hunting knife from a sheath on his belt. Alitha drew in her breath realizing that, except for the knife, he was unarmed. Was he mad? Pushing the branches aside, he advanced cautiously into the undergrowth, the brush closing behind him so that all she could see was an occasional flash of silver when the sunlight struck an ornament on his jacket.

She heard a low growl followed by a sudden thrashing in the brush, as though the bear was plunging down the hill at Esteban. The horses around her reared, the *vaqueros* fighting to control them. The branches swayed and she heard an animallike cry of pain. A few minutes later Esteban emerged from the gully, backing away his left sleeve torn and long, bloody slashes on his arm. In his right hand he still held the knife.

The bear crashed out of the brush toward him, loping on all fours, a brown bear larger than Alitha had imagined any bear could be. Was this a California grizzly? She looked quickly at the two men with muskets. Both were holding their weapons at their sides. Why didn't they fire? Could Esteban have told them not to shoot the bear, to leave the killing to him? But why?

Esteban stopped and the bear lunged at him. Alitha cried out as Esteban darted to one side, thrusting his knife into the bear and pulling it out again. With a roar of pain the animal clawed at him, one paw striking his shoulder and sending him sprawling to the ground. The bear rose on his hind legs above Esteban.

"Shoot him, shoot him," Alitha cried. "He'll kill Esteban if you don't."

The *vaqueros* raised their muskets to their shoulders but held their fire.

The bear hurled himself down at Esteban, but the don rolled away. The bear's claws snagged his boot and held it pinned to the ground as Esteban struggled to free himself. Yanking his boot away, Esteban closed on the bear, plunging his knife into the animal's side, darting away, returning to plunge the knife in again.

The bear, roaring with pain, struck out blindly. Esteban retreated and the bear lumbered after him, his blood darkening the ground. All at once the bear stopped and lurched to one side, looking around him as though puzzled. Slowly the bear turned and shambled up the hill toward the shelter of the rocks.

Esteban motioned with his hand and the two guns cracked simultaneously. The bear slumped to the ground and lay still.

Esteban walked down the slope, his shirt dark from sweat and blood, his face smeared with dirt, his clothing torn. Alitha saw bloody claw marks on his arm and shoulder. He embraced the two men who had shot the bear, then walked on toward her. When he was a few feet away, he hurled his knife to the ground, where the blade embeded itself between her feet. She stared down at the blood-smeared knife, her breath coming quickly, feeling the wild beating of her heart.

Esteban spoke so only she could hear. "Do you still believe me to be a coward?" he asked.

chapter 11

ALITHA AWOKE IN a dark, curtained room. She sat up and saw she was wearing a thin white nightgown. Whose? Her head whirled but she rose to her feet and made her way to the window, pulled the curtain aside and looked out at trees shrouded in a swirling white mist. Still lightheaded, she returned to the bed, where she lay on top of the coverlet, intending to rest for a few minutes, but she quickly fell into a fevered sleep.

She lay ill for a week, a time of strange dreams she couldn't remember in her infrequent moments of wakefulness. She was dimly aware of the comings and goings of Indian servants, of opening her fever-lidded eyes to see a heavyset middle-aged woman bending over her bed, of calling out for her father.

Esteban brought her a single red rose. She held it in both hands, smelling the heady fragrance as she looked from the flower to the don. Did she dream he knelt at her bedside, taking her hand in his and raising it to his lips as he kissed her fingers? Did she dream that before he left he leaned over and tenderly kissed her forehead?

When she awoke, clear-headed at last, she saw the plump woman reading in a chair near the window. The curtains had been looped back, but she could see only a gauzy mist outside. When Alitha lifted her head, the woman by the window closed her book and came to stand beside her.

"I am Maria Mendoza," she said in precise English. "The widow of the brother of Don Esteban."

Alitha looked at the black silk dress, its style ten years out of date, and realized that Maria Mendoza was still in mourning. She smiled at the woman.

"I'm sorry to be so much trouble," Alitha said. "Imposing on you, then getting sick."

"*De nada,* it is nothing—our house is your house. What can one expect but illness after having to live among savages?"

"No, it wasn't like that at all," Alitha said. "They never harmed me; they saved our lives, mine and Chia's." She rose on one elbow. "How is he? How is Chia? The boy with the broken leg."

"He is at the mission. The Indians there care for him."

Alitha sank back. Chia was safe. She gazed up at Señora Mendoza. "And Don Esteban?" she asked. "He is well?"

"Don Esteban is not at the *rancho.* He journeys north to the capital at Monterey to search for his sister and—"she paused—"for other reasons." Maria reached down and took Alitha's hand. "Don Esteban is not for you," she said.

"I don't understand what you mean." Alitha felt her face redden. She pulled her hand away.

Maria slid her fingers under the pillow and brought

out a somewhat bedraggled red rose. Alitha reached for the flower and Maria gave it to her.

"You wouldn't rest until the rose was with you," Maria said.

Alitha thrust the rose back under her pillow, out of sight. "I—the scent . . ." she began, then fell silent under the other woman's gaze. She pushed herself up in bed. "I left Boston to sail to the Sandwich Islands," she said. "I am betrothed to the Reverend Thomas Heath, a missionary there."

Maria watched her, waiting.

Alitha took a deep breath. "Reverend Heath and I planned to marry last year, but my mother fell ill and I took care of her until she died. Thomas—Reverend Heath—had to sail before we could be married." It was all true, and yet, Alitha thought, she couldn't bring Thomas's face to mind.

"I am happy to hear of your betrothal," Maria said. "All young women should marry. For ten years I was the wife of Don Tomás Mendoza, the brother of Don Esteban, until he was mortally wounded in the war against the tyrant Napolean. I loved Don Tomás." Maria lowered her face into her hands and began to sob.

Alitha threw aside the coverlet and sat up, reaching out to her.

"*Madre de Diós,*" Maria Mendoza murmured. "*Madre de Diós.*" Removing the black lace handkerchief from her sleeve, she dabbed at her eyes. "I beg your pardon," she said to Alitha. "I am such a worthless woman. The only man I could ever love is dead, a man I was not able to honor with children. All I have left is Don Esteban. Am I to be a Jonah followed by ill fortune all the days of my life? My husband was killed, Don Esteban's father died of the fever on the ship bringing us to this barbarous country, now my beloved sister-in-law, the sister of Don Esteban, has sailed away with an *Americano,* a man not yet her husband. What will become of us all in this strange land?"

"I find California even more strange than you do," Alitha said.

Maria returned the handkerchief to her sleeve. "A journey to one's beloved interrupted by shipwreck and savages—such misfortune! I am ashamed that I think only of myself and forget my duty. Before he left Don Esteban said, 'Care for the *señorita* as though she were your own while I am in Monterey. If I did not know she was almost well,' he said, 'I would not leave her.'"

Alitha smiled involuntarily, quickly raising her hand to her face to mask her pleasure. Esteban *did* care, she thought

"Don Esteban and the others return in ten days' time" Maria went on, "and a feast is planned to celebrate their homecoming."

"Let me help you. I'll do whatever I can to repay you for your hospitality."

Maria shook her head. "We have many Indian servants to do the work. You are a guest, and we will treat you as a guest until your ship arrives."

"My ship? The *Flying Yankee* was wrecked."

"No, no, not the *Yankee.* I meant the next ship bound for the Sandwich Islands. Many come here to Santa Barbara to be loaded with hides. There will be one soon, and you will be united with the one you love "

"Yes, of course," Alitha said.

'But, first, we must make you well again, find clothes for you. I want to show you our *rancho,* the mission, the village and something of this part of California. This is a beautiful country, though it is wild and uncivilized."

"You're very kind."

"Any Californio would do the same for a guest. Now, is there anything you want?"

"I'd like to read. Have you a book?"

"A book? The Mendozas have the largest library in all of California," Maria said, "but we have only one book written in English. I will bring it to you."

When she returned a short time later, Maria handed Alitha a thin, leather-bound volume with the title embossed in gold—*Pilgrim's Progress.*

Alitha leafed through the pages; at home she had read and reread the tale of Christian's adventures in the Slough of Despond, Doubting Castle and the Valley of Humiliation as he journeyed in search of salvation.

When Maria left, Alitha reached beneath her pillow, bringing the rose from its hiding place and pressing the flower between the pages of the book. She sighed as she held the book in her hands. She herself, Alitha thought, was as much a pilgrim as Christian, traveling to foreign lands in search of . . . What? Happiness? Love? What did she seek?

Alitha recovered quickly, and Maria was as good as her word—Don Esteban's house became Alitha's house as well. Dresses were lengthened for her, petticoats displayed for her selection. Maria led her through the kitchen garden, naming the herbs, and into the vegetable garden with its tomatoes, green and red peppers, cabbages, white onions, peas, watermelons and beans on high poles. They strolled in the orchards among the fig trees, oranges, limes and olives.

As they climbed hillsides painted a springtime yellow and gold by poppies, Alitha watched cottontails dart through patches of wild oats, listened to the cries of jays, the coo of turtledoves, and the echoing calls of the mockingbirds. Wherever she went she heard the tolling mission bells calling the Indians to work or to prayer.

They walked along the beach collecting shells, sat on the sand looking out over the Pacific.

"Soon," Maria told her, "the ship bound for the islands will come for you."

At the Mendoza *casa*, the preparations for the banquet quickened. Bread was baked in the huge ovens, grain was pounded, coffee beans roasted and ground in the kitchen courtyard, chickens plucked and dressed. The Indian women scoured bathtubs, scrubbed floors, made soap and tallow candles.

Despite the preparations for the coming feast, the day-to-day chores of the *casa* went on. The cleaning and cooking seemed never ending. The meals were elaborate. For breakfast Alitha might be served stewed beef and beans, tongue cooked with hot peppers and garlic, rice, pumpkin, cabbage, chicken and eggs, oranges and tortillas.

She was constantly reminded of Esteban's expected return. "When Don Esteban comes," Maria said five or six times each day.

"When Don Esteban comes," Alitha echoed.

On the day before the feast, Esteban had still not returned from the north.

"He will be here," Maria said. "Esteban instructed me to hold the feast tomorrow night. Already our guests are arriving. Surely he will be here."

Alitha looked from her window at the wooded mountains behind the house. What if something had happened to Esteban? Monterey was many miles away. What if he and his party had met hostile Indians? What if they had been stricken with the cholera? Or met with an accident on the trail?

The weather changed on the morning of the feast as a

dry, hot wind from the inland deserts blew the fog out to sea and the sun beat down with an intensity Alitha had felt only while the *Flying Yankee* sailed in the tropics. When she walked to the mission, the breeze hot on her face, she thought that all of life seemed to have come almost to a stop; even the Indians laboring in the fields worked more slowly than she had ever seen them work before.

Chia smiled up at her from his pallet in one of the Indian adobe huts, his leg encased in dried mud and bound by reeds. They talked in halting Spanish, for both had learned a few words of the language. Chia was impatient, eager to walk again.

Would he stay at the mission, she asked him.

Chia shook his head. He would go to his *rancheria* or to the mountains, he told her, wherever he could find his people. He made her understand, more with sign language than with his meager Spanish, that he saw the Indians of the mission as people who had traded their freedom for bread and shelter and received the worst of the bargain.

As they talked, the mission bells tolled. Chia hated the bells, for they spoke of his people's bondage as they called the Indians from their sleep, ordered them to make the sign of the cross, to begin work in the fields, to recite the benediction, to return to the mission for a supper of barley and porridge, to sing the *alabado* at sunset and to go to bed at night.

As Alitha left the mission, pensive and brooding, she walked past the stone fountain shaped like a bear in front of the church. A bear much like the one Esteban had fought. Esteban. What would her life be like if she were married to a don, she wondered. Would she be as enslaved as the Indians, not by the *padres* but by children, by the never-ending tasks of her *casa* and by the customs of this alien land?

While she walked, her head down, she was vaguely aware of horsemen riding by and of shouts from the village. At first, lost in her reverie, she paid no attention, but when she did look about her, she saw men hastening in the direction of the beach. Gazing out to sea, she drew in her breath as she saw the white sails of a square-rigger a few cable lengths offshore. This must be the long-awaited ship bound for the Sandwich Islands, the ship that would carry her to Thomas.

She made her way down the slope from the village to the beach to stand at the edge of the sand, staring at the ship flying the stars and stripes. As she watched, the anchor was lowered and the crew launched a boat, rowed through the surf and beached the boat on the sand.

The Spanish villagers clustered around the crewmen, but Alitha hung back, hearing the word *Islands* in English, hearing Spanish words she didn't understand. Finally gathering her courage, she approached a young seaman with curly blond hair who was standing guard at the prow of the boat.

"Where are you bound?" she asked him.

"To San Diego, *señorita.*" He smiled at her, frankly staring.

"And then?"

"Around the Horn to Boston."

"You're not bound for the Sandwich Islands?"

"No, ma'am, we're bound *from* the Islands."

She thanked him and ran along the beach, feeling her heart beating with thanksgiving. She did not have to leave the Mendoza *rancho* after all; she didn't have to sail to the islands. Her pace slackened. This was only a reprieve, she realized, not a pardon; another ship might drop anchor anytime, possibly as soon as tomorrow or the next day.

She climbed the stairs from the courtyard to the gallery and went to her room, where she sat in a chair looking from the open window. She took *Pilgrim's Progress* from the table next to her bed. The book opened to the rose, which was faded though still red and fragrant. Smiling, she stared down at the flower.

Has he bewitched you, Alitha Bradford? she asked herself. Admit the truth as you promised yourself you would. You've lost your heart to a man you scarcely know, a man who embraces a different faith, a man with a way of life alien to yours. Esteban can bring you nothing but pain and unhappiness; you hate him as much as you love him. Love? How could she ever think of loving Esteban? She loved Thomas; her feeling for Thomas was enduring, based on a shared life. How could she possibly describe this fascination as love?

What was it then if not love? Why did she toss and turn in bed at night, unable to sleep, her thoughts returning continually to Esteban—the way he looked at her, the inflection of his voice, the flash of his smile, the dark mystery of his eyes. She hated his arrogance, laughed at his grandiose figures of speech and was annoyed by his profuse flattery. She suspected she could never be happy with him.

At the same time she couldn't imagine life without him. If she couldn't see him again, if for some reason he never returned from Monterey, her life would be empty. Useless. Not worth living. If that was love, then she loved him.

But, of course, she was promised to Thomas.

That evening she laid the gown she would wear to the banquet on her bed. She stood looking at the figured white satin. She had learned from Maria that the gown had been intended for Margarita but hadn't been finished before her elopement. Now, altered to fit Alitha's body, it would be worn by another woman waiting to be a bride. The fabric was lovely, with the figured roses woven into the satin so that they seemed transparent.

Alitha took a chemise from the wardrobe, then hesitated. No, it was too hot; she wouldn't wear a chemise. She fastened her petticoats, slipped on her dress and buttoned it over her bare breasts. Surely the dress was modest enough, with its high neckline and the outline of her breasts concealed by a flounce of lace on the bodice.

She stepped to the mirror and adjusted a white mantilla on her head. She was dressed completely in white except for a silver pin in the shape of a rose fastened to an ornamental comb in the front of her hair. Her skin, browned by the sun, seemed to glow; the golden tan of her face, neck and arms contrasted with the white of the gown.

Maria knocked and opened the door. She was dressed in her customary black.

"You look enchanting," Maria said.

"Thank you. Is Esteban here yet?"

"No, but he will be soon," Maria assured her.

They descended arm in arm to the high-ceilinged dining room, where crystal glasses glistened and the silver table setting gleamed in the candlelight. The few women were elegant in their long gowns and mantillas, the men dashing in black and silver. Alitha felt their eyes on her, heard murmurs of curiosity from the women and saw smiles of admiration from the men. And still Esteban had not come.

The platters of food were passed from hand to

hand—turkey, chicken, veal, tomatoes, oranges, pomegranates. Alitha ate little. As she sipped the white wine, her gaze returned time and again to the doorway. Her ears were attuned not to the talk and laughter in the room but to the sounds from outside.

Hoofbeats. Alitha caught her breath; the talk in the room stilled and there was an expectant hush. Alitha turned in her chair as *Señor* Huerta entered, smiling and bowing. Two other men followed. Then Don Esteban was there, moving easily from one guest to another.

"Margarita?" they asked him.

Esteban shook his head. There had been no word of Margarita at Monterey.

Alitha's breath quickened as Esteban looked down the long table and saw her, his eyes holding hers. He walked directly to her, ignoring all others, took her hand and brought it to his lips.

"You are the most beautiful woman in the world," he said

Then Maria was at his side and he was gone.

After the banquet, after the singing to the music of violins and Spanish guitars, after the dancing, Esteban came to her, taking her by the hand and leading her from the house. He lifted her to his horse, mounted behind her and, with his arm about her waist, they rode to a knoll where a single pine leaned as though in flight from the ocean. The night was hot, though the wind had died with the setting of the sun. Below them, the American ship lay at anchor and the moonlight shimmered like a silvery ribbon on the sea.

Esteban took her in his arms and kissed her, his lips to hers, his hand to the nape of her neck. As she surrendered herself to his kiss, the world seemed to dissolve around her. As the kiss went on and on, she felt a warmth grow in her.

"You are my life and my love," Esteban whispered in her ear. "You are my heart of hearts, my beloved. I want you more than I can tell you."

"I missed you so much," she said.

"I want you with me always, Alitha. Ride with me. In two weeks' time I must go to Mexico. Will you come with me?"

She drew away. "To Mexico?"

"I go to Mexico City to convince the Spanish viceroy to send help to California."

"How long will you be gone?"

"The journey is one of many thousands of miles. Perhaps I will be gone for six months, perhaps a year."

A year. A lifetime, she thought. I won't be here a year from now. I'll never see him again.

"Oh, Esteban," she said, burying her face against his chest.

He kissed her, a long and lingering kiss, and when his lips left hers she felt his hand unbutton the top button of her dress. He kissed her bared neck and she leaned back against his arm. His hand cupped her breast, then fumbled at the buttons of her dress.

She pulled away and ran from him, down the hill to the beach and across the sand to the water's edge. She heard his footsteps following her.

I'll go with him, she told herself. We'll be married and I'll go with Esteban to Mexico City as his wife.

Her skin, her entire body was afire. Thomas's face flashed before her, but she shook her head. Thomas didn't understand her; Thomas thought there was something wrong with her. She glanced over her shoulder. Would Esteban feel the same?

Suddenly she felt she could no longer stand the weight of the heavy satin gown. She remembered the freedom of being on the island with Chia. She reached for the buttons of her dress, hesitated, then unbuttoned her gown, shrugged it from her shoulders, removed the dress and her petticoats, laying them on the sand. She stepped out of her satin slippers and stood naked in the moonlight for a moment, facing the Pacific, then ran into the sea, the water cold on her legs. She felt it rise on her body, to her thighs, higher, to her hips and to her breasts. She waded to the line of the surf, plunged into the oncoming waves as she had on the island, letting the breakers sweep her toward shore.

She stood up with the water to her waist. Esteban was a dark shadow on the sand. Around her the waves pounded the shore with their never-ending rhythm. The water had cooled her skin but the fire still flared within her. There was no one else in the world except herself and Esteban.

She walked toward him with the moon behind her, shadowing her body. He did not move. When she was a few feet from him he opened his arms and she ran to him, feeling the loops of his jacket press on her breasts and his breeches rub harshly against her legs.

He kissed her and, still kissing her, lifted her into his arms and carried her up the beach to where three rocks jutted up, and there he stopped, setting her down. He removed his own clothing until he was as naked as she.

He stood in front of her, taking her hand and urging her from the shadow of the rocks; and she realized he wanted to see her in the moonlight, so she let him pull her along as she followed his glance to the swell of her breasts gleaming whitely below her tanned arms and neck. He lowered his head to her breasts, kissing each nipple in turn, and she took him in her arms. Moments later he pressed her onto the sand, his body half over hers. She clung to him but he pulled back and gently spread her legs with his hands. Still kissing her breasts, his tongue going from one to the other, he slid his hand between her legs, touching her, caressing her, and she felt the warmth grow in her until it became a swelling need, a frightening, ecstatic rush of joy building in her legs and sweeping through her body.

His fingers left her body. When he entered her, she felt a stab of pain and she moaned. Suddenly frightened, she pushed him away and he drew back. After a moment she reached hesitantly for him, guiding him into her, enclosing him with her legs, and now her pain was mingled with her desire.

He thrust within her. At first she lay still, but then her body responded to his, her nipples hardening beneath his kisses. She reached down, guiding his lips up to hers. She felt his tongue probe into her mouth. Her tongue joined his, intertwined with his, and again she felt the throbbing beat of passion fill her body as she strained to him, trembling beneath him. He gasped and she felt him quiver and then he lay quiet in her arms and she could hear nothing except the beat of his heart next to hers and the insistent pounding of the surf.

chapter 12

"House," Maria said, pointing down the hill toward the cluster of adobe buildings.

"That was the first word I learned," Alitha told her. *"Casa."*

"Garden." From where they sat on a grassy knoll, they could see an Indian hoeing the rows of Mendoza tomato plants.

"Jardín," Alitha said.

Maria smiled. "Family."

"Familia."

"Friend."

"Amigo."

"That, as you know, is a man friend. If it was a woman?"

"Amiga."

"Bueno. Good. Now ask me English words and I will tell you how to say them in Spanish."

"Gentleman."

"Caballero. The word means horseman. *Caballo* is

148

horse." She nodded to their two horses grazing a short distance away.

"Ship." Alitha looked down to the harbor from which the American ship, loaded with Santa Barbara hides, had sailed the week before.

'Barco.''

"Journey."

'Viaje,'' Maria told her. "A long journey, such as your journey to the Sandwich Islands, is *un viaje grande.''*

"Marriage."

'Matrimonio.''

"California seems to have so many more men than women," Alitha said.

"Because this is the frontier of New Spain. Men come to the new lands first, then civilization comes with the women. Later."

"I hope you don't think me too personal, but I've wondered why you've never married again, Maria. After all these years."

"I do not take offense," Maria said, smiling. "I have thought of marriage many times, as what unmarried woman does not? There are many reasons I have not remarried. First, and most important, there is no man I love. I loved once and there can be no other for me—not that I have not been asked to marry many times. The man, however, must be of my station, and there are few who are in Alta California. The man must be someone like . . ." She paused. "Like Don Esteban."

Alitha glanced curiously at the other woman. Had she reddened slightly? It was difficult to tell. She had said Esteban's name fondly, as a lover might. As Alitha herself might.

She looked at Maria more closely. Speculatively.

Was the other woman as old as Alitha had first thought? She must be thirty-five at least, for she probably hadn't married before she was fifteen, but she was attractive, with her dark eyes and jet black hair. Though decidedly plump. She couldn't be too much older than Esteban, though. Alitha had heard of men marrying their brother's widow.

Maria sighed. "A man like Don Tomás is what I should have said. But you did not know him. Also, there is the matter of children. Spanish men wish to carry on the family name—our families are very important—so they want children, especially boys, and unfortunately I cannot have children."

Alitha covered Maria's hand with hers. "You're in love with Don Esteban, aren't you?" she asked softly.

Maria drew her hand away and straightened her *reboso*, the shawl she wore over her head.

"Don Esteban is a most attractive man," she said. "In many ways he resembles my husband Tomás, as Tomás was as a young man, when we married. The Mendoza men were all much alike, so I cannot help seeing Tomás in Esteban. I am much too old to ever think of marrying Don Esteban, even if it were possible."

Alitha noticed that Maria hadn't denied loving Esteban. Not directly.

"Almost the first words you spoke to me," Alitha said, "were to tell me that Don Esteban was not for me. Why did you say such a thing?"

"Do you believe I told you that because I wanted him for myself? No, no, not at all. I said that not because of me, but because it is the truth. Don Esteban is already promised to another. The marriage contract between the families has been signed and the dowry agreed to."

"He's to marry another?" Alitha heard her voice

rising. How could he have lied to her when he asked her to marry him and journey with him to Mexico? Although he hadn't mentioned marriage in so many words. But wasn't that what he'd meant? How could she go to Mexico with him otherwise?

"Are you well?" Maria asked. "I can see I have upset you. Didn't you know he was committed to marry?"

Alitha shook her head.

"He will marry Ines Gutierrez. The Gutierrez *rancho* is some three leagues to the east of Santa Barbara. They are a fine Castillian family."

Gutierrez, Ines Gutierrez. Alitha had never heard her name before. The name Gutierrez was familiar, though, there had been a Don Ramón Gutierrez in the raiding party that burned the Indian village. Not an older man, but a *caballero* Esteban's age. Perhaps he was Ines's brother. But why hadn't Ines been at the banquet if she lived only a short distance away?

Alitha stood up. "I—I—" she began, not really knowing what she wanted to say. She was overwhelmed by anger and humiliation. Esteban had deceived her!

She ran to her horse, untied the bay and swung herself into the saddle. She heard Maria's footsteps behind her.

"*Señorita,*" the Spanish woman said. "Alitha, wait."

Alitha, sitting sidesaddle, swung her quirt and the bay started down the hill. She swung the quirt again and again, wanting to ride as fast and as hard as she could. The horse galloped across a field gold with poppies, leaped a ditch and plunged through a grove of trees, making for the Mendoza stables. She let the bay have his head, feeling the wind sting her face as she exulted in the thrill of a fast horse under her.

The horse slowed and trotted into the stable area behind the adobe *casa*. A stable boy, an Indian no older than Chia, ran out to take the reins, and she slid to the ground, her exultation fading, replaced by despair. What a fool she'd been! She watched the boy lead the stallion to the barn, where he would unsaddle and brush him down. The Californios rode only stallions, Esteban had told her, or geldings. Never mares. A female of the species wasn't good enough for them.

Just as women themselves weren't good enough, Alitha thought as she dabbed at the tears in her eyes. She flicked the quirt against her riding dress, then stopped, remembering seeing Esteban flick his quirt in the same way. She didn't want to emulate him in anything.

She'd confront Esteban and make him tell her the truth. She had hardly been alone with him since the night on the beach. Every time she thought they would have a few moments together, Maria had appeared from out of nowhere.

Did Maria suspect there was something between them? Maria loved Esteban, despite her denials; loved her own brother-in-law, Alitha told herself. No wonder she's suspicious of me and tries to keep us apart.

But why blame Maria? If Esteban was engaged to marry Ines Gutierrez, it would be his doing, not Maria's. If. Could Maria have been lying to her? She had only to ask Esteban to find out, but knew she couldn't bear to face him. Not now. Not after he had humiliated her by offering to take her to Mexico when he was bound to another.

How she yearned to go with him! Even now she caught herself looking about her, hoping to catch a glimpse of him. For the hundredth time she remembered the thrill of his lips on hers, the feel of his hands and lips caressing her breasts, his bare flesh hard against hers.

Alitha felt herself reddening. How could she be so wanton, she wondered, the same question she had asked herself after they had lain together on the beach. Torn by doubts and second thoughts, she had been unable to sleep, finally watching from the window of her room as the sun rose over the ocean. What she had done was wrong, she told herself, for she was promised to another, to Thomas. Still, it had seemed so right at the time, so inevitable, so foreordained.

It must have been wrong, a sin. If she hadn't sinned, why was she being punished? And she was being punished—Ines Gutierrez was her punishment. What kind of woman was this mysterious Ines? Probably one of those docile butterflies with long fluttering eyelashes anxious to marry so she could bear a grateful husband thirteen children in the span of fifteen years.

Alitha paused in the kitchen doorway. She had to see Ines Gutierrez for herself, find out what she was like.

She had to do something, anything, to calm the fever raging in her blood, a fever every bit as virulent as the one she'd had when she first came to the *rancho*. All her thoughts turned to Esteban, were of Esteban. Nothing else mattered to her, only Esteban. She knew she was being wrong-headed, that her desires defied all reason, but there was nothing she could do to change the way she felt, nothing at all.

She returned to the stable and asked the Indian boy to resaddle the bay. As she rode from the *rancho*, she passed Maria.

"I'm going to the mission," Alitha told her, riding on before Maria could question her.

She rode through the village of Santa Barbara and

past the mission and to the road leading east, her mind in a turmoil, torn between her anger at Esteban and her need for him. If she chanced to meet him now, she would fly from him, though at the same time she couldn't bear the idea of never seeing him again once he left for Mexico.

When, after more than an hour's ride, she saw Indians working in a nearby field, she stopped.

"Gutierrez?" she called to them.

The laborers stared at her and then one of them nodded and pointed along the road. She went on, at last coming to a low adobe *casa* where, accompanied by barking dogs, she rode into the courtyard. Roses bloomed on trellises, sweetening the air with their fragrance—the same shade of rose, she noted ruefully, that Esteban had given her. The Gutierrez house, only one story high, was much smaller than the Mendoza *rancho*.

An Indian boy took the reins, and Alitha dismounted just as a woman came from the house. She was about thirty, fair-skinned and dark-haired with a *reboso* over her shoulders. Surely this wasn't Ines Gutierrez—this woman was heavy with child.

"*Buenos días,*" Alitha said. "I'm Alitha Bradford, a guest at the Mendoza *rancho*," she added in halting Spanish. The woman smiled and nodded her head.

"*Señora* Josefa Gutierrez." The woman motioned Alitha to follow her inside.

"I was riding in the hills and lost my way," Alitha said in English, crossing her fingers behind her back as she had as a child when she told a white lie.

"*Sí, sí,*" Josefa said.

They walked down a long, cool corridor to a room opening onto an outdoor patio where children played on a tiled floor. Alitha counted four girls in all, guessing their ages as two, four, six and eight.

"You have beautiful children," Alitha said, admiring the girls' bright faces and laughing eyes.

"Sí, sí," Josefa said, still nodding and smiling. She spoke in Spanish to a gray-haired Indian woman, and in a few minutes a bowl of chili beans and a mug of steaming coffee were placed in front of Alitha.

"I'm really not hungry," Alitha said.

"Sí, sí," Josefa said, smiling happily.

Alitha began eating the beans while she wondered how she could tactfully ask about Ines. She glanced through the archways leading into the other rooms of the house, hoping to catch sight of Esteban's elusive fiancée, but saw only an Indian servant girl carrying a basket of clothes on her hip. When she finished eating, Alitha smiled and stood up.

"Gracias," she said.

"De nada. Mi casa es su casa."

Still smiling, Alitha had started walking toward the corridor when she saw the oldest of the four girls standing in the doorway from the patio watching her. Though the girl's hair was black, her eyes were a startling blue.

"Muy bonita," she said to the girl's mother. *"Cómo se llama usted?* What is your name?" she asked the girl.

"Ines Gutierrez, *señorita.*"

Ines! No, this couldn't be Esteban's intended, the girl was scarcely eight years old. Or *was* it possible? There was a scarcity of women and a lack of eligible mates in California; Maria had said so only a few hours before. Perhaps Spaniards thought of family first, the appropriateness of a union, and let love come later if at all.

"Ines and Don Esteban?" Alitha asked.

Josefa broke into a broad smile, nodding vigorously as she answered in voluble Spanish. Though Alitha couldn't understand all the other woman's words, Josefa's meaning was clear enough. Yes, Ines *was* the intended bride of Don Esteban Mendoza who, Josefa fervently believed, had no equal among the gentlemen of this or any other world.

Alitha walked quickly to Ines, leaned down and kissed the girl on the forehead. Ines smiled shyly and curtsied. Amid protestations of mutual regard in English and Spanish, Alitha retreated from the Gutierrez *casa* and mounted her horse for the journey back to Santa Barbara.

So her rival was an eight-year-old, she thought as she rode into the setting sun. All at once Alitha smiled. Of course, she told herself, she should have realized the truth of the matter before this. The reason Esteban had not mentioned marriage, had not already married her here in Santa Barbara, was because of his friendship with the Gutierrez family. Esteban would wait until he and Alitha were in Mexico before he told Don Gutierrez he wouldn't marry Ines. Time and distance would soften the blow to the Gutierrez pride.

How could she have thought even for a moment that Esteban might feel bound to a wedding contract with an eight-year-old when he loved her, Alitha? And he did love her, Alitha assured herself, for he had told her so time and again.

She herself was at fault for even considering the possibility of Esteban wanting to take her to Mexico as his—she winced at the word—mistress. That was impossible no matter how much she loved and wanted him. Not only was it wrong—and it was—but she would be foolish to commit herself to any man with no assurance about the future.

How little Esteban understood her! He had tried to shield her from all knowledge of Ines so that she, Alitha, wouldn't be hurt. Smiling, she closed her eyes, picturing a great cathedral, hearing the organ music swelling with the first bars of the wedding march, seeing herself gowned in radiant white.

Alitha shook her head impatiently, opening her eyes. She must clear up the confusion. She would tell Esteban she knew of Ines and that he no longer had to hide his agreement to marry the girl. And then Esteban would be free to ask her to marry him and to tell her the future he envisioned for them both.

Looking around herself, she realized that the sun had set and shadows were gathering darkly under the trees along the road. From ahead of her she heard the bells of the Santa Barbara Mission. How wildly they rang! The tolling went on and on, almost without pause, and Alitha urged her horse on, anxious to discover the reason.

When she reached Santa Barbara, she found the village astir, with men riding frantically to and fro and heavily laden carts rumbling along the roads leading to the beach. Looking out to sea, Alitha spied a ship riding at anchor. She couldn't believe that all this hubbub had been caused by the arrival in the harbor of one merchant ship.

As she passed the mission, she saw a large group of Indians marching in front of the church, then disappearing behind it only to reappear on the other side. Talk of traveling in circles, she thought. Puzzled, Alitha urged her horse on to the Mendoza Rancho, leaving the lathered bay with the stable boy.

Just as she entered the main courtyard, Don Esteban rode up from the direction of the village and dismounted beside her.

"Alitha." Despite his frown, she saw his eyes glinting with excitement. "Where have you been?"

"I went for a ride." Though she felt guilty about her clandestine trip, she thought of adding, "To the Gutierrez rancho to visit your fiancée," but didn't. "What's happening?" she asked.

"That's Bouchard's ship you see anchored offshore," Esteban told her. "They're renegades who have come here, they say, for provisions. I signed an agreement to provide them foodstuffs in exchange for any prisoners they captured in California. I think at first they intended to raid Santa Barbara, but we've been marching the Indians around and around the mission until Bouchard must think we have a full-sized army here."

"Did they tell you who these prisoners were?"

"No, I met with them only an hour ago and they refused to say. We'll soon know." He raised her chin with his forefinger and kissed her, a quick promise of a kiss, his lips meeting hers so swiftly she didn't have a chance to draw away. Nor the will, she admitted to herself.

Esteban ate hurriedly and rode off. After she had eaten her own dinner, Alitha went to her room. From the window she saw lights coming and going along the road and heard men calling to one another. Hoofbeats pounded in the courtyard as messengers arrived and departed. At long last Esteban returned, and still later—it must have been nearing midnight—she saw a procession of torches advancing up the hill from the beach and, when the flaming pine brands drew closer, she made out riders escorting a closed carriage.

The horsemen galloped into the Mendoza courtyard, where their neighing horses milled around the carriage. Alitha ran from her room onto the gallery and looked down from the railing just as the door to the carriage swung open and a man stepped out.

She gasped when she saw his black hair and short black beard. Jordan Quinn, captain of the *Kerry Dancer!* She couldn't be mistaken, she knew, though she had seen him but once before.

The men who quickly surrounded Jordan looked about uncertainly until Esteban strode from the house. Taking Jordan by the arm, he led him beneath the gallery. A few moments later the two men reappeared at the top of the stairs, turning away from Alitha without seeing her and entering one of the *salas*. The other men stayed below in the courtyard.

Where was Margarita, Alitha wondered as she made her way cautiously along the gallery until she was beside the *sala*'s curtained entrance. Had Jordan been a prisoner of the pirates? She leaned forward, listening.

       should speak in English," she heard Esteban telling Jordan. "This house has a thousand ears." There was a long pause. Alitha held her breath.

"You wished to speak to me alone." Esteban's voice was like ice. "Now we are alone. Where is Margarita?"

"Your sister is dead." Alitha could read no emotion in Captain Quinn's voice. "Despite all I could do, she killed herself aboard Bouchard's ship."

To Alitha the silence seemed to stretch interminably.

"You have killed my only sister," Esteban said at last, "a woman I loved with all my heart. Not only is she dead, her suicide denies her a Christian burial. She is doomed to burn in hell for all eternity. I will never see Margarita again in this life or in the life beyond the grave."

"I did all I could," Jordan insisted.

Alitha heard a sliding sound as of a drawer opening.

"I must challenge you to a duel to the death," Esteban said. How melodramatic he sounded, Alitha thought, yet she knew he meant every word.

"I won't fight a duel with you," Jordan told him. "If you must kill me, kill me, but I won't fight you. I know you loved Margarita, but by God, I loved her too and I mean to avenge her death."

"You may have loved her in your way," Esteban admitted. "However, I have no choice; honor demands I kill you. If you refuse to meet me on the field of honor, then I must kill you here."

Alitha heard the click of a pistol being cocked. She pushed aside the curtains to see Esteban standing behind his desk, a pistol in his hand, with Jordan facing him from five feet away. The two men stared at her in surprise.

She ran to Jordan and flung herself in front of him. "No," she cried to Esteban, "don't kill him. You mustn't."

"Stand aside," Esteban told her. "This is between Capitán Quinn and myself. It does not concern you."

"There's no reason for you to kill him. If you do, his blood will be on your hands for the rest of your life."

"You told me you did not know Capitán Quinn," Esteban said, "and yet you plead for his life. Did you lie to me?"

"No, no, he means nothing to me." She took a step toward Esteban. "I'm trying to stop you because I love you. Don't you know that by now? All I ask is that you spare him. For me. Not for his sake, for mine."

"You ask a great deal, my Alitha," Esteban said.

She put her hand on his arm and gazed entreatingly into his eyes. "I've never asked you for anything before," she said, "and if you spare him I never will again."

Esteban lowered the pistol and turned to Jordan.

"If I ever see you again," he told him, "no power on earth will be able to save you."

Jordan wheeled about without a word. From the doorway he glanced at Alitha. His eyes met and held hers for an instant, but she could not read his look

When he heard Jordan's retreating footsteps on the gallery, Esteban returned the pistol to the desk drawer. He took Alitha in his arms, and she felt all the passion of the anger raging within him as he kissed her, his mouth hard on hers, his tongue seeking and finding its way between her lips.

As she surrendered herself to his kiss, she could think of nothing except Esteban, his arms gripping her and holding her to him, his body against hers from her thighs to her breasts. When his lips left hers and she felt his hands come up along her sides, she broke away and walked to the window, trying to quell the wild beating of her heart.

"Is something the matter, my Alitha?" Esteban asked.

She looked from the window at a row of orange trees. Their blooms were gone, replaced by small green oranges. In time the fruit would ripen and become sweet, but now it was still hard and bitter.

"I know about Ines Gutierrez," Alitha said without looking at him.

"Who told you of Ines?"

'Maria. She said you intended to marry her when Ines is old enough."

"Ines Gutierrez has never been a secret." She could picture Esteban's shrug. "She does not concern us, my Alitha. Ines is only a child."

"A child, yes, but a child you've agreed to marry."

Alitha swung about, her eyes flashing. "You do intend to marry her, don't you?" she asked.

Esteban gazed into her eyes; she saw his mouth tighten. "As I said, she does not concern us."

"In Boston," Alitha told him, "it's not customary for a man who's engaged to be married to ask another woman to accompany him on a journey."

"Your Boston is a strange city with strange customs. Someday I plan to visit this New England of yours to find out for myself if all the tales I hear of it can possibly be true."

"In Boston—" she began.

"Damn Boston." His anger silenced her. Alitha stared at him, for an instant half-expecting him to stride to her, sweep her into his arms and bear her away with him. She was alarmed, but even as she stepped back, she longed to feel his arms around her. A muscle twitched in Esteban's jaw, and then he seemed to make an effort to control his rage.

"To me," he said more quietly, "this matter is so simple. I do not see why you wish to make it so complicated. I love you with all my heart. You say you love me—"

"I *do* love you, Esteban," she protested.

"*Sí*, you love me. I must go to Mexico. We have a chance to be with one another there for many months, to love one another, to be as one. Life is short, my Alitha, shorter here in California than in your New England. I have lived the greater part of my life already. Who knows what the future holds for me or for you? Only today I discovered that my sister, my beloved Margarita, was dead. She was so young. My mother and father are dead, as is my brother. We Mendozas live life to the full, and we suffer for it. We die young."

"I couldn't bear it if anything happened to you, Esteban." Alitha crossed the room and put her hand on his sleeve, her fingers caressing his flesh through the cloth. He enfolded her in his arms, holding her gently, his cheek to hers, and as he talked, she felt his breath stirring her hair.

"We have been given one of the rarest gifts God in heaven has the power to bestow," he said, "and you talk of hurling it aside because of some puritan custom in this Boston of yours. If you truly love me, Alitha, you will ride with me to Mexico, where I will be your champion, your protector, your lover. I will garland you with roses; I will kill any man who dares to lift his eyes to gaze on you with desire. What more could any woman want from a man?"

She was tempted to say, "Nothing," but she could not because there *was* more a woman could want. *She* wanted more. She held Esteban at arm's length. "And still you can say you intend to marry Ines Gutierrez."

He swung away from her and stood with his hands clasped behind his back. "Ines Gutierrez, Ines Gutierrez. I never want to hear her name from your lips again. Never." He turned suddenly, grasping her arms even as she tried to draw back.

"A few minutes ago," he said, "when you were pleading for the life of Capitán Quinn, you said you had never asked me for anything before and would never ask me for anything again. Already you are breaking your pledge."

"That's not true!" she cried.

She tore herself from his grasp and ran along the gallery to her room, where she threw herself on her bed, tears welling in her eyes. Hearing footsteps on the gallery, she looked to the doorway, half-expecting to find Esteban there. Her door, though, remained closed. Through the open window she heard his steps descending the stairs to the courtyard.

Alitha pounded the pillow with her fist, hating him. Then she drew in her breath and clasped the pillow to her, wondering how she could feel such hate for the man she loved.

chapter 13

A WEEK LATER Alitha was tossing restlessly on her bed when she heard the strumming of a guitar and a man's voice singing. The music was slow, funereal, almost a dirge. She put on her slippers, drew a shawl around her shoulders and went onto the balcony. The music seemed to come from a nearby orchard. She had never heard such a sad song. All the cruelty and misery of the world seemed to be echoed by the singer's voice.

She crossed the bedroom to the gallery and made her way down to the courtyard. The *rancho* was quiet—it must have been long after midnight—and the fog high overhead hid the moon and stars. In a few hours the servants would be stirring, and by three-thirty the *casa* would be abustle, for Esteban planned to leave for Mexico before dawn.

Alitha hadn't been able to sleep well ever since she had realized that Esteban did not intend to marry her even if she went with him. She had tried to ignore him as, during the past week, he had directed the preparations for his journey to the south. Each time she saw him he greeted her courteously, his manner dignified and correct. His eyes, though, told her he was still waiting for her to tell him she had changed her mind and would go with him. When she did not speak, he shook his head sadly, his wan smile fading to a poignant look of reproach and regret.

Luckily, she thought, he didn't know how she longed for him, how constantly she thought of him in the endless hours of nights when sleep wouldn't come, how she dreamed of him when she finally dozed off in the hours before dawn. Dreams she blushed to recall. Her body might be weak, she told herself, but her will was strong. She vowed she would not go with Esteban no matter what he did or said.

Leaving the courtyard, she walked slowly across the wet grass toward the sound of the guitar. When she reached the orchard, the singing stopped and the night was quiet. She drew her shawl closer about her to ward off the damp cold.

There would have been a *fandango* tonight, Maria had told her, if the household hadn't been in mourning for Margarita. Many times in the days since the simple stone memorial was built beneath the orange trees, Alitha had happened on servants brushing tears from their eyes. How they all must have loved Margarita, she thought.

The music began again, and the man's voice was raised not in a dirge or lament but in a plaintive ballad, a love song. Alitha walked ahead and saw a dark figure standing alone among the trees.

"Mi amor, mi amor," he sang, his voice pure and clear

The singer paused as he saw Alitha approach and then went on with his song, singing now to her. She had thought she recognized the voice as Esteban's and now she was certain. She stood listening, enraptured yet at the same time sad, enveloped by feelings of loss and the fleeting brevity of life. All too soon the song, like life, was over.

"That was beautiful," she told him.

"My love," Esteban said. "Alitha, you are my love, my only love."

Placing the guitar on the ground, he came to her, his hand reaching for hers, and as their fingers touched, she felt a shock as though a spark of electricity had passed between them.

She gasped. What was she doing here? What had become of her firm resolve of the last week? She knew that if she did not flee now, she wouldn't be able to leave him, that Esteban would take her in his arms and, no matter how much she might try, she could never resist him. With a muffled cry, she turned and ran back to the house.

"Alitha," he called after her, but she didn't stop running until she was in her room.

Sleep wouldn't come. When the first sounds of the awakening house reached her, she rose from her bed, dressed and sat beside the window overlooking the courtyard. The early morning air was heavy with fog, and though lanterns had been hung around the court, the enshrouding mist made men and horses look like phantoms in the night.

Alitha watched as Maria clasped Don Esteban to her, kissed him on both cheeks and then stood to one side with her arms folded as the riders completed the final adjustments to their equipment. Besides Esteban, there were five *vaqueros* and seven extra horses laden with provisions.

Esteban was actually leaving, she realized. All along

she had hoped against hope that some miracle would keep him with her. Her future, Alitha thought gloomily, was as befogged as the day promised to be. She rose from her chair, clenching and unclenching her hands at her sides.

For a fleeting moment she thought of Thomas. In her mind she had long since placed him in a niche apart, almost as though she had erected a shrine to his memory. She could think of Thomas with affection, even with tenderness, but he was no longer real to her. It was almost as though he were dead. Biting her lip, she realized that, to her, he was. By falling in love with Esteban, she had killed him.

As for Jordan Quinn, she had not seen him since the night his life was spared by Esteban. When she had visited the mission to say good-bye to Chia, Padre Luis had told her that El Capitán Quinn was still in Santa Barbara waiting for a ship bound for the States.

Going to Chia's hut, she had found that the Indian boy had fled, returning to his people, she supposed. Chia had left without a word or sign of farewell. Whether his sudden departure stemmed from fear of the *padre* or whether the men of his tribe avoided leavetakings, Alitha did not know. Her hand touched the charm stone she wore around her neck; she would never forget Chia.

Esteban mounted his stallion to lead the *vaqueros* from the *rancho*. He appeared to have forgotten that Alitha existed, for he, like Chia, had not sought to bid her farewell. She held her head high even though she was close to tears as Esteban raised his hand. The other horsemen mounted and followed him from the courtyard.

As they passed through the gateway, she saw Esteban, his erect figure dark against the first light of the dawn. She would never see him again, never hear his voice, never feel his arms around her, never thrill to his lips on hers.

With a cry that was almost a moan, she ran from her room, along the gallery and down the steps.

"Alitha," Maria said, starting toward her.

Alitha brushed past the other woman and ran through the gate to the road. The men, their horses at a walk, were a short distance ahead.

"Esteban, Esteban," she called, running after them. Unheeding, the men rode on.

She stumbled and almost fell, recovered her balance and ran on, calling Esteban's name. Hearing her at last, Esteban wheeled his horse around. Alitha stopped, gasping for breath as he rode back and drew up beside her.

"Esteban," she said, looking up at him, "I couldn't let you go without saying good-bye."

He reached down and grasped her beneath the arms, lifted her and placed her in the saddle in front of him. The passion of his kiss took her breath away and she clung desperately to him. How could she have thought of letting him go without her? She loved him, he loved her. Nothing else mattered. Nothing.

"Ride with me, my love," he said. "Tell me you will."

"Oh, yes, Esteban, I will, I will."

His arm still around her, he rode to the waiting men. "Return and bring the *señorita's* belongings," he told one of them.

As they waited for the *vaquero* to return, Alitha heard a voice calling her name. Looking back, she saw Maria hurrying toward her. Alitha slid from Esteban's arms to the ground.

"You will go with him?" Maria asked.

Alitha drew in her breath. "Yes," she said, "I must."

"Wrong though it is, I understand." Maria embraced her. *"Vaya con Diós,"* she said, her voice choked by sobs.

"And you, too, go with God," Alitha said.

"See that no harm befalls him. Esteban is so rash, so headstrong, as all the Mendoza men are."

"I'll do my best, Maria," Alitha promised.

When Esteban brought her a horse outfitted with a sidesaddle, Alitha mounted and rode with him and the *vaqueros* from the *rancho*. Pausing beneath the twin oaks, she looked back at the house for the last time and saw, outlined in black against the light from the lanterns, the figure of a solitary woman waving to them.

The sky was brightening as they rode into Santa Barbara, though because of the mist Alitha could see only a hundred feet ahead. The mission loomed beside them, the tops of its twin white towers lost in the fog. Alitha heard the crow of a cock, and somewhere a dog barked.

They left the village and were passing through a grove of trees when Alitha came suddenly alert. Had she heard her name? A whisper that was a hint of sound rather than the sound itself? She shook her head, impatient with her daydreaming.

"Alitha."

This time there could be no mistake. Pulling her horse from the line of men, she rode a short distance to her right. A figure stepped from behind the trunk of a tree, a man made so indistinct by the fog that he seemed a part of the tree itself. Her horse skittered in alarm but she patted his neck, soothing him, and urged him forward.

"Many thanks, Señorita Bradford, for saving my life."

Jordan Quinn, captain of the *Kerry Dancer*. As she started to speak, he raised his hand to his cap in a salute and disappeared into the fog again. Alitha stared after him. She had seen Jordan Quinn three times—in Valparaiso, at the *rancho* with Esteban and now here in the mist. Were they fated always to pass like ships in the night, she wondered, never meeting? She sighed, slapping the bay with her quirt and rejoining the *vaqueros.*

"We will follow *El Camino Real,*" Esteban told her later in the day when he rode beside her. "The missions of the Franciscans extend along the King's Highway like pearls strung on the shoreline of the Pacific. We will go from mission to mission, to San Buenaventura, to San Juan Capistrano, to San Diego and on south to Baja California. There, in Loreto, my friend Coronel Morales commands the *presidio,* the military outpost."

The journey to Mexico City, he told her, would take more than three months, the exact time depending on the weather, the availability of food and water and the degree of revolutionary turmoil they found when they reached the port of San Blas on the western Mexico coast.

That night, camped on a bluff above the sea, Esteban and Alitha unrolled their *petates,* straw sleeping mats, apart from the rest of the company. Now that she was here, alone with Esteban in the wilderness, Alitha realized the enormity of what she had done by cutting her last ties to her past, to Boston, to Thomas. Feeling a twinge of panic, she looked up at Esteban, seeking comfort.

"You do love me?" she asked.

He pulled her to her feet and held her in his arms.

"How can you ask after I have told you so many times?"

"It's not just because my eyes are blue?" She smiled. "After all, Ines has blue eyes, too."

She felt him stiffen. "How do you know the color of Ines's eyes?"

"Why, I saw her when I was at the Gutierrez *rancho*."

"You lied to me." His arms fell away from her. "You said Maria told you of Ines, not that you journeyed to see her. How could you have gone there? What must Don Gutierrez have thought? You have disgraced me in his eyes."

He walked away from her, and when she came up behind him, putting her hand on his arm, he shook her off.

"Go to your bed," he told her.

She sank down on the sleeping mat. Esteban did not approach her nor did he speak, and though she was tired after the day's ride, she lay awake long after Esteban's measured breathing told her he had fallen asleep.

She wakened during the night, hearing animals howling among the trees, recognizing the cries as the same ones she had heard when she was searching for Chia's *ranchería*. Burying her head in her blanket, she turned away from Esteban—she would *not* wake him no matter how uneasy she became—and waited for sleep to return.

"Wolves?" Esteban repeated her question when she asked him the next day. "No, they are animals of a type between a dog and a wolf. We call them coyotes. They might kill a chicken or two but they are afraid of men."

All that day Esteban was solicitous, like a gracious host. He rode beside her and named the trees and animals they saw along the road to the Pueblo of Los Angeles. But again that night he lay on his *petate,* wrapped himself in his blankets and fell asleep almost at once.

The next morning Alitha woke before Esteban and sat up, watching until his eyes blinked open.

"You have no right to be still angry with me," she told him, keeping her voice firm with an effort.

"You visited the *rancho* of Don Gutierrez," he said. "You should not have done so."

"*You* should have told me about Ines."

"She is no concern of yours."

"To tell the truth, I was jealous. I didn't know until I saw her how young she was."

"You have no cause for jealousy. Don't you know you are my heart of hearts, my life and my love? Haven't I told you this time and again?"

"How can you say that when you're committed to marry another?" Anger flared in her. "How dare you try to make me feel guilty for doing something I'd never have done if you'd been honest with me. I wouldn't have ridden to the Gutierrez *rancho* if you had told me the truth in the first place."

Esteban threw aside his blankets and stood up. "I have heard enough," he said, walking away.

Alitha started after him, then stopped. No, she told herself, I won't apologize. If I was wrong to seek out Ines, he's equally at fault. She glared at his back, hearing the voices of the men in the main camp, smelling the smoke from their fire. She thought momentarily of mounting her horse and heading back to the *rancho,* but sighed and shook her head. Despite her anger, she still wanted to be with Esteban.

That night they camped along a stream. After she ate Alitha went to her saddlebag and found the cake of yellow soap she'd brought from the *rancho*. Skirting the fire where the men were singing sad love songs to the music of a Spanish guitar, she walked along the bank of the creek until she was almost out of earshot of the camp.

She stopped beside a small pool. After undressing she placed her clothes on a rock and stepped into the stream, lowering herself until the water just covered her body. She began soaping herself vigorously, though she still shivered from the cold.

"I would be glad to help."

Startled, she looked up and saw Esteban standing on the bank. He jumped from rock to rock until he was above her, then reached down and took her hand, drawing her to her feet. He took the soap from her hand and stood behind her, soaping her back, his hand gliding from her shoulders to her buttocks and down her legs to her feet.

"Turn around," he ordered.

Closing her eyes, she faced him, feeling his hands soap her breasts, fondling each in turn until her skin quivered under his touch. Kneeling before her, he started at her feet and soaped her legs, then the soap was set aside and his fingers fluttered between her thighs, teasing her.

A trembling began in her legs, growing until she shuddered with passion. Reaching down, she took Esteban's hand and guided it up between her legs. When his fingers entered her, caressing her, she put her hands to the nape of his neck, drawing his head to her breasts. She sighed, her head going back, her breath coming rapidly.

Suddenly Esteban stepped away from her, tore off his clothes and threw them to the bank of the stream. He came to her, pulled her against him, hard against him, and, with both of them still standing, he entered her. She moaned with desire as he thrust within her.

Esteban groaned, his fingers digging into her buttocks as he throbbed inside her. Finally sated, he lifted her into his arms and carried her to the bank, where he laid her on a blanket, kneeling between her legs, and then gathering her into his arms. When she felt him grow hard against her, she opened herself to him, whispering his name again and again, pressing herself to him until her passion was released in an overwhelming crescendo of ecstasy.

They rode inland to the Pueblo of Los Angeles and stayed overnight in that village of more than four hundred inhabitants. Turning their horses to the south, they felt the cool breezes off the sea again as they neared the mission at San Juan Capistrano. After pitching camp in the late afternoon just outside the mission walls, Esteban and Alitha rode to the sea.

When they approached the top of a high cliff overlooking the Pacific, Alitha was startled to see four men throwing objects down to the beach.

"What can they be doing?" she asked Esteban.

"Probably they're members of a crew from a ship anchored offshore," he told her. "Those are cattle hides—the mission here has thousands of head of cattle. The men are throwing the hides down to their shipmates who load them in a boat to take them to the ship."

As they dismounted a short distance from the men, Alitha saw that he was right: the men were throwing large, stiff hides, and there was a ship anchored a few cable lengths from the beach. When the sailors had tossed the last of the hides from the cliff, they rigged a line to a boulder and one of them descended with the rope tied to his waist. Alitha leaned over the edge watching as the seaman swung back and forth the face of the cliff, freeing hides that had lodged behind rocks. By the time he had sent the last of the hides plunging down to the beach and had been hauled back to the top of the cliff, the sun was on the horizon.

The four men tipped their hats to Alitha. As they trudged off to make their way down to the beach, one man turned and shouted, *"Adios."* Alitha waved.

What must they make of us, she wondered. Do they think I'm Spanish as Esteban so obviously is? Do they take us for man and wife?

Sighing, Alitha sat on a grassy verge at the top of the cliff with Esteban standing behind her. Leaning back, she rested her head against his legs as she watched the golden rim of the sun dip below the waves. The only sound she heard was the throb of the surf; it was as though, she thought, they were the only two people on earth.

"I wish it could always be like this," she said. "Just the two of us, together. No one else, Esteban, just you and I."

He leaned forward and put both of his hands on her shoulders. She reached up and covered his hands with hers.

"Alitha," he said. "I—" He hesitated. For once, she noticed, words didn't come easily to him.

"Alitha," he said again, "it has never been like this with anyone. The way it is with you."

"Esteban, do you love me? Do you truly love me?"

"I do; yes, I do, with all my heart."

He knelt behind her, and when she tilted her head back, he kissed her, his hands circling her waist to cup her breasts through the cloth of her dress. The night was darkening around them; already pinpoints of light shone from the ship offshore. Below them, Alitha heard the shouts of the sailors as they launched their boatload of hides into the surf.

"Undress me, Esteban," she told him.

His fingers went to the buttons on the front of her dress. He removed her clothes, garment by garment, and when she lay naked before him, he stood and took off his clothes and lay beside her, not touching her.

"Esteban," she whispered, reaching for him. Could he hear the pounding of her heart, she wondered. He took her hand in his and rolled her over so her back was to him. His arms came around her, caressing her breasts, his fingers brushing over her nipples. She felt his chest on her back, his legs to hers, his sex hard against her buttocks.

His hands slid down her body, across her stomach to her thighs until his fingers stroked the soft folds between her legs. She tried to turn, wanting to hold him in her arms, but he rolled her away from him until she was on her stomach. He knelt behind her, between her legs, his hands lifting her hips slightly so she rose to her knees. He reached around to take her breasts in his hands.

When she pressed back against him, his hands left her breasts and again went to her sex. Without warning her body began to tremble. He thrust into her, his hands still caressing her, and she moaned, wanting to clasp him to her but at the same time more aroused than she'd ever been before. She shuddered and then she felt an uncontrollable trembling shake her body over and over again. She drew in her breath in what was almost a scream, afraid she might never be able to stop the spasms of desire quivering up and down her body.

Esteban turned her over and entered her, gently this

time, and she felt the tremors gradually lessen. When her trembling stopped, she lay exhausted in his arms, still joined to him. She wanted to stay like this, she thought, forever.

"Oh, Esteban," she whispered, "I love you so much."

The days grew warmer as they followed *El Camino Real* along the coast from San Juan Capistrano to San Diego, warm but never hot. Alitha woke most mornings to find their camp blanketed with a cooling fog, and often, in the evening, she saw the fog swirl inland from the sea.

She was more accustomed now to rising before daybreak and setting off in the early dawn, to ride all day with only brief stops to eat and rest their horses. Though her body was sore after a day's long ride, she no longer woke still tired from the previous day's journey. Now she met each new day refreshed and eager for whatever lay ahead.

As they traveled south, the country became drier, more stark. There were few trees—the low, grass-covered hills to the east basked in golden splendor under the summer sun. Though hawks might circle overhead and rabbits run from cover as they passed, and an occasional deer might eye them with curiosity from afar, the land was becoming more and more a desert—a desert bordering on a benign summer sea whose waves swept endlessly onto the sandy stretches of beach.

Esteban was never out of her mind as she rode beside the sea. She wanted to ride with him, to talk to him, to share her innermost thought with him. She learned, though, to be wary. She found that when they sat beside the evening or morning campfire he liked her to bring his food and coffee and to ask him if he wanted more.

But in the presence of the other men, he didn't like her to touch him. When she did, he shrugged her away without a word, and so she had to wait until they were alone at night. Then he welcomed her embrace, her kisses. Were all Spanish men like Esteban, she wondered. So conscious of how they looked in the sight of other men?

She was scarcely aware of the five other horsemen in their party. Although she rode with them all day, often exchanging a word or two, she found they avoided staying near her for long and cast guarded glances at Esteban as they rode off. The men treated her with respect, but there was no question that Don Esteban would tolerate no familiarities with this blond-haired woman who rode with him to Mexico.

They entered San Diego in the evening, fording a river and climbing a hill to the Presidio, the Spanish fort. The gate stood open and the lone sentry, his hair in a queue, waved them inside the twenty-foot-high walls. She noticed cracks in the wall and saw piles of rubble at its base.

They skirted three cannons guarding the entrance and rode into the plaza, where all the buildings—the chapel, guardhouse, stores and homes—faced inward. In front of the barracks Alitha saw a soldier lowering the Spanish flag.

That night they slept in beds for the first time since leaving Santa Barbara. Alitha knew that Esteban was tired, for he didn't signal her—with a touch or a lingering kiss or by the way his fingers curled the hair at the nape of her neck—that he wanted her to join him in bed. Did all lovers have these signals, she wondered.

She woke in the first light of dawn. Hearing Esteban

sleeping soundly across the room, she went to the window and drew aside the curtains. In the distance she saw the white tower and red tile roofs of the Mission of San Diego de Alcala. Beyond the mission were barren hills outlined against a pale yellow sky.

She stretched, raising her arms to welcome the new day, knowing she had never been happier. All at once she shivered, seemingly for no reason since the morning was warm. She felt strangely vulnerable, as if some ancient god could see her happiness and, envious, would do all in his power to bring her low. She tried to smile at her foolishness. At the same time she found herself wishing she could believe that making the sign of the cross, as Esteban did, would ward off evil.

She left the window and went to kneel on the floor beside Esteban's bed. How peacefully he slept, she thought. Leaning over him, she kissed his eyelids and he opened his eyes, smiling up at her.

She pulled her nightgown over her head and dropped it to the floor. He threw his blankets aside and she saw he was naked. Esteban pulled her onto the bed so she straddled him, and as she bent forward to kiss him his hands found her breasts.

She lifted her hips so that he entered her and he drew her down on top of him, turned until she was beneath him and, in the early morning light in the Presidio of San Diego, they made love quietly and tenderly. When at last, fulfilled, she lay beside him listening to the sounds of the awakening fort, her unease was gone and she smiled, content.

chapter 14

"Do you mean to say, Captain Quinn, that you're asking me to take my ship and go hunting this pirate Bouchard?" John Cunningham, captain of the American frigate *Independence,* stared across his cabin table at Jordan.

"Yes, sir, that's exactly what I want. He's captured and looted at least one American ship—mine—and he's murdered American seamen. I submit that it's your duty to seek him, to find him and to destroy him."

"And who are you, sir, to presume to inform me of my duty?" Cunningham's voice rose angrily.

"Bouchard must be stopped." Jordan put his palms on the table and leaned toward Cunningham. "Have you ever lost a ship, Captain? Do you know what it's like?"

Cunningham rose, his voice shaking with emotion. "Sit down, Quinn. Did you hear me? Sit down!"

Jordan sank back.

"Lost a ship?" the gray-haired Cunningham asked.

"In '08 the *Puritan* went down with all hands off Cape Hattaras, all hands save one. Her captain was plucked from the sea a week later by a British schooner. I was that captain, Mr. Quinn."

"Then you know my feelings."

"Yes, I do." Cunningham sat down and went on in his quiet Southern drawl. "But you must realize it's been more than six weeks since Bouchard anchored here in Santa Barbara. Surely you, as an experienced sailor, are aware that by this time he may be off the northern California coast. Or he may be anchored in the Sandwich Islands enjoying the favors of the native women. Or he may be sailing south, bound for Acapulco. You do realize that, don't you, sir?"

"I do, Captain."

Slamming his fist on the table, Cunningham stood up and paced the narrow confines of his cabin.

"You possess a tremendous amount of gall, Captain Quinn," he said. "The very day the *Independence* anchors off Santa Barbara you stomp aboard demanding an interview with her captain. Since I'm an accommodating man who's always willing to go an extra mile for a fellow seaman, for a man who's a compatriot of mine besides, I consented to speak to you. And then without so much as a by-your-leave or an if-I-may-be-so-bold, you propose I use a ship of the United States Navy to play a game of hares and hounds up and down the length and breadth of the Pacific. Do I state the case correctly?"

"From your point of view, I suppose you do. Not, however, from mine."

"You're being damned stubborn and presumptuous. Do you know that?"

"I do, sir "

Cunningham clapped Jordan on the shoulder. "I

admire that, Captain Quinn," he said, smiling. "You're the sort of man I'd like to have serving under me. I can find plenty of the others, the boot lickers and the yea-sayers. Now listen to me, sir, and listen to me well." He sat across from Jordan, leaning forward and lowering his voice. "What you suggest is impossible, so put it from your mind. I have my orders and they don't include the pursuit of pirates unless we're fortunate enough to catch them red-handed."

"And what are your orders, if I may ask?"

"You may, sir, but I don't think I'm of a mind to tell you. Officially we're here to visit the ports of the Pacific coast to make known the peaceful intentions of the United States while at the same time trying to open California to our merchant fleet. I'm also bringing a message from President Monroe to countries that have thrown off the yoke of Spain, reminding them that the United States is the foremost revolutionary nation in the world today."

"And your message to Spanish colonies? Such as Mexico and California?"

"I bring them the President's assurance that the United States intends to continue to recognize legitimate governments; that we will give no aid or encouragement to revolutionaries. Though founded by a revolution, the United States is interested in maintaining the status quo in the Pacific."

"Where I come from," Jordan said, "we call that being two-faced."

"No, you're mistaken. It's known as diplomacy. Unofficially, Captain Quinn, I can tell you that I represent the traditional American policy of support for the underdog, for the downtrodden. If the Californios attempt to free themselves from Spain, I'll encourage them; if the Russians become discouraged with the fur trade and want to sell Fort Ross to Spain and sail back to St. Petersburg, I'll give them twenty excellent reasons why they shouldn't."

Jordan snorted. "And *I've* been called a cynic. You, sir, are the master cynic of them all. What you're telling me is that when the time comes, you hope California will be so weak it will drop into the waiting hands of the United States like a ripe apple drops from a tree."

"If we do inherit California," Cunningham said, "then the destiny of the United States will be fulfilled. We'll be a nation extending from coast to coast, from the Atlantic to the Pacific. Can you imagine it, Quinn? We'll border both oceans; we'll need a two-ocean navy."

"You're a dreamer as well as a cynic."

"Perhaps so. Wouldn't you like to be part of that dream, Captain Quinn? You could be, you know. Why don't you join us? I happen to have a vacant berth for an experienced officer on the *Independence.*"

"I'm bound for the East Coast to see about the insurance on the *Kerry Dancer.* I'm afraid there'll be trouble over the payment since my ship was neither sunk nor damaged."

"Troubles of that sort can be overcome. Have you found a ship yet to take you East?"

"No, sir, I'm on the beach," Jordan admitted.

"A hard berth in a foreign land."

"I speak the language, sir. I was engaged to marry a Spanish girl."

"Oh?" Cunningham raised his eyebrows.

"She died," Jordan said, abruptly getting to his feet. "Thank you for your offer of a berth, Captain. Even though you won't help me bring Bouchard to justice."

"Let me give you a word of advice from an older man

to a younger. Forget Bouchard. Revenge is more harmful to the man who seeks it than to his enemy." Cunningham held out his hand across the table, and Jordan clasped it. "I still can't believe a man such as yourself would turn down an officer's berth because of an insurance policy."

"You're right; that's not the main reason. With all due respect to you, Captain, I could never abide to serve in the navy, either as seaman or officer. I kowtow to no one. I never have and I never will."

"So be it then."

After Jordan left his cabin, Captain Cunningham sat thinking for a long time. Finally he knelt and unlocked the strongbox beneath his berth. He removed a pouch from the box, opened it and dumped silver coins onto the table, where they glinted in the lamplight. Yes, he told himself, my plan might work. It just might work

Walking boldly into Santa Barbara, Jordan headed for a spirit shop. Usually he avoided the village and its people, knowing their bitterness over Margarita's elopement and death, but today he didn't give a damn.

He bought a bottle of *aguardiente* and sat outside the shop at a table sipping the brandy while ignoring the hostile stares of passersby. Captain Cunningham would never know, Jordan thought, how close he had come to accepting the offer of a berth aboard the *Independence*. Jordan longed to be at sea again, to feel the deck roll beneath his feet, to hear the creak of the timbers, the wind in the stays. Still he'd made the right decision; he couldn't have abided life on a navy ship.

He recorked the *aguardiente* and, holding the bottle in one hand, strode through the village and along the track toward the Navarro *casa*. Eduardo Navarro, a half-breed who was as much an outcast as Jordan, had offered him a place to sleep in his small house in the hills behind the town.

Jordan left the track to follow his usual route, a path through the woods. Thinking he heard a sound behind him, he turned, but saw nothing. As he neared a thick growth of brush bordering both sides of the path, he slowed, recognizing it as a good spot for an ambush. His hand touched the butt of the pistol in his belt. He shook his head. You're leery of phantoms, Jordan Quinn, he told himself. The boredom of six weeks ashore had made him edgy about nothing.

"Señor Quinn."

He whirled and saw a *vaquero* with a long-bladed knife in his right hand approaching from twenty feet away. As he advanced on Jordan, he weaved slightly as though he'd been drinking. Jordan dropped the *aguardiente* bottle and drew his pistol.

"Halt," he said in Spanish but the man kept coming.

"You murdered Señorita Margarita," the man said in a slurred voice. Was he a fool, Jordan wondered, thinking he could match his knife against a gun?

Jordan heard a step behind him. Still holding the pistol trained on the advancing *vaquero,* he glanced over his shoulder. Too late. The point of a knife bit into his back.

"If you would drop the gun, *señor, por favor,*" a voice behind him said.

As the knife bit deeper, Jordan let the pistol fall to the ground. A hand went to his belt, took his knife and threw it aside. The first *vaquero,* smiling now, came and stood a few feet in front of him. The man no longer seemed drunk. The stagger had been a ruse, Jordan realized.

"We'll have a little sport with the murderer, eh,

Juan," he said to his companion. "Take the rope and bind Señor Quinn to that tree. It makes one skillful to practice by throwing a knife at a living target."

"Stop."

An English voice. Startled, the two *vaqueros* swung about to face a blond man, obviously an American. He held a book in one hand but appeared unarmed. The first *vaquero* leaped at him, slashing upward with his knife. The man blocked the thrust with the book, the knife embedding itself in the thick volume.

The American kicked the *vaquero*'s legs from under him, sending him sprawling. Jordan at the same time threw himself to the ground, his hand closing on his pistol. He stood and aimed the pistol at the armed *vaquero*.

"Drop your knife, *señor*," Jordan ordered. The Spaniard shrugged and let the weapon fall. "Now go," Jordan told them both. He waved his pistol, and the first man staggered to his feet and both men ran, hunching over as though fearful that Jordan might fire at them as they fled.

When the two *vaqueros* were out of sight, Jordan walked to the blond stranger and extended his hand. The other man, who was trying to dislodge the knife from his book, shook hands, then twisted the knife free. He was blue-eyed, with fair though sunburned skin and an open, engaging face, not a handsome man, but his smile was easy and friendly. He gave Jordan the impression that he was a man you could trust. If you could ever trust anyone, Jordan thought wryly.

"Do you often use your book as a shield?" Jordan asked.

"Often? I have all my life, in a manner of speaking." He turned the book over and Jordan read *Holy Bible* written in worn gilt letters on the front. "I'm Thomas

Heath," the young man said, "a minister of the Gospel."

"And a right handy man to have on your side in a brawl," Jordan told him.

"Because the meek are blessed doesn't mean all Christians are meek. Do you remember what Matthew tells us? 'And Jesus went into the temple and overthrew the tables of the moneychangers.' Surely not the undertaking of a meek man. But you don't want to hear my sermon on the subject."

"A man whose life has just been spared, even a Sunday Christian such as myself, is usually willing to listen to a sermon, good or bad. At least I am. I'm Captain Jordan Quinn, by the way."

"I know. It's not coincidence that brings me here. I asked after you at the livery stable in the village. I'm having my horse reshod. They directed me this way."

Jordan raised his eyebrows.

"You probably wonder," Thomas went on, "what on earth a roving preacher might want with you. Does he intend to attempt to convert me, you're asking yourself. Or to try to sell me a Bible?" Thomas opened the book to where the *vaquero*'s knife had pierced it. "Revelations has been somewhat damaged," he said, "but James, Peter and John seem to have escaped unscathed. To tell you the truth, I've never cared much for Revelations anyway. Raises too many questions that aren't easily answered."

"But what *do* you want with me?" Jordan asked.

Thomas's smile faded and he frowned. "A woman at the Mendoza ranch said you might be able to tell me more about what happened to Miss Alitha Bradford."

"Alitha Bradford." As Jordan repeated the name, he pictured the golden-haired girl riding away from him into the mist. "What is she to you?" he asked sharply.

"She's my fiancée. She was sailing to the Sandwich Islands, where we were to marry. I was a missionary there, but when I heard of the wreck of the *Flying Yankee,* I took passage as soon as I could on a packet to Yerba Buena, where I bought a horse. Not a very sound horse, I'm afraid, for I had to walk the last five miles into Santa Barbara this morning. I discovered from a Señora María Mendoza that Alitha survived the wreck, for which I was giving thanks to God when I was told she'd left here weeks ago for Mexico City under rather strange circumstances."

"Reverend, I think you've stated the case rather admirably. Except I wouldn't say the circumstances of Miss Bradford's departure are particularly strange."

"She left here with a Don Esteban Mendoza and five other men. And you say that's not odd behavior? Didn't she know she could have sailed from Santa Barbara to the islands? Or from here to San Francisco Bay and then to the islands?"

"I'm sure she was aware of that."

"Then why did she ride off to Mexico with strangers? Did this Don Esteban kidnap Alitha? Does he have some sort of hold over her?"

"In a way he does, Reverend. I'm convinced Alitha thinks she's following the dictates of her heart by going to Mexico with Esteban. When a woman thinks that, more often than not the end result is folly."

Thomas stared at him, slowly shaking his head. "I can't believe it, Quinn. The Alitha I knew in Boston would never go off with a man. Not of her own accord."

"This isn't the Alitha you knew. She's been through a great deal, and in California she's a stranger in a strange land."

"She can't have changed that much."

"Perhaps," Jordan said drily, "the young lady's not interested in Don Esteban as a man but took this wonderful opportunity to accompany a knowledgeable Spaniard to Mexico so he could provide her with a firsthand account of the fascinating history of that country. I expect that at this very moment he's identifying the exotic flora and fauna along the King's Highway in Baja California for her and explaining the strange customs of our neighbor to the south . "

"I've heard enough, Quinn." All at once Thomas's body sagged. He sat on a boulder, burying his face in his hands.

Jordan walked to him and gripped the other man's shoulder. "Women." He snorted. "You can't trust them, you can't . . ." He suddenly thought of Margarita, radiant in white, on their wedding day. He looked around him, thinking he smelled orange blossoms even though he knew that they had long since fallen into the dust.

"Damn it," Jordan said, "I'm sorry, Reverend. At times I speak without thinking."

Thomas stood up, pushing his blond hair back from his forehead and trying to smile. "Call me Thomas," he said. "Despite what you may think, I'm not afraid to face the truth about Alitha. 'And ye shall know the truth, and the truth shall make you free.' That's John. I expect she was injured in the shipwreck; perhaps she struck her head and is suffering from brain fever. She *was* ill, Señora Mendoza told me, after she first arrived in Santa Barbara. When she recovers, she'll be the same as she always was."

Man's capacity for deluding himself, Jordan thought, must be infinite.

"She'll need someone in Mexico to help her after she

recovers," Thomas said. "She'll be among strangers in a foreign land thousands of miles from home."

"You aren't telling me that you intend to follow her to Mexico City, are you?"

"I'm saying exactly that. Jordan, you're probably thinking I'm deluding myself, and perhaps I am, but one thing I know beyond all doubt." He smiled as though remembering a happier time. "I love Alitha. When you love someone, you have to believe in her; you have to have complete faith in her. So, yes, as soon as I can book passage, I'll go to Mexico. I've sent word to the bishop that I won't return to the islands until I've found Alitha."

"I suppose I should envy you your faith," Jordan said. "You were surely ill named, for I've never seen a less doubting man." Even though your faith makes you something of a fool, he added to himself. "I fear I'm the one who sees men as they are," Jordan said, "not as I'd like them to be. I see beyond their facades to their weaknesses and their evil intentions."

"I like to think I see men as they are, too," Thomas said. If you see men as weak and evil, he thought, perhaps it's because you're looking into a mirror without realizing it.

"You're tired," Jordan said, "and I imagine hungry as well. Come with me. I'm sure Señor Navarro has enough tortillas and beans to feed a traveling missionary. And don't forget to bring the Good Book, just in case we meet some more highwaymen."

Thomas retrieved the Bible from the ground, and the two men walked side by side up the path into the hills.

The sky was beginning to darken when Jordan came down the hill from the Navarro *casa*, leaving Thomas asleep. He skirted far around the village and made his way to the beach, where he walked along the ocean listening to the surf and letting the salt air fill his lungs.

He had gone only a short distance when he sensed someone behind him. Looking back, he saw the black shapes of three men in the growing darkness. He immediately increased his pace, but when he glanced back again, he saw that the men had also increased theirs. Damn, he thought, he wasn't about to run from a fight. One hand went to his gun, the other to his knife. He turned and waited, wishing Thomas were with him. The three men drew nearer, separating as they approached. Jordan took the pistol from his belt and braced himself for their attack.

"Put aside your weapon, Captain Quinn," a voice out of the darkness told him. Jordan recognized the Southern drawl of Captain Cunningham. He thrust his pistol back into his belt.

"I'd like to have a word or two with the captain," Cunningham said, and the other two men, both naval officers, walked ahead.

"I apologize for this rather unusual meeting place," Cunningham said. "But I thought it best that we not be seen together again."

"Is my reputation that bad?"

Cunningham ignored Jordan's remark. "I have an offer to make you," he said.

"As I told you earlier, I'm not interested in the navy."

"Not the navy, sir—a special assignment." He paused. "I want you to sail to Acapulco, make your way from there to Mexico City and, while you are in the capital, do all in your power to prevent the Spaniards from fortifying California. I've learned that a Don Esteban Mendoza left here some weeks ago to plead for more troops and more arms. We can't afford to have him succeed, and you're the man to stop him. You know Spanish, you're enterprising and you're not afraid of a fight."

"You're suggesting I become a spy?"

"I'd prefer to call you a confidential agent of the United States government. Your insurance matter, by the way, would be taken care of, and—" he reached into his pocket— "you'll be paid five hundred dollars in silver now and more when you reach Mexico City."

Taking a leather pouch from his pocket, Cunningham slapped it against his open palm. The coins clinked invitingly.

If he accepted Cunningham's offer, Jordan thought, he'd be on the move again and, in time, he'd have enough money for another ship of his own. Besides which, he wouldn't mind the chance to take that arrogant bastard Don Esteban down a peg or two if the opportunity offered itself.

And Alitha would be in Mexico City. Thomas Heath or no, he wanted to see her again.

"What do you say, Captain Quinn?" Cunningham asked. "Yea or nay?"

"I say aye aye, sir."

chapter 15

"BAJA IS NOTHING but poor shrubs, useless thorn bushes and bare rocks," Esteban said.

"But it has a certain beauty." Alitha said no more, knowing that Esteban soon became impatient when she disagreed with him. She liked Baja California—the dry clear days, the plains strewn with boulders and black lava rock, the impenetrable thickets of thorny shrubs and the small oases where date palms grew.

She was awed by the huge *cardones,* cactus with upsweeping ribbed arms extending more than thirty feet above her head. She'd seen the thick, swordlike leaves of the yucca before in the north, but here it had surprised her by sending up blooms of small, cream-colored flowers. Without the ocean, though, she might have agreed with Esteban, but the blue water was never far away on this narrow, fingerlike peninsula.

At first they had traveled along cliffs with the Pacific below them; days later, the Sea of Cortés was to their left, its shoreline indented by turquoise bays and coves whose beaches of white sand dazzled Alitha's eyes

They camped near one of the bays beside a spring whose water trickled from between rocks to form a quiet pool under overreaching palms. That night Alitha lay with her hands behind her head, staring up at the vault of the starry sky

"Last night I had a dream," she said to Esteban, who lay beside her on his *petate*. "I dreamed my father was waiting for me in a park of some great city, a park with green slopes and streams and willow trees whose branches trailed in the water. I wandered from place to place searching for him. At last I found him sitting alone on a bench, ramrod straight, with his hands clasped over the handle of his walking stick. I ran to him, and when he stood up to take me in his arms I realized it wasn't my father after all. It was you, Esteban. Before either of us could speak, I woke up "

"Am I like your father, then?"

"No, not at all. He was such a stern, forbidding man while you, you're   Well, you're different." She stopped, at a loss, realizing that at least in some ways Esteban *was* like her father. Demanding. Impatient

"I've never told you about my father," she went on

She described to Esteban how she had discovered that her father had been unfaithful to her mother and how she, Alitha, had been unable to forgive him until the day he died aboard the *Flying Yankee,* and how even now she did not understand why he had done what he did.

"You don't understand what men are like," Esteban said. "Men aren't fashioned for marriage. At least not marriage as women would have it."

"No, it's *you* who don't understand. I felt as though

my father had betrayed not just my mother but me as well. I thought . . ."

Esteban covered her mouth with his lips. After returning his kiss she drew away. "Let me tell you how I feel . . ." she began, but his hand had slid under her nightgown and along her bare leg. She sat up and pulled the gown over her head.

He entered her at once, thrusting inside her, and just as she felt her own desire beginning to grow he withdrew, turned her until she was on her stomach and entered her again. Again he withdrew after a few minutes. Finally he lay on his back with Alitha, also on her back, on top of him.

"Take that damn stone off," he said.

"I don't know what you mean."

"The charm, that pagan Indian stone you're wearing around your neck." He reached up and grasped Chia's charm stone and tried to yank it over her head, but it caught under her chin and she cried out in pain.

"You're hurting me," she told him. "Wait, I'll take it off." She lifted the cord over her head and placed the red stone on the ground nearby.

"I don't want you to wear it again, ever," Esteban said.

Alitha bit her lip to stifle an angry reply. Didn't he wear a cross of gold around his own neck? What right had he to tell her what to wear? She would never, never give up the charm stone. Still, she could keep Chia's gift without wearing it. Wearing the stone wasn't worth quarreling about.

She forced herself to relax and felt Esteban's fingers caress her breast. He touched her sex with the other hand, moving until he was within her again. She heard his hard breathing and felt the quickening of his thrusts. When he lay still beneath her, she rolled off him and huddled under the blanket with her back to him. For the first time her desire had not risen to join his. She took the stone from the ground, her fingers caressing its smoothness until she fell asleep.

The next day they rode down out of harsh, rocky hills into Loreto, the port town on the Sea of Cortés, where Esteban expected to find a ship bound for San Blas on the Mexican mainland. In front of them the sea sparkled under a hot noonday sun; they rode through groves of date palms, passed a weathered church and approached the *presidio*.

A soldier waved them through the gates of the fort while another hurried ahead of them to give Coronel Morales word of their arrival.

"I knew Manuel Morales years ago in Mexico City," Esteban told her, "when he was a lieutenant. Now he's a colonel."

Three men in blue uniforms, with shakos on their heads and swords at their sides, came out of an adobe barracks to greet them.

"Don Esteban," the taller of the men called. Esteban swung from his stallion and ran forward to embrace the *coronel*, while a soldier helped Alitha to the ground, where she waited a few feet behind the men.

Esteban embraced the other two men as Coronel Morales bowed to Alitha, raising her hand to his lips. "Señora Mendoza," he said as, in Spanish, he bid her welcome to Loreto.

He thinks I'm Esteban's wife, Alitha told herself. "Esteban," she said, wanting him to correct the *coronel*'s mistake, but Esteban, who was still talking to the other officers, shook his head impatiently and motioned her away.

Coronel Morales took her arm and led her along the side of the adobe building to a garden of cacti and succulents. Smiling at her, he pointed to the garden while he told her, she supposed, the names of each of the various plants. How proud he was of his tiny garden!

"I don't know much Spanish," she said in English. "And I—I'm not the wife of Don Esteban."

The *coronel* stared at her blankly. He looked past her, and in another moment she heard footsteps and Don Esteban was at her side, nodding in her direction while he talked to Coronel Morales. Explaining his presence here in Loreto, she guessed. Explaining that she was not his wife.

The *coronel* nodded as Esteban talked and tried to smile at her. *"Señorita,"* she heard him say. Alitha looked away, her cheeks flaming, wanting to flee but knowing she had nowhere to go. At last Esteban took her by the arm and led her into a building next to the barracks and along a corridor to a small room containing a table, a chair and a bed covered with netting.

"Stay here." Esteban went out, closing the door firmly behind him.

She sat in the chair and stared around her at the rough gray adobe walls. A spider, black streaked with yellow, crawled slowly up one of the walls, stopped, then went on until it reached a web stretched between wall and ceiling.

What am I doing here, Alitha asked herself. She stood and went to the window with its view of the rock hills behind Loreto. From another part of the fort she heard the tattoo of a drum followed by a shouted command in Spanish. She lowered her head into her hands and cried. She was still crying when the door opened behind her.

"You have brought great embarrassment to Coronel Morales," Esteban said.

"Damn Coronel Morales," Alitha sobbed. "What about my embarrassment? Don't you care about that? What did you tell him I was, Esteban? Your woman? Your mistress? Your—your whore?"

Esteban came up behind her and put his arms around her waist. "Ah, my Alitha," he said. "Forgive me, the fault was completely mine. It was my duty to explain to Coronel Morales when we first arrived and I neglected to do so. Humbly, I beg your forgiveness. Do not weep; you must know I suffer a thousand deaths whenever I see you in distress."

She wiped her eyes and leaned back against him, feeling his hands close tighter about her waist and his teeth nip her earlobe. He blew gently into her ear. His lips moved along her chin, and when they reached her mouth, she turned in his embrace, putting her arms about his neck and clinging to him as she kissed him.

"You mean so much to me," she said. "Esteban, you're all I have in the world."

When he began undoing the buttons of her riding dress, she looked up at him, all at once aware of men talking nearby and, farther away, the sounds of soldiers marching. In the distance she heard a blacksmith's hammer clang on an anvil.

"Here?" she asked. "Now?"

"Here," he told her. "Now."

When they were both naked on the bed, he gathered her into his arms, kissing and caressing her until she arched feverishly to meet him. Afterward she clung to him, wanting to hold him forever.

"You must never leave me," she whispered. "I couldn't bear to have you gone."

He didn't answer. His eyes were closed, and she tenderly kissed his eyelids. Suddenly she jumped.

"Esteban," she said and he opened his eyes. "That

spider." She nodded to the wall, where the spider had crawled to within a few inches of the white flesh of her leg.

Esteban reached across her body and with his thumb ground the spider against the wall. When he took his thumb away Alitha saw a black smear on the adobe. She clung to him, trying to recapture the contentment she had felt only a few minutes before, but she could not.

A week later Alitha was at the rail of the Spanish brig *Princesa*, looking across the blue waters of the Sea of Cortés. Esteban came to stand beside her.

"You're very quiet today, my love," he said. "You stare over the waters as though you could already see San Blas or even Mexico City itself."

"This is the first ship I've been aboard since the *Flying Yankee*. I was remembering our voyage around the Horn and the storm. I was thinking of my father."

Esteban covered her hand with his and she leaned against him.

"Oh, Esteban," she said, "when I was a girl, I thought I'd live forever. Each day seemed a lifetime, and a week was an eternity. Now, after what happened to the *Yankee*, I know life can be so—so fleeting."

"That's why we must live every day to the fullest. Why we must take the pleasures of this world where and when we find them. Who knows what lies beyond?"

"You don't believe in eternal life? That the body may die but the soul lives on?"

"Life eternal? Who knows? But it is not like you to be so gloomy, my Alitha. You usually greet even the dreariest of days with a smile as bright as the sun above. Besides, the worst of our journey is over. Loreto and

Baja are behind us, San Blas and Guadalajara and Mexico lie ahead."

"I liked your friend Coronel Morales." She hesitated, wondering if talking about the colonel would remind Esteban of the unpleasantness on the day they'd arrived. She hoped it wouldn't. "He seems such a gentleman for a soldier."

"Did Manuel tell you that he always wanted to be a botanist when he was young? As a boy, he avidly collected all the varieties of plants growing near his home in Córdoba. It is strange, the turns our lives take. Now he commands one of the most important yet Godforsaken outposts of New Spain."

Esteban leaned over the rail, watching the wake of the ship behind them. "Manuel told me what he knew of conditions in Mexico. The Spanish viceroy, Juan Ruiz de Apodaca, is in control, praise be to God, though a certain General Guerrero still leads a band of revolutionaries in the southern part of the country. The last word Manuel had from the capital was that the viceroy was sending his best general, Augustín de Iturbide, to the south to quell the revolt."

"I know there have been uprisings in Mexico for years. Why, Esteban? Why do these men revolt? Isn't there enough death as it is?"

"Most of them are opportunists attempting to create a place for themselves in the sun. They all have their endless lists of grievances, together with grandiose plans to resolve them. There is too much wealth in the hands of a few, they say, while the great masses of the people are poor. Prices are too high, some complain, while others claim there is little in the way of education for the young. Still others decry the great power of the priests, pointing out, truthfully, that the church owns half of all the land in the country. And certainly the

Inquisition left wounds that have not yet healed. We had a saying in Spain that one arrested by the Inquisition may not be burned alive but he will assuredly be scorched."

"My father didn't encourage me to be interested in politics. I'm not well informed."

"That is no failing, my Alitha; women have not the minds for it. In politics the more things change, the more they remain the same. As for myself, I only want to help save my homeland, my California. I'm a royalist, yes, and a Spaniard, of course, but California is first in my heart of hearts. Someday California will be independent, freed from Spain. I hope I live to see that glorious day."

Alitha glanced at him but decided not to argue. In Esteban's view women weren't meant to think She looked out over the water. "Esteban," she said, "is that San Blas? We seem to be sailing for the mouth of a river."

"Yes, at last." He put his arm around her shoulders and drew her to him. "San Blas! Mexico!"

Esteban sounded, she thought, as though he had found the promised land after years of wandering in the desert. The air was humid as they sailed into the bay of San Blas, and perspiration beaded their foreheads In the low-lying country behind the town, Alitha saw a forest of broad-leafed trees and, farther to the east, mountains. These weren't the barren hills of Baja but towering, tree-covered slopes.

"The South Seas must be like this," Alitha said. "The palms, the thatched huts on the sandy beach." And the Sandwich Islands must look like this, too, she thought with a sudden pang. How strange to think that she might never see Thomas again.

After docking alongside a wharf they waited on board while Indians unloaded the *Princesa*.

"Those men are *cargadores*," Esteban told her. "As you can see, they use straps to carry everything and anything on their backs. They carry as much as three hundred pounds, walking or trotting great distances. In the cities you often meet a *cargadore* with a man or woman seated in a chair on his back."

"The Indians here in Mexico seem so gentle, so quiet, as though they've endured without complaining for hundreds of years and will endure for hundreds more."

"They weren't always so. In the ancient days before the Spanish conqueror Cortés came, they were warlike, fighting not so much for land or gold or glory but to capture victims for their blood-lusting gods. They painted their prisoners blue before taking them to a sacrificial pyramid, where they stretched them across a stone altar. A priest with trailing hair matted with gore, wearing a bizarre costume and wielding a stone knife, would rip open the victim's chest, plunge his hand inside, and wrench out the man's heart which he threw, still pulsing and warm, into a stone urn on the altar."

"How horrible!"

"If the great Cortés accomplished nothing else, he brought Christianity to Mexico to take the place of the Indians' savage paganism, their worship of idols, their cannibalism. So you can understand why I asked you to remove that charm of yours from around your neck."

Alitha said nothing. How could a stone carved in the shape of a fish have anything to do with human sacrifices hundreds of years ago? Besides, hadn't the first Christians used the fish as their symbol?

Why was Esteban constantly finding fault with what

she said and did? He knew she was an American, not a Spaniard, and yet he seemed to expect that she act like a *señorita*. Even if she wished to she could not, because she didn't know all the customs, the manners of Spanish women. And though she wanted to please Esteban, she was determined to remain herself.

As soon as their horses and supplies were unloaded from the *Princesa*, they made preparations to leave San Blas.

"This climate is unhealthy for those of us who aren't used to it," Esteban said. "In San Blas we are in the *tierra caliente,* the hot country, far south of the Tropic of Cancer Many men die here of yellow fever.''

They struggled through swamps and tropical forests, where snakes slithered away into the high grass, where vines hung from rubber and mahogany trees. The forest was a lush green, for the summer rainy season was not yet over, although, except for an occasional shower, they hadn't seen rain since they had left Loreto.

On their second night out of San Blas, they camped on the top of a low hill, covering themselves with netting to ward off the flies and mosquitoes. Alitha woke abruptly, sitting bolt upright. Men were shouting nearby, the horses stomping and whinnying shrilly. She heard the terrible sound of an animal in pain. One of the horses? Lanterns bobbed among the trees. Esteban, she saw, was gone, his *petate* empty. A shot cracked a short distance away. A man called out in the night. She heard another shot and the thud of horses' hooves.

Throwing a shawl over her shoulders, she ran to the still-glowing campfire, where she found one of the *vaqueros* standing with his musket across his arm.

"Qué pasa?" she asked him. "What's happening?"

"Jaguar," he said.

The *vaquero* told her that the jaguar had killed one of the horses, and now the other men were hunting the night-prowling beast while he stayed behind to guard the camp. Not only did he guard against animal predators; when they were in San Blas they had been warned of marauding bandits, who were sometimes the remnants of revolutionary bands, along the route to Mexico City.

Alitha sat on the ground beside the fire and waited. Some time later she heard another shot in the distance, followed by silence. After what seemed an eternity she again heard hoofbeats. She stood up, staring into the darkness, and a few minutes later Esteban and the rest of the men rode into camp.

Esteban disappeared for a moment and returned with a bottle. After drinking deeply he gave it to the man next to him, and the liquor was passed from hand to hand until it returned to Esteban, who emptied the bottle and hurled it into the dark night.

He walked past Alitha, turning and motioning her to follow him. When they reached their *petates,* he said brusquely, "Take off your gown."

She let her shawl drop to the ground but hesitated an instant before pulling her nightgown over her head.

"Did you kill the jaguar?" she asked.

"Would I not have brought him back to the camp as a trophy if I had?"

He took off his clothes and knelt over her, his hands rough on her breasts. Still kneeling, he moved higher along her body and she felt his hands bringing her breasts together to imprison his sex between them. Her breathing quickened.

He hunched still higher until his knees straddled her

shoulders. She felt something smooth and warm touch her cheek. Instinctively she turned her head away

"What are you doing?" she whispered fearfully

"Take me into your mouth," he said.

"I can't. Oh, Esteban, I can't. Don't ask me to."

"You will do as you are told."

He took her head in his hands, and though she twisted away from him, he turned and lifted her head until her lips pressed against his sex. With her hands clenched into fists at her sides, her nails biting into her palms, and with tears scalding her eyes, she opened her mouth

The next morning the sky was blue and the sun bright as they climbed from the swampy lowlands into the cool, dry air of the mountains. Esteban rode ahead as always with Alitha behind him. She stared silently ahead. Everything will be all right once we get to Mexico City, she told herself. Look, even the weather improves as we go into the mountains.

Two days later clouds gathered in the west, and by evening she felt the first drops of rain on her face. The storm went on day after day, night after night, the rain heavy and unrelenting. When at last they entered Mexico City in the cold rain, the men huddled in their serapes and Alitha rode bundled in her cloak. The stone-paved streets of the city were slick, the buildings along their route a blur. She had never been more miserable.

chapter 16

ALITHA WOKE EARLY, as she had every morning since arriving in Mexico City, to the shrill cries of the street peddlers.

"Hay cebo?"

"Mantequilla!"

"Cecina buena!"

The last she'd just learned to translate. Good salt beef. She sat up in bed and looked toward the window

Alitha smoothed the coverlet and sighed. She was alone in the massive bed with the ornate gilt headboard. Esteban had made it clear that here in Mexico City they wouldn't share a bedroom.

"That does not mean you won't find me in your bed *mi corazón,* my heart, but there are certain customs to be observed."

"Won't they know that I—that we . . ?" she had asked.

Esteban had thrown back his head and laughed. "Of

a certainty everyone will know you are my *amante*, but still we shall abide by the ways of my people, as we did in *mi casa*. You are a *señorita* and must seem to sleep alone."

With this she'd given up any hope that he might pretend that she was his wife while in Mexico City. The trouble was, although he did come to her bed, she'd seen very little of Esteban otherwise.

"But I go to the *casa* of my third cousin," he would say. "I cannot take you with me to the home of a relative."

"Your sister-in-law knew about us. Maria knew very well we were—were lovers. Why should you care about a third cousin?"

Esteban had not smiled. "I cannot explain. It is the custom. One doesn't do certain things."

"Yet you say everyone is well aware of our relationship."

"I have walked with you in the Alameda, we have attended the theater, I shall accompany you to the costume ball in a few days. What more do you ask?"

Alitha sighed again as she remembered Esteban's words. He couldn't understand that she was bored and lonely. She was not allowed to venture from the house unless accompanied by a man. And no one visited when Esteban wasn't here, no one except Doña Anise, the only woman who had befriended her since their arrival in Mexico City. And though Esteban had been responsible for her meeting Doña Anise, he didn't like her.

"A meddler. One can never trust such a person."

Alitha rose and crossed to the marble-topped dressing table. The house Esteban had rented for them was a typical Spanish *casa*, built in a square with a gallery upstairs, but far grander than his own California home. A magnificent fig tree grew in the center of a courtyard graced with rosebushes and flowering vines. From below stairs she could hear the voices of the servants as they began their working day.

Why did she feel so desolate? She stared at her reflection in the silver-framed mirror. Was she as pretty as Esteban said? Somehow her blue eyes and blond hair seemed bland in this land of gleaming dark hair, skin like beige silk and brown eyes that flashed and danced.

Danced. There was the real source of her discontent.

She *was* beautiful, that dancer. And Esteban had done far more than glance. When he came to her bed at night, Alitha sometimes had the unwelcome notion that in his mind he made love not to her but to La Coralilla.

The dancer wore the brilliant reds and yellows of her namesake, the coral snake, and, with her black hair swirling as she writhed and twisted, Alitha thought the name fit. Beautiful but poisonous. Had she fascinated Esteban exactly as a snake fascinates its prey?

There'd been no one to talk to about how she felt except Doña Anise.

"La Coralilla is obviously a *mestiza*," Doña Anise had told her, "no doubt born of an Indian mother and a Spanish father. Such women are sometimes exotics. But acceptable, of course."

"You must know there are castes in New Spain," Doña Anise went on. "First we have the *gachupinos*, Spaniards who were born in Europe; next the *creoles*, as I am, a Spaniard who was born here in Mexico; next the *mestizos;* a very few mulattos who are white and Negro; the *zambos*, descendents of Indians and Negros; then, of course, the Indians and Negros themselves."

Alitha began to brush her hair. Doña Anise would visit later in the day to help plan her costume for the ball. Alitha had seen just the dress she wanted to wear on a Poblana peasant girl in the streets of the city—white muslin chemise, low in the neck and lace trimmed, with a multicolored petticoat shorter than the chemise. The bottom of the petticoat was scarlet and black, the top yellow. The girl had worn a vest—hers would be blue satin to bring out the color of her eyes—embroidered with gold and silver. Then there was the colored sash—blue again, for hers—which tied in back. She'd wear her hair braided up onto her head as the peasant girl had. The girl's legs had been bare, but Alitha decided she'd wear white silk stockings to match her white satin shoes trimmed in gold and silver.

Esteban can't help but notice me, she told herself. With silver chains around my neck, I'll be so colorful I'll put La Coralilla in the shade.

Doña Anise arrived soon after breakfast, which, as usual, was at ten o'clock. Esteban was out—meeting with some government functionaries, he'd told Alitha.

"Ah, my dear Alitha," Doña Anise said when she was shown into the *sala*. "I have taken the liberty of bringing my dressmaker, who waits outside. But I must warn you she is scandalized at the idea of a woman such as yourself dressing as a peasant. I fear you may provoke comment by your choice of costume."

"I don't care."

"I am happy to be of service to you," Doña Anise said, "but I felt I must warn you. Naturally, you must do what you wish."

Alitha smiled at the plump, older woman, who never seemed to dress other than in black. Did Spanish widows mourn forever?

"I have taken another liberty for which I fear you will scold me," Doña Anise went on. "Don Benito will be joining us later, after we have finished with the dressmaker. You know how sincerely he admires you."

Alitha frowned. Esteban had been most emphatic about gentlemen callers. If he was out, she was *not* to receive them unless they were accompanied by their wives.

"Oh, I trust you aren't furious with me? My only intent was to please."

"No, don't worry. It's quite all right," Alitha assured her.

Don Benito and Doña Anise were cousins. Surely Esteban wouldn't object. And if she alienated Doña Anise she'd have no one. Besides, Don Benito was at least fifty years old—though still distinguished looking.

"I find Don Benito a most intelligent man," she told Doña Anise.

"Of a certainty. Educated in Spain. And well known here in Mexico for his studies into this country's past. A true scholar."

The dressmaker proved capable, scandalized or not by the costume Alitha would be wearing. And yes, she would surely have it ready by the day of the ball.

"You are still fretting over Don Esteban, no?" Doña Anise asked after the dressmaker had departed. "This dancer, she is but *un momento*, a thing of the moment for him, while you are his eternity. That is the way of life. Men, they cannot be faithful, and women must understand."

"Esteban hasn't been unfaithful," Alitha said stiffly, sorry she'd ever spoken to Anise about La Coralilla.

Doña Anise raised her eyebrows knowingly. Outside the house a female peddler called, *"Tortillas de cuajada?"* The clip-clop of an approaching horse grew louder, then stopped.

"We will speak of this another time," Doña Anise said. "Don Benito is above *de boca en boca*, above gossip, and I'm sure that is he." She shook her head.

"We women can never measure up to a man's intellect."

"I don't agree with you," Alitha began but was interrupted by the servant announcing Don Benito.

Alitha managed to keep her costume a secret from Esteban. Though the evening of the ball was mild, she draped herself in a black velvet *manga*, a capelike affair that slipped over her head.

Esteban smiled at her. "An unusual arrangement for your hair," he commented.

She had wound gold chains into her braids and fastened braids and all atop her head with jeweled combs. Although Alitha knew by now that Mexican women wore many jewels and dressed resplendently when they attended any evening occasion, she still felt gaudy with the gold and jewels in her hair and the seven chains of silver about her neck.

"I've never been to a ball," she confessed. "We lived quite quietly at home. I've so looked forward to tonight!" She put her hand on his arm. "You look very dashing."

He'd chosen to come as a pirate and wore a black patch over one eye, a white silk shirt with a scarlet sash and black satin pantaloons tucked into black boots. Around his head he'd tied a white scarf hung with gold coins. A bolero of scarlet satin threaded with silver embroidery completed the costume.

"Is that how the French pirate—what was his name, Bouchard?—dresses?" she asked.

Esteban frowned. "He's merely a ruffian. No, I take my costume from the buccaneers of the Spanish Main."

"I doubt if there ever was a pirate as handsome as you."

He smiled again and patted her hand. How vain he

is, she thought. Would he still love you if you didn't always tell him how wonderful he is?

Alitha turned away from Esteban. What was she thinking? Why shouldn't Esteban realize how good looking he was?

Alitha tried not to look stunned at the size of the mansion where the ball was being held. So like a fairy-tale palace! Lanterns lined the drive; beside the entrance musicians played guitars and sang. As Esteban led her inside, a servant indicated where she was to leave her *manga*.

When Alitha returned to Esteban, she saw his eyes widen as he saw her costume for the first time. Before he had a chance to speak, another servant was announcing them.

Alitha stared into a sea of strange faces. Diamonds glittered on coiffures and bosoms, satin glistened, dresses of all colors swirled before her eyes. She recognized English and French queens, Cleopatras, dominoes and Greek goddesses. Most of them seemed even more intrigued by her than she was by them. Esteban had told her many times that her coloring was rare in Mexico and that that was why she drew so many eyes when they appeared in public. Alitha wondered if it might not be because everyone was curious to see Esteban's "friend."

Esteban's grip on her arm grew painful. She glanced at him but he was staring straight ahead, his face set and grim. What was wrong?

Several men approached, smiling, one dressed as a crusader, another as a sultan, but Esteban bowed slightly and turned away from them, almost dragging her toward a niche. Behind her she caught the Spanish words for lovely and for peasant.

"What are you thinking of?" Esteban demanded in a

low, furious tone as they were in the relative privacy of the niche. "Dressing like a nothing, a peasant—you humiliate me!"

"But—but you're a pirate."

"That's different. Do you see any other woman here gowned beneath her station? Do you?"

"There's nothing wrong with my costume!" she cried.

"Have the decency to keep your voice down. Had I seen your costume before we left the *casa,* I would never have brought you. You deliberately concealed what you were to wear. You planned this—you wanted to embarrass me."

Alitha blinked back tears. "No, no, all I wanted to do was surprise you."

"That you have done." His voice was icy with rage. "Unfortunately I've acknowledged you publicly, and leaving now will serve no purpose." He looked her up and down. "Such a dress is cheap and vulgar. Don't you understand that?"

Alitha gritted her teeth. He was being unfair! She wouldn't cry, she wouldn't give him the satisfaction of seeing her in tears. Lifting her head, she stared at him defiantly.

"Señorita Bradford," a man's voice said. Both she and Esteban turned.

Don Benito stood next to them, with Doña Anise on his arm. Neither were in costume.

"At last I have found you," Doña Anise said. "You look charming." She wore black velvet festooned with diamonds.

"If the girls of Puebla all resembled you, *señorita,* they would be the most sought after women in the world. I find your Poblana costume exquisite." Don Benito, also dressed in black, bowed slightly.

"Esteban!"

Alitha turned, already knowing whom she'd see.

Not only was La Coralilla's face veiled, her entire body was swathed in veils. As they watched, the dancer whirled about and stopped in front of Esteban with her face unveiled, the gauzy cloth in her hand. He smiled down at her. The diaphanous fabric of her body veils outlined her voluptuous curves.

"Ah, Salome," Esteban greeted her. *"Siete,* seven?"

"No, *seis,* six," she replied, tipping her head to smile teasingly back as she fluttered a loose veil at him. *"Cinco,* five?" she half-whispered as though she and Esteban were alone. She unloosened an end of material and pressed it into his hand. *"Cinco?"* she said again.

Alitha caught her breath as Esteban shrugged and said, *"Por qué no,* why not?"

He held the cloth firmly as the dancer gracefully twirled away from him until the veil unwound. Her dark nipples could now be clearly seen through the gauze of the remaining veils.

Esteban laughed and tied the veil around his waist. *"Cuatro,* four?" he asked.

La Coralilla danced away. Esteban took a step after her.

"Esteban!" Alitha spit his name from her lips.

He stopped, turning to frown at her.

"I should like to claim a dance with the loveliest peasant girl in the Western Hemisphere," Don Benito said, stepping between them. "That is, if I have your consent?" He bowed first to Alitha, then to Esteban.

Esteban shrugged. "As you wish," he said.

Reluctantly Alitha allowed Don Benito to lead her to the floor as she wiped away tears of rage and hurt. "You are far more beautiful than La Coralilla," he murmured into her ear.

"I—I don't think I feel like dancing just now," she said.

"Whatever you wish."

"I'm afraid Doña Anise's dressmaker was right about my costume," Alitha said. "I just don't understand Spanish customs." She pushed the words past the tightness in her throat.

"When one is as delightful as you are, my dear," Don Benito told her, "nothing is improper."

La Coralilla's behavior was far more vulgar than her peasant costume, Alitha told herself. Yet Esteban hadn't seemed to mind—he had, in fact, encouraged the dancer. She looked around but couldn't see either of them.

Laughter came from behind her. A man spoke in Spanish and she picked out several words. *Cabeza*, head. La Coralilla. Esteban. Salome. Were they saying the dancer would have Esteban's head on her platter instead of John the Baptist's?

Tears clouding her vision, she turned to Don Benito. "Please," she said. "Take me home. I—I don't feel well."

He hesitated momentarily. "I am at your service, of course. But Don Esteban . . . ?"

"I don't care!" Her voice rose. "I don't care about Don Esteban, do you hear?"

For once Alitha didn't wake early to the peddlers' cries. She'd lain awake most of the night waiting for Esteban. When, near dawn, she still hadn't heard him, she finally fell asleep and dreamed of sailing aboard a ship whose figurehead was La Coralilla, naked to the waist.

Alitha woke with a start. The brown face of the maid floated above her. The *galopina*'s Spanish was too rapid for her to follow but she gathered that there was a gentleman waiting in the *sala*.

Alitha sat up. Who . . . ? Oh, yes, she vaguely remembered promising Doña Anise she would accompany her today to the castle of Chapultepec, a short league from the city. Naturally they would have to be escorted by a man, as was the custom. Don Benito must have come for her.

She looked at Concepción, the *galopina*. "Don Esteban," Alitha said, then paused. What was the word for return? *"Volverá?"*

"No, *señorita*."

Alitha dressed in one of her newer gowns, a low-necked celestial blue taffeta with a bell-shaped skirt stiffened with buckram which cleared the floor when she walked to show her slippers. She took pains to twist her hair into a becoming chignon, determined to look her best when Esteban did come home. First, of course, she would have to dismiss Don Benito.

When she entered the *sala*, he rose, smiling.

"As beautiful as the day," he told her. "I trust you are over your indisposition of last night? Alas, Doña Anise lies ill—a headache—this morning. I fear she cannot come with us to Chapultepec."

When he smiled, she noticed, Don Benito looked younger, with his teeth white against his skin. He was a distinguished man, with graying hair waved back from his forehead and intelligent dark eyes. But as she gazed at him, Don Esteban's face superimposed itself over Don Benito's.

Was Esteban even now lying in the arms of that woman, that dancer? Why else wouldn't he have come home? Her eyes burned with unshed tears. How could he do this to her? Were all his protestations of love self-serving lies?

"I have taken the liberty of having my servants pack breakfast for us so that we might get an early start Don Benito said.

She focused her eyes on his with an effort. What was he saying? Breakfast? She never wanted to eat again

"I'm sorry, I hope you'll understand that I don't feel like going."

Don Benito inclined his head. "Naturally. I should have realized Don Esteban would not permit you to travel to the castle alone with me."

He thought Esteban wouldn't let her go? He was right—Esteban would be furious if he came to the *casa* and found her gone. Alitha took a deep breath Esteban deserved to be upset. And certainly there was little to fear from Don Benito. Damn Esteban; she'd go!

They drove through the city, passing the *leperos,* the beggars, in their rags; half-naked Indians, some of the women carrying babies on their backs in cloth slings; peasant girls in colorful dresses; and a few well-dressed gentlemen, both afoot and on horseback. It was too early for the Spanish ladies in their mantillas to be about.

Don Benito leaned across her to point out the cathedral. "If we are to believe de Castillo," he said "the chronicler of Cortés, the old Aztec heathen temple, the Teocalli, on this same site was far more impressive."

"*La Catedrál* is very beautiful," Alitha murmured.

The road they traveled was one of the better roads in Mexico, Alitha thought, paved and divided by an aqueduct with massive arches. She half-listened to Don Benito ramble on about the history of the city until they came to gates guarded by soldiers. Don Benito leaned from the carriage window and spoke to them, and the gates were thrown open. In a few minutes the carriage was passing beneath huge evergreens.

"The largest is Montezuma's Cypress," Don Benito said. "More properly Moctezuma's."

Gray moss hung from the branches, making them look even more ancient than they must be. The carriage climbed a steep hill, finally stopping in front of the castle. Don Benito got out first and helped her alight. Alitha stared at the huge arches and heavy walls of the castle.

"It looks more like a fortress than a summer retreat—isn't that what you told me it was intended for?" she asked.

"An early viceroy, Count Galvez, claimed he had such in mind. His superiors in Spain did not believe him and, as you can see, the castle was never finished."

"Doña Anise told me that according to the talk in the cafés, your present Spanish governor, Viceroy Apodaca, will soon be forced to return to Spain, and the government will be seized by the people of New Spain—the revolutionaries."

Don Benito shrugged. *"Quién sabe?* Of a certainty we have many able men in Mexico, but they fight among themselves. Ah, but you must know all this. They whisper about Don Esteban in the cafés, also. I shall be extremely sorry to see you sail for Spain."

"Spain? I'm not going to Spain."

"No? Perhaps the talk is wrong. Because of Don Esteban's friendship with old-guard monarchists, he is naturally suspected of being in on the plots."

She stared at him. "What plots?"

He shrugged. "It is nothing. Mere café gossip, which one should never listen to, much less repeat. There has always been talk of a secret place where Moctezuma's treasure is hidden. The monarchists intrigue to obtain

this gold for King Ferdinand. But enough of politics."
He waved his hand. "You are far more interesting."

When they had climbed to the terrace around the
castle, she saw that the building was falling to ruin. No
glass was in the windows, and the doors were warped
and weathered. From the terrace she stared out over
the valley toward the two snow-capped volcanoes,
Popocatepetl and Ixtachuatl.

"What an unbelievable view!" she exclaimed. "I
shall never forget being here."

Don Benito took her hand. "I shall never forget being here with *you*."

She disengaged her hand and moved away. "You
haven't told me all of the history of Chapultepec Hill,
have you?" she asked brightly. "Perhaps you could do
so while we walk back to the carriage." She started
toward the stairs.

After a moment he followed. "The beginning of the
Aztec civilization was on this hill," he said. "The
Indians who first settled here were nomadic barbarians
who dressed in skins and ate their meat raw."

"I thought the Aztecs were highly civilized when
Cortés arrived."

"So they were. Though they never lost the hideous
habit of making sacrifices to their gods. They skinned
human beings and performed their devil dances while
wearing the skins."

Alitha grimaced. Don Benito handed her into the
carriage, then climbed in beside her and the driver
started down the hill.

"The other Indian tribes in the area hated such
practices, even as you do, so the Aztecs were hunted
and killed," he said. "Eventually the survivors built
Tenochtitlan on an island in Lake Texcoco, the begin-

ning of our city. Their legend has it that they founded the city on that spot because they saw an eagle perched on a *nopal*, a prickly pear cactus, with a snake in his beak, and that was their prophetic sign."

"You are very knowledgeable," she said as the carriage pulled up beneath the giant cypresses. She looked at Don Benito.

"We have yet to breakfast," he said. "I thought we would eat in the garden."

"I should return home."

"It is early," he said, getting out.

Alitha stared down at him for a moment, then accepted his hand. She had grown surprisingly hungry, and surely she could discourage any advances Don Benito might make. He'd always behaved courteously.

He led her along a wide path bordered by wild and tangled shrubs to a garden where flowers bloomed. There he spread a cloth for her to sit on and opened the basket of food.

After they had finished breakfast Alitha's head drooped. She had scarcely slept at all last night, and now could barely keep her eyes open.

Don Benito waved his arm. "All this belonged to Moctezuma," he said. "He had gardens, aviaries, fish ponds. Even tanks for bathing. From the hill where the castle now stands, he looked out over his great Aztec city with its many lakes and its mighty temples to his gods. The mightiest of the gods was Huitzilopochtli, the armed protector."

Alitha only half-listened to the drone of his voice, hearing the strange Aztec words drift in and out of her consciousness. Sleep, she needed to sleep. She must tell Don Benito she had to leave . . .

A man's arms held her close, his mouth on hers. His

hand fumbled at the buttons on her dress and she opened her eyes. Suddenly very much awake, she found herself on her back, staring up at Don Benito. She tried to pull away.

"No," she gasped. "No!"

"My lovely fair-haired flower," he murmured, bending his head to her bared breast.

chapter 17

A SHADOW FELL across the struggling pair. Both Alitha and Don Benito froze, then looked up. A man stood beside them, a mocking smile on his lips. For a moment Alitha thought he was a stranger, but then with a start she recognized him.

"Your lecture on the Aztecs was most entertaining," Jordan Quinn said. "What you're doing now isn't."

Don Benito scrambled to his feet as Alitha, reddening, rebuttoned her dress. Jordan walked across the grass and bowed to her.

"Miss Bradford, if I may." He reached down and helped Alitha to her feet.

Don Benito dropped to one knee in front of her. "I was overwhelmed by my admiration for you," he said. "*Señorita,* if you will only forgive me. How could I help myself? Seeing you here in all your loveliness, being with you today, how could I resist my admittedly baser impulses? Can you ever forgive me? Will you ever forgive me?"

Alitha stared down at him, speechless. Don Benito seemed ludicrous with his disheveled hair and his flushed face as he protested his innocence. She didn't feel like laughing, though, for she realized too well what might have happened if Jordan Quinn hadn't intervened.

"I think you'd best leave," Jordan said to Don Benito, "while I escort Miss Bradford home. That *is* your carriage under the cypresses, isn't it?"

"My carriage?" Don Benito struggled to his feet. "No, not actually mine, I rented it for the day. I hope you'll have pity, sir, on a poor scholar who receives very little remuneration for his work. If it weren't for Doña Anise, my more than generous cousin, I would be forced to enter trade to earn my livelihood. Forgive me my circumlocution; it's the curse of the scholar to be less than direct. I beg you not to let Don Esteban know what occurred here today." Don Benito looked apprehensively from Jordan to Alitha.

Embarrassed, Alitha turned her head aside. Don Benito was not only ludicrous, he was making a complete fool of himself. How could she have ever thought him distinguished?

"I don't intend to tell Don Esteban," Alitha said.

Jordan nodded. "I suggest we all forget that this unfortunate scene ever took place," he said.

Don Benito took a large lace handkerchief from his pocket and wiped his face. "You, sir, are a gentleman," he told Jordan. "When I was a younger man, I would have challenged Don Esteban to meet me on the field of honor. However, when a man grows older . . ." He sighed.

"I think I hear your horses pawing the ground with impatience," Jordan said.

"My horses?"

"Your hired carriage, Don Benito. The longer you delay returning to the stable, the more *pesos* your carriage will cost you."

"Of a certainty, you are right." He bowed stiffly to Jordan, then took Alitha's hand and raised it to his lips before she knew what he intended. *Hasta luego, señorita,*" he said.

"No," she said, pulling her hand away. "*Adiós, señor.*"

Don Benito turned and hurried from the garden. A few minutes later they heard the cry of the coachman and the sound of receding hoofbeats.

"*Hasta luego,*" Jordan repeated. "Until later. I'll say this for your amorous friend, he's wonderfully optimistic."

Alitha straightened her dress, her mind still in a whirl. She had last seen Jordan Quinn in the fog at Santa Barbara as she had begun her journey south with Esteban. Now he was clean-shaven and dressed like a Spanish gentleman. What could Jordan be doing here in Mexico City? Not only in Mexico City but at Chapultepec Castle.

"I came here to see Chapultepec Hill," she said to cover her confusion. "I thought—that is, he really is most knowledgeable about the sights of Mexico City."

"I noticed his interest in sightseeing." Jordan glanced meaningfully at her breasts.

Alitha's face flamed.

"Captain Quinn," she said softly as she walked to him. Without warning she swung her hand and struck him full in the face. Jordan stepped back, and she saw his hands clench at his sides. With an obvious effort he smiled and swept off his hat.

"My humblest apologies," he said. "I spoke without thinking, as usual. Your loveliness makes a man forget himself. You are a beautiful woman, Miss Bradford. I've admired you ever since that day in Valparaiso."

Without answering, she walked past him, out of the garden and along the roadway. When she heard him following her, at first on foot and then on horseback, she ignored him. The guards at the castle gates bowed to her as she walked quickly by them down the hill.

Don Esteban. Don Benito. Jordan Quinn. Damn each and every one of them, she thought.

Last night at the ball Esteban had abandoned her for his dancer; there was no doubt in her mind about that. Did Esteban expect her to wait quietly at home, ready to throw herself in his arms on his return? And Don Benito. What must he, a man she hardly knew, think of her to try to force his attentions on her as he had? And Jordan Quinn, a man she knew not at all, to insult her?

She slowed her pace as her slippers began to pinch her feet. Jordan immediately rode up beside her. "May I offer you a ride?" he asked.

Still ignoring him, she walked quickly on, thinking that somehow, somewhere, she had let her life go horribly awry. All because I loved Esteban, she told herself. Am I to be punished forever for loving him?

She came to an intersection and was looking around her, uncertain as to what direction to take, when a man with curled mustaches and wearing a frock coat approached, raised his hat and asked her a question in Spanish that she didn't understand. She shook her head as his eyes roved down her body, lingering at her breasts and hips. Alitha hurried on, feeling his gaze following her as she crossed the street.

At the next corner she stopped again. Carriages rattled by, street vendors called their wares and across the way men played dice on a makeshift table. She was hopelessly lost.

"I'm impressed by your outraged virtue," Jordan said from behind her. "Now if you'll but allow me, I'd be most happy to accompany you home."

She turned to find him standing with the reins of his horse in his hand.

"I'm lost," she said, "and very tired." She drew in her breath and raised her head defiantly. "Although I don't forgive you, Captain Quinn, I do appreciate your offer of a ride."

He lifted her to the saddle and swung himself up behind her. When the horse whinnied and stepped sideways, Jordan tugged awkwardly at the reins to redirect him along the street.

"Damn all horses," he muttered. Alitha noticed that he rode stiffly erect as though expecting the horse to try to throw him to the pavement at any moment.

"Would you like me to handle him for you?" she asked.

Jordan didn't answer. She felt him urge the horse ahead with his knees, and in a few minutes they were making their way at a brisk walk along the avenue. She sighed, trying not to let herself relax against him—she was so tired, so terribly tired. When she got home, she'd go to bed and sleep for days.

Men. They were the problem, she told herself. If a woman could only do without them, what a wonderful world this would be. Or if only the good traits of several men could be combined into one. The gentleness, the tenderness of Thomas; the dashing grace of Esteban; the interest in learning of Don Benito; Jordan's tragic past. How terrible he must have felt, losing Margarita as he had . . .

"Here we are."

Jordan looked down at Alitha and saw that she was asleep on his shoulder. Dismounting, he lifted her from the horse, looped the reins on a hitching ring and carried her from the side street to the front of her house. I must tell her, he thought, of Heath. Jordan had left Thomas seriously ill with yellow fever in Acapulco. The poor bastard, Jordan thought, might even be dead by now.

He climbed the steps with Alitha in his arms, pausing at the front door and reaching for the bell pull. At the last moment he drew his hand back and tried the door, and found it unlocked. Alitha stirred in his arms as he carried her inside and shut the door behind him.

He glanced at the chandelier over his head, at the ornately carved moldings and the gilt-framed portraits. On the wall beside him a full-length mirror reflected a man in black with a golden-haired, blue-gowned woman in his arms.

The house seemed deserted. How like Mexican servants, he thought, always underfoot except when you needed them. He started to call out, checked himself and walked up the curving staircase. At the top of the stairs, Jordan stopped when he found himself facing a corridor of closed doors.

Gently, he shook Alitha. She stirred but didn't waken. He leaned down and kissed her on the cheek, his lips barely brushing her glowing skin. She was so lovely, he thought. At that moment his good intentions of telling her of Thomas Heath's journey to Mexico weakened. The news would only distress her. No, he decided, it would be best to say nothing.

"Where . . . ?" Alitha asked groggily, opening her eyes to stare at him in amazement.

"Which is your room?" Jordan asked. "They all look alike."

She gasped, twisting in his arms until he lowered her

feet to the floor. "What are you doing here?" she demanded.

"You were asleep, Alitha. It seemed a shame to wake you. Besides . . ."

"Listen!"

They heard the clatter of hoofbeats outside. The sounds grew louder and then suddenly stopped.

"It's Don Esteban," she said frantically. "If he finds you here he'll kill you. Your horse—he'll see your horse."

"I didn't leave him by the house," he told her.

Below them the front door opened.

Jordan strode past her to the first door on his right and hurried inside.

"No," Alitha whispered, "this is my bedroom."

As he crossed the room, Jordan was conscious of many shades of blue—in the wallpaper, the upholstered chairs, the canopy over the bed. He opened the French doors and stepped outside onto a balcony, closing the doors behind him. Alitha, who had run after him, turned just in time to see Esteban stride into the bedroom.

"Why did you leave?" he demanded.

"Leave?" she repeated, wondering how Esteban had so quickly discovered her trip with Don Benito to Chapultepec Hill.

"You left the ball last night without telling me. Without me." Esteban threw his hat onto a table.

How like him, she thought, to be questioning her angrily before she'd had a chance to ask him where he'd spent the night.

"Well?" he said. "I'm waiting."

Alitha felt rage rise in her. "I suppose you don't care that *I* waited all night? Why do you think I left the ball? You know very well."

"To humiliate me, was that your reason?" Esteban flung himself into a chair. "First you shame me by your choice of a costume, the dress of a peasant, then you leave with another man. Had it been anyone but that fool Don Benito, I should have been forced to kill him. Of course you will never see him again, nor that simpering cousin of his."

Alitha started toward him, her fists clenched. "Doña Anise is my only . . ." she began, then stopped as she passed the curtained doors leading to the balcony. One of them was ajar. Hadn't Jordan closed them both behind him? She looked away immediately, not daring to call attention to the balcony. "Doña Anise is my friend," she finished lamely.

"You will do as I say. Since you have no sense yourself of what is right and proper, I shall expect you to ask me before you . . ."

"Ask you?" Alitha marched up to his chair and stood over him. "How can I ask you anything when you don't come home all night? Don't try to shift the blame to me like you always do. What am I supposed to think about your conduct?"

"I had important business to discuss," he said stiffly, rising.

Alitha moved back, involuntarily glancing at the door to the balcony.

"We were awaiting the arrival of a gentleman from Vera Cruz who was delayed," Esteban went on. "You realize I tell you this only because I care for you, my Alitha. I do not have to justify what I do."

"Ha!" she exclaimed. "A gentleman from Vera Cruz. A gentleman wearing veils perhaps."

He gripped her arm. "Do not mock me."

Was that perfume she smelled on his jacket? Alitha jerked away. "You were with Coralilla, weren't you?

That—" the word *whore* came to her lips but she couldn't bring herself to say it. "That . . . trollop," she finished lamely.

"And you?" Esteban asked. "What do you call yourself?"

Alitha recoiled, hurt and angry. Stunned. Was that really how Esteban saw her? She had given him her love, and in return he treated her like his chattel or worse. He would not make her lose her temper, she vowed, stifling an embittered reply.

"Perhaps, as you say, I'm not acquainted with the customs of Mexico City." Her voice dripped honey laced with venom. "Maybe here dalliance is referred to as business."

"I do not know the meaning of this word *dalliance*, nor do I wish to. If I tell you I had important business matters to attend to, then that is what I was doing."

Alitha sighed. "All right, Esteban, tell me about this business. You've deliberately kept everything from me since we arrived here. Anyone would think you didn't trust me."

"What has trust to do with it? You are a woman and do not need to know. But, yes, you are right. The time for action is near and you must be told what will happen, what has been planned."

Alitha looked beyond him at the balcony door. "No, Esteban," she said. "Not now. I—I'm terribly tired. Do you know I hardly slept last night?"

He took her by the arm and led her to a chair, where he gently but firmly seated her.

"Women," he said, "I will never understand them. 'Tell me, Esteban.' 'No, don't tell me, Esteban.' My love, I will tell you and I will tell you now."

"Why don't we go downstairs? I'd so like a cup of chocolate."

"Downstairs? Where all the servants can overhear?" He crossed the room and pulled the bell cord. "What's wrong with you today, Alitha?" He smiled. "Is there, perhaps, a man hiding in your room?" She held her breath as he looked around him, playing the cuckold, finally dropping to one knee to look under the bed. "No," he said, "I was wrong. There is no one there."

Esteban rose to his feet and was brushing himself off when there was a tapping on the door.

"Chocolate for the *señorita, por favor,*" Esteban told Concepción. The maid curtsied and went out.

"All right, Esteban," Alitha said. "If you're through playacting, tell me what your business was all about."

"You may have heard that we were planning to sail to Spain."

"As a matter of fact, I have. Why am I the last to know? I've heard that it's common gossip in the cafés."

"It is common gossip because I want it to be common gossip." As he lowered his voice, she glanced toward the balcony. Did she see Jordan's shadow on the curtain? "In three days' time we leave Mexico for Vera Cruz," Esteban told her, "with our original party of five *vaqueros.* A ship sails from Vera Cruz in two weeks, bound for Havana and Spain."

"And we'll be on board?"

"No, the trip is a ruse to catch the rebels off guard. You see, the viceroy had bad news last week from the south, something the café gossips don't know as yet. General Iturbide, who was sent to fight the revolutionaries, is meeting with the rebel Guerrero instead. Viceroy Apodaca fears he's attempting to reach an understanding with him to combine their forces against the government. If this is true, it means Spanish rule in Mexico is almost at an end."

"What has that to do with us?"

"The Spaniards here in the capital have a great horde of gold hidden at the mint. They want to send that gold out of the country before it's too late."

"Montezuma's gold."

"You've been letting that fop Don Benito fill your head with fanciful tales. Where the gold comes from I don't know and don't care. But I do know the government is afraid to send it in a convoy to Vera Cruz for shipment to Spain, for fear the rebels will attack, overwhelm the Spanish troops and take the gold for themselves. As well they might. So they've devised a plan, a ruse. I, Esteban Mendoza, volunteered my services to help. Our services. We will conceal the gold in our equipage for the journey to Vera Cruz. Besides our five *vaqueros*, the government will supply a handful of outriders to accompany us, as they would in any case, to protect us from bandits. And in four days the gold will be in Vera Cruz, loaded aboard a ship bound for Spain, with the rebels none the wiser."

"And you and I? When the gold arrives, we'll leave Vera Cruz and not go on to Spain after all?"

"In truth, we won't even travel as far as Vera Cruz."

"I don't understand. If we're to deceive the revolutionaries, won't we have to go all the way to the ship with the gold? Otherwise they'll suspect we're not what we seem to be."

"Ah, but don't you see? I, Don Esteban Mendoza, will not be a party to this plot to smuggle gold out of Mexico to Spain. I will only pretend to be. How will the money help California once it is stored in the royal vaults in Madrid? The answer is simple: it will not."

"I've listened long enough to your riddles, Esteban. What *do* you plan to do?"

"I will play the Spanish game only in order to play another of my own. It will be like a box with a second smaller box inside, only this will be a ruse within a ruse. I'll take the gold—not I alone, but you and I, Alitha—and journey not to Vera Cruz on the east coast but to Acapulco on the west coast. And from Acapulco we'll sail for Santa Barbara with five hundred thousand dollars of gold. Enough gold to save California."

"And if you're caught?" She looked again at the door to the balcony. Was Jordan still there? Could he hear them? Surely Jordan, an American, had no interest in this plot.

"In Mexico," Esteban said, "the penalty for such an offense is death in front of a firing squad. If I'm caught, I'll die. So be it."

"Oh, Esteban." She ran to put her arms around him. "Is it worth it? Is the gold worth your life?"

"To me it is."

"It sounds so dangerous. Won't the troops be suspicious when you and I leave them on the road to Vera Cruz? Won't they stop us?"

"Ah, you'll have to wait and see how I manage it, my Alitha. My plan is dangerous but it can work. It will work." He smoothed her hair with his hand. "Alitha," he said, "your eyes keep going to the balcony. If I didn't know better—" he disengaged himself from her and strode across the room— "I'd suspect there was someone hiding there."

She ran after him, clutching at his arm, but he shook her off. He threw open the double doors and stepped outside, with Alitha a pace behind him. The balcony was deserted. He looked down into the courtyard. There was no one in sight. Alitha sighed with relief. Jordan was safe.

"I'm sorry, my Alitha," Esteban said, coming back into the room and closing the doors behind him. "This business of the gold has made me see spies everywhere.

My humblest apologies. After all, if I can't trust you, whom can I trust?"

"So last night," she said, "after the ball, you were planning this gold-smuggling venture?"

"Of a certainty."

"And this dancer, this Coralilla. What possible role can she play in your plan?"

"You will see, my dove. Wait and you will see. She plays a most important part."

Alitha wanted to believe him, in fact she willed herself to believe him. But once again she pictured the scene in the ballroom as Esteban wrapped the dancer's veil around his waist.

"Perhaps," Alitha said, "La Coralilla can signal the approach of bandits or revolutionaries by discarding some of her veils. One if by land and two if by sea. She would certainly attract the eyes of all the men if she did."

She whirled away from Esteban, imitating Coralilla's coquetry. "Six?" she asked, simpering. She fingered the top button of her gown. "Six," she said, undoing the button. "Five?" She unfastened the next button, exposing the swell of her breasts. She fluttered her eyelashes at Esteban. "Four?" she asked.

"Enough," Esteban said, "I'm tired of your suspicions. As I'm weary of your games." He came toward her, and she saw that he intended to take her in his arms, to smother her protests with his kisses.

She ran from him into the corridor, slamming the bedroom door behind her. As she crossed the hall, she saw Concepción approaching with a tray. Shaking her head at the maid, she ran into another bedroom, where she threw herself on a chaise longue. She heard the minutes tick by on the mantel clock. The door opened and she looked up to see Esteban just inside the room.

"Come here to me," he told her.

She rose but stood beside the chaise. Esteban hesitated, then crossed the room and enfolded her in his arms. "For me," he said, "there is no one in this world but you, Alitha."

If only I could believe him, she thought. As always when he held her, her heart beat faster and warm excitement rose inside her. What if he were caught trying to carry out his wild scheme? She closed her eyes and clung to him.

chapter 18

ON THE MORNING of their departure for Vera Cruz, Alitha was up at four. She drank hot chocolate, put on her *manga* and went to the courtyard to watch the preparations for the journey. The horses were saddled, the mules loaded and, when one was found to be lame, another was brought from the stable. Don Esteban arrived leading two more mules, laden, Alitha knew, with gold from the government mint.

They left the city by moonlight, passing along the broad and silent streets, the old buildings of Mexico City on either side of them, the spires of the ancient churches rising against the sky. In front of one church Alitha saw what appeared to her to be a statue of a kneeling figure bowed in prayer, but as they drew closer, she realized it was an old man kneeling motionless and silent on the pavement. He must be performing a penance, she told herself, for his sins and, perhaps, the sins of all the world.

"Pray for me," she whispered, "pray for all of us."

With the coming of dawn she saw the city gradually change before her eyes. The streets, so grand in the darkness, were in actuality littered with refuse; the seemingly splendid buildings were more often than not abandoned and in a state of decay, victims of time and of the revolutionary turmoil of the last ten years. The people who thronged the streets with the coming of the new day were mostly beggars—*leparos,* ragged and dirty, their bodies covered with sores.

Alitha closed her eyes, wanting to remember Mexico City as it had been in the silvered, moonlit darkness. Sitting sidesaddle, both hands on the pommel, she drowsed as she listened to the steady beat of the horses' hooves, the plodding rhythm of the mules, the creak of saddles, the jingle of spurs and the occasional words exchanged by the *vaqueros.* She was glad to be leaving the city, she told herself. Perhaps once they were underway she and Esteban could find what they seemed to have lost; perhaps they could recapture the soaring rapture of their journey south from Santa Barbara.

What had gone wrong?

Esteban seemed so different now, so changed. Were there really two Estebans, almost as different from one another as day from night? One the Esteban who had fought the wounded grizzly for her; the other the Esteban who appeared to be entranced by the wiles of La Coralilla. It was as though, Alitha told herself, she had been living in a moonlit world after she first met Esteban, a silvered world of love, and then quite gradually—so gradually that she had not realized at first what was happening—the sun had risen and everything had changed without her being aware of it. In the warm glow of love, she had ignored the decay and the cracks, but now she could ignore them no longer.

They passed through the gates of the city and, after climbing to the top of a hill, paused to look back at the valley just as the sun rose in the east. She saw the towers of the city, the lakes veiled by low clouds of vapor rising slowly from their surfaces, and the white summits of the two volcanoes still enveloped in mist. Mexico was so beautiful, she thought. What a magnificent yet troubled land.

As they rode on toward Puebla, she watched Esteban as six mounted lancers joined them, three of the uniformed cavalrymen riding ahead and three forming a rear guard some distance behind. How masterful Esteban seemed as he led their small troop forward. How graceful he was, how brave. Yet how cruel he could be, she thought, able to wound her with an unwitting word or glance. She sighed, realizing he could never be anything other than what he was.

How clearly she saw his faults now; how blind she had been to them when she had been at the Mendoza *rancho*. She had loved him, and, they said, love was blind. Did that mean she no longer loved Esteban? Alitha shook her head, refusing to answer the question.

A picture of Thomas's face came unbidden to her mind, and she remembered the night he'd asked her to marry him. Winter, a church sleigh-ride party, the gay jingle of bells on the trotting horses and the crisp swish of the runners on the snow. She recalled the innocent thrill of their first kiss—Thomas's face had been as cold as hers, but his lips were warm. At that moment she'd been certain of their love for one another.

How little she had known then! Alitha shook her head. Was she so much wiser now?

They passed an Indian with a blanket thrown over one shoulder, a farmer riding a mule, an old beggar in rags basking in the sun on a stone seat in a village doorway, an Indian woman with matted hair and a baby strapped to her back drinking *pulque* from an earthen jar, a portly friar smiling benevolently as he was greeted by a group of urchins, who removed their large, well-worn hats and shouted, *"Buenos días, padrecito."*

So like Mexico, so charming. Then why did she long to be somewhere else? She imagined herself on board ship, a fair wind at her back, the ocean's salt spray on her face as she sailed to . . . To where?

How could she think of leaving Esteban? Life without him would have no meaning for her. How her body tingled even now as she thought of being enfolded in the circle of his arms, with his bare flesh to hers, his lips meeting her lips while her passion rose to meet and join his. No other man could ever give her such pleasure.

As they entered a village, she saw fields of *maguey,* the fleshy-leafed plant from which the Indians made the liquor *pulque.* Esteban was like a heady draught of *pulque,* she thought, harsh and bitter yet intoxicating. Esteban—enough of Esteban!

She forced her attention to the scattering of village houses, the marketplace, the parish church, the narrow lanes, the Indian huts. She saw a profusion of pink and red roses, a bridge crossing a stream, scattered clusters of trees and a few larger houses where wealthy Mexicans came from the city in the summer to live behind grated windows amidst their gardens and orchards. Beside the road she noticed garlands of flowers lying against crosses. The crosses, Esteban had told her, might commemorate a murder or might have been erected as an act of piety.

Above her the sun shone brightly from the bluest sky she had ever seen. Now, in November, the days were as warm and invigorating as a May morning back home in New England.

"This part of Mexico," Esteban had said, "is a land of eternal spring." Esteban again. She found it impossible to put him from her mind.

During the afternoon they sighted horsemen following them at a distance. The other riders halted on a ridge and watched as they passed but made no attempt to approach.

"Bandits?" she asked Esteban.

"In all probability," he told her. "But no bandits are bold enough to attack a well-armed group such as ours. They may be ruthless, but they're not fools."

They entered Puebla in the evening, riding through the spacious plaza and past the magnificent cathedral to an inn on the far outskirts of the city. Alitha was tired from the long ride—she felt the first faint throbs of a headache—so after a supper of soup, fish, steak and frijoles, all well seasoned with garlic and oil, she went to bed and immediately fell asleep.

Voices awakened her. Rising on one elbow, she saw that the single window of her room was still black. The voices came from the next room, Don Esteban's room. Alitha threw a shawl around her shoulders and crept to the door on bare feet. The voices were so low she couldn't make out the words, nor could she tell who was speaking.

Then she heard a woman's deep, husky laugh. Alitha drew in her breath. She'd know that laugh anywhere. Coralilla was in the next room. Esteban's room.

Alitha raised the latch and threw open the door. La Coralilla stood facing her, wearing a blond wig. Esteban's back was to her.

"Esteban!" she cried.

The man turned and Alitha stepped back, startled. It

wasn't Esteban after all. Though the man had a small mustache as Esteban had, and though he was Esteban's height and build and coloring, the man most definitely was not Don Esteban Mendoza.

"*Muy bien.* Very good."

Alitha whirled to see Esteban in the room's other doorway, nodding with satisfaction.

"If we were able to deceive you from a distance of only a few feet," he said to Alitha, "we'll have no trouble deceiving the Spaniards."

Only then did she realize that the stranger not only resembled Esteban but was dressed as Esteban had been the day before. She looked at Coralilla again. The dancer wore a riding hat and *manga* of the same style and color as Alitha's own. They certainly didn't become her, Alitha thought. In fact, Coralilla looked much older than she had at the ball.

So that was Esteban's plan, Alitha told herself. While she and Esteban rode west to Acapulco with the gold, these two would replace them for the remainder of the journey to Vera Cruz. That was Esteban's ruse within a ruse.

She smiled at Esteban. So Coralilla *was* an essential part of his plot to outwit the Spaniards, just as he had claimed. Coralilla was to take her, Alitha's, place. She wanted to run to Esteban, throw her arms about him and tell him she should never have doubted him. She *would* tell him, she promised herself, once they were alone.

After a hurried breakfast of eggs, well-fried chicken, bread and coffee, Esteban led her to the shadowed rear of the inn, where he lifted her into the saddle.

"We'll travel light but with much speed," he told her. "You and I and the two horses carrying the gold. There will be risks, of a certainty, grave risks—bandits, revolutionaries. Are you certain you wish to come with me?"

"Oh yes," she said. "I'd rather face danger with you than be safe anywhere else."

"Good. *Un momento.*" Esteban walked quickly back to the inn.

A moment. The words Doña Anise had used when talking of La Coralilla and Esteban.

Alitha dismounted and ran to the partly open kitchen door. A single candle glowed on the table, and by its light she saw a man and woman clasped in one another's arms. Esteban and Coralilla. It was all she could do to stop from flinging herself at them. Trembling, she closed her eyes and drew in a shuddering breath. Finally controlling herself, she turned and stumbled back to her horse and mounted, and when Esteban returned a minute later, she was sitting just as he had left her.

Esteban swung into his saddle and looked across at her. "Are you ready, my Alitha?" he asked.

"Yes," she said, her voice cold.

She found she had no tears left; he would never make her cry again. Instead she was furious, hurt and angry. Coralilla wasn't only taking her place today on the journey to Vera Cruz, Alitha thought bitterly, she had taken her place at least once before. In Esteban's arms.

Had Coralilla taken Alitha's place in his heart as well? No, she didn't think so. Doña Anise had probably been right when she said that, for Esteban, Coralilla was a thing of the moment. But passing fancy or not, Alitha knew that her love for Esteban could never be the same again.

The road from the city of Puebla to the small village of Río Frío passes through flat and fertile farmland.

Río Frío—Cold River—is in a valley surrounded by woods. Beyond the village the way becomes hilly and even more densely wooded as the trail enters a tract of somber oaks, pines and cedars known locally as the Black Forest. Only an occasional cluster of wildflowers growing in a forest glade brightens the dark and gloomy green of the woods.

It was in the Black Forest that Jordan Quinn intended to ambush Don Esteban.

Jordan lay concealed amid thick brush at the top of a hill thirty feet above a particularly narrow stretch of trail where horses were forced to proceed in single file between the trees. From where he lay he could also see, across a valley and through a gap in the woods, a length of trail two miles farther back. He would have more than adequate forewarning of anyone riding from Puebla and Río Frío.

The chance that Don Esteban would pass this way, Jordan calculated, was better than four out of five. The best and quickest route to Acapulco lay three leagues nearer Mexico City so, with Esteban having every wish to stay as far away from the capital as possible, he would have to ride through Río Frío and into the Black Forest.

Jordan glanced at the rifle lying on the ground beside him. At a range of thirty feet he could kill Don Esteban with one shot. Mightn't Esteban bring some of his *vaqueros* with him? What then? Jordan thought it more than likely that he would find Esteban and Alitha traveling alone, for that had been his impression from the conversation he had overheard while he stood on the balcony of Esteban's house, before he had been forced to climb to the roof and lie hidden while Esteban searched for him. But even if Esteban brought men with him, Jordan still had the advantage of surprise and an easily defended position.

He saw movement on the distant section of the trail. Raising a spyglass to his eyes, Jordan swept it across thick-growing pines to the open glade. There were two riders, a dark man and a woman, the pair leading two heavily laden horses. Jordan smiled. Good. Even though the woman's hair was covered by a shawl, he recognized Esteban and Alitha. He slowly swept the glass back and forth along the trail, looking for other riders. Finding none, he lowered the glass, returned it to its case and settled down to wait.

It would take Don Esteban at least thirty minutes to reach the narrow trail below him. Impatient, Jordan raised the rifle to his shoulder, sighted and imagined squeezing the trigger. In his mind he saw Esteban jerk back and fall, thrown from his horse by the impact of the bullet. He pictured Esteban lying motionless on the trail as Alitha slid to the ground, ran and knelt beside him, cradling his head in her arms.

Jordan imagined her turning from Esteban's body and looking up at him as he approached to make sure Esteban was dead. He recognized the look in her eyes as one of implacable hatred. As Jordan stared down at the circle of dark blood staining the Californio's jacket, Esteban's eyes seemed to look up accusingly at him.

Damn it, Jordan told himself, he had no choice but to kill Esteban Mendoza, kill him as quickly and cleanly as he could and then bury his body. Esteban had to disappear from the face of the earth, the victim, or so everyone would believe, of bandits or revolutionaries.

If Esteban lived, he would pursue Jordan relentlessly. One of them must die. Better it be Esteban; better that Esteban die here and now. If Jordan succeeded, the Californios would be denied the gold—the money would be his, Jordan's. Just as Alitha would be his.

Jordan ran his hand along the wooden stock of the rifle. He would kill Esteban with his first shot.

He heard the steady clop-clop of the approaching horses before he saw them. He raised the rifle and aimed at the spot between two pines where Esteban would emerge from the woods. Yes, there he was, dressed in black, with a wide-brimmed hat set rakishly on his head, his eyes darting from side to side, perhaps suspecting an ambush. Jordan sighted on Esteban's chest and his finger tightened on the trigger.

From the corner of his eye, he saw Alitha follow Esteban from the trees, riding sidesaddle, her golden hair hidden by her shawl, her lovely face expressionless as she stared straight ahead, looking as though her thoughts were miles away. Jordan caught his breath, struck by her beauty as he always was, as he had been on that foggy morning when he first saw her on the deck of the *Flying Yankee* in Valparaiso.

Jordan shook his head to banish thoughts of Alitha from his mind and sighted on Esteban. Again Jordan's finger tightened on the trigger, again he pictured Esteban falling to the ground, mortally wounded. All at once Jordan lowered the rifle. Goddamn it, he thought, I can't shoot him down in cold blood. He watched as Esteban drew nearer—the Californio would pass almost directly below his hiding place—and realized that all he had so carefully planned was slipping away.

Without giving himself time to think, Jordan raised the rifle and fired. Esteban's horse shuddered and fell with a bullet through its eye, but Esteban leaped clear of the horse at the last minute, falling to the rocky ground. Jordan, pulling his neckerchief up to cover his lower face, sprang from the concealing brush, reloading as he scrambled down the hill toward Esteban, who was lying stunned on the trail.

Esteban staggered to his feet and stared dazedly at Jordan. The Californio's hand went to his belt, only to discover that his pistol was not there. Jordan saw it lying a few feet away from where he had fallen. Esteban took his knife from its sheath, advancing on Jordan as though oblivious of the rifle in the American's hands.

"Esteban! Don't!"

Esteban, confused, glanced at Alitha, and as he did, Jordan kicked out at him, his boot striking Esteban's hand and sending the knife flying into the brush. Esteban leaped at him, his arms outstretched, but Jordan stepped aside at the last moment and brought the butt of the rifle thudding down on the back of Esteban's head. The Californio grunted, staggered forward, then collapsed to the ground and lay still.

Alitha slid from her saddle and ran to Esteban, cradling his head in her arms exactly as Jordan had pictured her doing. She stood up and Jordan saw that she had retrieved Esteban's pistol and now grasped the gun in both of her hands, pointing it at his chest.

As Jordan walked toward her, he drew the neckerchief down from his face.

"You!"

Alitha's hands wavered. Jordan gripped the gun by the barrel and twisted it from her hands.

"You killed him," she said.

Jordan put the pistol into his belt and knelt beside Esteban. The Californio's color was good and his breathing was firm and regular.

"No, he's not dead. Far from it."

Jordan went to one of the pack horses, returned with

a length of rope and bound Esteban's hands and feet.
Alitha watched him in mute anger. When he had
finished, Jordan placed the muzzle of the pistol to
Esteban's knee.

Alitha gasped. She ran to Jordan and grasped his
hand, pushing the gun to one side.

"What are you doing?" she demanded.

"I have to lame him to make sure he's in no condition
to follow us."

"Us?"

"I intend to take you with me as a hostage. I could
have killed him a few minutes ago; I was a fool not to.
Now I have to make sure he won't kill me."

"I'll not go with you. I'll fight you every step of the
way if you try to take me with you by force. You'll have
to cripple me as well as Esteban."

Jordan cocked the pistol.

"Wait," she said desperately, her eyes glistening with
tears. "If I give you my word I'll cause you no trouble,
if I go with you willingly, will you spare him? Esteban
couldn't bear to live as a cripple. He'd rather you killed
him here and now."

Jordan hesitated. He'd already spared Esteban's life.
To leave him unharmed and able to pursue him and the
gold would be the height of folly.

"For my sake," Alitha said.

Jordan thrust the pistol back in his belt.

"Get ready to ride," he told her. He climbed the
slope, going past the place where he had waited in
ambush and into the trees.

Alitha brought a canteen of water from her saddle,
took a handkerchief and wet the cloth and used it to
wipe the blood from Esteban's head wound. She held
the canteen to his mouth, but his lips remained closed,
so the water ran along his cheek and dribbled to the

ground. Placing the canteen at his side, she bent down and kissed him gently on the lips.

"Esteban," she said. "I did all I could."

She remembered opening her eyes long ago near the Santa Barbara Indian village and seeing Esteban for the first time, remembered thinking she had never seen a handsomer man.

"Esteban, my love," she whispered.

She rose and went to Esteban's dead horse, took the pistol hidden in his saddlebag. Hearing a sound behind her and realizing that she didn't have time to load the pistol, she thrust it into her own saddlebag. She turned to see Jordan ride from among the trees. He reined in next to her and dismounted, coming toward her to lift her into the saddle.

"Don't touch me," she told him. Her voice was like ice. "I'll come with you because I promised I would, but if you ever touch me, Captain Quinn, I swear to God I'll kill you."

chapter 19

THEY RODE FROM the forest in silence. When they came to a crossroad, Jordan reined in and looked at Alitha. She knew he wanted to ask her which route she and Esteban had intended to take so she turned her head away, determined to keep silent. Jordan said nothing.

After a moment he swung his horse to the left, and soon they were climbing along the side of a mountain on a trail winding among great volcanic rocks. When they reached a treeless crest, Alitha had a sweeping view ahead and behind her of farmland and wilderness, while to her left were villages with their groves and gardens. To her right rose the higher reaches of the mountain, with its dark forest of pines.

They met few other travelers and those eyed them warily, not speaking, riding faster until they were past. As they alternately descended into and climbed from a series of *barrancas,* narrow rocky ravines, Alitha noticed that one of their pack horses was favoring its right foreleg. Glancing at Jordan, she almost told him but then closed her lips in a tight line. She'd be damned if she'd lift a finger to help him!

She closed her eyes, picturing Esteban as they'd left him, bound and unconscious beside the trail, and murmured a prayer for him. Would she ever see him again? Her heart ached to be with him, and yet she couldn't hide from herself the release she also felt.

No longer did she have to glance at Esteban, wondering if he approved of what she wore or what she said and did, ready to brace herself against his disapproval. She could say the things she felt without thinking first of how Esteban would receive her words. No longer would she have to try to fit herself into his narrow code of feminine behavior, his unseen but definitely drawn line of what was right and wrong. Yes, if she was to be truthful to herself, she'd have to admit that Esteban never had and never would treat her as equal to him. She knew she couldn't have stayed with him much longer.

How free she was now! Yet she still missed Esteban terribly, and for some strange reason she felt guilty, as though to be free was wrong. Why is it wrong, she asked herself. I *am* free. From this time forward I mean to be beholden to no one but myself.

They stopped in a grove of pines off the trail and ate dried beef and drank wine. When Jordan spoke to her, Alitha turned her head, and he soon fell silent. As she remounted, she saw him watching her with frank admiration, and her hand briefly caressed the leather flap on her saddle where she'd hidden Esteban's pistol. She couldn't harm Jordan without provocation, but she knew that if he touched her, she meant to kill him.

Shortly after they left the grove of trees, the pack horse that had been favoring his foreleg began limping noticeably.

"Damn," Jordan said, slowing their pace.

He has no choice, Alitha thought, but to go on, hoping for the best while trying to replace the injured animal in one of the Indian villages along the way. She also knew that horses were scarce because of the banditry and the fighting.

They were riding along a dusty trail with a sloping field rising to their left when a horseman rode from the trees at the field's upper boundary some two hundred feet above them. The man, lean and dark and wearing a black sombrero, rode parallel to their trail while glancing down at them from time to time. She saw Jordan's hand slide along the stock of his rifle as he urged his horse on.

Another rider came from the trees into the field. As soon as he had galloped past the first man, he slowed his pace to match theirs. Alitha felt her heart begin to pound as she spurred her horse to a trail lope.

"Bandits," Jordan said.

A third rider left the woods on the hill above them and followed the first two. Alitha's gaze searched the trees but she saw no more men. All at once the lead rider spurred his horse to a gallop until he was well past Jordan, then raised a musket over his head and, at the signal, all three men wheeled down the hill and galloped toward them.

"Cut the pack horses loose," Alitha shouted to Jordan. "Let them have the gold."

Jordan shook his head. "This way," he called to her and wheeled his horse to the right down a steep slope. They rode in and out of a gully and over a rise into a waterless *arroyo*, a dry creek bed, the pack horses scrambling after them. Behind them she heard horses' hooves thudding on the hard-packed earth and the shouts of the bandits.

The lame pack horse stumbled and fell. With a curse Jordan reined in, waving her past him as he cut the rope leading to the fallen animal. He sprang to the ground and opened a pack on the horse's back, and Alitha saw the glint of gold in the sunlight.

She spurred her horse up the side of the *arroyo* to the crest of a small hill, stopping and waiting a short distance farther on until Jordan, leading the other pack horse, joined her.

"This way," she said, pointing to a defile between the high rocks ahead of them.

"No." Jordan clambered to the ground and looped the reins of his horse around a dead branch. "Get down," he ordered her.

She hesitated, but when she saw him start toward her, she swung from her horse. Jordan, using his rifle to motion her to follow him, climbed back to the top of the rise, where he threw himself to the ground. Alitha dropped to her knees and crawled up to lie beside him.

Below them the injured pack horse lay on his side on the rocky bottom of the dry creek bed. As they watched, the horse tried to struggle to his feet but with a whinny of pain he fell back, his legs kicking futilely in the air. Gold coins and jewelry lay scattered on the ground near the open pack.

"They'll find the gold," she whispered.

"I intend them to," Jordan said.

The first of the three black-garbed riders crested the hill at the top of the *arroyo*. The rider, seeing the fallen horse, rode cautiously down the gully with his eyes scanning the silent rocks on both sides of him.

"Do you know how to use this?" Jordan handed her a pistol.

Alitha nodded, grasping the gun in both hands.

"It's loaded," Jordan told her. "Here's the fixings to reload. Can you do that, too?"

"Yes."

The second rider came into view farther up the *arroyo*, and they heard the hoofbeats of the third horseman off to their right.

"*Oro!* Gold!" The first rider rode into the creek bed, leaped from his horse and reached into the pack, his hands coming out clutching gold ornaments and coins.

"*Oro!*" he shouted again to his two companions. They spurred their horses toward him.

"When I tell you," Jordan said, "shoot the man kneeling next to our horse. Shoot to kill."

"I can't . . ." she began.

"Do as I tell you," he insisted, "or they'll kill us both. Or worse."

The other two men dismounted and ran to where the first rider was scooping gold from the injured horse's pack. They knelt on either side of him and plunged their hands into the pack, laughing and talking loudly.

"Now," Jordan said.

He fired as he spoke and the bandit on the left spun around and fell to the ground. Holding her pistol in both hands, Alitha pulled the trigger and the gun bucked back. She saw the center man jerk upright, a black hole in the upper shoulder of his jacket. The man on the right whirled about, his musket in hand. A bullet zinged past Alitha's head, and she smelled the acrid odor of gunpowder. The man she had wounded was firing now, and a bullet struck a rock a few feet from her and ricocheted away.

Jordan fired again. The man on the right dropped his

rifle, grasped his stomach with both hands and plunged face first to the ground. The bandit with the shoulder wound fired again, wildly this time, then turned and ran to his horse and leaped into the saddle.

Jordan came quickly to his feet and stood taking careful aim as the bandit, riding low in the saddle, urged his horse up the *arroyo*. Jordan fired, and as the man spun from the horse to the ground, his foot caught in the stirrup and he was dragged until his body struck a boulder and he tumbled free to lie motionless in the dust. His riderless horse galloped on out of sight.

Grunting with satisfaction, Jordan scrambled down into the gully with his rifle reloaded and ready. He used the toe of his boot to turn the three men over. As she watched, Alitha felt bile rise in her throat and she stumbled a few steps away, where she leaned against a boulder and was sick.

When she returned to the gully, Jordan had pulled the three bodies into a ditch, where they lay piled on top of one another in a grotesque tangle of arms and legs. He began covering the bodies with rocks as she stared first at him and then at the three dead men. She had shot one of these men, she reminded herself. Perhaps she hadn't killed him, but she knew she had meant to. She shook her head.

"That last man," she said to Jordan, "the one who rode off. Did you have to kill him, too?"

Jordan finished piling rocks on the bodies before he answered. "If I hadn't killed him," he said, "he'd have spread the news of the gold from here to Mexico City. Every bandit, revolutionary and government soldier in the country would have been on our trail. Besides, don't you think they would have done the same if they had managed to ambush us?" When she didn't answer, he asked again, "Don't you?"

"I suppose they would have," she said. She slumped down to sit on a boulder facing away from the grave.

Jordan came up behind her, his hand gripping her shoulder so tightly she winced. "Listen to me," he said angrily. "We're in a foreign country in the middle of a revolution, carrying a fortune in gold in our packs. Do you think bandits are going to stop and ask for our calling cards or that we should do the same?"

When she didn't answer, he swung her around and tilted her face up so that she was forced to look at him. "This is American gold now, and you and I are going to see that it gets to Acapulco and aboard a ship bound for the States. If you're not going to help, I'll go on alone. I don't have the time to wait while you sit around feeling sorry for yourself."

As she stared up at him, a seething rage coursed through her. I shot one of those bandits, she told herself; what does he mean about not helping? He's being unfair. She took a deep breath. That's what he wants, to make me angry, she thought. I won't give him the satisfaction.

Brushing his hand aside, she stood up, hiding her clenched fists in the folds of her gown. Her eyes stung with tears she refused to shed. She longed to strike out at him, to hurt him, while at the same time she longed to have someone comfort her. She turned away and stared up at the barren rock hill and the pine-covered mountain beyond.

"Do you understand what I'm telling you?" Jordan demanded.

"I quite understand." She faced him and spoke as calmly as she could. "I'm ready to ride when you are."

Jordan looked at her for a long moment; then he drew in his breath and let it out slowly. "At least we've gained a new pack horse," he said finally, "and an extra mount besides." He nodded at the bandits' two horses farther down the *arroyo*. "Come along," he told her, "and help me reload the gold."

By three that afternoon they were descending into the tropical lowlands, the *tierra caliente*. The country grew more arid and the heat became so intense that they were forced to stop near the trickle of a stream and rest until the sun dropped behind the mountains. They went on in the half-light of early evening along a road winding through a succession of boulder-strewn badlands and woods. After they passed an Indian village of cane cottages in an oasis of flowering shrubs, the country became even drier, with the only trees an infrequent palm or two.

As the sky darkened overhead and the first stars appeared, Jordan called a halt. They made camp off the trail on flat ground sheltered by huge boulders. Afraid to attract attention by building a fire, they ate bread, cheese and dried beef.

"Listen," Alitha said.

They heard a muted rumbling from a great distance. Thunder? Alitha wondered. Or gunfire? She glanced at Jordan's dark form seated a few feet from her.

"A storm in the mountains," he said, and in a few minutes she saw lightning, not jagged streaks but a dim, pulsing glow above the horizon.

"Good night, Alitha," Jordan said. When she looked, she could no longer see him in the darkness and knew he must be lying on his pallet.

"Good night," she said tonelessly.

She lay on her back, pulling a blanket to her chin as she felt a chill breeze sweep between the boulders. She stared overhead at the stars, reliving in her mind the long journey from California to Mexico with Esteban. She remembered making love beside a stream after

Esteban had soaped her body, remembered watching
the sailors throwing the hides from the cliff at San Juan
Capistrano, remembered reaching out for Esteban in
the night and feeling him enfold and comfort her as his
hands moved along her body, teasing and caressing her
at the same time.

She closed her eyes, imagining she was with him
again, not the Esteban of these last weeks in Mexico
but Esteban as he had been at first, loving and
attentive. And passionate. She sighed as she drifted
toward sleep.

She heard a slithering sound somewhere in the
darkness to her left. Opening her eyes, she drew in and
held her breath. As they had entered the *tierra caliente*
earlier in the day, she had seen lizards scurrying away
from the hooves of their horses to seek shelter in
crevices in the rocks. Now she remembered Esteban
telling her of the many and varied venomous creatures
that thrived in the hot country.

"There are the scorpions," he had said, "whose tails
carry poison deadly to a young child or to an old
person, so you must always examine your bed and the
walls of your room before you extinguish your candle.
Then there is the *vinagrillo*, an insect like a large
cricket, orange in color and always smelling of vinegar.
And spiders without number, one in particular whose
body is red and black and whose bite sends pain into all
your bones. And, of course, there is the tarantula."
Alitha had shivered when he said the word. "The
tarantula is soft and fat and covered with dark hairs like
a great ugly beast. And the coral snakes and the
rattlers."

Again she heard the slithering and imagined snakes
and scorpions crawling toward her in the dark night.

"Jordan," she whispered urgently.

"Jordan," she said again. When he didn't answer, she repeated his name a third time, more loudly than before. She heard him stir, then sit up abruptly.

"What is it?"

"Listen," she told him. A moment later the sound came again, nearer than before.

Jordan stood and lit a lantern, and she heard him tramping about in the scrub brush near their sleeping place. She heard the sound of rocks scattering, and then it was quiet. When Jordan returned, he stood over her with the light from the lantern mottling his unshaven face.

"Just a lizard," he said. "I used a stick to toss him away from the camp."

"Oh," she said. She lay back on her pallet in some embarrassment. Jordan continued looking down at her. "Thank you," she said. "I'm not usually so—so nervous."

He extinguished the lantern, and she heard him return to his pallet. Why did she always encounter Jordan Quinn at the wrong time and in the wrong place, she wondered. In other circumstances she might have liked him. She shook her head. It was their fate, she thought, to meet and then go their separate ways, following their separate destinies.

"Jordan," she said, "why are you in Mexico? Why were you at Chapultepec Hill?"

She heard him sigh, but when he said nothing, she turned on her side, looking away from him, thinking he wasn't going to answer.

"I'd been following Don Esteban the night before," he said at last. "I lost him after he left the costume ball, or rather he lost me, and so I was watching his house the next morning when I saw you leave with Don Benito. I followed you, thinking you'd lead me to Esteban, but instead you led me up Chapultepec Hill."

"You were following Esteban? What on earth for?"

Jordan hesitated, then, seeming to make up his mind, told her of his meeting with the American navy captain in Santa Barbara and of his own trip south by ship to Acapulco, carefully omitting any mention of Thomas Heath. The missionary couldn't have survived the yellow fever, sick as he'd been when Jordan had left him in the Acapulco convent hospital.

"Then, in Mexico City," Jordan told her, "the American consul alerted me to the rumors of a plot to smuggle gold out of the country to Spain. The café gossip had it that Don Esteban was one of the ringleaders."

Esteban would never have told me if he hadn't needed my help, Alitha said to herself, yet everyone else knew what was going on. Everybody except me!

"The shipment to Spain," Jordan said, "was none of my concern, but I suspected that Don Esteban might have his own plans for the gold. Which he did. So the gold became my concern. I have to keep it out of the hands of the Californios. You know the rest—how I was lucky enough to be able to overhear Esteban when he told you of his plan. His ruse, I think he called it."

Alitha lay listening to the sounds of the night. She imagined Jordan smiling in the darkness, for he had managed a ruse of his own. Gold means so much to men, she thought. They kill for gold, risk their lives for gold, and it's really so unimportant.

She must have fallen asleep, for when she opened her eyes, the night was brighter and she saw a crescent moon overhead. Certain that a voice had awakened her, she sat up, listening. Yes, Jordan's voice. What was he saying? As she strained to hear, she realized he was talking in his sleep. All at once he groaned, and she threw off her blanket and rose to her feet. A name, that was it, he was repeating a name over and over.

"Margarita."

He moaned as though in pain, and Alitha knelt beside him. Suddenly he shouted hoarsely and she shrank back, startled. His moaning resumed and again he muttered the name. "Margarita."

Alitha reached down and shook his shoulder. He muttered something, turning away, so she shook him harder. With an oath Jordan sprang to his feet, sending her sprawling to the ground. She got up, backing away.

"You—you were having a nightmare," she told him.

"I should have warned you." He stood a few feet from her, his face shadowed by the moonlight. "I often dream. At times I dread going to sleep because of the dreams."

"Do you want to tell me about them?"

When he didn't answer, she said, "You were repeating Margarita's name over and over in your sleep."

He drew in a long breath. "I still can't believe she's dead," he said quietly, sadly. "She was so alive and vibrant, so young; she had her whole life to live. Until I killed her." He kicked at the ground and dirt sprayed into the dry undergrowth.

"You mustn't blame yourself," Alitha said. "You didn't kill her, Bouchard and his men did."

"If she hadn't sailed with me, he wouldn't have had the chance. It's all so senseless. Why did she have to die? There was no reason for her to die, none at all. It would have been a thousand times better if I had died in her stead." He reached down and she saw that he was picking a handful of rocks from the ground.

"Why?" he shouted into the night. He hurled a rock into the blackness. The rock struck a boulder and thudded to the ground. "Why did you let her die? Why did you?" He flung rock after rock into the darkness. When she heard him sob, she went to him and he turned and gripped her arm so fiercely she cried out.

"Tell me, Alitha. Why? Why did God, if God there be, let Margarita die? Answer me. Why did He?"

"God works in mysterious . . ."

"No! I've heard that evasion too often. I don't want to be told that I can't understand God's ways now but that someday, in the hereafter, perhaps, I will. That answer's for children. I'm a man and I want to know. I deserve to know."

"Why do you deserve to know?" she asked softly, "when no one else knows either?"

He released her, and she watched him walk to his pallet and throw himself down. She wanted to run to Jordan, to kneel beside him to hold and comfort him. With a shiver she remembered holding Esteban in her arms only hours ago, after Jordan had almost killed him.

Alitha sighed and lay on her *petate* to stare up at the stars. Jordan's question echoed in her mind.

"Why?"

chapter 20

JORDAN REINED IN his horse at the top of a rise and watched Alitha as she rode to join him. Damn, but she was beautiful. He never tired of looking at her. Not because of her hair, though its soft blondness made him want to reach out and touch it; not because of her eyes, though they seemed to change from one entrancing shade of blue to another; not because of her fair skin, nor her small yet sensuous mouth, nor her full figure.

No, none of her features in and of themselves so intrigued him. Rather it was Alitha herself, the harmony of her features, her steadfast good cheer, her spirit, her intelligence. The reason, he thought, mattered little; all that was important to him was that she held him in thrall more than any other woman ever had.

Even more than Margarita? Despite a twinge of guilt—the feeling that he was betraying his beloved Margarita—he admitted the truth to himself: Alitha had come to mean more to him even than Margarita.

Alitha stopped beside him, and they looked around

at the desolate landscape. A steep slope rose to their right, and a ravine fell away to their left.

"We're entering rebel territory," Jordan said, deliberately keeping his eyes on the vista before him, tempted though he was to stare admiringly at Alitha. "I saw fighting not far south of here on my way from Acapulco to Mexico City last month. The rebel general Guerrero was raiding government convoys sent to bring supplies to their outposts in the provinces. Guerrero had his men under control for the most part, but there was so much killing and looting that the rich landlords were abandoning their haciendas and fleeing to their homes in the cities till the fighting ended."

"That may be soon," Alitha said. "If what Esteban heard is true, then the viceroy's own general, Iturbide, will make peace with the revolutionaries. Without consulting the viceroy. With the idea that he might eventually join the rebels against the Spaniards. If General Iturbide does, Esteban said it would mean a quick end to the war."

"Once a revolution succeeds," Jordan said, "you have rejoicing in the streets for a time and then a short while later the revolutionaries begin quarreling over the spoils and there's more fighting and bloodshed, until the people forget their grand-sounding slogans as well as the reasons they fought the war in the first place. That's when they look for a man on a white horse, a strong leader to bring peace to the country. The result is that a tyrant takes over. Like Napolean. The same will happen here. The only question is who the tyrant will be. Guerrero? Iturbide? Santa Anna?"

"You're too cynical. Look at the United States. We fought a revolution without a civil war afterward. And without a tyrant."

"The army wanted Washington to become king,"

Jordan said, "but he turned them down. America's the exception, not the rule. Mexico won't be an exception; the army's too strong here, too powerful. The first revolt ten years ago was led by priests like Hidalgo; now it's the generals fighting one another here in the south. We'll have to be on our guard every minute."

They rode on side by side. For the last two days, as they made their way across the countryside, shunning the villages and the well-traveled roads, Jordan had treated Alitha as he would have treated another man, a trusted comrade-at-arms. At times he had seen her glance at him in surprise when he asked for her opinion. Knowing Esteban, Jordan guessed the don had treated her as he would a chattel. Esteban was a pompous fool. Any other man would be proud to have her for a companion, not a bond maiden.

As the day grew hotter, Jordan saw beads of perspiration form on Alitha's forehead. Her dress, a heavy, high-necked black muslin, was streaked with dust. Finally she undid the two top buttons of the dress and, though he tried for the rest of the day to keep his eyes on the trail ahead, Jordan was acutely conscious of Alitha's white flesh leading in a vee down between her breasts.

The next morning Jordan woke first and, in the half-light of the predawn, knelt beside Alitha. He drew in his breath. Her dress and petticoats lay folded beside her. She faced away from him, her golden hair loose on her bare shoulders, wearing only her chemise. The thin garment had pulled up on her body as she slept, revealing her long, slender legs while barely covering the curve of her hip.

Desire stirred in Jordan, forcing him to stand and turn away in order to marshal his self-control. Only after long minutes was he able to kneel beside her again. He put his hand on her bare shoulder to wake her, feeling her warm skin quiver beneath his touch.

Alitha came awake with a startled cry. Sitting up, she clutched a blanket to her.

"It's time to ride," Jordan said gruffly, standing and looking away before she could see the pain of denial in his face. As he began saddling the horses, he heard the rustle of her clothing as she hurriedly dressed. When he turned to look at her, he saw that she had buttoned her dress to the neck once more.

The day proved hotter than any that had gone before. A wind came up in mid-morning, and dust devils swirled across the dry land, the dust coating their faces with grime, streaking their clothing, even filtering through the handkerchiefs tied over their mouths and noses. Dirty and thirsty, they rode on with the sun rising ever higher in the sky overhead.

Just as Jordan was about to call a halt to rest, Alitha spurred her horse ahead, stopped and turned to him, removing the handkerchief from her face. "Water," she called back. "I've found a stream."

As she trotted ahead, he was about to shout a warning, then hesitated. They had seen no other riders, friend or foe, all morning. He was being overcautious, Jordan told himself; the rebels had probably left the area weeks before to move south.

Digging his spurs into his horse's flanks, he followed Alitha, swinging to the ground beside her tethered horse. She knelt a short distance away beside a fast-flowing rivulet. When she heard him behind her, she looked up, frowning.

"The water's hot," she said, "and has a strange salty taste."

The small stream, he noticed, was clouded. A hundred feet ahead of them a rutted track followed the stream. His gaze went along the track up the side of the mountain and, behind a cluster of trees partway up the slope, he saw the wall of what appeared to be a building.

"The water must come from a mineral spring," he said. "That building might be an old Spanish bathhouse."

"A bathhouse! Then I can wash. I feel so dirty after all these days on the trail." She looked at Jordan. "Let's ride up the hill and see." When she noticed him hesitate, she said, "Please."

"When you look at me like that," he told her, "I can't deny you anything."

She glanced sharply at him. As soon as he'd spoken, he regretted his words, for he had promised himself that he would treat her coolly, with indifference. After all, she loved another man, Esteban. Hadn't she been prepared to die for the don when Jordan had ambushed him on the trail?

"We'll take a look to find out if the baths are safe," Jordan said, his tone again distant. "They'd make a good hiding place for bandits or rebels."

They rode up the side of the mountain in a great circle so that they approached the building from above. They saw no signs of life at all.

"Look." Alitha pointed to three cone-shaped hills farther up the mountain. The hills were barren and littered with black rocks.

"They must be volcanic," Jordan said. "I've read that there's a great fissure running beneath this part of Mexico. Humboldt says that from time to time molten rock from the center of the earth forces its way to the surface to create volcanoes and hot springs."

"Oh, Jordan," she said, smiling, "you sound exactly like a schoolmaster."

Despite himself, his face reddened.

"Jordan," she said quickly, "I meant no harm. I've always liked schoolmasters, as a matter of fact."

When he saw her pause in confusion, he rode ahead, examining the ground for tracks of either men or animals, smiling to himself. Finding no evidence of life, he said, "I think it's safe."

They rode slowly from a fringe of trees, crossing open ground to the low stone building. The scene was one of complete desolation: shards of earthen jars lay scattered on the ground; the walls of the bathhouse were cracked, as though by an ancient earthquake, and the thatched roof had been darkened by weather and time. At the downhill side of the building, the stream flowed sluggishly from a stone duct with steam rising from the yellow-green water.

After they tied the horses to a dead tree, Jordan held out his hand to keep Alitha behind him. Pistol ready, he went to the doorway and peered inside. The interior was dark, for the baths were enclosed by stone walls with only small apertures near the roof to admit light. As Jordan stepped inside, a great whirring sound erupted. Swinging his gun up, he was about to fire when he saw a large bird take flight, circle the room and fly through a rent in the roof and disappear.

Alitha hurried past him and knelt beside a pool, testing the water with her hand. The mineral water in the bath was captured in a series of terraced pools. Steam rose from their surfaces; the odor in the building was sharp and medicinal.

"The water's delightfully warm," she said. "At last we can bathe. Do you want to be first or second?"

"I'll wait outside." Jordan walked to the doorway. "I'd best keep an eye out for trouble, just in case."

She followed him into the glaring sunlight, and when

she led her horse to the doorway and retethered him there, Jordan smiled knowingly to himself. He paced back and forth on the crest of a rise before sitting with his back to a tree, from where he could see up and down the valley. Taking his handkerchief, he mopped his face. God, but it was hot.

He heard a sound behind him and, looking back, realized it was Alitha singing. He stood up. Beside the doorway to the baths he saw a pile of clothing—Alitha's black dress, her dark petticoats and, on the top, her white chemise. He drew in a long breath as he closed his eyes, picturing her as she bathed, imagining her raising cupped palms and letting the warm water run from them down over her naked body, across her breasts to her hips and down along her legs.

He blinked, surprised to find himself just outside the doorway to the baths. Who was Alitha Bradford, after all, he asked himself, that he should be so circumspect? She was no better than she should be. Hadn't she traveled to Mexico with Esteban? Hadn't she these last few days been tempting him by sleeping in her chemise, by exposing her body to him?

Alitha had stopped singing, but he could hear the splash of water from inside the baths. Jordan stepped through the doorway and stared into the gloomy darkness. Steam rose in front of him like an early morning mist at sea; the air was warm and damp on his face. As his eyes grew accustomed to the darkness, he saw, through the white haze, a darker form. Alitha stood with her back to him, her body outlined in the clouds of steam.

Jordan felt a pang, almost an ache, as he saw her hands lave her body, and he moaned, his desire rising. Turn back, he told himself, before she sees you. Turn back while you still can. Alitha leaned over so that he saw her in profile, her hair falling free across her face. He saw the enticing curves of her breasts and buttocks. Standing again, she raised her arms above her head, stretching, almost as if she were reaching out to him and inviting him to come to her.

Jordan strode into the steam. When she saw him, Alitha cried out, shielding her breasts with her arms. He stopped a foot from her, his heart pounding in his chest as his eyes roved down over her body, taking in all of her pale, glowing loveliness.

"Alitha," he murmured.

Slowly, ever so slowly, he reached toward her, his hand going to her face until his fingers touched her cheek in a tentative caress. She stared at him as though frozen, and for a moment he thought she was about to turn her face and press her lips to his fingers.

She placed both of her hands on his chest and shoved. Jordan stumbled back, tripping on a stone ledge and falling into the bubbling water, where he flailed about until he was finally able to sit up, spluttering, in the two-foot-deep bath. He heard Alitha's bare feet race across the stones to the entrance.

Jordan stood, shaking the water from his clothes. He must look like a sopping wet dog. He glanced down at his soaked trousers. Sudden immersion was a sure cure for passion, he thought, smiling ruefully.

He climbed from the pool and walked to the door. Alitha, now wearing her chemise, stood next to her horse with a pistol in her hand.

"Don't come near me or I'll shoot," she warned.

Jordan reached for the gun.

"I mean it," she insisted. "After what you tried to do to me, after what you did to Esteban, I'll not hesitate to kill you."

"Give me the gun," Jordan said, calmly stepping toward her until the muzzle pressed against his stomach.

He saw her finger tighten and thought she was about to pull the trigger, but then her hand relaxed and her arm dropped to her side. Jordan took the gun from her and thrust it into his belt.

"I couldn't," she said. "I wanted to shoot you—I should have shot you—but I couldn't."

Jordan smiled. "It would have done you no good. The first night we were on the trail I searched your saddle after you feel asleep and found your pistol. I emptied it. Pulling the trigger just now would have produced nothing louder than a click."

"I don't believe you."

He removed the gun from his belt and handed it to her.

"Here," he said, "try to shoot it and see."

Alitha held the gun gingerly in both hands and aimed to one side of Jordan's head. When she pulled the trigger, the gun roared, filling the air with the stench of gunpowder.

"I'll be damned." Jordan stared at the gun, feeling a sudden queasiness in his stomach as he realized he'd been but a hair's breadth from death a few minutes before.

"The gun was loaded after all," Alitha said. "That just shows you, Jordan Quinn, you can never be sure of anything—not about guns or about me. You might think you know the truth and later find out you don't. To your discomfort."

"I could have sworn I unloaded that gun." Jordan shook his head. "I must be losing my mind."

"No," she said. "I don't think that's the case. Or at least not completely. I woke up and saw you unload the gun, so after you'd gone to sleep, I reloaded it." She turned from him. "Now why don't you take your turn in the baths? I'm quite through. And I can assure you I won't interrupt your pleasure as you saw fit to interrupt mine."

He started to speak, shrugged instead and entered the bath, where he slowly began removing his clothing. By God, he told himself, she's a match for any man. The one who gets her will have his hands full, no question of that; and she'll be worth every battle of wills, there was no question of that either.

As he began to rinse himself off, he wondered what she had meant when she told him not to be too sure about her. He'd never understand her, not in a thousand years. He'd give a great deal, though, to have the chance to try.

When he was dressed again and came out into the sunlight, he saw that Alitha had put on her petticoats and the black muslin dress over her chemise. She stood near the tree where he had gone to wait for her. She was staring down into the valley.

"I was about to call you to come," she said when he stood beside her.

Following her pointing finger he saw, in the distance, a lone horseman riding at a gallop toward them from the direction of the territory held by the revolutionaries.

chapter 21

"THAT'S NO ORDINARY horseman," Jordan said after studying the oncoming rider for a few minutes. "Look at his brown robes and the cowl. It's a priest."

"A Franciscan *padre*."

"Come along; we'll ride into the valley and find out what he can tell us about conditions to the south."

At their approach, the *padre* pulled up his lathered horse and waited for them to reach him.

"Father," Jordan said, "we ride to the south, to Acapulco. Is there fighting ahead?"

"Go no farther," the *padre*, an emaciated-looking man with close-cropped gray hair, told them. "Renegades are in control from here to the jungles near the sea. A foreigner courts certain imprisonment, a foreign woman risks worse." He glanced at their pack horses laden with the sacks containing the gold. "Anyone with valuable possessions faces death."

"I feared as much," Jordan said.

"Why don't you ride with me?" the *padre* suggested. "My brothers at the monastery ten leagues from here will harbor you until this danger passes."

Jordan, thinking of Esteban in pursuit of the gold, shook his head. "No," he said, "we must go on."

The *padre* shrugged. "May God have mercy on your souls," he said.

"We'll travel by night," Jordan said to Alitha as soon as the priest was out of earshot. "Even if it slows us down."

They camped for the rest of the day, rising as soon as the sun set behind the mountains. At first they rode in moonlight, but then clouds swept in from the west to darken the sky and force Jordan to slow their pace. Finally he dismounted to lead the horses himself as thunder growled in the distance. Suddenly a jagged streak of lightning crackled earthward, followed by a drumroll of thunder, and Alitha's horse whinnied in fright. The sky blackened until she could no longer see Jordan walking ahead of her, nor his horse nor even her own horse.

A drop of rain struck her cheek. Her horse stopped, and a moment later Jordan was standing at her side.

"Best put your cloak on," he said. "It looks like we're in for it." Already the rain was beating a tattoo on the hard earth around them.

Alitha pulled her *manga* from her pack and slipped it over her head. Once more they started forward, plodding on with the rain driving down on them until Alitha's hair was plastered to her head. The *manga* clung wetly to her body as the water soaked through to her dress.

Again Jordan stopped. "I'll go ahead and look for shelter," he called to her through the rain.

"Yes," she shouted back. They could make little progress in this storm. A barn, an Indian hut, a cave among the rocks, anything would be preferable to slogging on in the drenching downpour.

Lightning sliced across the sky, and in its glare she saw two stone pillars with a road between them. When the thunder boomed, her horse reared, forcing her to tighten her grip on the reins. She leaned forward on the stallion's neck, talking to him, comforting him until he quieted.

"I saw a gate," she called to Jordan.

He didn't answer but led the horses on, and in a few minutes they turned in the direction of the pillars. The way leveled and she knew they must be on a road. In the next flash of lightning she saw trees arching above her head and, farther along the road, a looming mass of buildings.

Jordan walked back to her. "A hacienda." He had to shout to make himself heard above the steady roar of the rain.

"No lights," she shouted back. Even this late, and it must have been nearly midnight, Mexican houses were usually lit by at least a single lamp or candle.

"Wait here," he told her.

She lowered herself to the ground and huddled beside the horse's flank. When Jordan returned, he leaned to her and spoke into her ear. "Seems deserted," he said. "We'll go in, then I'll find shelter for the horses."

He took her hand, led her along the road and up the steps to a massive door. He pushed open the door, and as soon as they were inside, he released her hand.

"The door was bolted," Jordan told her. "I had to break a window to get in."

The flicker of lightning through the windows on

either side of the door showed her they were in a high-ceilinged entryway with chandeliers over their heads, the candles unlit. She saw chairs along the walls but no other furniture; the floor itself was bare brick. Brown drapes covered the windows.

A spark flared near her, and a moment later a candle flamed in Jordan's hand. He held the candle out to her and she took the holder in her hand while he found another. After he lit it, they advanced side by side into the dark hacienda, holding the candles in front of them.

Going through an archway, they entered a lofty room furnished only with a deal table and a few chairs. Old pictures of saints and the Virgin Mary hung askew on the stone walls. Jordan strode across the room to a fireplace recessed in the far wall. He took wood from the pile on the hearth and soon had a fire crackling in the grate.

"I'll see to the horses," he told her.

She nodded, going to stand in front of the fire with her hands stretched out to receive its warmth. As the flames leaped higher, she pulled the wet *manga* over her head and spread it on the table to dry.

"Why don't you see if you can find some food," Jordan said from the doorway.

She reluctantly left the warmth of the fire and, taking a candle, searched among the cavernous rooms, shivering in her damp dress. One room, a bedroom with two green-painted bedsteads, a bench and more pictures of the saints, had clothing strewn on its wardrobe floor as though the occupants had left in haste. Other rooms were empty, but whether they had never been furnished or had been stripped bare by the hacienda's departing owners or by marauding revolutionaries she could not tell.

At last she came to the kitchen, with a pump above a

washbasin. In the pantry she discovered food—lidded earthenware jars partly filled with dried beans and dried corn. Although she searched every cranny of the two rooms, she found no more food. She sighed; while she was tired of trail food, dried beans and corn were little better. Discouraged, she made her way back to the room with the roaring fire, where she found Jordan waiting for her. He had a broad smile on his face as he stood holding one hand behind his back.

"I've a surprise for you," he said. Bringing his hand from behind him, he held aloft a chicken, its neck wrung.

"We'll have stewed chicken," she said, catching some of his enthusiasm. "I saw some old pots in the kitchen and a pump that actually works."

"And while you're cooking the bird, I'll have a look around and see what else I can find. One thing I can tell you for sure, we're the only ones here."

They ate the chicken stewed with beans and corn on the deal table in front of the roaring fire. Afterward, ignoring the thunder crashing outside, they sipped red wine as the fire cast their wavering shadows on the stone walls of the room.

Jordan stood and raised his glass while Alitha stared as though mesmerized at the light glinting from the crystal.

"To Valparaiso," Jordan said grandiloquently. "To Santa Barbara and to Chapultepec Hill. To you, Alitha Bradford, in all your many manifestations, in all your moods and with all your caprices, to your courage, your perseverance and most of all to your golden loveliness."

"You'd best have no more to drink, Jordan Quinn," she told him. But she smiled as she raised her glass. "To a safe ending to our journey," she said.

"No, to a journey without an ending. We'll drink to a journey to all eternity, to the pale moon above, to the stars, to the end of time."

After they had finished the wine, Jordan stood again and raised his hand. "I found no more food or drink while you were stewing the chicken," he said, "but I did find something else. Something just as wonderful as wine or women."

"What?" she asked, seeing nothing.

"Wait and you'll see. And hear."

He walked into the entryway, seeming to place his feet with great care as though the wine had gone to his head, Alitha thought. In fact, she felt light-headed herself. When Jordan returned, he held a guitar in his hand and stood beside her, tentatively plucking the strings.

"Only one string is broken," he said. "Not that I could play this damn device well anyway."

He began strumming, then sang in a high clear voice. She recognized the chanty as one the seamen on the *Flying Yankee* used to sing as they worked. Jordan kept time by thumping his foot on the stone floor.

"Heave, ho, aye the tall ships," he sang.

"Do you know it?" he asked, and when she nodded, he flung his hand wide. "Now, once again," he called out, "and will the entire company join me if you please."

She sang along with him—

Heave, ho, aye the tall ships
Heave, ho, aye the tall ships
See the tall ships, sail the tall ships
Aye, aye, aye the tall ships.

Jordan laid the guitar on the table, bowed to her,

extending his hand, and she rose, curtsied and let him lead her to the middle of the empty floor. He clasped his hands to her waist and spun her in a polka as he sang the chanty. Around and around they whirled until, flushed and laughing, he stopped, with Alitha still held in his arms.

He drew her to him, paused, then kissed her. So sudden was his kiss, so unexpected, that she drew in her breath, feeling his hand pressed hard to her back, his lips pressed hard to hers. She pulled away from him, staring up into eyes made black by the shadows from the firelight.

"Alitha," he said, "I've wanted to hold and kiss you ever since the first day I saw you." His voice was soft; he seemed to have suddenly sobered.

She touched her lips with the back of her hand, still light-headed from the wine and the dancing, her mind in a turmoil. This warmth I feel is from the fire, she told herself, glancing at the now-dying flames. Jordan drew her to him again, and his movement seemed to break the spell and she twisted free and fled. She ran from dark room to dark room until, exhausted, she stopped and rested her head against the glass of a window. The rain beat against the sides of the house, water streamed down the pane and the dull rumble of receding thunder came from without.

Hearing a sound behind her, she swung around and in the next flash of lightning saw a window curtain rippling inward. She felt a pang of disappointment when she realized that it wasn't Jordan coming to look for her.

No! The wine had befuddled her, not Jordan Quinn. The wine and her weariness. Jordan could rot in hell for all she cared. Alitha's hand came up to cover her mouth. You're lying, she accused herself. You're lying

now and you lied a few minutes ago when you told
yourself Jordan's kiss was unexpected. You knew he
meant to kiss you when he held you in his arms after
the dance was done. You said you'd never lie to
yourself again, and yet you have time after time these
last six months. You've lied about your feelings for
Esteban. And now about Jordan. So much for that
pistol you hid; you'll never use it.

I pity Jordan, I admit that, she told herself, but I
don't love him.

Alitha walked to the blowing curtain and drew it
aside and found the window was broken. She leaned
forward until her face was in front of the shattered pane
and let the cool rain strike her forehead, her nose and
her cheeks, the water running down her neck and
under her gown to her breasts. She shivered and turned
from the window, sighing and shaking her head. Will I
ever understand myself, she wondered.

When, much later, she walked slowly back through
the deserted hacienda, Alitha found Jordan gone and
the fire reduced to glowing coals. She laid another log
on the fire but the wood failed to catch and lay cradled
darkly in the smoldering embers.

Taking a candle from the table, she walked from
room to room as the thunder rumbled in the distance.
Above her head she heard the rain falling steadily,
drumming on the tiles of the roof. In the bedroom the
brass beds were empty, and she felt a thrill of panic.
Where was Jordan? She opened the far bedroom door,
almost stumbling over—What? She lowered the candle
and saw Jordan on his pallet. His eyes were closed and
he breathed steadily and deeply. There was no doubt
but that he was asleep.

Alitha closed the door again and went to sit on one of

the beds. It was so soft! She sighed, placed the candle on the floor and lay back with her hands behind her head, staring at the ceiling, the candle throwing flickering shadows on the walls. She reveled in the luxury of a real bed after the endless days on the trail.

She stood up, stretching. Holding the candle in front of her, she found her way to the kitchen, where she filled a small tub with water from the pump. She unbuttoned her dress, let it fall to the floor and, after stepping out of dress and petticoats, drew her chemise over her head. When she had finished bathing, she put her clothes over her arm and returned to the bedroom, where she laid them across the back of a chair. Naked, she slipped beneath the blankets, crossing her arms over her breasts and hugging herself, feeling the blankets harsh against her flesh. Smiling, she closed her eyes.

An all-encompassing red glow surrounded her. A fire sprang skyward in flames of yellow and orange, warming her, caressing her as the colors changed and deepened to a magenta red whirling around and around above her head in an exotic Spanish dance, swirling up above her higher and higher as the fire decreased in size to form an inverted funnel.

Flashes, brilliant as lightning; lightning without thunder.

She lay on an altar at the top of a great stone pyramid hundreds of feet high. Naked, her body gleaming. A man came up the stone steps toward her, his bronze body suffused by moonlight, the light from the fire in the pit beside her glinting from the knife in his hand. He stood over her and she recognized him.

As he raised his knife, she screamed his name.

"Esteban! Esteban!"

He dropped the knife and came to her, his brown eyes flashing, a slight smile on his lips.

She opened her eyes and he was beside her, as naked as she, his hand between her thighs, caressing her, his fingers running up and down her leg making her flesh quiver under his touch. The room was dark, completely dark, and it was a moment before she realized where she was. The storm. The hacienda. Jordan.

She sat up, suddenly alert. "Jordan?" she said.

His arms enclosed her and his mouth found her bared flesh, closing on her breast with his tongue to her nipple. Involuntarily she arched toward him as she felt the fever rise in her legs and pulse upward through her body, the burning fever she couldn't control, the red glowing need.

Jordan's hand came between her legs, forcing them apart, his fingers finding the lips of her sex, touching her, caressing her as her whole body shuddered. His mouth left her breasts and slowly came higher, to her neck, to her lips, and he kissed her, a long lingering kiss. She turned her head away.

"No, Jordan," she whispered. "No."

Alitha wrenched herself from him, her hands clawing at his face, her legs closing against him. She fought until he grasped her two wrists in one hand and held them over her head, kissing her again. She bit his lip so that he cried out in pain and she tasted blood but his mouth still held to hers as he thrust his other hand between her legs, not caressing her now, forcing her, his hard body following the path of his hand, his leg pushing hers apart.

He entered her and she moaned.

As he thrust inside her, she felt the fire return, a fierce red blaze that seared her, threatened to consume her, and she tensed in his arms, then tried to lie inert but the burning need within wouldn't let her and she opened her arms and legs to him. As his passion mounted, she felt her body respond, rise to his, and the fire exploded inside her in a burst of crimson as she arched to him, responding to him thrust for thrust until, spent, he lay exhausted beside her.

chapter 22

ALITHA OPENED HER eyes, shivering in the cool of early morning. She lay naked on top of the blanket with Jordan beside her, his hand thrown across her stomach. She moved his hand aside, taking care not to wake him, and then pulled another blanket over them both. Hugging herself, she scarcely felt the roughness of the blanket on her body as she relived the night before in her mind, feeling at peace with herself and with the world.

The two uncurtained windows across the room were gray with the first light of dawn. Water streamed down the panes, and she became aware of the steady thrum of rain on the roof over her head. Lying snugly in bed with Jordan beside her and with the rain falling outside, she felt warm and content, as though wrapped in a luxurious cocoon.

She hadn't believed that another man could make her feel the same excitement Esteban had. But with Jordan there had been the excitement and much more.

Passion, yes, rapture, yes, but also a feeling of sharing. Jordan's lovemaking, so tender yet so fervent, made her feel whole and fully alive, made her want to please him as she'd never wanted to please Esteban.

Looking at Jordan, she smiled as she gently brushed a black strand of hair from his forehead. He stirred but did not waken. At last, she thought, she was freed from Esteban; the thrall in which the don had held her was broken.

Sitting up, she drew in her breath, all at once alarmed. What kind of woman am I, she asked herself. Had Thomas been right? Am I a wanton? She had bedded the night before with Jordan Quinn and, she admitted, she had wanted him. Still wanted him, for that matter. She had bedded with him in part from pity because of Margarita, in part from her own affection for him, and in part because of her own need. But there had been more than pity or affection or need.

Jordan shifted on the bed beside her, and his hand found and clasped her hip. Alitha lay back, staring at the whitewashed ceiling, all her senses alerted by his touch. She bit her lip. Was she once again in danger of confusing desire with love? She had thought she loved Esteban and found she didn't. She mustn't make the same mistake again. Besides, Jordan didn't love her, had never said he loved her. He had forced her, after all, and no man who loved a woman would do that. Jordan still loved Margarita, so how could he possibly love her?

His hand slid from her hip to cup her buttocks, and when she looked at him, she saw him staring raptly at her face.

"Alitha," he said slowly as though savoring the sound of her name. When he started to draw her to him, she slipped away and left the bed. Going to the clothes she had piled on the chair the night before, she searched in the pocket of her dress.

"What are you doing?" Jordan asked. He raised himself on his elbow to watch her.

"Looking for this." She dropped a looped cord over her head and lifted her hair so the cord fell around her neck.

"What in the devil is it?"

She came to the bed and knelt on the blanket, facing him. He lifted the reddish stone from between her bare breasts and held it in his hand.

"Why, it's just a stone carved in the shape of a fish of some sort," he said.

"That's all. An Indian boy gave it to me months ago in Santa Barbara, an Indian boy I was very fond of."

"I've never seen one like it. Does the fish have a meaning in his religion?"

"I don't know, but the charm stone has a meaning to me. I can't explain why, but wearing it is sort of my declaration of independence."

"Alitha, my love, I really don't know what you're talking about. And this morning I don't think I really care." He took her by the upper arm and pulled her to him so that she lay on top and Jordan beneath the blanket while he kissed her, his lips parting, his tongue probing for hers. As their tongues met, she felt the fire kindled within her once more.

She drew away. "It's still raining," she said.

"It may rain for days; it does here in *tierra caliente*. But this isn't the time to discuss the weather. Come here, Alitha, lie next to me; we have plans to make. Where we'll go from Acapulco, where we'll live once we're back in the States. We have a lot to decide."

She shook her head. "No, Jordan," she told him, "we'll make no plans."

He stared at her. "Last night . . ." he said before she interrupted.

"As long as it rains," she told him, "as long as the storm continues, we'll lie together. But once the rain stops we'll ride to Acapulco and everything between us will be the same as it was before last night."

"Alitha, I think you've ridden too long in the moonlight. You've become slightly mad. Nothing can ever be the same as it was before."

"It can and it will."

"I understand what you say but I don't believe you." He drew her close. "I don't want to believe you."

"Wait." She raised the blanket and pulled it over them both, and then he took her into his arms and their bodies met and joined.

Much later Alitha wakened to find Jordan lying beside her, staring down at her.

"I was thinking I've never seen hair so golden or skin so fair or eyes so blue," he said.

She smiled and sat up, the blanket falling away from her breasts as she stretched lazily. His fingers trailed up her legs to her thighs.

"It's still raining," he told her and, when she looked to the window, she saw that he was right. When he knelt above her, she gasped; when he entered her, she moaned; and when at last he lay sated in her arms, she sighed with pleasure.

The storm lasted for two more days . . .

They rode from the hacienda in the muted light of early morning, through a land refreshed by the rain. The sky above them was a pale blue, the breeze cool and pleasant, the grass and trees a bright green.

Jordan looked at Alitha and wondered if she would

pass a close scrutiny. Wondered if he would. They both wore the robes and cowls of Franciscans, fashioned from the hacienda's drapes; crosses hung from their necks. Alitha's face was smeared with mud.

They had traveled only a few leagues when four horsemen galloped from a ravine beside the trail to ride on both sides of them. The leader, black-garbed, with black mustaches curling luxuriantly, stared at them without speaking.

"One who travels in times such as these," he said finally, "must have a great need to reach his destination."

"True, my son," Jordan said in Spanish. "We ride to the village of Acapulco to take passage to the north. We travel to the mission of our brothers at Loreto to bring instruction to the Indians in the doctrines of Christianity."

"A worthy endeavor, surely, father." The rider slowed until he rode beside one of the pack horses. As he reached into one of the packs, Jordan said, "Wait—" but the man thrust his hand inside.

He withdrew it with a yowl of pain.

"I tried to warn you, my son," Jordan said. "We carry specimens to a horticulturalist at Loreto for his cactus garden. We also bring seed and tools for the Indians."

As the rider shook his stinging hand, he stared at Alitha. "Your companion is young for the priesthood," he said.

"Some men see fit to dedicate their lives to God after sampling the pleasures of the flesh, others before. God accepts them all if their hearts are pure."

"Your companion is also very silent. And in need of a bath, perhaps?"

"Padre Juan performs a penance. He will neither

speak nor bathe until he reaches our destination in Baja."

"A penance is to expiate sins."

"True," Jordan said. "Padre Juan has the curse, as you no doubt have noted, of great natural beauty. Some women found him attractive and he was tempted. He did not succumb, but a sin of intention can be as great as a sin of commission."

"I would think the young father might have tempted some of the men as well as the women."

"We do not find your jest amusing," Jordan said.

The mustachioed rider slapped the flank of Jordan's horse with his quirt, laughing. "May God go with you both," he said.

"*Vaya con Díos*, my son," Jordan said.

When he looked behind him five minutes later, the four riders were nowhere to be seen.

The lush growth of the jungle had all but completely reclaimed the mule trail leading over the mountains to Acapulco.

"It's the revolution," Jordan told her. "Commerce has been at a standstill since the fighting began in 1810. There have been no ships sailing from Acapulco to Spain and few to the ports of the Pacific."

Alitha nodded, paying little attention to his words as she stared about her at the exotic jungle growth, the flaming flowered shrubs, the arching broad-leafed trees, the delicate beauty of the orchids. Birds flaunting their outrageously colorful plumage flitted from tree to tree over their heads; she heard a raucous squawk and looked up to meet the beady eye of a green and gold parrot.

Soon after they left the jungle they came out on a height overlooking the fishing village of Acapulco.

"This must be the most beautiful bay in the world," she said. "Look—the white sand, the palms, the thatched huts, the ships in the harbor, the blue blue sea."

Jordan, however, was frowning. "Only a hermaphrodite brig and a schooner," he said. "I was hoping to find more ships here than that."

As they rode down the mule trail into the village, Jordan glanced from side to side at the walled San Diego Fort, at the outrigger dugout canoes drawn up on the sandy shore and at the Indians who mended their nets nearby.

"You look wary," Alitha said. "As though you expect to find someone here you'd rather not see."

Jordan glanced at her. "Esteban could well have followed us," he said.

"I don't think he could have recognized you. And if he doesn't know who has the—"

"Don't say the word," Jordan cautioned her, "not even in English. Esteban may have been able to pick up my trail in Mexico City if he had the nerve to return there; I'm certain there were those who suspected I was an American. Carrying what we do in our packs, even a more trusting man than myself would see dangers where none exist."

Jordan led her into the courtyard of a one-story inn and dismounted. When an Indian boy ran to take the reins from him, Jordan spoke to him in Spanish. At first the boy looked surprised, then nodded.

"I told him I'd look after storing our supplies myself," he said to Alitha once the boy had led their two riding horses into the stable. Seeing a gap-toothed Indian watching them from where he sat with his back against the adobe wall of the inn, Jordan lowered his voice. "I'll carry the packs. I'm not about to let them out of my sight."

After eight trips the gold was all stacked on the floor of their room. When he was done, Jordan slid home the bolt on the door and sat on the bed to catch his breath.

"I'll visit those two ships in the harbor next," he told Alitha. "The sooner we're able to find passage out of Acapulco, the better."

There was a knock on the door. Jordan glanced at the packs before he slid the bolt aside and opened the door. The gap-toothed Indian stood in the corridor holding his stained sombrero in his hands. He smelled, Alitha noticed, of garlic. As the man spoke rapidly in Spanish, he looked down at his feet, avoiding Jordan's eyes.

"No," Jordan told him. The man asked a question. "No, no, *gracias,*" Jordan said. Nodding, the Indian backed away and Jordan rebolted the door.

"He said his name was Enrico and if there's anything we need, anything at all, he's most humbly at our service. You heard what I told him."

Jordan walked to the window, pushed it open and leaned on the sill to look through the black metal grating toward the harbor. Over his shoulder Alitha saw a golden sun settling toward the sea.

"I'm going out to the two ships while it's still light," Jordan said. "Keep the door bolted. Don't open it no matter who comes, no matter what they may say. When I return I'll knock twice, then once again."

"I understand," she told him.

Jordan took her in his arms but when he leaned forward to kiss her, she turned her head from him. Frowning, he kissed her cheek.

"I'll bring you back food the likes of which you've never seen before," he said, trying to manage a light tone. He released her and walked to the door. "I'll bring coconuts, melons, papayas and bananas," he said. "You'll think you're the queen of some far Pacific isle."

"Godspeed," she told him.

She slid the bolt home behind him and sat on the bed staring at the packs of gold in the corner. Gold. Already Esteban and Jordan had been enslaved by this gold, she thought, and now the yellow metal had made her its prisoner as well.

Jordan walked quickly along the street fronting the bay. Once out of sight of the inn, he turned from the beach. Ten minutes later he stopped in front of a grilled gateway between adobe walls, rang the bell and waited.

Presently a black-robed sister appeared, nodded to Jordan and opened the gate. She led him through a garden of flowering vines and along dim corridors to the top of a stairs, where she tapped on a rough-hewn wooden door. When a woman's voice bade them enter, the sister opened the door, smiled at Jordan and slipped silently away.

Mother Superior Angelica was alone in the sparsely furnished room. She nodded to a chair. "You seek your friend," she said, looking at Jordan across her bare oak desk.

"I do, Mother Superior. For months, while I've been in Mexico City, I've feared the worst. As you are aware, he once saved my life."

"I have good news for you. Your comrade, Señor Thomas Heath, recovered from the yellow fever. His strength returned, and he left the convent hospital more than a week ago. I must say he is a most determined young man."

"That is good news. When I rode into Acapulco earlier today, I kept a weather eye out for him. I didn't see him in the village then and I haven't seen him since. Do you know where he lives?"

"When he left here, he told us he intended to travel to Mexico City, and I presume he did so. I have heard no more of him since he left here. In the convent, as you know, we receive little news from the outside world."

"Thank you for all you did for Señor Heath. When I carried him here, I thought he was dying. Your sisters have performed a miracle in saving his life."

She smiled. "I must correct you. Only God can perform miracles, Señor Quinn."

Jordan stood up, reached into his pocket and crossed the room to place a pouch on the mother superior's desk. "This is a small offering to help with the work of the hospital," he told her.

"May God bless you. A thousand thanks, Señor Quinn."

"You shouldn't thank me." Jordan smiled. "You should thank God."

After leaving the convent Jordan went directly to the harbor, where he hired a boat to row him to the schooner. The ship, the captain told him, would sail north the next day, intending to trade at the ports along the Mexican coast. Jordan frowned as he listened. The schooner would be of no help—he had to get as far from Acapulco as he could.

The brig, though, held out more hope.

"She's bound for South America and will visit New York before she sails for London," Jordan told Alitha when he returned to the inn. "We can probably book passage aboard her to the States, though I have to talk to the captain first. He was ashore visiting at a hacienda some miles from here; they expect him back on board tomorrow."

"When does she sail?"

"In two or three days."

Jordan began taking tropical fruits from a net bag.

"The dinner I promised you," he said. When he had piled all the fruit on the table, he went to the corner of the room and knelt beside the gold.

"That Indian we saw in the courtyard," he said over his shoulder as he removed coins to pay for their passage. "Enrico. There was no sign of him while I was gone?"

"None. As far as I could tell, no one has the slightest interest in us."

When Enrico left the inn after having his offer of his services spurned by Jordan, he walked along the dusty road to the center of the village, where he entered a *cantina*. At the bar he asked, as he always did, for *pulque*. The *cantinero*—the bartender—a grossly over-weight man, nodded, waddled away and returned with the drink.

"Thank you, Juan, my friend." Enrico leaned over the bar and lowered his voice to a whisper. "I think the fish are beginning to run," he said.

"You have always had an eye for the fish, Enrico. What do you expect, a large run or a small?"

"Large. Perhaps the greatest we have ever seen." He put his empty glass on the bar for Juan to refill.

"Large enough to interest those who hunt only the biggest of fish?"

"Yes. Though only God can say for sure." He hesitated, wondering how to put the words. "There is also a golden-haired mermaid of great beauty," he said finally.

Juan laughed and poured him another drink. "If you are right, Enrico, my friend, you will be rewarded with a portion of this spectacular catch. As usual."

Enrico smiled as the *pulque* sent fire through his blood. He closed his eyes, imagining riches—singing, dancing, drinking, women. Life was good, he told himself.

As he walked unsteadily back to the inn, he heard a horse approaching from behind him. When the rider galloped by, Enrico raised his hand in greeting. The horseman ignored him, riding on toward the south, leaving Enrico coughing and cursing in the dust raised by the horse's hooves.

Juan wasted no time, Enrico thought as he entered the courtyard of the inn. He glanced in the direction of the stranger's room, the man who had walked eight times from the stable to the inn, his back bowed beneath his heavy packs. These fish won't get away, Enrico told himself.

The messenger from Juan's *cantina* galloped south along the shore of the Pacific in the gathering dusk. After more than an hour's ride, he left the road to follow a trail, slowing when he saw a tree felled across his path. A harsh order to halt came from the darkness.

"The password," the same voice demanded.

"The fish are running."

A light flared. A lantern was raised and the rider saw a bearded face. "Give me your message," the sentry said.

"No, I speak only to the captain."

"I'll take your message to him myself."

"No, I must speak to the captain. Those are my orders."

The sentry shrugged. "Your message best be important," he said. "Jorge," he called over his shoulder. A man walked his horse out of the darkness. "Take this one to the camp," the sentry told him.

The two men rode on with the rumbling surf to their right. They were passed through two more guard posts before coming to a row of fires burning in front of huts clustered above the beach. In the light of the fires, the messenger saw men sitting about drinking and gambling. A ship lay careened on the shore for repairs; another was anchored in the bay.

Jorge led the messenger to a thatched hut set apart from the rest. When he rapped on the door, they heard a man curse and a woman laugh. In the ensuing silence Jorge stepped aside. After some minutes the door opened and a man wearing a red sash stood facing them. He stared coldly at the messenger.

"Your message had better be worth my while," Hippolyte de Bouchard said. In spite of himself the messenger felt a quiver of fear course along his spine.

The next day Jordan booked passage for himself and Alitha on the British brig *Redeemer* bound for Valparaiso, New York and London.

"Valparaiso," Jordan said. "That's where I first saw you." He was lying on his pallet on the floor of their candlelit room; Alitha was in the single narrow bed.

"It seems so long ago," she said. "So much has happened since then, so much has changed. It's almost as though I'm a different person."

She sighed and closed her eyes, remembering Valparaiso. Her father had been alive then, and she had been on her way to the Sandwich Islands to marry Thomas. She had never heard of Esteban Mendoza. And Jordan Quinn was a handsome sea captain sailing from the harbor aboard the *Kerry Dancer*.

Where was Thomas now, she asked herself. Lately she had thought of him often, wondering how he had fared in the islands. Life in the West was nothing like she had imagined it, and probably not as Thomas had imagined it either. She and Thomas had expected the dangers, the storms, the turmoil of the times. The greatest danger, she thought, to a person like Thomas, a man who was gentle and trusting yet unbending, would come from a more subtle source. Neither the Indians nor the Spaniards viewed life as the Yankees of New England did. They lived more fully, more passionately, as though there were no tomorrow.

"You seem to be miles away," Jordan said. He leaned over and blew out the candle on the floor beside him.

"I was thinking of Boston and whether I could ever be happy living there again."

"You don't intend to go on to the Sandwich Islands?"

"Someone must have told you about Thomas. I don't know whether he'd still consider us betrothed. It must be over a year since he last heard from me."

"I have a confession to make." Jordan paused, then plunged on. "Thomas came to Mexico looking for you. In fact, he sailed with me from Santa Barbara and I had to leave him here in Acapulco when he came down with the fever."

"Thomas followed me . . ." she began.

"I visited the convent hospital where I left him and found out that he'd recovered and set out for Mexico City some weeks ago."

Alitha sat up in bed. "And you never told me," she accused him, her voice shaking with anger. "How could you have been with me all this time and never told me?"

"I didn't know whether he'd live. Besides—" He stopped. "Listen," he said.

"What is it?"

Footsteps pounded along the corridor. A door slammed in another part of the inn.

"Do you smell something?" Jordan asked.

She sniffed the air. "Yes, smoke. I smell smoke."

"*Fuego!*" a voice cried from outside their door. "*Fuego!*"

Jordan scrambled to his feet and ran to the window, a bandana shielding his nose and mouth from the smoke pouring through the grate. He gripped the iron bars with both hands and shook them, but they refused to budge.

"Alitha," he called, stumbling to the bed, "give me your hand. The inn's on fire."

She reached out and touched his arm, and his fingers closed on hers.

"Stay as low as you can," he told her. "We'll be all right once we're outside."

They groped their way to the door, coughing in the now dense smoke. Jordan slid the bolt aside and opened the door. The smoke was even thicker in the corridor. They ran to the outer door. Jordan threw it open and they staggered into the courtyard.

A club thudded down on Jordan's head and he fell face forward to the ground. Strong hands grasped Alitha, and though she struggled a gag was thrust into her mouth and tied behind her head. She was lifted, kicking and flailing, to a waiting horse and thrown across its back. Rope bit into her wrists and ankles, and the bindings were tied beneath the horse's belly. Men shouted. She still smelled the acrid odor of smoke.

"Oro!" someone shouted. They had found the gold. A rider sprang into the saddle behind her and with a cry of triumph urged the horse from the courtyard and into the night.

chapter 23

JORDAN QUINN OPENED his eyes and saw a white ceiling above him and a white wall to his right. His head throbbed and he groaned as he shifted his body on the narrow cot.

"The wound, while painful, is superficial. At least that is what I am told."

Jordan jerked his head to his left to stare at Don Esteban, then glanced quickly about, looking for his pistol. His clothes were draped over a chair, but the gun was nowhere to be seen. Had Don Esteban been the one who had attacked him? Was he being held prisoner?

"Do not seek your weapon," Don Esteban said calmly. "I have declared a truce in our personal war. For the time being I suspect I need you, my friend, as much as you need me."

Jordan struggled up to sit with his back to the wall, the pain in his head blurring his vision. Don Esteban observed him coldly from a chair next to the bed. Jordan recognized his cell-like quarters as one of the sick rooms in the convent hospital. So he wasn't Esteban's prisoner. If he could only remember what had happened.

"The gold," Jordan said. "What became of the gold?"

Esteban raised both hands, palms up, in a shrug. "I thought you might be able to enlighten me, Señor Quinn. About the gold and the present whereabouts of Señorita Bradford."

"Alitha? Alitha's missing?" Wisps of memory began to return. When Jordan touched the bandage on his head, he winced. "I remember the fire at the inn. Alitha was with me. We groped through the smoke to the courtyard. I heard someone behind me. After that—nothing. Nothing at all."

"Because you were struck on the head and have been unconscious ever since. After the attack on you, the gold was taken and Señorita Bradford was abducted." Suddenly Esteban leaned close to Jordan, fire in his brown eyes. "You fool. You let them dupe you. They set small fires among rags and you thought the entire inn was aflame."

"They have Alitha." Jordan spoke as though realizing the fact for the first time. "When did this all happen? I've lost track of time."

"Last night. The entire charade was over by the time I arrived at the inn. I've been sitting here since five this morning, over an hour, waiting for you to become conscious."

"How did you track me down?"

"I suspected the gunman on the trail was you because anyone else would have killed me. You wouldn't have, not from ambush and not in cold blood. And then the Indians in the villages told me of the foreigner who rode with the woman of the golden hair. Once I found that you and the *señorita* were journeying west, I knew you must come at last to Acapulco."

Jordan swung his legs from the bed. Standing, he swayed on his feet, but when Esteban stepped to his side, Jordan shook off his steadying hand. He began pulling on his clothes.

"We must act without delay," Esteban said. "Already we've lost valuable time. Have you any idea who attacked you? I learned nothing at the inn. It was too dark, they told me; it happened too quickly, they said."

"I have no idea who it was."

"Who knew you had the gold?"

"No one. Only Alitha and myself. We'd only arrived the day before."

"Whom did you speak to?"

"No one." Jordan paused to think. "That's not true. I talked to the mother superior here at the convent. I'd left a friend in their care the last time I was in Acapulco. But he had gone. And I talked to the captains of the two ships in the harbor. About passage."

"Did you pay them in gold?"

"No, I hadn't paid for our passage yet." Jordan rubbed his forehead in an attempt to ease the pain as the events of the last two days began falling into place in his mind. "I gave the mother superior a pouch of gold coins to repay her. You don't think—?"

Esteban shrugged. "Anyone else?"

His head whirling, Jordan closed his eyes and leaned against the wall beside the window. When he opened his eyes, he was looking through the grated window. He remembered another grated window, the one at the inn.

"There was an Indian," he said slowly. "Name of Enrico. A gap-toothed Indian who offered his services at the inn. I turned him down. He was there in the courtyard when I carried my packs to my room. But he had no way of knowing I had gold inside."

"I'll start with him. Can you walk to the courtyard? I have a horse for you outside."

"I can walk. No," Jordan said when Esteban started to take his arm. "I don't need your help."

"I think you need my help as much as I need yours. How else will we find Alitha and recover my gold?"

"Your gold, Don Esteban? Somewhere I remember hearing that the gold belonged to the Spanish government."

"Let us say our gold. If we are so fortunate as to recover it."

"Fifty-fifty? Half for each of us?"

"I agree," Don Esteban said. "Fifty-fifty."

They didn't find Enrico at the inn. "Look for him at Juan's *cantina*," they were told.

"What do you intend to do to him?" Jordan, remembering the attack by the two knife-wielding *vaqueros* at Santa Barbara, nodded at the knife on Esteban's belt. "Use that to make him talk?"

"Torture has its place, but only in an extremity. Have you any of the gold left?"

Jordan hooked his finger in his money pocket and brought out four coins. "These were for our passage," he said.

"One should be more than sufficient to entice Enrico to tell all he knows. You must wait here at the inn. I'll speak to Señor Enrico alone."

Esteban's face was grim when he returned to Jordan's room. Shutting the door behind him, he went to the window and glanced into the courtyard before sitting on the edge of the bed.

"It is much worse than I feared," he said. "They are not bandits who attacked you and took Alitha. It is the pirate Bouchard and his men."

"Bouchard!" As Jordan breathed the name, his hand gripped the butt of the pistol in his belt. He clenched his teeth thinking of Alitha as a captive among that crew.

"I'll kill him," Jordan snarled. "Kill that bastard Bouchard and all the scum who follow him."

"We'll ride to his camp at once," Esteban said. "Wait until nightfall and then swoop down on them and carry Alitha and the gold off with us."

"No." Jordan shook his head. "First we have to plan, to reconnoiter their camp so we know the lay of the land. We have to find out how many men Bouchard has, how well armed they are, where they have Alitha, where they've cached the gold."

"We can't wait!" Esteban spoke passionately, pounding his fist on the small table. "Such as they are not fit to even look on Alitha, much less touch her with their filthy hands. Men lower than dogs! We must count on surprise to overcome them. If we pause to deliberate, they may scatter to the four winds, each with his share of the gold, and we lose all."

"By God, Esteban, I'm surprised you've managed to stay alive as long as you have. They might have two hundred men in that lair of theirs, all armed, all desperate, all hungry for the gold and willing to kill us on sight. I don't like to think of Alitha there any more than you do, but we'd be fools to attack them as though we were a cavalry troop when we're but two men against two hundred. We have to approach their camp not from the land but from the sea; they'd never expect that."

"Are you afraid of Bouchard?" Esteban mocked.

"Afraid?" Jordan took his gun from his belt and slapped it on the table. "Pistols at twenty paces. Now, in the courtyard. Does that suit you, Mendoza? We'll decide matters between us once and for all."

"I do not want to take advantage of an injured man."

"Are you a coward as well as a rash fool, Don Esteban?"

Esteban's face flushed a dark red. "Pistols at twenty paces, then. I don't fight you for myself but for Margarita. For Alitha. I should have killed you long ago."

As they turned to leave the room, the door swung open and a blond man stood barring their way.

"From what I've heard, gentlemen," he said, "this is a time for prayer, not for dueling."

Jordan stared. "Thomas!"

"Your friend from the hospital?" Esteban asked.

Jordan nodded. "Thomas Heath. The man Alitha meant to marry in the islands."

"Ahhh." Esteban looked at the blond man's rough black pants and shirt, his Mexican hat, the Bible in his hand.

"Are you both mad?" Thomas demanded. "Ready to fight one another when Alitha's in the hands of Bouchard?"

"How did you learn that?" Jordan asked.

"By standing outside the door listening, as anyone in the inn could have if they understood English."

"This damn fool of a Californio wants to attack

Bouchard's lair," Jordan said, appealing to Thomas. "Just the two of us riding into their camp in the middle of the night firing our pistols. He thinks the pirates will flee from us in terror, leaving Alitha and the gold behind."

"This *estúpido* American proposes to procrastinate," Esteban said. "To scout the enemy position for days looking for a weakness that in all likelihood does not exist. He proposes to debate endlessly and finally to act with too little and too late. As a coward would."

At the word "coward," Jordan started for Esteban but Thomas stepped between them. "Forget what you think of each other," he said. "At least for the time being. Our first task is to save Alitha. Are you agreed?" He looked at Jordan.

"Agreed." Jordan glanced at Esteban, then went to the window and stared into the courtyard.

"Don Esteban?" Thomas asked. "Do you agree?"

"Of a certainty. Alitha is our paramount concern. She must not be left to suffer Bouchard's hospitality while we quarrel among ourselves like children. While we waste time."

"Good." Thomas knelt on the floor. "This is a time to pray," he said. "Both of you will join me in prayer." It was a statement, not a request.

Esteban immediately dropped to his knees beside Thomas. Jordan looked down at the two kneeling men, raised his eyes heavenward in exasperation, then joined them on the floor.

"Bow your heads," Thomas said. Both men bowed.

"Almighty God, hear this day our prayer." Thomas's tone was conversational, as though he often talked to God. "Give us the wisdom to know what is right and the courage to act on that knowledge. Protect your daughter, Alitha Bradford, from harm in the dark hours to come. Amen."

"That's all?" Jordan asked.

"I think it's sufficient under the circumstances," Thomas said. "I agree with Don Esteban that every minute counts. We have to find Alitha before it's too late."

"But—" Jordan began.

"I also believe, with you, that we can't act impulsively. We must have a carefully thought out plan. Now then, Esteban, tell us what you found out from this man Enrico."

Esteban nodded. "Enrico has been to the pirate camp but once," he said. "It is in a cove some fifteen miles to the south, a place where they bring their ships for repair. Not all the pirates are there now—some are still at sea—but Bouchard is there, or so Enrico's been told. One of the ships is on its side so the bottom may be scraped, they have . . ." He paused, searching for the right word.

"Careened her," Jordan put in.

"Yes, the ship has been careened and so is out of action. One other ship lies at anchor in the cove, prepared to put to sea at short notice. For the most part the pirates live ashore in huts behind the beach. They have guards on the only trail leading to their camp. Many guards, Enrico says."

"These ships in the cove," Jordan said. "Could one of them be the *Kerry Dancer?*"

"I asked him about the ships, but Enrico could not tell me."

"They're well armed, of course?" Thomas asked.

"With pistols, sabers and knives. Their cannons are on board the ships. My idea is to use our remaining gold coins to recruit mercenaries and attack by land."

"They'll overwhelm us," Jordan said.

"We must outwit them," Thomas put in. "If we can't outman them we must outthink them. It's our only chance. And Alitha's only chance."

Jordan hit his open palm with his fist. "I have a plan," he said, going to the window and glancing out into the empty courtyard. "Check the corridor," he told Thomas.

Thomas opened the door and looked up and down the hall. "All clear," he reported.

"My idea is risky," Jordan said, "and the chances for success are less than poor. But as Thomas would tell us, no one expected David would slay Goliath."

"Tell us your scheme," Esteban said, "not stories from the Bible."

"We're all of us right and all of us wrong," Jordan said, ignoring Esteban's remark. "We should use the gold, we should go by sea, we have to outwit Bouchard. This is my plan . . ."

After a long ride Alitha was untied, pulled down from the horse and carried to a hut, where she was pushed inside and left alone in the darkness. She lay huddled on the ground for a moment listening to the sounds around her—the pounding of the surf, the drunken shouts of the men, the neighing of horses, the barking of dogs.

She pushed herself to her feet, ignoring her bruises, gathered her flimsy nightgown about her and tried the door. It was barred from the outside. With her hands she searched the walls of the hut for an opening between the bamboolike poles. She found none.

She heard the bar withdrawn from the door. A man holding a lantern stepped into the hut, a short man with curled mustaches who wore a waistcoat and breeches.

A pistol and a knife were thrust in the broad crimson sash around his waist.

Bouchard placed the lantern on the earth floor and stood with hands on hips, appraising Alitha as though she were a captive at a slave auction. He nodded.

"Remove your gown," he ordered.

Alitha stepped back, trembling. She was numb, frozen; she could think of nothing except the horror awaiting her. She clenched her hands into fists at her sides, trying to calm herself, trying to think.

Bouchard took the knife from his sash, tossed it spinning into the air and caught it deftly by the handle. He made a downward slashing motion with the blade as though ripping her gown from neck to hem.

"Remove your gown," he said again.

Alitha reached up and slipped the cord from around her neck, holding it in her hand, with the red charm stone dangling from the end. Impatient, Bouchard took a step toward her. She drew in her breath and, with the cord looped around her wrist, grasped the hem of her nightgown and pulled it over her head. She forced herself to watch his reaction as she dropped the gown to her side and stood naked before him.

Bouchard stared at her, transfixed, his eyes roving from the swell of her full breasts down over her white body glowing in the light from the lantern.

"I have never beheld such loveliness before," he murmured, stepping forward.

Alitha took the end of the cord, swung the charm over her head and, still holding the cord, whipped the stone at Bouchard. The stone struck his temple and he grunted in shock and pain. His knees buckled and she thought he would fall, but he recovered enough to stagger to one side, his hand reaching for and grasping the wall of the hut.

She swung the stone again but his arm deflected the blow and the cord wrapped itself around his sleeve. She pulled the stone free, then reached down, grasped the handle of the lantern and hurled it at Bouchard. The lantern smashed against the wall in a burst of flame. Snatching up her nightgown, she ran to the door and flung it open.

Outside the hut, the night was lighted by the glow from the beach. Between the dark outlines of the huts, Alitha saw men clustered around campfires and the white line of the surf beyond. Palm trees arched behind her. No one was near, no one seemed to have seen her leave the hut.

She ran between huts, away from the beach and toward the trees. Away from the fires, away from the men. When she reached the first of the palms, she put the charm stone back around her neck and slipped her nightgown over her head. She looked over her shoulder. A man's voice—Bouchard's—called out, but the hubbub of drunken laughter and shouting went on. She saw a flash, heard the sharp report of a shot. A dog barked. The laughter stilled.

She turned and ran under the palms. Get away, she told herself, get as far away as you can. Don't stop to hide; they'll find you if you do. If not now, they'll wait and search for you again and find you by the light of day. Keep running until you're as far from here as you can go. Only then can you risk resting, only then can you find a place to hide and wait for Jordan. Was Jordan alive? If he was, she knew he'd set out to find her, would find and save her.

Her foot caught on a root and she fell headlong, slamming to the ground, where she lay gasping for breath as behind her she heard men shouting. She heard the ominous baying of dogs. Still lying on the ground, she looked back and saw the bobbing of many torches.

Alitha pulled herself to her feet and went on, more carefully now, her hands groping in front of her, her feet feeling their way across the uneven ground. Branches of shrubs caught her gown and she pulled herself free, the fabric tearing. Still she struggled forward, impelled by the growing tumult behind her— not only behind now but on both sides as well.

More palms arched over her head, their fronds etched darkly against the starry night. She heard the crash of surf in front of her. Running from the shelter of the palms, she found herself on a white sand beach. Had she run in a circle in the dark? No, looking both ways along the beach she saw no sign of the pirate campfires. Instead of fleeing inland as she had thought, she must have crossed the neck of a spit of land and emerged on the beach on the far side.

Disoriented, she hesitated. Which way should she go? She didn't want to be trapped on a point of land thrusting into the sea. To her left. Safety lay to her left, amid the dark mass of trees along the shore. She turned that way, only to see lights ahead of her and on both sides. Voices shouted, a line of men advanced toward her, their torches hissing, and she heard the barking of the dogs. Her escape route sealed off, she had no way to go but toward the sea.

Alitha fled into the trees. As she ran on with the surf to her left, the trees on her right thinned and after a few minutes she saw the ocean beyond them and, in the distance, the fires on the beach.

She had been right, she was on a small peninsula, a Florida-shaped mass of land jutting into the Pacific. Again she stopped and looked behind her. The torches were closer now, and she saw the bearded faces of the buccaneers in the flickering lights. She ran from the trees and on all sides saw nothing but sand and sea. She had nowhere left to go except into the sea or back toward the advancing men.

She turned and reentered the darkness beneath a cluster of palms. Where could she hide? There. In that dark hollow under a wind-bent shrub. She lay on the sandy ground, pulling her legs close to her body and clasping her knees with her hands, huddling in the darkness. As a torch came toward her, she put her head down and closed her eyes. A man shouted a few feet from her.

Opening her eyes, she saw him—black-bearded, a bandanna around his head, a torch in his hand. He looked about, cursed and went on. She sighed with relief—he hadn't seen her. More men passed, their torches crackling. She heard the men a few moments later milling about on the beach. They had all gone past her hiding place without seeing her; their querulous tones told of their confusion.

She heard a sniffing and tensed as a lean brown dog stopped above her. As he sniffed at her, she reached out her hand to pat him. The dog barked.

"Shhh, shhh," she whispered. The dog growled, pawing the ground, then raised his head and began to bark again.

A pirate approached, calling to the dog, and the animal whined and sidled away from Alitha into the night. She relaxed as she let out her breath in a shuddering sigh. Suddenly a torch flared over her head. The flame was thrust at her, and behind it she saw a grinning face.

"Here she be," the man cried.

His hand grasped her wrist and pulled her stumbling to her feet. Torches formed a circle around her. Men's faces leered at her. One man, a giant redhead, stepped forward and stared down at her breasts, which were partly revealed by the torn gown. He put his hand to the neck of the gown and pulled.

Alitha's scream went unheard amid the shrill and lustful laughter of the men.

chapter 24

THE SMALL MAN who had found Alitha's hiding place sprang at the giant redhead with the harelip. "She's mine," he cried, grabbing the big man's arm. "Grosbeck, you shan't have her."

Grosbeck shook him off. "She belongs to whoever's man enough to take her. I'm man enough, Ferret, and you're not."

Grosbeck turned to Alitha, who was clutching the edges of her ripped gown together to cover her breasts. He took her by the arm and yanked her to him just as the man called Ferret leaped onto his back and began pounding him about the ears with his fists.

Grosbeck snarled, releasing Alitha. He reached over his head, grasped Ferret's jacket and, bending forward, hurled Ferret head over heels into the crowd.

"Wait, Grosbeck." One of the pirates stepped forward. "Fair's fair. Ferret found the wench, after all. Let Bouchard decide who's to have her first."

"He'll want her for himself," Grosbeck protested sullenly.

"He's had his chance with her. We'll see he don't have her again. Am I right?" He appealed to the men around him, and they murmured their approval.

"Let Bouchard decide," Ferret whined. He was on his feet again, warily keeping out of Grosbeck's reach. "Fair's fair," he said.

Grosbeck shrugged his massive shoulders. "We'll see what the captain says."

He swept Alitha into his arms and carried her into the crowd in the direction of the pirate camp. The men stood aside to let Grosbeck through, falling in behind him, torches held high as they surged forward in a grotesque parade.

Alitha crossed her arms over her breasts as she felt one of Grosbeck's hands on her leg, the other on her side below her arm. She twisted to free herself from his grasp only to have Grosbeck cradle her closer to his hard body. She struck his cheek with her fist but he only laughed, cupping her breast with his hand and twisting her nipple. When she cried out in pain, Grosbeck laughed again.

"I like a lass with spirit," he told her, "a wench who makes a man fight for all he gets."

Grosbeck strode from the trees onto the beach, and in the light from the first of the bonfires Alitha saw Bouchard leaning heavily on a walking stick, his head swathed in a bandage. When Grosbeck carried Alitha to him, Bouchard stared glassily at her.

"Bring the captain his judge's chair," someone called.

Timbers were cross-hatched on the hard ground at the top of the beach, boards were laid on them and a

chair was placed on top. Two men lifted Bouchard onto
this platform and into the chair, where he sat staring
down at Alitha. Torches formed a semicircle around the
judgment seat.

"I'm glad to see the bitch didn't get far," Bouchard
said slowly, smiling at Alitha. "Let her stand on her
two feet," he said to Grosbeck.

The big man lowered Alitha to the ground, keeping
his hand on her shoulder. Ferret sidled from the crowd
to stand on the other side of her.

"You wouldn't disrobe for me," Bouchard told her.
"You should have—you would have found me the most
appreciative and civilized of men. Now let's see how
you enjoy these"—his gesture included all the men
pressing close to her—"these other gentlemen."

"Remove her gown," he told Grosbeck.

The redhaired pirate spun Alitha around to face him,
grasped the already torn nightgown in both hands and
split the cloth down the middle. He stripped the gown
from her arms and Alitha stood naked except for the
charm stone on her neck. Closing her eyes, she buried
her face in her hands.

"Now tell me the nature of your dispute." Bouchard
nodded to Grosbeck and Ferret.

"I found her," Ferret said, "after all the others
passed her by, and so by rights she's mine. Fair's fair."

"Did he indeed find her?" Bouchard asked
Grosbeck.

"He may have, he may not have. Perhaps his dog
found her. What's the difference? She's mine because I
have her." He gripped Alitha's upper arm. "Possession's nine points of the law. Any man who wants her
first can fight me for her. Including you," he told
Bouchard.

"I want no more of the bitch," Bouchard said. "She

had her chance to be treated like a lady; now let her be treated like an animal." He looked from Ferret to Grosbeck. "Settling this matter calls for the wisdom of Solomon." Bouchard began to laugh, almost giggling. With an effort he quieted his laughter and stood up, leaning on his walking stick.

"And we will decide the matter much as wise King Solomon did," Bouchard said. "Ferret, you found her, so you will have her first."

Grosbeck took a step toward the platform, but Bouchard waved him back.

"Grosbeck," he said, "you appear to have appropriated the young lady, so you will have her first. You both shall have her. And when you have done with her, let anyone who wishes have her, and when all that want her are through with her, break her back and bury her beneath the earth and let the maggots have her."

Bouchard sank back in his chair, his hand to his forehead. Grosbeck picked Alitha up in his arms and carried her to one of the huts as Ferret ran along behind him.

"Bring a light so we can see her," Grosbeck ordered, and Ferret darted outside. He returned with two lanterns and placed them at the side of the room.

Alitha began to scream. Grosbeck laid her on the ground where she curled herself into a ball, screaming, her eyes closed.

"Make her stop screaming," Ferret said. "For God's sake, make her stop."

"You're too soft-hearted for your own good, Ferret." Grosbeck snorted but he took a bandanna from his pocket, twirled it and put the gag in Alitha's mouth, tying the ends of the bandanna behind her head.

Alitha tried to scream but the sound was choked off to become a thin wail. She tried to speak but couldn't.

Though her eyes were closed, she saw brilliant flashes of red as pain sliced across her forehead.

Grosbeck pulled his shirt over his head and threw it into a corner of the hut. He unlaced his boots and tugged them off. He was unbuckling his belt when he glanced at Ferret. The small man stood staring down at Alitha, his eyes wide, a look of horror on his face.

"Well, Ferret," Grosbeck said, "aren't you going to prepare for action? Battle stations, Ferret, battle stations."

Ferret turned from Alitha and walked to the side of the hut, where he leaned against the wall. "I can't stomach it, Grosbeck," he said. "I thought I could but I can't. It's her screams. When she screamed I thought of—of someone I once knew."

"A lass who wouldn't have you, Ferret? All the more reason to skewer this one."

"She was my sister, Grosbeck. She was the same age as this wench here. Something burst inside her gut and she screamed for hours before she died. I can't do it, Grosbeck."

Ferret turned and clutched Grosbeck's arm. "You won't tell them?" he asked, looking pleadingly up at the other man. "You won't tell the men, will you?"

Grosbeck took Ferret's hand from his arm and shoved him aside. "I won't tell them, Ferret. Sit yonder and watch how a man goes about his work."

Ferret went to the corner of the hut, where he sat and buried his face in his hands.

Grosbeck removed his trousers and kicked them away. Naked, he looked down at Alitha, huddled on the ground at his feet. She had stopped trying to scream or to call out. When Grosbeck grasped her ankles and straightened her legs, she didn't struggle, nor did she resist when he spread her legs nor when he unfolded her arms, uncovering her breasts. For a moment he stared greedily at her golden hair, her breasts, her white body, before he knelt between her legs . . .

Alitha reached up to take her father's hand and he led her along a country lane, through fields and woods and across green pastures to a road with arching stone bridges, across the bridges to a stream with pools of still water. They climbed a hill and at the top Alitha saw a profusion of blooms so she let go of her father's hand and ran to throw herself on the ground amid the flowers . . .

Her father was real to her, the flowers were real and the stream gurgling nearby was real. Nothing else was. All the rest was a horrible nightmare that might never end. Nightmares weren't real, though; only her father and the flowers and the quiet stream were real.

"Esteban found out that the revolutionaries gather here," Thomas said, nodding to a small café. Jordan crossed the street and pushed open the door. When he came out ten minutes later, Thomas met him on the road. "It went well?" he asked.

"They all know about the gold now. How much was stolen from me and where I suspect it's cached. Soon the whole village of Acapulco will know."

A horseman rode past them, raising dust.

"Good," Thomas said. They walked to the inn and were about to enter the courtyard when Esteban rode up from the opposite direction.

"How did you fare?" Jordan asked him.

"*Muy bien.* The fishing boat is at our disposal, as are two men to row us. Gold coins work many miracles." He dismounted and clapped Jordan on the shoulder. "Your scheme is mad and dangerous, Capitán Quinn. That is the reason I like it."

Esteban looked at the Bible in Thomas's hand. "I think you'll need a more powerful weapon tonight," he said.

Thomas opened his jacket, revealing a pistol and a knife. "Not more powerful weapons, merely different ones," he said. "The Lord will understand."

The sun was setting in a splendor of gold and yellow when Thomas, Esteban and Jordan pushed the dugout canoe into the surf and scrambled aboard. The two Indian rowers, clad only in breechclouts, began paddling with long, steady strokes. No one spoke as the canoe glided south a few hundred yards offshore.

The sky darkened, the evening star shone brightly in the west and the other stars began to appear overhead. They rounded a point of land and saw the blaze of three fires punctuating the night. A ship lay on its side near the fires, and another rested at anchor in the bay.

"By God," Jordan said, "it *is* the Kerry Dancer. Look at her, isn't she a beauty?" He studied the ship. "She's rigged to sail. They must want to get themselves and the gold away from here as soon as they can."

They rowed into the bay, keeping the ship between the fires on the beach and their canoe. Slowly, silently, the oarsmen approached the *Dancer*. There was no sign of life aboard as the canoe slid closer and closer, finally nestling against the ship's side.

"Eight bells," someone called out in Spanish from the deck above them. Again there was silence.

"Here," Jordan whispered. His searching hands had found a ladder on the ship's side. He grasped a rope rung and climbed up, with Esteban and Thomas behind him.

Jordan cautiously raised his head over the rail and glanced around the familiar quarterdeck. He saw no one; the only light came from aft near the wheel. Swinging himself on board, Jordan crouched low and padded aft. No one was at the wheel, but he saw a seaman standing at the starboard rail looking toward the beach and the fires.

Jordan crept up behind him, circled the man's neck with his arm and plunged his knife into the man's side. The pirate groaned and collapsed into Jordan's arms. After lowering him to the deck, Jordan turned swiftly, but the poopdeck was still deserted.

Hearing a muffled shout forward, he ran back to the quarterdeck, where he stopped and looked about him. Again the ship was quiet; he saw no one in the darkness. Suddenly a figure loomed up in front of him. Thomas.

"We found two men," Thomas whispered. "We disposed of them. We've searched the deck and found no more of them."

"The rest are probably below," Jordan said. "Three more, most likely. If I were Bouchard I'd have two watches on the ship while she's anchored like this."

Esteban joined them. "Prisoners," he said. "Would they have prisoners aboard, Capitán Quinn?"

"They might. They'd be men they've impressed from ships they've captured, seamen who refused to join them. Or pirates who broke the articles they signed when they came aboard. Why?"

"The noise you heard. My man almost eluded me. He thought I was a prisoner escaping. They'd keep prisoners in the hold, would they not?"

"We planned to seal the hold shut," Thomas said, "and we should. It's too dangerous to go below."

"Could we use the prisoners if they would sail with us?" Esteban asked Jordan.

"We can use all the men we can get."

"Then I will go below and discover if there are actually prisoners aboard."

"No," Jordan told him. "I'll go. I know this ship and you don't. We can only risk one man."

"Listen." Thomas turned toward the shore. In the distance they heard the pop-pop-pop of musket fire. "Look." Thomas pointed. They saw torches bobbing along the beach and flashes of gunfire to the north.

"By God," Jordan said, "we did bring them. My talk of gold in the café did pay off. Revolutionaries or whoever they might be, they're attacking the camp. We got aboard the *Kerry Dancer* none too soon."

"The power of gold," Thomas murmured.

"I'll secure the hatches," Jordan said. "We've no time to go below now."

As Jordan bolted the hatch covers shut, the other two men watched torches approaching the fires on the beach as though the pirates were retreating from an attack on their guard posts. They saw men running, heard their cries and shouts of alarm.

"They're not launching a boat," Jordan said. "They mean to fight it out on the beach."

"They're fools if they do," Esteban said.

"Wait," Thomas said, scanning the shoreline. "Be patient; it's still too early to tell. They will come to us; they'll bring Alitha to us. They must."

The firing ashore grew louder and spread up and down the beach. Men ran to the pirate camp while others ran from it. The bonfires began to die down.

"There!" Thomas shouted.

They saw men, they counted nine or ten, launch a longboat into the surf. In a few minutes the pirates were rowing toward the *Kerry Dancer*, while behind them a new blaze erupted as the careened ship was set afire.

"Take your stations," Jordan ordered, "as we planned." This was his ship and, by God, he meant to be her captain.

Thomas and Esteban crouched behind the rail next to the only ladder on the starboard side as Jordan stood watching the approaching boat. The shooting had died down, but the fire on the careened ship blazed higher, the glow shimmering on the sails and rigging of the *Kerry Dancer*.

"Ahoy!" a voice from the boat hailed them in Spanish.

"Ahoy!" Jordan called to the men in the boat. "What's happening?"

"We were attacked. We bring the gold to the ship."

The boat thudded against the *Dancer*'s side and they heard men clamber up the ladder. As the first pirate reached the deck, Thomas grabbed him by the collar and pulled him aboard as Esteban struck him over the head with a belaying pin. The pirate groaned and fell to the deck.

The first four boarders were quickly disposed of in the same way, but the next man, seeing that something was amiss, let out a cry and hurled himself at Thomas. Esteban grasped his shoulder, pulling him away, but as he did, two more men climbed over the rail onto the deck. One flung himself at Thomas while the other drew his sword.

"Bouchard!" Jordan called to him.

The pirate captain advanced with sword drawn. Jordan, a knife in his hand, retreated toward the mainmast.

Bouchard slashed out with his sword. Jordan stepped

aside, but Bouchard recovered quickly and thrust at Jordan's body. Jordan threw himself to the deck as the sword sliced through his jacket, drawing blood, and buried itself point-first in the mast behind him. Though Bouchard tugged mightily, he could not free the sword from the mast.

"I've waited a long time for this," Jordan said.

As Jordan advanced, knife in hand, Bouchard abandoned his sword and backed away, drawing a pistol from his sash as Jordan leaped at him, driving upward into Bouchard's body with the knife. Bouchard grunted and the pistol dropped to the deck. Jordan thrust again, twisting the knife as it entered Bouchard's belly. As he withdrew the blade, he felt Bouchard's blood on his hand.

Bouchard, clutching his stomach, staggered toward the rail. Jordan followed, grasped him beneath the arms and heaved him overboard, smiling grimly when he heard the splash from below. He turned in time to see Thomas's fist strike a pirate's jaw. The man's head snapped back and he crumpled to the deck. Esteban, one arm hanging limp at his side, smiled wanly from the rail. A pirate lay unmoving at his feet. Jordan, suddenly light-headed, touched the wound on his shoulder and felt the warm ooze of blood.

Thomas ran to the rail and looked down. The longboat, with two men still aboard, had been shoved away from the *Dancer* by one of the pirates. He saw a figure huddled in the stern.

"Alitha!" he cried.

Thomas unlaced his boots and pulled them off; he dropped his knife and pistol to the deck. Climbing to the rail, he dived into the sea, surfacing a few feet from the longboat. When one of the pirates—a short, feral-appearing man—thrust at him with his oar,

Thomas grabbed it in both hands and yanked, and with a scream the man tumbled forward into the water.

As Thomas swam to the boat, the second pirate raised his pistol. Thomas ducked beneath the surface of the water. When he came up, he saw smoke curling from the gun. He grasped the side of the boat, rocking it up and down as the pirate tried to reload his pistol. Cursing, the pirate stomped with his boot on Thomas's fingers clutching the boat's side.

Thomas grunted with pain, released his hold and plunged into the water, intending to surface on the boat's other side. He felt a dull pain in his shoulder. Had the pirate's bullet struck home after all? He tried to swim under the boat but his right shoulder was numb and he had to resurface. Looking up, he didn't see the pirate. Thomas grasped the boat's side once more and heaved himself aboard.

The pirate, waiting for him on the other side of the boat, turned and fired. Missed. The redhead picked up a sack of gold and, as Thomas hurled himself forward, he threw the sack, catching Thomas full in the chest and sending him thudding to the deck. Thomas struck the back of his head on the seat and lay still.

Jordan, using his uninjured hand, carrying a knife in his belt, clambered down the ladder and leaped into the boat where, weak from loss of blood, he staggered and almost fell. The red-haired pirate swung about, again lifting a sack of gold over his head. Before he could throw it, Jordan lunged with the knife at the man's midsection and Jordan, the pirate, and the gold all disappeared over the side.

Esteban dropped into the boat and leaned over the side, searching the dark water. He saw nothing. Both men and gold had been swallowed by the sea.

Thomas rose groggily to one knee, bending over

Alitha, who lay naked in the water at the bottom of the boat. He took her into his arms while Esteban grappled with a hook to bring the boat alongside the *Dancer*.

"Alitha," Thomas said. She didn't move. "Alitha," he said again, "are you all right?"

She opened her eyes, staring through him as though she neither saw nor heard.

"Alitha," he murmured, "Alitha." Her head fell back and she closed her eyes.

"Hurry," Esteban called. "More boats are putting out from shore. We must release the prisoners and sail." He helped Thomas carry Alitha to the deck of the *Dancer*.

"What about Quinn?" Thomas asked.

"There's nothing we can do for him. He's been drowned."

chapter 25

ALITHA STOOD IN the doorway looking across the sparkling waters of the Sea of Cortés, breathing deeply of the salt air as she listened to the morning songs of the birds. The day was cloudless and the sun warmed her even while the breeze off the water teased her hair.

It was too early for the fishing boats to come in. She knew this, but nevertheless she couldn't help watching for Thomas's return. She was safe enough here in the house that Esteban's friend, Coronel Morales, had found for her above the village of Loreto, and she really wasn't frightened now that she'd left her nightmares behind, but she was lonely.

Alitha stepped back from the open door and returned to her bedroom to dress. There were no mirrors in the primitive dwelling, but when she pulled off her sleeping shift to put on her dress, she looked at her body, at the white curve of breast and hip. I'm no longer ill, she thought.

Alitha touched her lips with her fingers. The time she had lain unable to talk or to take in what went on around her was weeks lost from her life, weeks she'd never be able to remember clearly. She was grateful, because the moments she did recall, the horror of being a captive of the pirates, were blurred and faded as though they had happened to someone else.

Alitha straightened her simple peasant dress, brushed her hair smooth and left the bedroom. Outside, she blinked in the strong sunlight. A small yellow and green bird alit on one of the prickly pears in the garden and cocked its head to stare at her.

This was hardly the Garden of Eden, Alitha thought as she glanced about at the thorny cactus plants. Her motion startled the bird and it flew off. Beauty was fleeting; her life seemed as barren as the dry and rocky land of Baja. And as desolate. She must learn to face the truth, she told herself, for nothing on earth could change it.

The truth was that Jordan Quinn was dead. She folded her arms about her, suddenly chilled.

True, Esteban had recovered a portion of the gold. True, he had shared this good fortune with Thomas. But what did gold matter when Jordan was dead, a victim of the sea he loved so well? Not only was Jordan dead but his beloved *Kerry Dancer* had been impounded by the Mexicans at San Blas until they determined the ship's rightful owner. Esteban had returned yesterday, Thomas had told her, from an unsuccessful attempt to retrieve the *Dancer*.

She had not been well enough to talk to Esteban since he had helped rescue her from Bouchard and his men. She thought of him often, recalling the time they had once been so happy together here in Baja.

Once Alitha had thought she would hate to leave Mexico, for she loved its people, its contrasts, its beauty. Even here in the desert land of Baja, she enjoyed the warmth of the sun, the palm fronds rustling in the wind and the ever-changing panorama of the sea only a short walk from her doorstep. But now, with Jordan gone, she was indifferent to her surroundings.

So it mattered little to her that the time was fast approaching when she must leave.

Alitha shook her head, unable to recall when she had been so torn by indecision. What did she want now from life? Love, of course, she wanted love. What had happened to her with the pirates had nothing to do with love. And yet a man and woman who loved one another came together in passion. Could she forget her ordeal as a captive if she should find a man to love? Would this man be able to put her ravishment aside and love her? Perhaps not. Maybe no man would offer her love again.

But she wanted more than love. She had a passion for living—at least she had before the last few weeks—a penchant for daring, for voyaging into the unknown.

Her gaze left the choppy waters of the Sea of Cortés, wandered in to the white-tipped curl of the surf, to the cluster of thatched huts of the fishing village of Loreto, finally to the gray buildings of the mission and the *presidio*.

A lone horseman rode up the hill from the *presidio* toward her. Alitha gripped her hands together as she recognized him. She'd know him anywhere. How graceful he was, how dashing. With a stab of excitement she remembered the first time she'd seen him at the Indian *ranchería*. How handsome he'd been then; how handsome he was now.

Esteban swept off his hat as he reined in his horse in front of the gate. Dismounting, he walked slowly to her, smiling. He tossed his hat to one side and bowed, taking her hand and raising her fingers to his lips. What would happen if he kissed her, she wondered. Would she feel the same overwhelming passion she'd once felt?

"Alitha, my love," he said. "My dove, my heart of hearts. Now that you are well again, I have come to take you with me to my *rancho* at Santa Barbara. All will be as it once was. You and I will be together, Alitha, only you and I."

"Esteban," she murmured, turning from him to hide her confusion. "You're expecting a ship?" she asked to give herself time to recover from the unexpected rush of warmth she felt for Esteban. He wanted her, she thought. After all that had happened to her, he still wanted her as much as ever. Perhaps more.

"A ship arrives tomorrow," Esteban said. "Bound for Alta California and the Sandwich Islands. I hurried here to you as soon as Coronel Morales informed me. I never want to be away from you again as long as I live."

"Aren't you forgetting something, Esteban? Aren't you forgetting someone?"

"How is it possible for me to keep anything else in my mind when all my thoughts are of you?"

"Aren't you forgetting Ines?" Alitha remembered the blue-eyed little girl smiling at her at the Gutierrez *rancho*. "After all, you're going to marry her."

"I knew I had something to tell you before your loveliness drove it from my mind. But first—" Esteban brought a dark red hibiscus from behind his back and put the flower in her hair. "How beautiful your golden hair is, my Alitha," he said.

"You were about to tell me of Ines," she reminded him.

"Ah, of a certainty. Ines, a lovely girl. I intend to speak with Señor Gutierrez when we return to Santa Barbara, and I am confident that he will graciously agree to release me from my commitment to marry his daughter."

Alitha wondered if gold coins would have to change hands before Señor Gutierrez showed his graciousness, but she said nothing.

Esteban dropped to one knee in front of her.

"Alitha," he said, motioning behind him with his hand, "imagine that Spanish guitars are softly playing a love song. Imagine it is night, with the moon full and bright above our heads, that the stars in the heavens are as numberless as the grains of sand on the shore. Do you remember our journey to Mexico? Do you remember, my Alitha?"

"I'll never forget. How could I?"

"Do you remember the many nights beneath these same stars when I held you in my arms and you whispered of your love everlasting?"

"You were my first love, Esteban."

"And you were mine, my Alitha. No woman was ever like you; I never loved a woman as I love you and I never will. I want you to sail with me; I want you to be my wife."

He rose and took her in his arms, and when his lips found hers, it was as though she were no longer in Baja but in Santa Barbara again, and she loved Esteban more than she had ever thought it was possible to love anyone. For a long moment she surrendered herself to his kiss.

She heard him draw in his breath and felt the passion

mount in him. He drew her closer until she felt the charm stone press against her breasts. She pulled away, stepping back.

"What is it, my Alitha?"

"I—I thought I heard a sound in the garden near the tall cactus. It's probably just another lizard."

"I do not see—" he began, lifting an arm of the prickly pear with his boot. All at once he stomped the ground with his heel. "A snake," he told her. "A small coral snake. A lovely creature, but deadly. Do not fear, I have killed him."

She almost said, "I always thought of coral snakes as female rather than male." Instead she turned from him, her hand touching the charm stone through the cloth of her dress. As she looked out over the sea, Esteban came up behind her and circled her waist with his arms.

"Will you marry me, my Alitha?" he asked softly, his lips to her hair.

"Do you want me to sail with you to Santa Barbara, to live in your *rancho* as Maria does, to have your children, to make my life there? Do you expect me to adopt your ways, the customs of the Californios?"

"Yes, of course I do. As I said, I want you to be my wife."

Alitha felt tears sting her eyes, for she knew Don Esteban Mendoza was offering her the most he could offer any woman. She turned in his arms and looked into his brown eyes.

"Why do you cry, my Alitha?" he asked. "You know I cannot bear to see you cry."

"Oh, Esteban. I'm crying because I did love you. I was a girl when you found me at the *rancheria,* and you made me a woman, for better or for worse. I'll never, never forget you or how much you meant to me. But marry you? I can't, Esteban, I can't marry you. I wouldn't be happy as a *señora;* I'd be lying to you if I said I would. The fault's not yours or mine; it's what we are, all that's happened to us in all the years of our lives, everything that's made us the way we are."

He stared at her in disbelief. "You cannot be serious," he said. "Perhaps you need time to consider. Perhaps I have been too impetuous."

"I've never been more serious; I don't need time to consider." Alitha went to him and clasped his hand in both of hers. "I can't marry you, Don Esteban," she said, ignoring the tears coursing down her cheeks. "I loved you once. I no longer love you."

Esteban frowned and walked away from Alitha to stare at the ground. Finally he turned to face her, a wan smile on his face. He bowed, taking her hand and raising it to his lips. *"Hasta luego, mi amor,"* he said.

"Until we meet again, Esteban," she said, knowing she would never see him again. Never.

He turned, retrieved his hat and swung effortlessly into the saddle. Spurring the stallion, he galloped down the slope in front of the house, across the valley and up the hill toward the *presidio.* At the hill's crest he stopped and swung his horse about so he faced her. He swept his hat from his head and bowed. And then he was gone.

Alitha removed the hibiscus from her hair and held the flower cupped in her palm, remembering the rose Esteban had given her when she lay ill in Santa Barbara. The hibiscus was so beautiful. And so fragile. She knew the bloom, once picked, soon withered, just as she would have withered if she had journeyed north with Esteban. As her love for him, once so vibrant and so beautiful, had withered long ago.

There was no book here in which to press the hibiscus as she had pressed Esteban's rose between the pages of *Pilgrim's Progress*. Would Ines one day find that faded flower and wonder who had placed it there?

As for me, Alitha told herself, like Christian, I've dallied in Vanity Fair, journeyed over the Enchanted Ground, and I've been forced through the Valley of Humiliation. Now at last I should be able to see the Celestial City in the distance. But will I ever, she wondered. And will I recognize it if I do?

chapter 26

ALITHA PICKED UP a stone with a pointed end and scratched at the hard-packed earth. Gently she laid the already shriveling hibiscus blossom in the small hole and buried the flower. Rising from her knees, she brushed at her skirt and walked slowly toward her adobe house. How she longed for Thomas's return! Thomas, kind and thoughtful, would comfort her.

He'd told her of the Sandwich Islands these past weeks while she recovered her strength, about the customs of the people and of the problems the missionaries faced. Thomas seemed to assume that she'd return to the islands with him, although he hadn't spoken of it directly. Now a ship was due tomorrow. Thomas would certainly plan to sail on that ship.

Alitha knew that they wouldn't marry until they reached the islands. Thomas wouldn't accept a Mexican priest, even if the priest could be persuaded to marry them. Nor a ship's captain. And, of course, Thomas would insist on their sleeping in separate berths on the way. His manner toward her in Loreto had been entirely proper—he hadn't even taken the minor liberties allowed a fiancé.

She entered the house and looked about at her meager belongings. There'd be little packing to do. Why did she feel such reluctance at the thought of leaving on that ship? Thomas had always been her friend; he still was and always would be. Didn't she *want* to marry him?

She'd once planned to be a missionary's wife, looked forward to traveling to foreign climes. If she didn't now feel a wild thrust of passion for Thomas, at least she was fond of him. They'd grown up knowing one another and had a way of life in common. Passion wasn't the only possible bond between a man and a woman. Passion was all she and Esteban had shared, and it hadn't been enough. As for Jordan . . . But, no, she couldn't bear to think of how it had been with Jordan.

She heard two quick taps on the door and turned to open it. Thomas was back.

"I didn't expect to find you still here," he said, placing a fish wrapped in leaves on the crude table.

"I made my trip to the village earlier today," she said.

"That's not what I meant. I thought you'd leave with Esteban. I knew he was coming to see you, and you did leave with him once before. In Santa Barbara."

"Is that why you spent the whole day on the fishing boats? Must you be so noble?"

"I didn't think I was being noble." He drew in his breath and took her by the hands.

Alitha pulled away. "And must you always hold my hands as though you were a minister and I one of your parishioners?"

"I can't help but be the way I am. Noble, though? I don't think so. I just want to do what's best for you."

"Did you really expect me to go off with Esteban, Thomas? To leave you without a word?"

He bowed his head momentarily, then looked at her again. His appearance was a far cry from the Thomas she'd known in Boston. In his rough peasant shirt and pants, with his blond hair curling below his neck, no one would take him for a man of the cloth.

"When I suspected that Esteban might have forced you in some way to go with him," he told her, "I followed you two thousand miles from Santa Barbara to Mexico. But I came to believe you wanted him. So this morning when he came for you, I stood aside."

Alitha shook her head. Inside, he was still the same Boston Thomas no matter how his appearance might have changed. Why, when Thomas wasn't with her, did she always forget how he really acted? He'd said himself he couldn't help being what he was.

"You've been so good to me," she said. "So kind. All the visits you made when I was sick. Delores said you often sat all day by my bed during the time she cared for me. And now staying on in Loreto until I recovered. I can never repay you."

"There you're mistaken. You can repay me by keeping your promise to me."

"What promise, Thomas?"

"To be my wife."

Alitha took a deep breath. As Thomas's wife she'd be loved and protected. And she loved Thomas in her way. But she was no longer the Boston girl he'd asked to be his wife; she could never be that girl again.

"I'm afraid you wouldn't be happy married to me," she said, "and I'm certain the bishop wouldn't consider me an ideal wife for one of his missionaries."

"I'm not required to petition for the bishop's approval before I wed," Thomas said stiffly.

"I realize that. Don't be so literal—I know you've always been your own man." She smiled at him, and after a moment he smiled, too.

"Oh, Thomas, you'll be my friend forever," she said. "I don't imagine I'll ever meet another man with such true nobility of character as yours. I certainly have very little nobility in mine. Why, if I loved a man I wouldn't stand aside and let another woman claim him. I'd fight for him!"

"But I love you, Alitha." He tried to take her hands again, but she put them behind her back.

"In Boston," she said, "do you remember the night by the Charles when we almost made love? I've thought of that night many times. I believed then that you thought I was sinful. Do you want to live with a sinful woman, Thomas?"

"It was myself I was ashamed of, not you." Thomas lowered his head again. "A man has an obligation to keep from arousing a woman's passion. It wasn't your fault."

"My fault! You still don't understand how far apart we are. My passion is my own to control or not."

"The Bible tells us the woman is the weaker vessel. Don't upset yourself, Alitha, over a matter beyond your nature to . . ."

"Thomas, let's not quarrel. I can't marry you, dear as you'll always be to me. We've grown away from each other since those days in Boston. I'm not suited to be a minister's wife, nor would I be happy as one." She reached up to brush his hair back from his forehead. "Do you realize you've never called me Leeta since the night by the Charles? I think you gave me up then without understanding what you'd done."

"But you know I'll sail on the next ship to the islands. The fishermen say one is expected tomorrow. How can I leave you here in this barren land, alone and unprotected?"

"I imagine Coronel Morales will see to my safety," she said drily.

"Come with me, Alitha—sail with me on that ship to the islands. We'll be married there. You know the bishop prefers missionaries to be married men. He'll not jibe at you because of what you've been through. He'll realize you were an innocent victim."

Alitha shook her head. "No, I'm not as innocent as you make me out. Don't keep trying to convince me how it was. I know how it was."

"Your mother would have been anguished to think of you left alone in a foreign land. And your father . . ."

"My parents are dead. My mother, God rest her soul, was a different kind of woman than I, Thomas. And my father . . ." She paused, then went on. "I rather believe my father would understand."

"My dear." He captured her hands at last. "I wish there was a way to convince you that marriage to me is the best future for you."

Alitha let him keep her hands in his warm grasp. Warm but somehow impersonal. He doesn't really see me as I am any more than Esteban did, she thought. Thomas has built an image of his Alitha that he'll never relinquish. If I married him I'd have to spend a lifetime trying to live up to that image, and I could never do that.

Tears came to her eyes at the thought of losing him. They had known each other for so long; she liked him so much. And if the truth be told, she admonished herself, she also felt a flicker of disappointment at rejecting a journey to the islands.

She withdrew her hands gently, standing on tiptoe to kiss Thomas on the cheek. "You've honored me by asking me to be your wife," she told him. "I do love you, but not in the way a wife must love a husband." She sighed. "Good-bye, Thomas," she said.

For a long moment he held her against him, and she realized what he had said was true. He did love her. But she could never make him happy, and Thomas deserved to be happy.

She managed to smile as she saw him to the door, but as she closed it behind him, she felt as though everything familiar to her had left with Thomas. Now she was truly alone among strangers.

What was there to do but return to Boston? She owned the small house that had belonged to her parents, and eventually there'd be money from the insurance on the *Flying Yankee*. She'd still be alone, but she had to begin to sort out her life somewhere.

If she never found a man to love, she could still find contentment in doing what she felt was right for her. Was it possible that somewhere there were boys like Chia, or like the *mestizo* children in Loreto, who needed to be taught to read and write? Weren't there children right in Boston who would never have a chance at schooling unless someone sought them out?

I'd be happy doing that, she told herself. But an image of Jordan laughing down at her, his eyes lit by candlelight, made her throat ache with grief.

chapter 27

CORONEL MANUEL MORALES laid aside his trowel, brushed the dirt from his blue uniform and smiled almost apologetically at Alitha.

"You must think I spend too much time with my garden," he said. "After all, I am supposed to be a soldier, not a horticulturist."

"I only wish I had your love for plants."

"I will tell you a secret," the Coronel said as they walked beside the *presidio* wall to the bluff overlooking the Sea of Cortés. The sun, setting behind the barren hills, threw their shadows on the ground in front of them. "All the news from Mexico is of victories for the revolutionaries. Soon the viceroy must flee to Spain; soon General Iturbide will take his place. There is even talk of crowning Iturbide emperor of all Mexico."

"Will you have to leave the country, too?"

Coronel Morales shrugged. "Most of the Spanish officers in Mexico will merely change their uniforms for those of the new government. Soldiers are paid to fight, not to be politicians, and no matter whose government controls Mexico, life will go on. There will be more wars, more killing, more proclamations, more revolutions, new champions of the people, new despots."

"You're very cynical, Coronel," Alitha said. "Not unlike someone I once knew."

"You left him because of his cynicism?"

"No, he was killed."

"Ah, el Capitán Quinn. Such a pity. He was, from all Don Esteban told me, a brave and gallant man."

Close to tears, Alitha nodded and said nothing.

"But the success of the revolution," Coronel Morales said, "is not my secret. When the chance presents itself, I plan to sail home to Spain. Not because of the revolution; I have decided to leave Baja regardless. After more than twenty years I intend to give up my commission in the army."

"Won't you miss being a soldier? The life? The adventure?"

"Ah, of a certainty I shall. Any great change is a kind of dying. But the time for change has come. I became a soldier because my father was one before me and his father before him. In my family the first son enters the priesthood, the second son joins the military. There was no choice, or at least I thought there was none. Now, before it's too late I will return to my first love, the earth and the plants it nourishes. Like Candide, I must cultivate my garden before it is too late."

"If only all of us could know what we should do with our lives before it's too late," Alitha said. For Coronel Morales, she thought, the coming years would be a new beginning. For her, without Jordan, they seemed more like an ending.

The coronel nodded. Looking up into the darkening

sky, he said, "Such strange weather for this time of year. See how the fog comes in from the sea."

Alitha pulled her shawl closer around her.

"I must prepare to inspect our troops at the lowering of the flag," Coronel Morales said. "I wonder how many more days the flag of Spain will fly over Baja." Bowing to Alitha, he strode away to the barracks.

She walked slowly out onto the bluff, where she stood looking at the mist swirling above the sea. Closing her eyes, she remembered the morning in Valparaiso when she had stood at the rail of the *Flying Yankee* and seen the *Kerry Dancer* for the first time, remembered how Jordan Quinn had saluted her as his ship disappeared into the fog.

Opening her eyes, she stared across the smooth waters. All at once she gasped in disbelief. Her heart leaped. No, it wasn't a vision, not a mirage. A ship sailed through the mist. She strained to see the masts. Two. The lines of the vessel were familiar, so like those graven into her memory.

Alitha watched, her heart thudding in her breast, as the ship sailed into the harbor. By the time it had anchored offshore and a boat was launched, there was no doubt in her mind that it was the *Kerry Dancer*.

The Mexicans were returning the ship, she told herself, realizing the foolishness of her first wild hope that Jordan Quinn was in command. They were bringing the ship back, but days too late, for Esteban and Thomas had already sailed from Loreto. Alitha turned away. It was too painful to look at the *Kerry Dancer* now that Jordan Quinn was gone.

No, she told herself, she would *not* spend the rest of her life turning her back. She must face life just as Coronel Morales had finally decided to do after all these years. Biting her lip, she turned and watched as the ship's boat nestled beside the quay and a man climbed the ladder to the dock.

No, it couldn't be! Holding her skirt in one hand, she ran down the path to the shore and along the dirt road to the beach. He waited for her, his black hair curling over his forehead, his eyes dancing.

Jordan opened his arms to her and she threw herself into them, laughing and sobbing.

"Jordan," she said, burying her face against his chest. "I thought you were dead."

"Only the luck of the Irish saved me. And kept you here in Baja until I was well enough to travel."

"I must have been waiting for you without knowing it. I think I must have been waiting for you all my life."

"As I was about to tell you when I was interrupted—" Jordan began. When she looked up at him, puzzled, he went on, "At the inn, when Bouchard's men came. As I was saying then, the reason I never told you that Thomas was in Mexico was because I love you, Alitha. I was jealous, I was a fool, but when a man's in love—"

She raised her lips to his. When he kissed her, she felt the familiar excitement and more, the aliveness she knew only with him, the desire to share, the need to be with Jordan Quinn as long as they both should live.

A cannon boomed a salute from the fort, and one answered from the deck of the *Kerry Dancer*. Keeping his arm around her, Jordan turned to look at his ship and the ocean beyond.

"Australia's out there," he said, "and Tasmania and all the isles of the South Pacific. Someday we'll cross this ocean, you and I, to India and the Cape of Good Hope and the Congo. There are so many wonders you've never seen that I want to show you, so many lands I've never sailed to that we can discover together."

She rested her head against his shoulder, smiling. No, she told herself, this wasn't an ending after all. This was only the beginning.

Romance & Adventure

New and exciting romantic fiction—passionate and strong-willed characters with deep feelings making crucial decisions in every situation imaginable—each more thrilling than the last.

Read these dramatic and colorful novels—from Pocket Books/Richard Gallen Publications